FOREVER Freed

NEW YORK *TIMES* BESTSELLING AUTHOR

Laura Kaye

PRAISE FOR FOREVER FREED

"Laura Kaye's *Forever Freed* is unlike any vampire romance I've read to date. With characters that grab you from the start, this is a book that will stay with you long after you finish....Laura Kaye has been added to my auto-buy list!" ~Vampire Romance Books

"*Forever Freed* has something a little different. Packed with memorable characters and very distinctive and well written, Laura Kaye pulls out all the stops....More than just a paranormal story, you get exceptional entertainment." ~Sizzling Hot Book Reviews

"Who knew such a heart-warming story could have you so on the edge of your seat? I absolutely loved this book!" ~Were Vamps Romance

"I can't say enough how much I enjoyed reading this story. The writing flows seamlessly, the editing is great, and the story is engaging to the point I was unable to put it down once I started. I highly recommend this story to anyone who believes in second chances at love and who likes paranormal romance." ~Paranormal Romance Guild

To my family, for helping me make my dream come true

And for everyone who has already loved Lucien, Sam, and Ollie

.

CHAPTER 1

The sleek silver Beemer swerved roughly to the curb in front of my driveway, cutting me off as I pulled out. The bike fishtailed underneath me as its tires fought to grab the concrete.

"What the hell?" My boot heel caught the kickstand. I dismounted as I tore off the glossy black helmet. I hadn't eaten in over a month. I was in no mood.

The passenger window eased down. "Lucien Demarco," a deep voice called. "Thought that was you. This must be fate."

"Langston?" I peered in the window and found his trademark grin. He stuck his hand out and we shook across the empty passenger seat. I leaned against the door frame, helmet in hand. "Holy shit. Good to see you. Been a while."

"What? Ten, twenty years?" "That's about right."

Langston's pale yellow eyes glowed against the warm brown of his skin. He appeared to be in his mid-thirties, but was more like seventy-five. "Look, man," he said, "I gotta be somewhere five minutes ago. Here"—he thrust a business card into my hand—"I'm thinking you might want to come see me."

The embossed lettering read:

LANGSTON BROWN
DIRECTOR
DETROIT MEDICAL CENTER BLOOD BANK

My eyes snapped back to his, which were full of the same humor I'd started tasting. "Well, that's...interesting."

"Tell me about it. I work again tomorrow. Come see me in the evening, around seven?"

Distracted by the realization of what he was offering—a much-needed alternative—I murmured, "Yeah. Okay."

"All right, then. I'm outtie." He tapped his hand twice against the center console. I saluted him with his business card and stepped back up on the sidewalk as he pulled away from the curb.

I scrubbed my hand through the length of my brown hair, still trying to wrap my brain around the coincidence of Langston's offer just as I was heading out to hunt. Filled with an unusual hopefulness, I walked the Harley back into the garage. I was used to going hungry. What was one more day?

The next evening, energized by my anticipation of guilt-free sustenance, I approached the hospital just as the spring sun dipped below the city's skyline.

Out of nowhere, feelings of amusement and awed curiosity filled my chest with intense, comforting warmth. I had learned to control my empathic ability and could generally tune out others' emotions if I concentrated, but there was always a low buzz of perception in the back of my mind, one that flared when the emotions had to do with me. A defense mechanism, of sorts. I turned and scanned the plaza.

A little girl's blatant stare caught and held my gaze. "Hi," she said with a smile. She waved her tiny hand. The evening breeze blew long strands of gold across her face.

She was so focused on me she stumbled, which only brightened her smile. She continued to grin and look at me over her shoulder as an elderly black woman drew her toward the entrance and through the automatic doors to the lobby. Then she was gone.

I was stunned.

Humans generally didn't interact with me unless I wanted them to.

Yet, the girl *saw* me. Not only that, she met my eyes and held them. I smelled no fear from her at all, just that unbelievable curiosity and amusement, and an inexplicable touch of affection.

Her unusual attention made me feel present in the world, for once. The goodness of her emotions felt warm, tasted sweet.

I craved more. I wanted her to see me again. Which was why I needed to get the hell out of there.

I flipped open my cell phone and made a call, then left a message: "Hey, Langston. Sorry. Tonight's not good after all. Can we do this in the next day or two? Let me know."

My hunger too greatly tested my control, my judgment. I couldn't risk staying. So I retreated through Detroit's blighted streets back to my hulking, dilapidated manse on Edmund Place. The crumbling dark red sandstone, rusted ironwork, and numerous boarded windows were more than good enough for me.

The house's poor condition brought me no special attention given the surroundings. Once posh, the Brush Park neighborhood had decayed with the rest of the city during the twentieth century. Abandoned mansions stood guard over debris-filled vacant lots. Just across the street a Gothic-style church sat empty—even God had forsaken this place.

I entered my dark parlor, knelt down before the hearth and built a fire. Starvation clawed at my gut. The girl's unprecedented observation nagged at my mind. I needed a distraction.

Pulling a chair closer to the radiating heat of the fire, I bent and flipped the latches on the antique case. Raising the lid revealed one of the few mementos I permitted myself from my human life. The neck of the reddish-brown instrument filled my hand and felt like the only home I'd ever known. Nothing helped fill my endless time like my violin.

The instrument smelled of pine rosin, reminding me of idyllic days in Italy. Whenever I played, my human memories echoed as loud in my head as the notes sounded in the room.

Any pain those memories brought...well, it was deserved.

Soon, rich yearning tones filled the room. The melancholy of the anniversary hung over me still, and my dire need for sustenance didn't help. It didn't take long, therefore, before the image of the smiling blonde girl transformed in my mind's eye into another girl, with olive skin and chocolate ringlets.

A girl who had once been my whole life. A daughter whom I had failed.

Two days later, I was back again to see Langston, finding myself in more urgent need of his assistance.

From the empty waiting room of the blood bank, I sensed him immediately. He had an expectant smile on his face when he came around from the back to the reception counter. "Well, well. Look what the cat dragged in. How the hell are you this fine evening?"

"Okay, Langston." I surveyed the laboratory space behind him. "Interesting work you're doing here."

"You have no idea. Come on back through that door," he said as a buzzer sounded. I walked through, and he extended his hand, which I shook as the door clicked behind me. "So, what have you been up to all these years?" He led me into the more private space in the back.

"I've been around. Lying low. You know." "Yeah, I know."

We stared at each other. "So..."

"Laumet finagled me this job," he offered. "Been in it about a month now. He figured a more formalized relationship with the blood bank was overdue." He smirked as he leaned against a counter and crossed his arms over his chest.

I frowned at the mention of Laumet's name. "Well, there aren't many of us who could do it, I guess."

Langston broke into a grin. "That's for sure." From Langston's first moments as a vampire, he'd been completely free of bloodlust. It was his special gift, one Laumet found quite useful.

So here was my biggest concern about being back in touch with Langston: Antoine Laumet. Laumet was the oldest and most powerful vampire in the city, and we'd both worked for him. In fact, I'd already been with Laumet for two decades by the time Langston was turned and had helped train him. Having fought free of Laumet's criminal underworld, however, I had no interest in interacting with him again. But Langston was still under his thumb.

Yeah, but you need this blood source, Lucien. It was a chance I had to take. "So, can you supply me from time to time?"

"Yeah, man, of course. I figured you might be interested... with everything." The compassion that filled his words also warmed my chest. I was so unused to someone looking out for me I found myself surprised he had thought about me. But I wasn't surprised he knew what feeding did to me, knew my empathy forced me to suck in my victims' emotions with each accursed draw of blood. We'd worked together for over two decades, after all. "Just, Lucien, you realize Laumet will have to know."

"I know. *Cazzo*," I grumbled. "I expected as much. You can pass on that this is just a business deal. That'll make it more acceptable to him."

Langston nodded. We worked out cost, transport, and storage arrangements. He agreed to contact me in a day or two when he had extra again, the blood he'd set aside for me before having been used in a trauma. I only hoped it wouldn't take too long—my pallor, dropping body temperature, and the dark circles beneath my eyes all reflected the nearly five weeks since I'd last fed.

This new source promised freedom from my ancient dependency on the weak blood of animals and the punishing blood of evildoers. Imagining what that freedom could mean for me, I wound my way through the hospital corridors toward a side exit.

And gasped as I walked into a haze of pure bliss. A young woman approached the same exit, wearing the green scrubs of a doctor or nurse. Her golden blonde hair hung in a thick braid well past her shoulders. Her arms were tanned and, as I caught up with her, I could see where the sun brought out a light freckling across her upper cheekbones and nose. The color of her eyes was striking—a dazzling blue-green with nearly black edges around the iris. She was young and vital and pretty in a girl-next-door kind of way.

As beautiful as she was, her most remarkable quality had captured my attention in the first place: the extraordinary feelings of joy, affection, gratitude, and contentment washing off her. Her emotions tasted sweet and gripped every part of my body in warmth and pleasure. My borrowed euphoria left me dumbstruck as she hurried through the door and around the hospital drive. The intensity of the feeling diminished in direct correlation to her growing distance from me.

I gasped for more. Having lived without such feelings for so long, this reminder of true unqualified happiness beckoned to me. So I followed her. I stalked her emotions, grateful for the cloud-covered evening, and learned the location of her residence.

And then an unbidden thought entered my brain: If her emotions felt this good, what would it be like to consume her blood?

Certainly I'd feel her regret. But what came out of her would also be life-giving, humanity-restoring, beautiful, and sweet.

The thought of it was intoxicating. She was a temptation of such magnitude, I lost all capacity for reason or rationality. I simply had to have her, had to have that one fleeting feeling of light in the darkness, that one richly sweet moment free from pain and grief.

In that instant, I was so far gone it never occurred to me that my efforts to avoid the blood of bad humans 'led me to plan to kill a good one.

~

Driven by the promise of rapturous relief, I lurked around the edges of the beautiful woman's life that night, but had no opportunity to claim her. She always seemed to be surrounded, as if the humans she knew were equally drawn to her.

I wasn't interested in taking out others to get to her— hell, going after her at all was unconscionable, violated the rules I'd created to try to bring meaning and structure to my unnatural life. But defying her pull was about as possible as a moth resisting the lure of a flame.

The following night, I made my way under cover of darkness back to her townhouse on Farnsworth Street. She lived in an unusual enclave in this city— a full square block of adjoined tan townhouses, arranged around new streets carved out of the interior of the block. I stood in the shadows on the side of her building until I captured the feeling of her mind. To my relief, I found her easily, the sweetness of her contentment palpable even as she slept.

A long branch of a thick oak tree passed within feet of her window. I jumped onto it and moved as close as I dared, knowing she was unreachable within the confines of her home but needing to see her nonetheless.

The sheer curtains interfered little with my view as she lay sleeping on her side in the wide bed, her hands tucked under her chin. She appeared to be sleeping peacefully, though the whirlwind of her emotions revealed the intensity of her dreams.

Oh *Dio*, her feelings felt good. Too good. But good enough to harm an innocent, something I'd avoided since I'd largely harnessed the bloodlust over a century ago?

I hated how flippant it sounded, but this woman was simply in the wrong place at the wrong time. When I saw her, I had not fully emerged from the melancholy of the anniversary of my human family's murders at the hands of my maker. Each May, I attempted to pay penance for failing my wife and daughter by secluding myself and observing the old Italian mourning rituals I'd known in life. And I denied myself all sources of pleasure, all means of distraction from my loss of them: no television, no music, no Internet, no books, no violin, no companionship, no blood.

Encountering the woman less than one week after my seclusion ended, before I'd had the chance to feed, made her a temptation of unimaginable proportions. It made her joy not just appealing, but vital to restoring any peace to my state of mind.

For hours, I sat and watched and savored and imagined. When the rising sun turned the edge of the nighttime sky pink, I jumped down from the tree and headed back to

Edmund Place, realizing as I did so how close I lived to this woman—no more than sixteen city blocks. Even at a human pace, it was no more than a half-hour walk. To think relief had been so close all this time.

Now I just needed to make her mine.

～

L angston called me to pick up blood two days after our reunion at the blood bank. Carrying a soft- sided cooler, I approached the entrance to the hospital for my evening meeting—and stopped short upon feeling and then seeing the woman sitting on a bench ahead of me. Unless I looped around to another entrance, I would have to walk right by her to get inside.

How ironic I'd been stalking her for days and now encountered her out in the open—though the comings and goings of patients, staff, and visitors continued to protect her. I swallowed thickly, acknowledging my rather dire under-nourishment. Nearly six weeks had passed since I'd fed on a trio of wolves on the shores of Black Lake north of the city.

I scoffed. I'd gone this long before without feeding, and now she had me doubting my control as if I were a neophyte. I was used to the clench of hunger in my gut, had forced myself to endure it for much of my existence. I usually didn't tempt myself by intermingling with humans, let alone with one who was so appealing, but I was eager to taste and feel her happiness again.

So I resumed walking. Her feelings intensified within me as I approached. Forty feet, then thirty. By the time I was within ten feet, my mouth was so alive with the rich sweet-ness of her joy, I was salivating and struggling to keep my fangs retracted.

Her emotions provided such exquisite relief I couldn't

force myself to pass her by. Without a conscious decision, I stopped in front of her, her allure locking me into place as surely as if I were shackled. She looked up and smiled. Her teal eyes settled on me like a caress. In that instant, I needed to be in her presence. I hadn't intended to, but I was going to have to talk to her now.

"Would you mind if I asked you a question?" I finally asked, working hard to make my voice relaxed, casual—the exact opposite of the tense anticipation that shivered over my skin.

Her brow dropped and her expression became a little guarded, but she smiled. "Sure." Her eyes widened and her heart rate increased as she took me in.

I walked over to the bench and hesitated as my nine-teenth-century manners resurfaced. "May I?"

She nodded uncertainly, her pose less relaxed. So close to her for the first time, it took everything I had not to reach out and cup my hand behind her neck and pull her into me, particularly as her pounding heart pumped blood into a blush that spread from her face down her throat.

Touch her. Feel her. Taste her. I shook the urges away.

"I've noticed you once before when I was here visiting a friend. Please feel free to tell me to mind my own business, but both times I've been struck by how incredibly happy you…look. Such happiness seems a rare quality."

Her blue-green eyes sparkled, reflecting the inner light I could feel. Her smile was reserved at first but more open as she spoke. "Uh, well, a lot of times working at a hospital can be emotionally draining. The hours, the pace, the stress, and especially losing patients can all take it out of you. But on occasion working here can be the best thing *ever*." She paused in thought.

I found myself having to concentrate to keep my breathing normal. The strong mixture of her joy and love was arousing—a sensation I hadn't experienced in far too long. The tingling around my canines intensified.

"Do you mind if I ask what happened to make it feel like the best thing recently?" I smiled and searched her eyes. With effort, I restrained myself from charming her.

Her surprise at my interest rang through my gut as she shrugged. "Well, I've been doing a rotation in the pediatric oncology department, and one of my favorite patients found out recently she's in remission. It's been such a wondrous week, because her family has been through so much. She's always reminded me of my daughter Olivia—I couldn't imagine something threatening to take her away. So, I've just been riding on cloud nine ever since. I've never seen anyone more appreciative of life than this girl and her family. It's just really been...great to know they won't lose each other, you know?" For a brief second, a sharp torrent of loneliness underscored her words. I frowned and studied her thoughtful expression, but as quick as the bitter-tasting sadness came, it was gone. Her joyfulness returned, immersing me once more.

I listened and nodded in the right places, but was overcome with the certainty her happiness was my irresistible siren song. Like the mariners of old, I would be wrecked in my pursuit of her.

My devoted attention apparently made her feel self-conscious, because I tasted her self-doubt just as she said, "I'm sorry, I didn't mean to go on forever—"

"Not at all," I began, forcing myself to relax as I considered her words. "Thank you for sharing that. It is certainly something to feel good about."

She nodded her head and smiled as she looked down. I took the moment to study her profile. She had a small scar that cut through the edge of her right eyebrow and ran into her temple. I fought the urge to run a soothing finger over it.

At first appearance, she seemed so young and carefree.

But the set of her shoulders, the pale purple beneath her eyes, and her obvious compassion for others spoke of a woman who knew a little something about hardship. Though her emotions at the moment well concealed whatever difficulties life had thrown at her.

The soft evening breeze blew long tendrils of gold around her face and stirred up her intoxicating scent, at once luscious and fresh. I swallowed hard against the sensory assault. She was too appealing for her own good.

More. I wanted, *needed*, to learn more so I could convince myself she was nothing special, no one to regret killing. "How long have you worked here?" I asked before the pause in the conversation turned awkward.

She looked up at me and then shrugged. "Actually, I don't formally work here. I'm a nursing student. I have one semester left at Wayne State and am finishing a clinical practicum. But hopefully I'll get a job offer before the end of the fall semester." She cut herself off and glanced over at me through the wisps that had fallen free of her braid.

"Interesting," I reassured before her self- consciousness returned. Inwardly I grimaced, because it was true. Before me sat a woman with ambition, purpose, compassion.

She glanced at her watch. "I'm sorry, my break is about over. I have to be getting back." She smiled and rose from the bench.

I panicked. *Stay*.

She hesitated and looked down at me a little dazed, as if she had gotten up too fast.

I stood and offered a steadying hand under her elbow. "Are you okay?" The warmth of her skin and the rush of her quickened pulse in my palm thrilled my senses.

"Yes, I..." She placed her other hand on her forehead. "I just got a little dizzy for a second." Her embarrassment washed through me. "Um, thank you."

"Of course." I soaked her in through all my senses. I stood a full head taller, but her presence was the one that filled the darkening courtyard.

Free of my charm, she stepped back and smiled up at me. "It was nice talking to you."

"To you, too. I'm Lucien, by the way. Lucien Demarco." I offered my hand, eager to assess her reaction.

She reached out and shook with a firm grip. "Hi, Lucien. I'm Samantha Sutton."

She touched me voluntarily and with complete ease. *Remarkable.* "Glad to meet you, Samantha." My voice sounded different, lower, as I met her eyes. Her body heat soaked into me where our palms pressed together. Her hand was small and soft, but strong.

She blinked lazily. "Sam. Everyone...calls me Sam." She took an unconscious half step toward me.

I relished the proximity. "All right, then, it's nice to meet you, Sam." A couple passed us on the sidewalk. I reluctantly released her hand and her will.

She shook her head. "See you 'round," she murmured as she turned away. "I hope your friend gets better."

I nodded and watched as she walked up the sidewalk toward the doors, so bewildered by the loss of her emotions I hadn't thought to correct her assumption about my friend. Not that it mattered.

"Samantha," I whispered as I pressed the hand that had touched her to my mouth and tasted her there. I closed my eyes against the pleasure of her scent. Finally I glanced down, replaying the unexpected conversation in my head. The blue cooler bag was still in my hand.

Cazzo! Fuck!

Looking at the sky, I knew I was late for my appointment with Langston. I hurried through the hospital and ignored the pull of Samantha's scent. When I pushed through the door to the blood bank, Langston called me back to the laboratory space in the rear. I followed his voice and found him standing near a large refrigeration unit.

"Thought you were gonna stand me up," he said without any particular annoyance as he held out his hand.

We shook. "Sorry, Langston, got sidetracked."

"I figured. Just glad you made it. I held aside ten units for you. Hand your bag here." He arranged them. "These should keep refrigerated for four to six weeks. You can freeze them for longer. Did you get the equipment I suggested for all this?"

"Yeah."

"You should be set then. Just give me a shout a few days before you want more." He zipped the packed cooler shut and handed it over to me. In exchange, I passed him an envelope, which he tucked inside his lab coat.

I looked at him and debated whether I wanted the answer to the question in my head.

"Yeah, Laumet knows," he said, guessing what was on my mind.

"And?"

"He said he's looking forward to catching up with you soon."

Damn. I was going to have to be careful to keep out of Laumet's orbit. I didn't have a particular interest in being caught up with. I nodded and slung the pack onto my shoulder.

"Don't worry about it, man," he said. "I'm sure it's nothing."

We spoke for a while longer, then I made my way back out of the hospital. I half hoped to see Samantha again but didn't want to make her suspicious. I needed her to stay happy.

A bright moon lit my way through Detroit's urban decay back to Edmund Place, where I had recently refitted a base-

14

ment closet to conceal a refrigeration unit for the contents of my cooler. I drank five of the pints immediately, grimacing at the coolness of the liquid as it flowed down my throat but feeling the relief and the power of it hum through me.

With effort, I convinced myself to save the rest—though my body craved more. But I wasn't sure how frequently Langston would be able to do this for me. I opened the refrigerator and stored the remainder, suddenly restless from a combination of the rejuvenating jolt of the blood and the earlier conversation with Samantha.

Samantha. I had not planned to speak with her before having her. It was pleasurable to have done so, but it unnecessarily complicated the matter. She had proven interesting, selfless, and giving in the course of our brief conversation. She'd demonstrated the very specialness I'd hoped to disprove. But I couldn't resist what I had to do.

She was the light, and I had been drinking the dark for so very long.

CHAPTER 2

The next morning, I emerged from a normally restorative trance—a semi-conscious state that was my only form of rest—agitated and strung out. My body craved more blood, my mind yearned for Samantha's joy. Jesus, I was just *hungry*.

One thing was for sure: I had to get out of my head.

All night, the most punishing memories had assaulted me. I thought of Lena, my beautiful wife who crossed an ocean at my request, her body rounding with our second child, only to die at the hands of a monster who forced me to watch. I saw the tumble of my little Isabetta's dark curls sprawled out over a blood-covered blanket. My conscience also pulled in Catherine, my best friend in this dark existence and also my lover for a time.

I had loved all of them. Failed them. Lost them.

I muttered my aggravation in my mother tongue as I stalked into the bathroom. Setting the shower water just shy of scalding, I stepped in.

My skin was hotter than normal from feeding, so the heat was tolerable. When I fed infrequently, my skin paled and cooled, and hotter water became less comfortable. Minutes later, I twisted the nozzle to off and grabbed a thick towel.

The steam from the shower distorted my reflection in the mirror—a fitting analogy for what my unnatural existence had done to the man, the husband and father, I'd once been. *Cazzo*. There was one way to stop all this pathetic self-flagellation. Samantha. *Today she becomes mine*.

With renewed purpose, I dressed in my typical worn jeans, long-sleeved shirt, and work boots. I walked to the window and tugged the layers of heavy drapes aside. *Cloudy. Good*. Detroit's frequent overcast weather was part of why I lived here. The city's large criminal population and proximity to my adoptive coven in North Ithaca, whom I avoided because I felt such a burden to them, were other considerations.

The city was just stirring. As the morning dawned, an occasional car sped down Woodward Avenue on the side of my house. At a human pace, I ghosted through the dark gray of the morning.

When I reached Samantha's neighborhood, I surveyed the block to determine where best to intercept her. From Brush Street, I turned right on Frederick. A park sat opposite on my left, empty in the early morning gloom.

I followed the driveway into her development and then cut along the rear of the row that included Samantha's unit. The large oak tree that served as my nocturnal post obscured most of her house and provided cover as I came close enough to assess with frustration she wasn't home.

I pushed forward with my reconnaissance, circling an abandoned brick house behind Samantha's and fronting Frederick. Its boarded bay windows created an asymmetrical façade capped by a few randomly situated dormers and a conical tower. The deep-set covered entryway shielded the front door.

It was another of the city's endless inventory of late-nine-teenth century houses. Unlike many such structures, however, this one looked relatively well maintained from the outside—cut grass, clean yard and, except for the first-floor bays, intact windows.

I noticed Victorian-era houses like this all the time. Since I'd come to Detroit sixty years before, I'd honed the carpentry skills I'd learned in life to restore dozens of houses. This work was just one way I kept myself busy, distracted.

These houses fulfilled another purpose as well: I'd promised Lena a home of her own when I'd convinced her to travel to America. To be sure, I hadn't kept my most impor-tant promises to her, but I kept this one. Once, she'd given me everything. The least I could do was build her these small memorials to her life, and her death.

My previous surveillance of Samantha suggested it would be hours until her shift ended and she returned home. I ducked into the arched entryway of the old house and, intent on a diversion to pass the time, fished my silver cell phone out of my pocket and hit a number on speed dial.

On the fourth ring, the voice mail of James Bryant at LeClare Bryant LLP picked up.

"Mr. Bryant, this is Lucien Demarco. Take down the following information and get back to me. I am interested in learning the status of"—I looked more closely at the front of the house—"448 Frederick Street. Find out who owns it and whether it can be purchased. If not, persuade the owner to consider a long-term lease. Make this happen as soon as possible."

The phone snapped shut in my palm. As my long-time and well-paid attorney, Bryant routinely performed a variety of seemingly odd requests for me. He was conversant with my interest in the city's abandoned historic homes and wouldn't think twice about it.

I jumped down off the porch and gazed up at the dark red façade, impatient about the house. It would provide the perfect retreat once I captured Samantha. Then I could enjoy her at my leisure. I didn't want to have to rush. If I was going to do this, I was going to savor it. I tugged my hair back and walked around the corner of the Victorian.

Just then, a high-pitched laugh captured my attention. The tenor of the laugh, so joy-filled and innocent, called to me. I opened my senses and felt the warmth of sheer glee. It was mesmerizing.

"Slow down, Ollie!" an old man's voice shouted from down the street to my left.

My gaze followed the sounds, and I was startled to see the little girl from the hospital gliding down the sidewalk on a scooter. The man was a fair distance behind the girl. Noticing, she stepped off the scooter, turned it around, and propelled herself back to him.

"I can go fast, Grampa!" she called.

"Yes, I see that. But I can't. I'm barely awake, ya twerp." He mussed her hair. "Just don't go too far ahead, 'kay?"

"Okay." She turned her scooter around and headed in my direction again. Her eyes connected with mine before she looked back down to coordinate her foot with the pavement.

I stood and stared, her childish enthusiasm warming my chest, providing such comfort. The part of me that wasn't entranced by the girl was frustrated by my interest in her. How could any *other* girl interest me?

I shook my head and felt awkward, exposed. She'd already seen me. Again. Now she would have to pass me. I wondered if she would speak to me like last time but thought not, *hoped* not. I felt oddly cemented in place as she neared.

Stopping about ten feet away from me, she looked back over her shoulder for her grandfather, still a good sixty feet behind her. Then she turned to me and smiled. Her carefree disposition tasted refreshing, rejuvenating. I'd never been stared at so intently.

Finally, she said, "You're that…um, from the hospital—"

The ringing of my cell phone interrupted her curious speech, but I'd become as interested in observing her as she seemed to be with me.

Her eyes cut from my face to the silver rectangle in my hand and back. "Your phone's ringing. Aren't you going to answer?"

"Yes." It was the first word I'd uttered to any child since Isabetta.

The girl's intense curiosity felt warm and tingly in my gut. But most notable was what I *didn't* feel. No fear. Again.

"I suppose I should," I added.

She cocked her head and met my eyes. "Yeah. Somebody wants to talk to you." Then she shrugged, hopped on her scooter and pushed herself past me. "See ya later."

Remarkable! My eyes followed her back until I stepped under the cover of the deep porch once again. I answered my phone, pleased to hear Bryant's formal voice, and picked the lock to the door before the girl's grandfather ambled by with a steaming mug in his hand. Because the house wasn't currently inhabited by humans, there was no barrier to letting myself inside.

As I looked around, Bryant detailed the information I'd been waiting for: "The house is owned by a development company that held the whole block at one time. They leveled most of it in the late eighties to build townhouses but left two historic homes standing, then still inhabited. Four forty-eight was one of those. I've worked with that company's attorney before and just got off the phone with him. He recalled the property and feels certain his clients would be willing to lease."

"Good. Insist on my usual terms and offer whatever they require."

"Of course, Mr. Demarco."

"I'll wait to hear about the paperwork. We can take care of it by fax."

"Certainly. I'll be in touch." We both hung up.

Free of the phone, my mind doubled back to my most recent interaction with the girl. How extraordinary she is! Twice now she'd spoken to me and had neither shown nor felt fear. The conversations themselves were trivial, but it was the very fact of the interaction with her, with a human child…I shook the thoughts away. Fascinating as she was, the girl was not my focus.

Samantha was my purpose; she was the one who'd drawn me to this place. I pondered whether to prepare the old house for her arrival. It wouldn't take much to make it presentable, and the work would offer a distraction. I made a mental checklist of projects, materials, maybe even some furnishings. The property owners were apparently eager, as Bryant's call came within the hour. I signed the contract early that afternoon.

A thunderstorm darkened the late afternoon, and I ducked into the downpour with hopes of claiming Samantha. When I found her already protected within the confines of her home, I resolved to fix the new house up a bit and collected some supplies from another property. With the image of Samantha standing in the middle of my living room in mind, I labored, painting, sanding, and staining for hours on end. Working with my hands was one of the few productive outlets besides playing my violin that allowed me to pass time and redirect my thoughts away from the past.

A little before seven the next morning, I stepped outside to meet a delivery truck arriving with additional materials. I was gazing up at a sky promising to be problematically sunny when a horn blared.

I jumped down off the porch in time to see the blonde girl standing in the middle of the street. The truck wasn't going to stop in time. The girl froze in the face of her oncoming demise. I spat out a curse and bolted into the street. The truck's brakes screeched, and its tires squealed as they locked against the pavement.

I grabbed the girl around the waist and curled my arms, chest, and shoulders around her so when we tumbled to the ground on the far side of the street, my body absorbed all the punishing impact.

The driver jumped down from the cab, frantic with concern and apologies. His colleague ran around from the other side, pale despite his black skin. I waved my hand. They fell unnaturally silent and still, the darkly appealing smell of their fear dissipating from my charm.

I unfolded myself from around the girl and sat up. She remained on my lap and blinked up at me, huge tears waiting to spill down her face. Her bottom lip quivered. Her body trembled. I inhaled and was relieved the only blood I smelled was my own. My shoulder and side screamed from the road burn but were already trying to heal.

"Are you all right? Were you hurt anywhere?" I asked as gently as I could manage.

In answer, the large tears fell and her lip shook harder, but she still said nothing.

Her closeness and the smell of her tears set my throat to burning. "I'm going to take you over to sit on my porch right there, okay?"

She nodded as I cradled her in my arms and rose easily. Her eyes never left mine, and her shock from the near accident began to fade. I still didn't smell fear, which meant my proximity, incredibly, didn't faze her.

As I passed the men, I allowed them to reanimate. "Do you have anything to drink in your truck?" I asked as I remembered something I'd seen Langston do years ago for human witnesses of a shooting.

"Yeah, man." One ran to the truck and returned with a warm can of soda.

I sat the girl down on the front step of the house and opened the can, which I held out to her. "Here. Drink." Her shaking hand reached out for the soda and told me to moderate my tone.

I glared at the anxious men, surprisingly furious with them. "Take the materials inside, and place everything on the tarp in the front room."

The driver nodded, and they both moved to the rear of the truck, clearly relieved to walk away from me. I sat down on the other end of the stoop from the girl, thankful the large porch cast the steps in shade.

She continued to stare at me, then her eyes flickered to the can. "My mom doesn't let me have pop."

"Drink, please. It'll help you feel better."

Finally, she put the can to her mouth and tilted it. Her nose twitched as the fizz sprayed, and her hand shook still. While she drank and calmed down, I had my first opportunity to observe her in an unhurried manner. She had long straight strawberry blonde hair and bright aquamarine eyes. She was small and beautiful. Her innate goodness was calming, comforting.

"Where are your parents?" I asked quietly, the idea of conversing with her like this strangely...nice.

"Still sleeping."

I shifted further away on the step. The purity of her scent —like the smell of hyacinths on a spring breeze—was mouthwatering. I appreciated the intrusion of the delivery men's more corrupted scents as they passed between us with my supplies.

"Does anyone know where you are?"

The abrupt smell of fear surprised me. Given the context, it could only mean she was out without permission.

I changed tack. "What were you doing?" I pointed to the street.

"I was going to go over to the playground for a few minutes until Mom woke up." She became very interested in the soda can's design.

"What's your name?" She looked up at me. Her surprise tingled in my gut. I remembered that guilty-child look. She had expected me to reprimand her.

"Ollie."

"It's nice to meet you, Ollie. I'm Lucien."

"Hi," she whispered. She stared at me a beat longer. "I've never seen gray eyes like yours before."

I blanched. No one had ever commented on the color of my eyes, though they were unique. All vampires began their lives with red, blood-filled eyes. But our bodies had means of shielding our identity from humans. It took time to learn, but it was possible to drain the blood from our eyes, leaving them a markedly paler shade of their human color. Brown in life, mine were now a pearly gray.

Just then, a panicked woman's voice called in the distance. "Ollie? Ollie, where are you?"

The color drained from Ollie's face. She set the can down and rose. She looked me square in the eyes for several seconds in a way that was completely disarming. "I have to go." Then she turned and ran around the side of my house, her long blonde hair streaming behind her.

At that moment, the deliverymen stepped up to me with a clipboard. One began going over the invoice, but I cut him off by grabbing the clipboard and signing.

"We got a first aid kit in the truck if you wanna use it, man," the driver offered.

I knew they had seen my blood-soaked and torn shirt as they walked in and out of the house. The rawness burned, but it would heal. I handed the clipboard back and waved him away, needing them out of my presence. Seconds later, the truck rumbled down the street.

Never had I interacted like that with a child— that is, not in *this* lifetime, not since Isabetta.

Two reactions coursed through me: the grief and sadness for Isa I expected. But I also felt something I didn't expect: I felt…good. Holding and talking to her, even for those few minutes and under such distressing circumstances, felt almost…hopeful, in an unexplainable way.

And the way she looked at me, *really* looked at me. That's why I'd saved her. It made no sense for me to do so, really. As a general rule, I didn't get involved with humans.

But if she died, the one human who saw me, who made me feel like I existed in the world, would be gone. My gut tightened. I couldn't fathom the meaning of my reaction, nor did I fully understand the protective feelings I was developing for the unusual child.

I just knew, if I could help it, I wouldn't allow anything or anyone to hurt the beautiful little girl with the seeing eyes.

CHAPTER 3

Apparently, even the damn sun was on the woman's side. Days and days of brilliant weather had trapped me indoors, kept me from my prize. Daywalking I could do, but not in direct sunlight without some immediate third-degree pain. It hadn't been my intention to do a full renovation given my purpose, but it provided something to do while forced to cool my heels.

During the nighttime, I camped out near Samantha's townhouse, unable to claim her within the confines of her dwelling but relieved to find her continued joy. I'd been right: the anticipation of her blood coursing through my veins was nearly intoxicating.

I imagined how I would lure her to my new home, what she would look like standing in my living room, how her curves would feel in my arms, and how the column of her slender throat would taste against my lips. I found myself building a wall around my bloodlust for her—one that needed reinforcement daily.

As the sun set on Friday night, I gathered my tools and moved everything out to the front porch to make room for a select few pieces of furniture arriving the next morning. Once the sun was sufficiently low in the sky, I carried my things out to my black Silverado pickup parked at the curb.

I was almost done loading everything into the bed when I tasted intense sweetness. My eyes threatened to roll up into my head from the sheer pleasure of it. I knew instantaneously she must be close. I inhaled deeply, catching her scent. Footsteps echoed some distance behind me.

Samantha and an older man walked up the sidewalk on the other side of the street. I feared under the cover of darkness I wouldn't be able to restrain myself from taking her and I'd end up attacking him, too, so I flung the last of my gear into the back. Salivating hard, I rushed around to the driver's side and reached for the door handle.

Someone ran up behind me. I turned defensively, nearly dropping into a crouch, and was floored to find Ollie darting across the empty street while Samantha gaped.

"Lucien!" Ollie cried as she flung herself around my legs.

I froze. My mind was everywhere at once. The girl. Her heat. Her touch. Her scent—the spring hyacinths again. I held my breath, a last-ditch effort at restraint.

Samantha's confusion rolled through my body and played out across her face.

The two humans who'd filled my thoughts and senses over the past weeks stood before me...together? The woman I planned to kill. The child I vowed to protect. *Together*.

Questions and sensations inundated me. Amid it all, I was careful to keep my hands pressed back against the truck. I didn't want Samantha to be any more alarmed than she already was. And I didn't want to chance harming Ollie.

Ollie. Olivia. *Cazzo!* This was the daughter about whom Samantha spoke so lovingly. The blonde hair, the aquamarine eyes. How had I not put them together?

"I never really thanked you," Ollie gushed in a loud whisper.

"Olivia! What do you think you're—" Samantha's heart skipped a beat as she focused on me and recognition dawned. "I...I know you...from the hospital?" She placed a hand on Ollie's shoulder and prodded the girl to release her grip on me and stand back.

Undeterred, Ollie beamed up at me. So striking was the girl's attention it took a concerted effort to focus on Samantha's lovely voice.

I chanced a breath. "Yes. Sorry," I said, not sure exactly what I was apologizing for but feeling it necessary nonetheless. "Lucien Demarco," I reminded her.

An awkward silence filled the air for a few long moments, and then Samantha asked, "Um, I'm sorry, but how do you know Olivia?" Her fear smelled appealing though the acridity of her anger tasted sour.

"Right. Sorry. I helped Ollie the other morning," I began. "She...fell down in the street. I was working here," I said, nodding to the house behind us, "and saw her. I invited her to sit on my porch until she felt better." As I spoke, I could feel the wheels in Samantha's brain moving. The flavor of her relief began to replace the scent of her fear.

She looked down at her daughter. "When was this?"

Ollie shuffled her feet, the smile gone from her face.

"Ollie, answer me, honey."

"On Saturday morning." Ollie sniffled. "I woke up early and I got bored, so I went outside—"

"You came all the way over here to the street?" Samantha asked, alarmed again.

Ollie was too scared to answer as the tears streamed down her face.

Samantha knelt. "Olivia Sutton! How many times do I have to tell you? You cannot just wander away from the house like that!" Samantha thought for a moment, then a new wave of frustration came from her. "Were you trying to go to the *playground*? *By yourself*?"

A fresh round of tears sprung from Ollie's eyes as she nodded.

Samantha closed her eyes and took a deep breath. "*Promise* me you will not do that again, Olivia. You could have been hurt. You could have been...Promise me."

"I promise, Mommy," Ollie whispered.

Throughout this exchange, I felt like a caged lion, held in place by the force of the drama unfolding before me—a drama powerful only because of who was starring in it. At the same time, my throat was starting to burn from the prolonged exposure to their scent, their blood, their emotions. I snapped out of these considerations as Samantha stood up and addressed me.

"I'm sorry, Lucien. I'm sorry Ollie bothered you, and I'm sorry I...lost it...a little...here."

"Not at all," I replied thickly. "And Ollie was no bother, really. I was going to walk her home when we heard you calling for her. She's a sweet girl. You're very lucky," I said, my voice trailing off toward the end. Those words held more truth than she'd ever know.

"Yes, I am." Samantha ruffled her daughter's hair. Ollie's eyes were drying as she stood shyly against the man. "Oh," Samantha said, noticing, "this is my father, Joe, by the way."

The man and I exchanged nods, and Samantha looked back to me.

"So...do you live here? I've always wondered about this place. I love old houses."

We all walked around my truck to the curb. Her movements were easy, graceful.

"I've just finished renovating it for the owner and am

leasing it. It's sort of a hobby for me. I love old houses and enjoy bringing them back to life."

"That's really great," she said, looking the house over.

"Would you like to see the inside? You're more than welcome," I offered, looking at all of them. My earlier imagining of Samantha in my living room came to mind. I licked my lips but then shook the image away. I diverted my eyes so as to not influence her.

"Well..." Samantha glanced down at her watch. The sun was fully set now. "Maybe another time? It's Ollie's bedtime, and we should probably head home."

"Of course."

"Good night," Samantha said, "and thanks again." Her happiness resurfaced, warm and sweet. "Olivia, say 'good night' to Lucien."

"Good night, Lucien." She turned and whispered something to her mother, though it didn't escape my ears.

I found myself stunned, again.

"Uh...I don't know, honey. You'll have to ask him," Samantha said, a mystified undercurrent to her voice.

Ollie looked at me uncertainly for a moment, and then the bright smile returned to her face. "Lucien, can I give you a hug good-bye?" she asked unselfconsciously.

After a few seconds, I closed my gaping mouth and lowered myself to one knee, working hard to remain casual. "Sure, Ollie." I held my breath and threw walls up around all the reasons this was so wrong.

She ran the four steps between us and flung her arms around my neck.

Oh Dio! Her skin was so soft against me. With surprise, I recognized the warmth that ran up my spine as affection.

"Good-bye, Lucien. Good night," she sang.

I patted her twice on the back and looked up at Samantha's dumbfounded expression. She and Joe exchanged a meaningful glance, then she smiled and shrugged her shoulders. "Sorry," she mouthed.

I shook my head and tried to make her understand I didn't mind. Not at all. In fact I craved the innocent, affectionate touch more than I realized. More than I should. "Good night, Ollie," I breathed. "Sweet dreams."

She smiled, then turned and skipped down the sidewalk with Joe. I stood back up.

"She *never* does that." Samantha looked at me. "You should feel really special."

I flinched at the kind words.

"Well, see you around then," she said, turning to catch up with her family. "Thanks again."

"You're welcome, Sam." I regretted seeing them leave and immediately missed their company and the pleasure of their emotions. I sucked in a deep breath as the atmosphere around me seemed to change in composition. My head was spinning.

What are the chances? The woman I planned to kill—the *innocent*—was Ollie's mother, the very girl whom I had just saved and pledged to protect. I walked to the porch railing and threaded my fingers through it, then leaned forward and banged my head against the thick ornate woodwork. *Humans are so fucking messy, Lucien! This is why you should stay away!*

But I wasn't sure I could.

My longing for Samantha drew me to her window just after midnight. I was surprised to find a dim light on in her room. She sat in her bed with her back against the headboard and her knees drawn up. She was writing and, even from outside, the warmth and comfort of her love radiated.

She wrote for half an hour, occasionally leaning her head back against the white headboard and putting the pen in the corner of her mouth. She finally closed the book and slipped it into the top drawer of her bedside table. She sat for a moment and then reached over to shut off the light. Her body slid down into the covers and pillows. Soon she was asleep.

I dissected the evening's events from every conceivable angle and particularly noted the intensity of my bloodlust. That would need to be addressed if I hoped to draw this out.

But what is "this" now?

I kept vigil until the first warm pink touched the edge of the sky. My emotional tank more filled than I could ever remember it being just from hours in her presence, I finally returned home.

The furniture delivery truck arrived at nine o'clock that morning. Several rooms' worth of furniture took an inordinately long time for two human men to unload and set up. I itched to just do it myself.

Why am I so impatient, anyway? Restlessness unsettled me, filled me with nervous energy. Arranging the furniture the way I wanted it was useless as a distraction.

Downstairs, a knock sounded against the open front door. A moment later, my senses told me who'd arrived. *Dio* help me, I wanted to see them. I had to see them—it was obvious I was here. But it seemed like such a bad idea considering my desire for Samantha and protectiveness for Ollie. Those two imperatives were in direct conflict.

Knuckles rapped against the door frame again. "Hello? Lucien?"

I debated for one last moment, then attempted to restrain the speed of my movement as I rushed downstairs. Samantha and Ollie filled the doorway, both looking around with wide, curious eyes. Samantha smiled up at me as I came down the last few steps.

I drank her in through all my senses. Saliva filled my mouth, and I forcefully swallowed and took a deep breath.

"Hi," she said.

"Hello," I replied, a hopefully warm smile on my lips. The calmness that now spread through me seemed to explain my earlier anxiety—I'd been anticipating seeing them again.

"Happy house, Lucien," Ollie said enthusiastically. She held out a foil-covered plate. The space was so thick with her excitement I was swimming in it.

I took the plate from her and met her eyes. "Thank you, Ollie. How thoughtful of you."

"This looks like a bad time. We can stop back later," Samantha hedged.

Silencing the nagging voice in my head, I said, "It's no problem, Sam. The delivery men are just finishing up. I'm glad you came." And it was true. Her presence centered me. When she wasn't around, I felt literally depressed. When she was near me, a weight lifted off, like I could stand straighter.

I could only imagine how much more potent that sensation would be if it was running through my veins...I shoved the thought away. Samantha's relationship with Ollie undid my plans, even though a small part of me remained desperate to have her.

Ollie's excitement regained my attention. Hands clasped underneath her chin, she danced from side to side. "Aren't you going to open it?" she finally asked, pointing to the plate.

I laughed. *Laughed.*

"We're a little excited about what's on that plate, if you couldn't tell," Samantha joked.

"I would love to open it. Come on, let's go in the kitchen."

Her little face lit up further.

We stepped around broken-down boxes and other moving

mess in the living room on our way to the kitchen at the rear of the first floor. I set the plate down on the counter.

"Shall I?" I asked Ollie with my fingers poised to lift the foil.

"Yes! Let me help." She moved her hands to the other side of the plate and began unwrapping. "Ta- da!" she sang as she pulled off the foil with a flourish, revealing a round golden cake drizzled with a thin white icing.

"This looks delicious, Ollie. Thank you."

She was bouncing again, bursting with anticipation. "Mommy and me made it!" The fervor of her emotions reminded me of the nervous energy that had filled me earlier.

I smiled at her. "You made this?" I asked as she nodded eagerly at me. "You are really something. This is very thoughtful." I looked at Samantha. "Thank you, Sam. Truly."

"You're welcome. Just a little something to welcome you to the neighborhood. It's so nice to see this place lived in and looking so nice. You've really done a wonderful job in here," she said as she looked around.

"Mo-ommm!" Ollie cried to recapture our attention.

Samantha looked down at her playfully. "Wha-at?"

Ollie turned her attention back to me. "Do you know what it is, Lucien?"

"Um, a cake?" I hadn't eaten one in one hundred thirteen years, since my last birthday, in fact, but I was fairly certain I recognized a cake when I saw one.

"But what *kind* of cake is it?" she asked, as if I was missing an obvious point.

My sense of smell was of no help. It just smelled sweet to me. I looked down at the cake again. It was white. So I ventured a guess. "White cake?"

"Noooo!" She giggled at my mistake. "Guess again!"

"Um..."

Samantha looked at me curiously. A mild sensation of amused disbelief rolled off her.

Clearly a normal person would recognize what was on that plate.

So I made a game of it. "Chocolate cake?"

"NOOO!" Ollie laughed hard now. "*Lucien!*" She giggled impatiently.

"All right. I give. What kind is it?" I asked her.

"It's angel food cake!"

"Of course. Angel food cake. That's great, Ollie. Thanks so much, again."

She deflated at my reaction.

What am I missing? I couldn't come up with anything, so I deflected. "Well, since I'll never eat all of this by myself, will you two please have some?"

Ollie looked at Samantha hopefully.

"Okay, a small piece." Samantha smiled and looked at me. "She's been busting at the seams all morning to try it." She set the plastic bag she'd been holding on the counter. "I figured you wouldn't have your kitchen set up yet, so I brought some paper goods."

"Thank you, Sam." I made a mental note to buy kitchen supplies in case they came again.

As I turned to fill the plastic cups with water, Samantha offered to cut the cake. She laid a thick slab of the fluffy-looking confection on a plate and pushed it toward where I had been standing. Then she proceeded to cut two smaller pieces for herself and Ollie.

I turned toward them with the drinks. "Shall we sit?"

Ollie scampered over to the table balancing her plate and fork. She pulled out a chair and climbed up. "I want Lucien to sit next to me," she said, looking between Samantha and me.

I withheld any reaction to her words, though they lit me up inside, and pulled the chair out for Samantha. When I took the seat next to Ollie, her fork was poised above her cake. She looked at me expectantly, so I picked up my fork.

There was no way I was going to be able to avoid eating.

It had been a long time since I'd needed to ingest human food. Back in my earliest days at my adoptive family's New York estate, Orchard Hill, my "brothers," William and Jed, had enjoyed watching me try to learn how to eat food. Knowing my stomach would revolt, they would snicker and howl with laughter when my body violently rebelled. It was exhausting.

And they tested me too—the better I got at keeping the food down, the more exotic the food and the larger the portions they offered. Indeed, more than a few dares and bets circulated amongst the men during my years at Orchard Hill. However repulsive, it was necessary to master the consumption of food. Doing so was a safety measure; we needed to be able to pass as human in all conceivable ways.

But there was a cost to our bodies. The food either had to come back up or be destroyed internally. Our bodies were simply not equipped to process it. Whereas for humans the consumption of food was nourishing, for vampires the consumption of food was draining. Ridding ourselves of the foreign matter necessitated an expenditure of blood and energy.

Ollie was still looking at me expectantly, so I sliced my fork through the spongy cake and scooped a bit into my mouth. "Mmm," I said as I beat down my gag reflex.

They began eating too.

"Do you really like it, Lucien?"

"Absolutely. It's delicious." Another bite slid dryly down my throat. *Why am I putting myself through this again?*

"We were going to bring chocolate chip cookies," Samantha chimed in, distracting me. "But Ollie absolutely insisted we make angel food. I had to send my dad out to the market for all the eggs and sugar." She laughed.

"I *told* you, Mommy, it had to be angel food," Ollie said in exasperation.

Eager to get the cake over with, I choked down a large bite while they were looking at their plates. "It really is good, Ollie," I offered, then pushed the plate away.

"Aren't you going to finish it?"

"Absolutely. But...I just finished breakfast. So I'll have some again later."

For a moment she frowned, but then shrugged and took another bite of her piece.

Just then, the delivery men called from the front hall. "Mr. Demarco? We're all done."

"Excuse me, please." I walked out to the foyer to the man holding the clipboard.

"Do you want to walk through and inspect everything?" he asked.

"No. I've worked with your company before. If I see a problem, I'll call." I took the clipboard and signed where required. The men stepped out and closed the door behind them. I inhaled a deep breath of air less tinged with Samantha's and Ollie's scents. When I returned to the kitchen, Samantha was replacing the foil on the cake.

"Would you like a tour?" I asked hopefully.

"Sure," Samantha said, smiling.

As I walked them through the house, I delighted in Samantha's observations, questions, and compliments. I reveled in her seeming ease with me.

Ollie danced around us, trying out the furniture here and hiding behind it there.

I basked in their light. Their happiness was sweet and warm. Parts of me felt tempted to life that had long ago been buried.

As we made our way back through the house, Ollie's exuberance continued, and she skipped and jumped and sang.

"Sugar," Samantha said ruefully.

Ollie began down the steps ahead of us, then turned to say something to Samantha. The next thing I knew, she was in a free fall. Before I'd even thought through the consequences, I jumped down eight steps and caught Ollie mid fall.

"Whoa—you okay?" I asked a startled Ollie. She nodded vigorously.

I looked up. Samantha stood, frozen, at the top of the steps. Her mouth gaped. I probed her emotions, but...nothing, no emotions, seemed present. *Not good.* I met her eyes.

She was glancing back and forth between Ollie and me. Her brain apparently restarted itself then, because the smell of fear and sour taste of panic rolled through me. "How...?"

Ollie started giggling, grabbing both Samantha's and my attention. I realized I was still holding her and placed her back on her feet. A rectangular piece of soft Styrofoam packing material stuck to the bottom of one of her shoes. I pulled it off and held it up for Samantha to see. "Sorry."

Ollie made it down the rest of the stairs without incident, I followed after her. Samantha stood still.

Please let this go. Ollie looked at me strangely as I muttered a soft plea in my native tongue. Finally, Samantha came down and joined us.

"Mommy, can we go to the playground?" Ollie asked with her face pressed up to the sidelight to the left of the front door.

"Um...I don't...know. We'll see." Samantha looked back up the stairs with a frown.

"Lucien, can you come play with us?" Ollie asked.

"Ollie, I'm sure Lucien has a lot to do today," she

murmured, still not looking at me. Ollie opened the door and skipped out to the front porch. Samantha seemed torn between a desire to flee and to confront me.

The smell of her fear was becoming problematic. Fear was an especially attractive scent to my kind. With difficulty, I swallowed the bloodlust down. "Sam, I am sorry. I should have been more careful to ensure the floors were—"

Her wide eyes flew up to meet mine, resolved now. "You just saved Ollie. You saved her. You…flew…you *flew* down the steps and caught her in midair." The words came more quickly. "You didn't hesitate—one minute you were beside me and the next…and you were *perfectly calm* about it. I didn't even hear your feet…"

"Sam—"

"No! Don't get me wrong, Lucien. I can't thank you enough. I appreciate what you did. In those few terrible seconds, I had already played the whole awful scene out in my head. I saw her lying crumpled at the bottom of the steps. But…but…*how?*"

Anticipating this question, my brain had already begun evaluating possible explanations, discarding some as unworkable and placing out for my consideration a few possibly convincing ones. Hopefully one of these would work, or I was going to have to charm her to see it my way. I didn't want to have to do that with an audience; I certainly didn't want to have to charm a child as well. There was no telling what the effects of that would be on one so young.

"It was no big deal. I was only a couple steps away when she started to wobble, so I slid down the banister to her. I used to love sliding down stair railings when I was a boy," I added with a smile, trying to distract her.

"Wait. What? You weren't…already on the stairs. You were standing just by me…a little behind me, actually."

"No, Sam, really. I had just begun down the steps—"

"Mo-omm!" Ollie called from the porch. "Can we go to the playground now?" Her interruption shook Samantha's determination to have her version of events confirmed. I silently thanked the child for her impatience.

"Coming, Ollie. Don't go near the street." She looked back to me. "I'm sorry. Obviously it doesn't matter. I just got so scared seeing her fall like that." She took a deep breath and laughed a little. "God, you would think since I'm becoming a nurse, I would be a little more able to deal with stressful situations."

"Everyone would be scared for their child in that situation, Sam." We stood there awkwardly for a moment. "Well, I'd say please come back any time, but I suppose after that, you won't be wanting to visit my old deathtrap again." There was more disappointment in my voice than I had intended. Or expected.

She laughed. "Oh, stop. Of course we'll visit again. Thanks for showing us around your place. It looks great." She stepped out the open door.

Ollie sat on the front steps in nearly the same position as the first day I'd saved her. "Mom, can we go to the playground *now*?"

"Uh, okay. Just for a little while, though." Samantha turned to me. "Would you like to take a brief break from house work?"

I stepped out onto the porch with them but noted with disappointment the bright sunshine flooding the grass and sidewalk around the porch. I squinted against the uncomfortable brightness. "I would love to come with you another time, but I should really finish getting settled here today."

"*Please*, Lucien?"

I smiled at Ollie, marveling at the warmth of the affection coming from her. "I'm sorry, Ollie. Another time, though."

The salty taste of disappointment hit me. A passing sense

of that came from Ollie, although her excitement about the playground trumped it. My eyes flashed to Samantha—the feeling was hers. While she smiled her goodbyes at me, those smiles never reached her eyes.

She wants *me to come with her*. My chest tightened and I swallowed hard. *Damn, I am getting in too deep.*

And worse, I wanted more.

CHAPTER 4

I cursed the sun as they walked away, then turned and walked back into the house. The place positively vibrated with their scent.

Just then, my cell phone came to life in the pocket of my jeans. I whipped it out, not recognizing the number.

"Yes?"

"Ah, Lucien. How very good to hear your voice." I froze, recognizing the accented voice immediately, despite the decade since I'd last heard it. My hesitation didn't go unnoticed.

"Really, Lucien, where are your manners?"

"Monsieur Laumet." *Cazzo!*

"Lucien, we have known one another for half a century." Amusement rang through his words. "Why the formality?"

"Fine, Antoine. I wasn't sure if we were still on a first-name basis."

"You're hurting my feelings, Lucien. Of course we are. Why wouldn't we be?"

"Antoine, may I ask what you want?" I worked hard to

moderate my tone, though the hairs on the back of my neck rose. No good could come from reassociating with Laumet.

"I always did appreciate your directness." He chuckled. "I was simply pleased to hear from Langston you were alive and well and wanted to check in on you for myself," he said with an innocence he didn't possess.

"Well, I appreciate that. I'm good, but of course, I have no illusions you didn't know perfectly well I was still around." Laumet had a large vampire guard and a huge staff of human employees, most of whom were not in on his secret life. Still, there were plenty of Laumet-loyal goons running around Detroit keeping an eye on every aspect of the city for him.

"Be that as it may." He hesitated—his purpose in calling was coming.

I distracted him with more small talk. "Since we're exchanging pleasantries, Antoine, how have you been?" I paced the length of the first floor.

"Oh, Lucien. Thank you. I thought you would never ask. I am old and under-appreciated. The times aren't what they used to be. All this effort at economic revival and urban rede-velopment in my old city complicates my life. But, of course, I am managing to adapt to the changes. Business is growing, and we do our best to identify new opportunities," he said, as if he was talking merely about overseeing a small family business.

"Hmm" was all I could think to say.

"I want you to come see me, Lucien. I would love the opportunity to catch up with you in person and reminisce about old times." So this was the real reason for the call, then. He was summoning me to him. Given it was *his* city in just about every sense of the word, one simply did not refuse such a request.

I sighed. I'd give it one try: "Of course I appreciate the

offer. But, begging your indulgence, I remain rather fond of our current arrangement. I—"

"Tomorrow night. Nine p.m. The Boat Club on Belle Isle. I *will* see you then." The line went dead.

"*Cazzo!*" I roared as I threw my phone, lucky it landed against the soft cushion of a distant chair before clattering to the floor.

I spent the rest of Saturday waiting impatiently for the sun to set enough to return to Edmund Place. As soon as I got home, I flew to the basement and wrenched open the refrigerated storage unit, then consumed the remaining pints right out of the plastic.

The blood began to work its magic within my body. I hadn't fed so frequently in a long time. My senses immediately heightened, and my muscles tingled with an electric energy. The air felt cooler against my now-blazing skin.

Unusually sated and satisfyingly warm, I could think of only one other way to prepare for tomorrow's reunion: rest. As I willed myself into the trance, lying in the coolness of my drape-darkened bedroom, I thought about my arrival to this city and everything that flowed from it.

Coming to Detroit sixty years ago began the darkest chapter of my existence. Still guilt-ridden from my human family's horrific deaths and infuriated at my inability to find and exact revenge upon my maker, I had willingly associated myself with the worst of the vampire race. I deserved little better and went out of my way in those years to punish myself. Knowing I would see Laumet again brought the memories of those dark times into sharp relief.

Finally, it was time.

I made my way through downtown to Belle Isle. I hadn't been on the island in the middle of the city's river for years. Making no effort to conceal my arrival, I crossed the cracked parking lot to the path that led across a raised footbridge to the abandoned Boat House's entrance. The canopy and awning over the walkway were long gone, leaving only the metal skeleton that had once held the fabric. I pushed through the front door into a dark vestibule—left dilapidated to discourage curious trespassers, as was the usual practice— and came to a set of heavy double doors.

Two thumps of my fist served as my knock.

After a moment, the door opened. Langston stood before me with an apologetic expression on his face. I walked in and clapped him on the shoulder. I didn't blame him for this situation—not that I knew if there was a situation yet. I paused while Langston secured the door. Then he led me through a once- grand lobby space into a ballroom.

Laumet always surrounded himself with the most beautiful spaces in Detroit—this Boat House was no exception. Ornately molded wood paneled the walls, and a beautiful balustrade featuring carved sea horses framed a balcony around the top of the room. Heavy blue velvet curtains hung at the windows, effectively shielding the abundant candlelight in the room from outside notice.

As was his style, Laumet sat as if holding court in an oversized chair at the head of the room near the fireplace. His hair was silver, although his former black color still revealed itself in its undertones. His silver eyes were filmy around the edges. He was the oldest vampire I had ever seen in every sense of the term—at least sixty or seventy when transformed nearly three centuries ago. His finely tailored black suit accentuated his dark brilliance and aura of power. The silk was so fine the candlelight danced off it.

I approached but paused just a few feet in front of him. His smile was wide and genuine. Encouraged, I stepped forward and offered my hand. "Good evening, Antoine."

He shook enthusiastically. "Yes, Lucien, it is. I am so

pleased you came to see me tonight." He held on a moment longer than seemed natural and studied my eyes and face all the while. "You look well."

"Thank you." I let pass the fact that he'd given me no choice but to come. Laumet's good humor surprised me. He had a volatile personality, so I never knew what to expect from him.

That was perhaps because of his line of work. He ran some legitimate businesses, but most of his wealth and power came from his black market operations and illegal entertainment activities. It was dangerous to trust the people who operated in these arenas, so Laumet's group of confidantes was quite small and for the most part consisted of the people sitting in the room, myself included, despite a number of recent clashes.

"You remember Jacques and Magena, of course." The pair of them sat on a brocade sofa a few feet from Laumet. Jacques was short, slight, and olive- skinned, with black hair pulled back into a tight ponytail with a leather cord, while Magena was exquisite—dark skinned with waist-length iron-straight black hair and high pronounced cheekbones that set off her sparkling silver eyes.

"Of course." I nodded to them.

Magena offered a warm smile, her emotions full of affection for me as they had always been. Jacques managed a sort of a grimace then looked away. His continued hostility toward me was no surprise.

"Won't you please sit, Lucien? Langston, you too." He motioned to a second brocade sofa opposite from Magena and Jacques. The fire was a little too warm against my blood-heated skin, but I offered no complaint.

Everyone looked uncomfortable to some degree—except Laumet.

"Ah, it's so nice having all of you together again." Laumet

crossed his legs and smiled at us. Awkwardness hung in the air like a fog.

Finally, Magena said, "So, what have you been up to all these years, Lucien?"

"Truly? Nothing remarkable, Magena. Existing." Jacques rolled his eyes.

"Do you still work renovating old houses?" she asked.

Her efforts were paying off. The small talk relaxed everyone. "Yes, occasionally. I have restored nearly four dozen houses, many of which I still own. It helps pass the time. And seeing the end result is satisfying. I just finished one this week, in fact."

She smiled back. "How fascinating. The city should give you a medal—you're a one-man force for historic preservation."

I smiled at Magena, grateful as the last of the awkwardness faded. She and I had always had a special relationship, born of our shared misgivings about what we were. "That might be a little more attention than would be in anybody's best interests. Not to mention the city seems to be more interested in tearing things down than building them back up again."

"True in the neighborhoods"—Antoine joined in—"but downtown, the city has been attempting a resurrection with new buildings, new sports fields, and waterfront development. It's been quite a renaissance."

"And new casinos, too," I added.

"Indeed. I have been particularly pleased with that development."

"I assumed as much. And how is that business treating you?"

He chuckled. "If I had known how lucrative casinos could be, I would have built one myself. It is a sad testament to human nature that people without sufficient money to feed their families or pay their obligations will come to a casino and put their whole paycheck on the line."

"We don't feel too sad for them, though, do we, Father?" Jacques smirked at me as he addressed the vampire who had been his human father; they had been changed at the same time. "You should add stupidity to your list of death-deserving human failings, Lucien. You would never run out of a fresh supply of blood if you did. We certainly don't."

"Very good, Jacques. You managed to make it a whole"—I made a show of looking at my watch— "wow, twenty minutes, before starting in on me."

Looking down, Magena tried to hide her smile. "Yes, yes," Antoine interjected, amused. "Just like old times indeed. I do wish my sons could get along better."

Jacques blanched. Laumet frequently used family metaphors to talk about the vampires who served him, but his designation of me as one of his sons always rankled Jacques. Laumet liked me as well as and treated me nearly the same as one of his real sons. Maybe that was because one of his sons had died, and Jacques was the only one remaining.

Whatever the case, Jacques was clearly shocked to hear Laumet still considered me that way after my long separation. Jacques's jealousy of me was and had always been palpable. And with that comment, his father had just reignited the smoldering burn of his hatred for me.

As the conversation continued, I kept waiting for something bad to happen, sure Laumet had summoned me for some purpose I wasn't going to like. However, the night passed in storytelling about our shared pasts. Aside from Jacques's black emotions, it wasn't altogether unenjoyable.

With an affectionate chuckle, Magena recalled my confusion regarding Laumet's possessiveness of Detroit. She'd long ago been the one to explain to me when he said it was his city, he really meant it was *his* city: in the late seventeenth century, Laumet, who claimed for himself the title Sieur de Cadillac, founded Fort Pontchartrain, the forerunner of the modern city of Detroit.

However, ruthless even as a human, Laumet had earned the ire of the powerful Jesuit priests, who exiled him to face imprisonment in France for illegal trade with the natives. The king soon pardoned him and rewarded his New World service with a governorship in the south of France.

"That was when I met my maker," Laumet reminisced. "A servant girl had accused the lord of an aristocratic family of witchcraft. Curious, I looked back through the records to discover the family had been accused twice before. Each time the accuser either died or disappeared. It was all very convenient."

Jacques shifted in his seat as Antoine spoke. His dread of the memory suffocated me. Knowing I would sense his discomfort, he glared at me.

"Henri Malenfant was all that the girl had said, and more. He promised me power and immortality if I could eradicate the evidence that led me to suspect him. How surprised I was to learn what he was." Antoine paused.

We all knew where his mind went. Jacques's recall of the pain of their transformation washed through me. The Laumet men had all been perfectly healthy when Henri changed them. Their bodies, their blood, had therefore fought the change, which made their experience sheer agony.

Antoine sighed. "Returning to my old domain made everything worthwhile. Even when things were hard here"— he gazed at Magena with a small smile—"I was satisfied to be back in the wilds of my American empire."

Magena offered a shy smile in return, although her emotions were less composed. A flash of rage chilled me before she reined herself in, then her eyes flickered to Langston before looking down.

Magena resented her transformation. Mortally wounded during the conflict between the British and Indians under Pontiac's leadership, Antoine saved and transformed her, wanting her for a mate.

She stayed with him initially out of fear and despair, the spiritual beliefs of her people making her transformation particularly hard to accept. Later she grew to appreciate Laumet's protectiveness toward her in a world where all the rules had changed.

But though she held a certain respect for Laumet, she never loved him. She thought herself incapable of it—she saw herself as a monster, as evil incarnate, though in truth she was one of the most gentle of my kind I'd ever known.

Like me, Magena bore a gift she believed a curse. Her telepathy meant she could literally hear the fearful thoughts her presence caused in humans. It made her especially aware of her effect on others. The flip side of her self-hatred was an ever-present resentment of Antoine for putting her in this position in the first place.

This was something he did not know, but I could easily feel. And I had always kept her confidence.

Laumet interlaced his fingers and laid his hands in his lap. "The rest, as they say, is history." He radiated a smug satisfaction at the recounting of his history—though parts of his story had reawakened the group's discomfort. Jacques's phantom pain and Magena's turmoil settled on my shoulders like a lead weight.

With some effort, Magena lightened the mood. She recalled the city's golden age when the auto industry brought wealth and society to Detroit. The elite found Antoine and Magena fascinatingly exotic and dangerously mysterious, and they were frequent guests at the city's best addresses. Antoine had loved the attention.

Langston regaled us with Motown stories. He'd seen Stevie Wonder play in Detroit as a kid. And the other artists he saw or met read like a who's who of great American musicians. Magena laughed and smiled warmly at Langston's stories. They had been good friends since Magena and I had helped him through his transition to this life.

Jacques was reluctant to participate. Ever since Antoine told the story of their transformation, he'd stood stone still near the fireplace. When Antoine pushed him, I was not at all surprised at the kinds of stories he chose to tell.

A dark humor came over him. He went into explicit detail regarding the number of humans he'd been able to consume during the city's two notorious race riots in 1943 and 1967. Remnants of the latter remained visible all over.

"It was bacchanalian. Blood, violence, the freedom to attack—in broad daylight. And the fires, they were everywhere, perfect for disposing of those pesky bodies." He folded his arms over his narrow chest and fixed a do-something-about-it stare on me. "Two of the best days of my life."

Magena glared at Jacques. But it was the barely audible growl rumbling in Antoine's chest that forced him to end his story abruptly.

Still, Jacques was riled up enough to spit out one last taunt: "Why, Lucien, you haven't regaled us with any stories of your own. Surely you intend to remind us what a *hero* you are."

I shot up and stalked toward him.

Jacques's reference to *that* story pushed me to my limit. I had saved his and his father's lives from an assassination attempt by a power-hungry human who had allied with some of Laumet's vampire enemies. But Jacques's brother, François, died in the battle, and Jacques blamed me. When Antoine freed me from my obligation of service to him in recognition of my actions, Jacques had become incensed.

Magena jumped up and grabbed my arm, saving me from being stupid. I glared down at him; the angst I'd experienced in recent weeks itched to find release. I would have loved to unleash it on Jacques, who ranked only above my maker as my least favorite creature in the world.

"Enough!" Antoine commanded both of us to settle down, although his order was more aimed at his son than at me.

Jacques's rage chilled me to the bone, and his humiliation tasted sour. My words came low and fast. "Antoine, I appreciate the pleasure of your company. But I should leave. Now."

His eyes made a circuit from Jacques to the velvet-covered windows that hid the impending dawn and back to me. "Yes, I believe you are right. It is time for you to be going." He looked up at me. "It was nice to see you again."

His sincerity was disarming. I didn't know what to make of it. Laumet had always valued me for my honesty and frankness; few others were willing to risk his wrath, but when we'd first met I hadn't cared enough about myself to fear him.

I nodded good-byes to Magena and Langston, then crossed the ballroom. With my hand on the door knob, I hesitated. "Antoine, is there truly no other reason you wanted me here tonight?"

In an instant he was standing beside me, his right hand curled around the back of my neck and his face close to mine. "Do not be concerned. I only wished to see you. Your candor and loyalty were always a comfort to me and not at all easy to come by. I know those days are gone. You earned your independence. But allow an old man to reminisce."

A touch of warmth revealed his affection for me and made me believe him. I nodded my head, and he squeezed my neck before dropping his hand. In the same instant, he disappeared from my side.

Without looking back, I fled out the door, through the building, and into the night.

CHAPTER 5

Jacques's black feelings infected me as I returned to Edmund Place just as the sun fully broke over the city. I cursed myself for letting him get under my skin. He'd always had a knack for exploiting my vulnerabilities. My years apart from him had clearly left me out of practice for dealing with his invective, which pissed me off to no end.

I showered and regretted my earlier consumption of the remainder of the blood. A fresh infusion would have gone a long way toward easing my discomfort. Instead, I sprawled out on my bed in my darkened room, the air cool against my still-wet skin, and forced myself into another long, deep trance.

Thirty-six hours later, I awoke as the sun set on Tuesday night. I had been out a long time, but despite the attempt at rest, recent infusion of blood, and distance from him, Jacques's twisted mind continued to taint my well-being.

There remained only one thing I hadn't tried: Samantha. I growled at the thought. Ollie's near fall on the stairs, Samantha's observation of my abnormal actions, and my bloodlust were all reasons to stay away from the Suttons. I lulled myself back into a trance.

Samantha's image moved in and out of my thoughts all night. I finally gave up on rest as a means of distracting myself from my want of her. Three movies, half a book, and a violin concerto later, she remained the center of my focus.

As I threw on clothes, my resolve crumbled. I fled out the door and headed north. The darkening sky allowed me to move swiftly through the warm summer night. Five days had lapsed since I'd last been at the Frederick Street house and, more importantly, since I had last seen—felt—the girls.

I ignored the nagging voice that told me I should be distancing myself, not seeking them out. My eagerness to be in Samantha's presence built as I walked up Brush Street. I needed her.

I unleashed a tirade of colorful Italian expletives at Jacques. His contagious vitriol raised my bloodlust and forced me to imagine, for just one last moment, Samantha's blood flowing into my mouth and down my throat. The most thrilling part of that vision was not the warmth, nor the quenching, nor the sweet flavor; it was the pain-relieving ecstasy her emotions would bring to my body.

I stopped in my tracks. *But then she would be gone. And what would happen to Ollie?*

Cazzo! I shuddered this whole train of thought away. *You. Will. Not.*

Faintly, I tasted the sweetness of Samantha's happiness. I shook my head to break the daydream, but I wasn't imagining the sensation after all.

Inhaling deeply, I caught her scent—she was in the park across the street. Now that I focused, I could hear and feel them both. While I debated, my feet made the decision, and I crossed Frederick and followed the diagonal sidewalk that led to the playground.

Samantha and Ollie's presence pushed the last of Jacques's poison from my mind, and my shoulders relaxed. Guilt over using them attempted to worm its way into me, but the relief of their healing influence was stronger.

Maybe I'd been thinking about this all wrong...

Ollie saw me first. "Lucien!" She threw herself around my legs.

Having advance warning this time, I was prepared for her contact and could manage a more normal reaction than I had when she'd surprised me at my truck that night. "Hello, Ollie."

She squeezed harder.

"Hey. There you are." Samantha followed Ollie across the playground and stopped several feet in front of me. She looked so lovely with her blonde hair down over a form-fitting white V-neck T-shirt and a pair of jean shorts. Her blue-green eyes sparkled at me.

"Hello, Sam." I nearly sighed. "How are you?"

"We're good."

Ollie stepped back but was holding onto my right hand. The contact was an amazingly satisfying sensation. She tugged once as Samantha and I talked. "Lucien, do you want to play?"

Play with me, Papa!

I winced. "Uh..." The memory of Isabetta's voice caught me off guard, rattled me.

Samantha looked at me with an amused grin. Ollie tried again. "I know! You can push me on the swings!"

I tugged my hair back off my face. "Um, sure." Ollie ran over to the swing set and pulled herself up onto the plastic seat. As I pushed her, Samantha came over and leaned against the closest metal support pole. Her obvious pleasure in watching me with her daughter helped soften my feeling of betraying my own.

57

Ollie laughed. Between fits of giggles, she sputtered, "Wow, Lucien! You push higher than Mommy by a lot!"

I tore my eyes away from Samantha and gaped. At the top of the high arc, the chain slackened for a few seconds before jerking Ollie back in the other direction. I let her go for a few swings without pushing and allowed her to return to a more reasonable height. "Sorry," I said.

Samantha laughed. "Don't worry about it. She loves it. Nothing scares her."

I already knew that was true.

Samantha made small talk with Ollie for a few minutes before her daughter announced she was done swinging. She hopped down and ran to the sliding board. I became aware of eyes on me. Samantha was watching me watch her daughter. I looked to the ground.

"You're her new favorite person. She talks about you nonstop."

My eyes widened as I looked up at her. I opened my mouth to respond but nothing came out. My brain froze with unexplained emotion.

"I'm sorry. I didn't mean to embarrass you."

I met her stare and laughed despite myself. To laugh, to smile—both so foreign—Jesus, being near her made me dizzy with life. I swallowed. "No, no. Don't apologize. I, uh, I really like Ollie, too. She's a great kid."

Samantha smiled. "Yeah." She held my gaze for a moment, and her heart rate jumped. A slight flush colored her face. It was stunning. "So…" She stepped away from the bar against which she had been leaning and moved toward a bench on the side of the playground.

The next thing I knew, she pitched forward. I caught her with one hand around her waist and another around her arm. I overcompensated slightly, distracted by the feel of her warm silkiness against my skin, and pulled so her back momentarily pressed against my front.

A torrent of competing emotions erupted. The taste of embarrassment. The smell of fear. The heat of lust. I couldn't sort out which were mine and which were hers.

She chuckled nervously. "Thanks."

"Are you okay?"

"I think so. Let's just sit for a minute."

I dropped my hands and motioned for her to continue over to the bench. I stepped over the small hole in the blacktop that had caught her foot and stayed next to her in case she was unsteady.

She sat on the edge of the bench and rotated her ankle. "Eh, I'll live."

We smiled, then sat awkwardly for a minute. Samantha's heart rate remained elevated.

Finally, she broke the silence. "Hey, Lucien? Are you feeling all right?"

I frowned. "Me? Yes. Why?"

She reached her hand over to my face, pausing to silently ask permission before continuing.

I nodded, still not understanding. Then I registered her worry.

She pressed the palm of her hand to my forehead and then slid it down to my cheek. I wanted to lean into her touch. "Lucien, you're burning up. I can't believe you're sitting here so easily with a temperature this high."

I flinched and pulled back.

She dropped her hand. "Sorry to go into nurse mode on you, it's just—"

"No, don't apologize. I'm fine, really. I...tend to run a little warm. You shouldn't worry about me." My inexperience around humans had finally proved a liability. I should've realized my recent meals would elevate my body temperature and been more careful.

"Lucien, you don't feel just a 'little warm.' "

I stood up and stepped away. "Why don't I walk you two home?"

She sighed, seeing through my effort at distraction, but agreed. She rose and tested her ankle, taking a couple of tentative steps and favoring the uninjured side.

I steeled myself. Her injury made her vulnerable. Her vulnerability made her even more appealing. I cursed my instincts for evaluating her this way.

"Ollie, it's time to go, honey."

"Can I have five more minutes, Mommy?" She looked up at us expectantly as she came over.

"No, honey. Let's go. It's late. Besides, Lucien offered to walk back with us."

"Oh! Okay!" Ollie skipped and sang in front of us as we walked across the park to the street.

"I knew that would be the selling point," Samantha said as she elbowed me softly and smiled.

Out of the park, we ambled along the bush-lined side-walk. It was dark along this stretch of Frederick. The monster within me reared up again and begged to be sated by Samantha's blood. Luckily, Samantha didn't notice my struggle.

"Unbelievable."

"What?" I tasted the tartness of her annoyance, but had been so caught up in my own thoughts I wasn't sure what caused her mood shift.

"I've called about replacing that street light"— she pointed to a dark pole about ten yards in front of us—"four times in the last three weeks. This street seems so dark without it. I mean, this neighborhood is a lot better than some, but still…"

"I'll call too. Maybe if more than one person complains,

it'll get fixed." The exchange proved an effective distraction from my bloodlust. Plus I would do anything to make her happy. *What a remarkable thought.*

"Hey. Thanks. I'd appreciate that." She smiled. Her heart rate picked up again.

As I met her eyes, she leaned in to me. My mouth watered. My desires warred. I looked away and took a deep breath, shoving down the urge to kiss her. *What am I doing?*

At my house, a piece of paper stuck out from the jamb of my front door. "Oh, that's from us. We came by to visit you on Sunday afternoon."

"Well, I'm sorry to have missed you."

"Me, too," Samantha said as she peeked up at me. Her heart rate accelerated yet again and, as if her happiness by itself wasn't attractive enough, she began projecting the warmth of affection and the heat of desire for me. It was intoxicating.

We passed my house and crossed the grass field toward the back of Samantha's. I asked her a few questions about her work, eager to hear her voice and heighten her feelings of happiness. My interest pleased her. She was proud of becoming a nurse.

We stepped up to the front porch of their townhouse. Ollie had exhausted much of her energy and yawned. Samantha put a hand on Ollie's shoulders and hugged her in, then smiled at me. "Thanks for walking us home, Lucien. I'm glad we ran into you."

"You're welcome. I'll see you."

She hesitated for a moment. "I hope so." The blush was slow in coming, but I could feel the heat of it from where I stood.

I smiled back and nodded. "Good night, Ollie. Dream good dreams."

The words came out of my mouth effortlessly, and I

sucked in a breath in surprise. I hadn't uttered them in well over a century. *Dream good dreams*—my bedtime wish for Isabetta every night of the forty-one months of her short life.

"G'night," Ollie mumbled. Then she turned and grabbed the storm door handle, and they both walked through. Samantha waved over her shoulder before shutting the door.

I walked away smiling. As I left the radius of the porch light and stepped into the dark shadows on the side of her house, a startling thought hit me. *I have feelings for her. For them.*

No, not possible. Can't be. My guilt had eaten my capacity for love a long time ago.

Disconcerted, I crossed the field to my new house and decided to stay there for a while. I often familiarized myself with my new properties by residing in them for stretches, particularly after completing a renovation. I jogged up the porch steps and fished my key out of my jeans pocket.

The papers Samantha had left were wedged into the jamb. I grasped them as I pushed through the door and flicked on the light. I walked into the living room and sank into the leather couch. My boots fell to the floor with a couple of thuds, then I propped my feet up on the coffee table.

With pleasure, I noted I'd retained some of Samantha's happiness despite my distance from her, similar to the way I'd held on to Jacques's darkness earlier. I shifted and my arm brushed the papers lying next to me on the couch. Samantha's and Ollie's scents hung on the pages as I unfolded them and found Samantha's handwriting.

> Hi, Lucien—Just stopped by to say hello. Hope
>   you're getting settled in. Ollie wanted to
>   drop this off for your fridge. Let us know if
>   you need anything.
> Sam & Ollie (Sunday @3 p.m.)

I shuffled the note behind the second page, a child's drawing of a man, sort of. From the man's back two white triangles protruded. There was also a yellow circle over the man's head. Ah, an angel. I smiled, then leaned forward and laid the papers on the coffee table.

I frowned. Written in the bottom corner of the drawing were three words: "Lucien, by Ollie." I stared at the drawing. Ollie's words confounded me, but after a minute I realized she simply forgot to write the word "for" in front of the other three.

I rose and paced the first floor. I'd always appreciated the serenity of the night. But my restlessness was unsettling. I fought the urge to go to Samantha's tree. More temptation was the last thing I needed.

Instead, I ran through the moonless night to Edmund Place, lucky the darkness concealed my unnatural pace. I built a fire, crashed on the couch, and spent the night drifting in and out of a trance. Just before daybreak, crashing thunder convinced me to give up on trying to get any meaningful rest. I showered, changed, and retrieved a few belongings to take to the new house.

It was both selfish and masochistic to spend any more time there, but the idea of not going, of not seeing them…So I went.

And the restlessness maddeningly returned. But I couldn't make any sense of my emotions. There was no one around, so they were clearly mine.

A knock at the front door interrupted my thoughts. I sensed immediately who stood on the other side. *Don't answer.* I nodded, agreeing with myself.

But then she knocked again and called my name. When I still didn't answer, she chanted, "Please be home, please be home, please be home."

Extending my empathic abilities to seek her out, the most

comforting affectionate warmth embraced me. Shaking my head at my weakness, I worked at a smile and opened the door. "Hi, Ollie."

"Hi, Lucien! How are you?" she asked with a big grin as she twirled a clear umbrella with sea creatures on it.

"I'm good."

She laid the umbrella on the porch, then walked in and flopped down on the couch like she owned the place.

I watched her in amazement. "Um, does anyone know where you are?" I closed the door and leaned against the arch separating the foyer from the living room.

"Yep. I asked Mommy last night if I could visit you today, and she said yes. As long as I came straight here and told Grampa and didn't interrupt anything important you were doing."

I marveled at Samantha's trust in me, especially as it was so ill placed.

"I told Grampa, and he just said I needed to be home for lunch at twelve o'clock." She looked down at the plastic pink watch on her wrist. "It's only five after eleven o'clock now. See?" She held her arm up to me. "Were you doing anything important?"

I laughed and shook my head. "No, definitely not." As I spoke, I ignored that the restlessness was dissipating in Ollie's presence.

"Good." She leaned forward and grabbed her drawing. "Did you like my picture?" She held it on her lap and smiled up at me expectantly.

"Yes. Very much. Thank you."

"Can we hang this on your refrigerator?" She stood up in anticipation.

"Uh, sure. Let's see what I can find to hang it." I pushed myself off the wall and headed to the kitchen.

Ollie followed. "We use magnets at home. Or tape. Do you have any tape?"

"Good idea." I opened the utility closet in the back hallway next to the kitchen and found some remaining painting supplies, including a roll of blue tape. I ripped off a piece, and we walked to the fridge.

"Here," she said. "You hold the paper still, and I'll put the tape on." She pulled the tape off my fingers and applied it to the corners of the paper.

I watched her while she worked and sensed nothing but the warmth of affection from her. Which wasn't nothing, at all.

"That makes it much homier, Ollie. Maybe you can draw me something else to fill up the rest of this empty space." She beamed at my invitation.

I scratched my head. She simply reached a part of me I didn't even know still existed.

Ollie moved curiously around my kitchen. After a few minutes, her eyes settled on the black case on the kitchen table. She walked over to it and ran her index finger down the marred surface. "Is this a guitar?"

I walked over to the other side of the table. "A violin. Would you like to see it?"

"Yeah." She took a step back but leaned her head forward excitedly.

I spun the case around and unclasped the latches. "You can hold it if you want. Just sit down." I pushed the chair out for her, and she scooted herself up. I laid the violin in her arms, and she cradled it uncertainly like a baby. I smiled. "Do you want me to show you how to hold it?"

She nodded eagerly.

I knelt down next to her and double checked my control. Though she smelled and felt good, my protectiveness of her had overridden my bloodlust, for which I was incredibly grateful—I would never be able to forgive myself if I stole the lifeblood from a child, particularly this one.

I positioned the violin on her collarbone and showed her where to place her hand and chin. Then I handed her the bow and invited her to move it across the strings. The screeching noise made her grimace and me laugh. I offered her more guidance, and she attempted to play again.

Then she stopped and held the instrument out to me. "Do you play?"

I pulled out the chair next to her and sat down. "Yes. Do you want to hear something?" The adoration in her lovely blue-green eyes melted me. I just couldn't fathom it.

She wanted me to play for her. So I played. She started clapping immediately. "That's 'Twinkle, Twinkle, Little Star'!"

Encouraged by her requests for encores after each song, I played for her for almost a half hour before we ran out of time.

"Thanks, Lucien. You're good at the violin."

"Thanks," I said as I secured the instrument in its case. "Come on. I'll walk you home."

"Okay."

We walked out of the house as she chattered. The rain had stopped. A muggy haze hung over the midday. I was just thinking how much I appreciated the overcast day when Ollie did the most shocking thing—for me at least.

She took my hand.

I looked down. Her hand was engulfed by mine and so filled with life. She was oblivious to the significance of her actions. To her, the idea of holding my hand—a grown-up's hand—was commonplace. To me, it offered a sense of connection I'd never had. I reveled in her touch and memorized everything about the moment.

Ollie ran inside her house with a wave. I stood on the sidewalk, dumbfounded. She had seen me, met my eyes, volunteered interaction, spoken to me, touched me, embraced me. It was wondrous, but...completely fucking unprecedented.

Wasn't it? Lost in thought, I meandered back over to my place, wondering how to determine if Ollie's reaction was typical of children in general. The sound of cheering pulled me out of my head.

The park. Other kids would be at the park. I passed my house and walked with purpose.

As I approached, a group of boys of all ages played touch football. They skidded on the wet grass and laughed and jeered at one another. None were as young as Ollie, but they were still kids. I grabbed a nearby bench at the side of the makeshift field and watched.

Twenty minutes lapsed without a single apparent notice. When an errant pass sent a boy tumbling within feet of me, my stomach tingled with his surprise at my being there. When another overshot sent the ball end over end near my bench, I retrieved it and threw it to the boy who had missed the pass. I smelled his fear even as he thanked me.

Maybe it was me being a big white guy and him being a black teenager, but I didn't think so. I left them to their game and followed the sidewalk to the central playground.

A boy and a girl nearer to Ollie's age alternated sending action figures and matchbox cars down the wet slide so they landed in a puddle at the bottom with a splash. They didn't look up or acknowledge me, but their heart rates increased. The longer I stood there watching them, the more inappropriate my observations felt, so I left.

Still, I'd gathered enough evidence. It wasn't just that I'd avoided children for the past century. Nor did all children react with as much acceptance.

Ollie was special.

I hadn't really needed an experiment to prove that. It

simply confirmed what I already knew. But could I really keep that specialness in my life? My heart railed against the resounding NO my conscience offered up. *There is one way to lessen the risk…*

The thought energized me, and I left the park on a mission.

CHAPTER 6

A little before six o'clock, I shelved the procured flasks in the cabinet next to the kitchen sink. I felt the girls' presence before they even knocked on the door.

Samantha and Ollie stood on the front porch and invited me to walk over to the playground with them again. More hopeful now that this...friendship with them could work, I was only too happy to agree.

Ollie entertained herself on the playground while Samantha and I sat on a bench talking. I focused the conversation on her and was so engrossed in hearing her thoughts vocalized and feeling her happiness a whole hour passed without notice.

Finally, Ollie danced in front of us. "Can we go home now, Mommy? The 'squitos are eating me."

"Okay, honey. Let's go."

Back at their house, we stood on the front porch making small talk. Samantha looked up at me. "Would you like to come in?"

My mind erupted with want and regret. I managed to nod

and followed Samantha and Ollie into their house, awed to actually be inside.

By issuing the invitation, Samantha had unwittingly lost her last line of defense. My control and the contents of those flasks had just become even more important. Samantha's father walked into the room, and we exchanged hellos. He remained wary of me, his reaction the more typical.

Ollie asked to watch a television show before bedtime. Joe took Ollie's hand. "I'll watch with you, Ollie. Come on." He led them to a room on the other side of the kitchen and looked back at Samantha. "I'll keep an eye on her if you want to go out for a while or something."

"That's great, Dad. Thanks." She walked over and kissed Ollie on the head. "Be good for Grampa, 'kay?"

"Okay, Mommy. Bye, Lucien," she called, already getting herself settled in front of the television as Joe worked the remote.

Samantha looked at me expectantly.

While I wanted to remain in her presence, I wasn't convinced I could trust myself alone with her. So when it came, Samantha's innocent question disarmed me. "Do you want to get some ice cream?"

My only response was a laugh.

"What? I'm dying for some ice cream. I was going to get some at lunch today and decided against it. And I've been thinking about it ever since." She smiled a little self-consciously.

I couldn't contain my continued mirth. "Sure. Ice cream it is. Where do you want to go?"

She walked toward me and our eyes met, drawing me to her until I had to look away. "How about the Ben and Jerry's downtown? I love their vanilla chocolate chunk."

I nodded and we walked outside. "May I drive? My car's just over on the street."

"Okay." As we approached the classic Z28—my first car—she whistled appreciatively. "Nice car. Wow. It's in really great condition."

"Thanks. I don't drive it often, but was just in the mood today." I held the door for her, and she got in. I took a deep breath before opening the driver's door and sliding in. We arrived at the newly rebuilt area around the ice cream shop in less than fifteen minutes, which was good, as the interior of the car was so thick with her sweet scent I was salivating.

True to her word, Samantha got a big cone of vanilla ice cream with huge chocolate chunks protruding everywhere. I avoided getting one for myself, much to her chagrin.

We walked the avenue for a few minutes and before long found ourselves in Cadillac Square, a large oval plaza in the middle of downtown. Samantha pulled herself on top of a table and rested her feet on the attached metal bench below.

I sat next to her and watched her lips and throat work while she ate. The tightness in my jeans finally forced me to look away.

"Are you *sure* you don't want to try some? It's really good."

I glanced back to her and found her smiling. "No. Thanks, though." I tried like hell not to focus on her long pink tongue.

"Oh, come on. Are you really going to make me eat alone?" She held the ice cream closer to my face.

I smiled in defeat. It appeared I was going to have to eat some ice cream. When I still didn't take her up on her offer, she tilted the cone toward me and touched it to my nose.

I flinched. I didn't know what facial expression I wore, but it set her off laughing with abandon. She laughed so hard she almost dropped the cone. It was irresistible. I had to join her.

"I'm...I'm sorry. I don't know what came over me.

71

Here…" She held up a napkin and wiped the cold cream off my face. The smell of her radial artery set my mouth to watering, and I longed to lean forward and lap at the slender length of her exposed wrist.

I smiled and looked at her intently. "This is a dangerous game you're playing, Samantha."

She shivered. "Oh really? How's that?" The flirtation in her voice was unmistakable. And enthralling.

Before she even saw me do it, I scooped some of the offending cream on my finger and wiped it messily across her lips and chin. She screamed and laughed. I swallowed hard at the soft feel of her lips.

She turned to face me on the table. When our laughter settled, I sat holding my cream-covered finger up in front of her. She used the soiled napkin from my face to clean off her own. Then she saw the ice cream still on my hand.

"Sorry, that was my only napkin." I grimaced at the ice cream, and Samantha huffed. "Who doesn't like ice cream? Do you want me to get rid of that for you?" She met my eyes and arched one eyebrow.

The mild scent of her adrenaline intrigued me. "Please," I said quietly, observing her with interest.

She grabbed my hand by the wrist and pulled it down to her face.

I gaped at what she intended to do but was so captivated, my finger was in her mouth before I'd grappled with whether or not to allow her to do it. My brain exploded with the sensation.

Ah, Cristo. So warm. So wet.

Her pulse beat through her tongue. I fought not to gasp out loud. My eyes stung as blood threatened to rush in, the normal reaction to feeding and feeling threatened or aroused. It took all my concentration to will the blood away.

"There," she whispered as her lips slid off the tip of my

wet finger. Her heart thundered in her chest. The blossoming scent of her arousal was mouthwatering. "All better."

The heat of her lust traveled down my abdomen, and my own rose up to meet it. She released my hand and hopped down off the table, then walked over to a trash can and discarded what she hadn't finished. I tracked every sway of her hips and movement of her lithe frame, the predator in me now wanting something entirely different from her.

She returned and stood in front of me as I still sat on the table. "So, um, tell me about you, Lucien." She laced her fingers together behind her back and looked up at me.

"What do you want to know?" My voice was low, strained by the thrill of her actions.

"Well, what do you do?"

"I'm a real estate investor, both commercial and residential."

"Wow. Are you from Detroit originally?"

"I was born in New York, but I've lived here most of my life."

"Is your family here?"

I swallowed my discomfort. "No. I don't have much family. What I do have is all in New York." I kept my answers short, purposely vague. Her questions helped me refocus and calm down.

"Ollie told me you play the violin. I hope she didn't bother you by coming over today, by the way." Samantha moved a full step closer to me as we spoke.

"No, she didn't bother me at all. We had fun. I gave her a quick violin lesson, and then she twisted my arm and got me to play for her."

She smiled and more affectionate warmth flooded me. "She told me all the songs you played. I would love to hear you play some time."

"I would love to play for you. Any time."

She stepped forward again and stood just at my knees.

I watched her movements with wonder and need. The atmosphere between us thickened and sparked. Samantha looked up at me shyly, but with clear purpose.

"Lucien?"

"Hmm?" I gripped the edge of the table lest I reach out and pull her flush against my body.

She leaned in further and placed her fingertips on my knees. Electrical impulses ripped up my thighs and settled into the thick organ between my legs.

"Kiss me?"

My breath caught in my throat. My original plan for her made it blasphemous for me to consider accepting her affection. But I wanted it desperately. Wanted her.

We leaned toward one another. I met her lips tenderly, not wanting to take more risk than I already was. But then she took another step forward and fit herself tight between my legs. She moved her hands to my shoulders. Her heart hammered between our chests.

I needed to be careful, but I had to hold her. I released the table's edge and wound my hands around her, tangling one in the soft, fine hair behind her head and snaking the other around her narrow waist. Her life thrummed in my arms. I had gone so long without affectionate touch that this felt beyond miraculous. It was simply irresistible.

I was so hungry for her, but not for her blood. I deepened the kiss and stroked my tongue with need and want against hers. Exploring her mouth with abandon, I groaned at the sweetness of her taste and thrilled at being inside of her.

Oh, *dolcezza*. The taste of her joy, her vivacious personality, the way she loved Ollie, her acceptance of me—everything about her bespoke her sweetness. Her heat seared me. I pulled her in tighter and relished the throb of her pulse against my skin.

She moaned. Her hands found my hair, stroking, pulling, fisting. Had my eyes been open they would have rolled back into my head. Hot feelings of ecstasy roared out of her and into me, and I groaned as I struggled to keep my fangs from stretching out. I pursued her touch, her kiss, again and again. She returned what I gave her with equal fervor.

Minutes passed before she finally pulled away. I released her reluctantly and smiled when she bit her lower lip and grinned up at me. I tasted her happiness and her exhilaration, but some of what I was feeling was my own. And that was a miracle.

She leaned in to kiss me again, this time just on the corner of my mouth. But having had a taste, I needed another —I turned my head to capture her lips again. She moaned into my mouth and pulled my hair, causing a groan to rumble low in my throat. A smile played on her lips.

I pulled back to look into her eyes. "What?"

She shook her head and laughed softly. "I don't want to," she murmured in a seductive voice as she stroked her fingers through my hair, "but I should probably head home. I might be able to catch Ollie to say good night."

"Okay." I impressed myself with the fake nonchalance in my tone; I was nearly out of my mind with delight and lust.

She took a step back, and I slid off the table and stood in front of her. I towered over her, forcing her to tilt her head back to maintain eye contact. I couldn't resist. I cradled her face in my hands and greedily lowered my lips to hers one last time.

Her feminine curves melted against me as we kissed, then she finally stepped back and turned around. Our arms brushed as we walked back to the car. She intertwined her fingers with mine and smiled up at me.

Too fast, we were back to her house. As I walked

Samantha to the door, I truly regretted the end of our evening.

She reached up on tiptoes to kiss me again and stepped away far before I was ready to release her. We said good night, and she slipped inside. *Dio*, I wasn't ready to part from her.

The positive energy coursing through my body freed me from my usual melancholy. I felt better—content, whole, happy—at that moment than probably at any time since I'd been changed. So I went around the back of the townhouse and jumped up onto the tree branch where I had on previous occasions pondered Samantha as she slept.

A little over an hour later, she came into her room. I looked away as she changed her clothes, protectiveness now flooding me where Samantha was concerned. She crawled onto her bed and pulled open the drawer to her nightstand, then yanked out a book and a pen and flipped the book open in one fluid motion.

She wrote furiously. I occasionally caught a smile or thoughtful look, but most interesting were the feelings radiating from her. Happiness was the baseline emotion, but added to that were feelings of nearly uncontainable excitement and desire. I wished I could see the words flowing from her pen.

Finally, Samantha closed the book and hugged it to her chest. She shut her eyes and rested her chin on the book's edge. Then she stretched to the side and slid the book and the pen back into the nightstand drawer and switched off her lamp.

She lay still for a moment. Then she caught me completely off guard: just as I sensed an intensified wave of excitement, she started kicking her feet and smacking her hands against her bed, her face alight with a brilliant smile. Her absolute delight was contagious.

Without thinking, I laughed out loud.

She bolted upright, her gaze directed at her window. *Uh oh.*

I flew from the tree and across the grassy field to the front corner of my house in a flash. As I peeked around the corner, she pulled her curtains apart and surveyed the area outside her window. She disappeared after a moment, her curtains closing behind her.

I chided myself for my stupidity with a smile still plastered on my face. If it hadn't been so dangerous, it would have been funny.

Back in my own house, this newfound happiness demanded expression. The violin case was still on the kitchen table where I'd left it after Ollie's morning visit. I undid the clasps and pulled out the instrument, then settled myself in the same chair I'd used earlier. I set the bow on the strings, closed my eyes, and allowed my mood to dictate the song.

The upbeat sound of Brahms's Violin Concerto in D Major filled the house. As the closing chords of that concerto rang out over twenty minutes later, I moved right into Stravinsky's Concerto in D Major. I allowed the instrument to take me from one high-spirited piece to another and reveled in the feeling and sound of the music.

Looking up, I was surprised by the LED display on the oven: 1:32 a.m. I could not recall the last time I'd played so long, so intently, or with so much joy. I placed the violin back in its case and stood for a long time at the table with my hands flat on its surface.

Then I paced, walking the length of the first floor several times. Finally I stopped in front of a side window in the living room. I ran my hands through my hair and interlaced them on top of my head.

My eyes focused; I was standing in front of the only first-floor window that allowed a view—partial though it was—of Samantha's house.

Samantha.

God dammit, I want her. Now. I want them. Could I be falling...? My brow furrowed. I shook off the errant thought. *I'm not that reckless or delusional. Am I?*

No. That is simply the influence of her emotions talking. I nodded in agreement, then flopped down onto the couch and clicked on the TV. The black-and-white images of the old movie did little to pull my mind away from the momentous events of the day.

∼

A t three o'clock the next afternoon, there was a soft but insistent knock on my front door. Alarming emotions vibrated from the other side.

When I opened the door, a tear-streaked Ollie flew into my arms. My protective instinct engaged immediately. I stifled a growl, surveying the streetscape for potential threats.

I crouched down to her level. "What's wrong?" My voice was raw. She sobbed against me and curled her little hands around my neck. I picked her up and kicked the door shut, then carried her into the living room and sat us down on the couch. "It's okay, Ollie, just tell me what's wrong."

Her fear filled my nose. I vowed in my mother tongue to avenge her if she'd been harmed. Finally she responded. "Mommy's gonna...be...be...maaad at me." She cried harder.

"Why do you think that? What happened?" I sat her up and brushed her tears off with my thumbs. A fleeting image of Isa sitting crying at the bottom of a set of stairs with a skinned knee ran through my mind. I breathed deeply and willed the comparison away before I gently moved Ollie from my lap and sat her on the couch. "Here. Take a minute to stop crying. I'll get some tissues and a glass of water."

She nodded and her breath hitched as she tried to breathe deeply.

In the kitchen, I grabbed an empty cup from a new set I'd purchased and one of the two flasks I'd had filled. I poured some of the clear liquid into Ollie's glass, then filled it with tap water. Drink in hand, I ripped a paper towel off the roll and returned to the couch. "Here, Ollie."

She took the glass and a long drink, swallowing around the hiccups she'd given herself. She looked at the paper towel, then shrugged and wiped her nose.

"Okay, now, what happened?"

She placed the empty glass on the table and fiddled with the paper in her hands. "I was playing dress-up in Mommy's bathroom. And I...I..."

"It's okay. I promise."

"I was trying on her jewelry. And I dropped a ring my daddy gave her in the sink. And...and...it..." The tears started again. "It went down and now it's gone." She looked pitifully up at me, her breath still hitching.

I closed my eyes and heaved a deep breath. She hadn't been hurt. "Okay. It's okay. I bet we can still get it, Ollie. I have tools that can help me take the pipe apart. We can look for it, okay?"

"Really?" The relief poured out of her and compounded my own.

"Yes. Really. Okay? But you have to try to stop crying."

"Okay."

I patted her knee, then moved to the utility closet in the back hall and grabbed several tools. On my way past the kitchen, I noticed the time: 3:35 p.m.

"Does your mom know where you are?" Samantha was

usually home from work by now. I shouldn't have known that, but I did.

Ollie shook her head.

"Come on, then. We don't want her to worry."

I walked Ollie across the grassy field, her little hand gripped tightly around mine once again. Sure enough, Samantha flew out the front door just as we rounded the corner of the townhouse. She was still in her scrubs.

"Olivia Sutton! Where have you been? Grampa didn't know where you were. You just left the house without saying anything! Again! How many times have we talked about this?"

Just then Samantha saw the tools in my hand and cocked an eyebrow.

"It seems we had an accident, Sam." I glanced down meaningfully at the back of Ollie's head. "But I think I can fix it."

"Uh, okay. What happened, Ollie?" She knelt down in front of her daughter. "Come on and tell me. It'll make you feel better."

The words rushed out of her. "I was playing dress-up with your jewelry and dropped Daddy's ring down the sink." She looked up at her mother's eyes from under wet eyelashes.

"You know I don't mind you looking at my things. But only when I'm here, and only when you've asked permission. Do you understand?"

"Yes, Mommy."

"Okay. Go on in, then." Samantha smiled at me. "You really don't have to do this, Lucien."

"I don't mind, unless you'd rather I not." I sounded nonchalant but really wanted to take care of this for them.

"No, no, of course. Come on."

We paused in the living room while Samantha recounted the story to Joe, who stifled a smile while looking sternly at

Ollie. I asked her to grab a bowl before she showed me upstairs.

As we approached her bedroom door, she turned to me. "Um, sorry. Would you mind waiting a minute?" Embarrassment radiated off her.

"Sure. No problem." Samantha scurried into her room. I heard her throwing clothing and pushing drawers shut and smiled to myself.

I wandered down the hall and stopped in front of what was clearly Ollie's room. A princess border ran around the purple walls of the small room along with dozens of princess wall stickers. Baskets of stuffed animals and shelves of books crowded the space. It was perfectly charming. But what most caught my attention were the dozen or so pictures taped to the wall above her bed—some hand drawn, some cut from books or magazines. Angels.

Samantha's hand rattled the doorknob. I flew back to the side of her door.

"Sorry. Okay. It's safe now." She grimaced at me, still embarrassed. "Bathroom's over here."

It was odd being in this room and looking out the window at the tree, but I pushed that thought away and followed Samantha into the bathroom. I knelt down and opened the vanity cabinet, then placed the tools and the bowl on the floor next to me. "Do you have a towel I can use?"

She turned and pulled an old brown towel out of the narrow closet in the corner. "Here you go."

I moved a couple of bottles of various toiletries out of the way to make room for the bowl. Within minutes, I fished the diamond ring out of the pipe's contents that had spilled down into it. I handed it to Samantha, whose embarrassment I tasted again. I reassembled everything, then dumped the wet contents into the sink and watched as I did so to see if any water would drip from the pipes below. When everything remained dry, I closed the vanity and stood up, then collected my tools and placed them on the countertop. I washed my hands and dried them on the still-clean towel.

"Thank you, Lucien."

"No problem."

We stood awkwardly for a moment. She was between me and the door to the bathroom. She realized this and rushed backward to move and in the process tripped over a scatter rug not fully flat on the linoleum.

I reached out and caught her, and she threw her arms around my neck to keep from falling. When I righted her, she didn't drop her arms.

Hunger lit her eyes at the same time her lust blazed through me. She wanted me. It was all the invitation I needed.

I pushed her back against the bathroom wall and lowered my mouth to hers. I cupped her face in my hands. She threaded her fingers into my hair, grasping at long thick locks of it as she attempted to pull me closer. She opened to me, a small moan escaping her throat as our tongues touched. I explored the warmth of her mouth, tasting her sweetness, always her sweetness.

The kiss became urgent and needful, full of stroking tongues and sucking lips and hungry moans. The most intense feeling of possessiveness gripped me. I wanted to claim her, mark her, have her.

She ran her hands over my chest, forcing a hiss from me as she unknowingly brushed over a sensitive patch of skin. My insides went molten, making it nearly impossible to pull away. But this was neither the time nor the place. I slowed our kisses, pressing a final one to her forehead before leaning back.

Breathing hard, we smiled at each other. Then our eyes descended to the ring she held in her fingers between us.

"Oh." The embarrassment again. "Since you had to fish this out of the muck, you deserve to know what it is." She held the engagement ring up for me to see more clearly.

"I don't deserve anything, Sam. You don't have to tell me." I took a small step back.

She frowned. "Well, I want to." She looked up at me and I nodded.

"Olivia's father, Jensen, was my college boyfriend. I thought he was great. He gave me this and called it a promise ring. I expected we would get engaged when we both graduated. But then at the beginning of my junior year, I got pregnant. And Jensen couldn't deal with it. He wanted me to have an abortion, but I didn't want to. Olivia was born the week before he graduated. He was headed off to law school in the fall, and he broke up with me. I dropped out of school to raise Olivia, which is why I'm just now finishing up." She glanced at me through her lashes, judging my reaction to her story. "Ollie knows her father gave me this ring and absolutely adores it. When she's older, I'll give it to her."

An unreasonable fury seized me at this man I didn't know who hadn't been in Samantha's life for years, apparently, but I moderated my tone. "I'm sorry he treated you that way."

Her eyes flashed to mine. "Yeah. But I'm not sorry I kept Ollie. As hard as it's been sometimes, she was entirely worth it."

I smiled. "I have no doubt about that."

"So, are you completely freaked out yet?" She held her smile, but it didn't reach her eyes.

I frowned. "By what?"

"We've known each other for, like, three weeks, and I'm revealing all my deep, dark secrets." She made a joke of it, but her feelings told me she was serious.

I shook my head and laughed out loud. She smiled uncertainly. "Samantha, your secrets are neither deep nor dark. Trust me. So, no, I'm not freaked out."

She grinned self-consciously. "Really? Um, okay. Good." She looked down for a moment and fiddled with the ring before shoving it in the pocket of her scrubs. "Lucien, can I tell you something else?"

"Of course." Her feelings gave away the direction this conversation was about to take.

"Okay, so, I didn't exactly picture this conversation happening in my bathroom, but, um, I just wanted to say I really like you." She leaned back against the wall and looked up at me appraisingly.

I cautiously opened a part of myself I had long kept buried and took a deep breath and a leap of faith. "I like you, too, Samantha." She smiled hopefully. So did I.

We'd barely voiced our declarations before Ollie pushed through the door behind us. I stepped back several paces before she got fully in the room.

"Crisis averted," Samantha said as she pulled the ring out for Ollie to see.

"Yay!" She looked at me. "Thank you, Lucien! You're the best!"

"You're welcome, Ollie. Any time." I squeezed her shoulder.

"Now remember"—Samantha recaptured Ollie's attention —"you need to ask first."

"Okay. I will."

"And no more running out of the house without permission. I'm getting tired of having that conversation, Olivia."

"Okay, Mommy." We all stepped out of the bathroom and headed downstairs together.

"Well, I should be going."

"Do you want to stay for dinner? Just spaghetti. Nothing fancy. But you're more than welcome." Samantha's desire radiated. "It's the least I could do to repay you for your plumbing expertise."

I smiled and hated the thought of disappointing her. "Thank you. But I have some errands I need to run yet this afternoon."

Her smiled faltered. "Oh, okay."

"I'm free later though," I said, pleased to see her grin return.

"Sure."

I stepped toward the door and called back, "Bye, Ollie."

"Bye," she replied distractedly as she twirled in circles next to her mother, all traces of her former fear gone and replaced with a playful happiness.

Samantha stepped out on the front porch with me. Peeking back over her shoulder to check Ollie hadn't followed us, she reached up quickly and kissed me on the mouth.

I smiled at her. "See you later," I said as I resisted pulling her into my arms.

She nodded, then went back inside.

I could still taste her on my lips.

CHAPTER 7

I loved the smell of the girls on me, but it was so distracting I could barely think, so I showered and changed. But then I was without something to do again. Somehow I'd gone from an eternity of keeping myself company to going stir-crazy after just an hour of being apart from them.

Still warm inside from their affection, I ducked out and bought some groceries, just in case. Then, because my violin had always served as my most effective form of distraction, I ran through the same repertoire of songs as the night before.

Before long, the light in the room faded, and I found myself playing in the near dark. I was so focused on the music, the knock on my door caught me by surprise. I put the instrument down on the kitchen table and walked with a smile to the door, then flicked on the foyer light as I opened it.

Samantha stood in the doorway looking as beautiful as I'd ever seen her. A seductively natural ponytail turned her hair into a golden stream. Long wisps hung down along her face. The deep V-neck of her ivory satin blouse exposed a wide expanse of flawless skin. Two loops of a long beaded necklace surrounded her neck, suggesting a path for my lips, and a longer one dangled down the front of her blouse.

"Wow."

She grinned crookedly and leaned against the door jamb. "So, I realize I'm being presumptuous here, but I was hoping you would want to take me out."

I motioned for her to come in and shut the door behind her. "It would be my pleasure. Did you have anything in mind?"

"Actually, yes. One of my friends at work raves about this jazz bar up by Eight Mile."

I smiled. I knew the one she was talking about and had gone there with Langston a number of times years ago. "That sounds great." I looked down at my jeans and T-shirt. "I should put on something a little nicer. Do you mind waiting?" I motioned to the couch. Then, noticing the only light was in the foyer, I walked into the living room and turned on a lamp.

Samantha followed me. "Not at all. Go ahead."

I ran upstairs to the master bedroom. I didn't really have any dress clothes here, but I did have a pair of black jeans and my brown leather coat. It would do. Most of my belongings remained at Edmund Place.

I hurried back downstairs but didn't find Samantha in the living room, so I continued into the now-lit kitchen. She stood fingering the body of the violin. I watched her for several minutes and thought I could look at her forever. I shook my head at myself.

"Oh, God! You scared me!" She clasped her hands to her chest. Her heart rate escalated wildly. Her surprise tingled in my gut.

"Sorry."

"I just didn't hear you." She laughed, then looked back

down at the violin again. She reached out one hand to touch it. "This is beautiful, Lucien. It looks very old."

"Thank you. It is. It's been in my family for generations. My grandfather gave it to me when I was a teenager."

"Were you playing when I came to the door?" She peeked up at me through the fallen wisps of her hair.

I nodded.

"In the dark?"

I smiled and shrugged. "Sometimes I lose track of what's going on around me when I'm playing."

She traced the strings absentmindedly. "The music of the night."

"What?"

"Oh, for some reason your playing in the dark reminded me of that song from *Phantom of the Opera*. Do you know it?"

I took a step forward, and she took a step back. I picked up the violin and the bow and, standing before her, positioned the instrument, closed my eyes, and played. The sweet melody rang out in the room until she gasped.

When I hit the high note midway through the song, I smelled the salt. I opened my eyes to see two tears had snuck out of the corners of hers.

I'd never thought about it, but the lyrics of the song were applicable to our situation. I played it with reinvigorated enthusiasm, willing her to hear the words—words I couldn't say about things I had no business wanting. When I hit the high note at the end, she lost her fight to cry quietly and let out a small whimper.

I lowered the instrument, completely taken with her reaction.

"Oh God, Lucien. That was incredible." She fanned herself with her hands and took a deep breath, then laughed. She wiped at her tears with the back of her hands. "That is my favorite musical. I've been to see it three times. I cry every time. That was the most beautiful version of that song I've ever heard."

I set the violin down and turned to her. Cupping a hand around each side of her face, I brushed away the last of her tears with my thumbs.

Then I lowered my face to hers and slowly kissed the salt off her skin across both cheekbones. She brought her hands up and grabbed my biceps. Her heart raced against my chest. I walked her back into the island and lifted her up onto the cool hard surface.

I worked my lips down to hers as she trembled against me. Her hands slid up around my neck, and she pulled me further into her. The kiss was slow and sweet and filled with longing.

Could this really be happening? And what is "this"? I pushed the inner turmoil away. *Just be, just feel, Lucien. For once.* So I did. I wrapped a hand behind her head and pulled her into me. I licked at her lips, and she opened. We moaned into each other's mouths as our tongues traded caresses.

"Lucien."

The sound of my name falling from her lips unhinged me.

I needed more.

I ran open-mouthed kisses across her jaw and down her neck, breathing in her feminine scent and tasting her sweetness. She threw her head back and threaded her fingers into my hair. I hardened and, all at once, the smell of her throat and the intensity of her heat were too much. I pulled back, panting, while I still held her face in my hands.

She smiled.

"Shall we go?" I rubbed my thumb over her lower lip.

"We should." She gripped my arms as I helped her down from the counter.

I took her hand in one of mine and led her out of the house to my car. I tugged at my hair as I brushed it back off my face and struggled to find the will to use caution, have patience.

In less than half an hour, we pulled up in front of the club. The large white neon sign of Baker's Keyboard Lounge illuminated the street in front of the building.

An older man in a sharp gold suit coat and black tie showed us to a table in the second row. Samantha smiled excitedly and pointed to the famous keyboard design of the curved bar and the framed photographs on the surrounding walls of all the jazz greats who'd played here over the years. The waitress came up to our table, and we each ordered a glass of red wine.

The jazz quartet had a lean, exhilarating sound. Several songs and another glass of wine for Sam later, the saxman exchanged his tenor for a soprano and launched into a tender, lyrical piece.

Samantha leaned against me. I wrapped my arm around her, relishing her warmth as she stayed in that position through the rest of the set. Everywhere we touched, the soft rush of blood through her veins caressed me. I found it a comforting sensation.

When the set ended, Samantha excused herself. I rose when she returned, earning a kiss on the side of the mouth. Again, I had to resist turning it into more.

"That was wonderful. This place is great. Thank you so much for bringing me. I never have the chance to do something like this."

I tucked a strand of gold behind one ear. "The pleasure was mine, Sam. Truly." I ushered her to the door and out into the night.

I offered to drive her right to her front door, but she insisted we park on the street by my house. Smiling at her feistiness, I came around and opened her door. In one fluid move, she stepped out of the car and curled her arms around my neck.

The kiss started soft but became urgent.

Wrapping my arms around her body, the heat of her lust hit me again. I pulled her tight to me. When my erection came to life, I couldn't resist pressing into her hips. Her soft moans turned into a groan that thrilled me. I slid my hand up to the back of her head and tugged gently on her ponytail, tilting her head back until her neck opened. I kissed and licked across her jawline to her ear, then ran my tongue down the side of her neck.

Don't fucking mess this up, Lucien! I clamped down any hint of bloodlust and kept my eyes drained and fangs retracted as I worked over her carotid artery. Her sweet essence tantalized, tormented. I shuddered.

She moaned and fisted her hands in my hair. I loved the way she pulled at it. I groaned and skimmed my lips back up the elegant column of her throat, the tingling in my canines growing fierce, before finding her mouth again and again. I throbbed from the pressure our embrace created. She tilted her hips into mine, and I grasped her bottom and pressed her into me harder. She whimpered. I grunted. Our mouths and bodies hungered and sought out the pleasure of this connection.

Between kisses, she rasped, "I want to stay, but I have to go."

I pulled her more tightly to me. "Don't go."

"God, Lucien," she murmured around the edge of a kiss.

The sound of my name out of her mouth in this moment was fascinating, particularly joined as it was by the rich smell of her arousal.

Mine. I groaned at the thought and the feeling.

Needing this so damn bad, I pulled her harder against me and settled us back against the car. Her body fell between my legs, and I ground my length against her stomach. My desire for her went from "I should stop this" to nuclear in seconds.

Oblivious to my ever-present overthinking, Samantha smiled against my mouth, then panted, "I don't want to. But I have to go. I have to get up for work in five and a half hours."

"Hmm" was all I managed as I continued to kiss and caress her.

She chuckled, and I pulled back, still concentrating to keep my eyes clear and my teeth human. I stared at her for a long moment and brushed my thumb against her cheek. *La perfezione. She is perfection.* "Let's get you home then." I held my arm out to her, and she wrapped hers through it. "Before I forget..." I reached into my coat pocket, pulled out a plastic square.

"Oh, Lucien. This is the quartet we just heard?" I nodded, smiling.

"That's fantastic! Thank you so much!" She kissed me on the cheek as we headed across the field. In too-few minutes, she closed her door behind her. I returned home, amazed by the current of joy and need and tension still running through my body.

Without turning on any lights, I went right upstairs. I stripped and stepped into the shower without waiting for the water to warm.

My body was on fire with her need and mine. The spray of the shower jets against my skin intensified my arousal. I reached down and grasped the heavy weight of my hard length, then closed my eyes as I stroked and ran a series of memories by my mind's eye: Samantha's lips wrapped around my finger, the smell of her arousal as she pressed herself between my legs, the taste of her mouth, the feel of my tongue penetrating her pink lips, the sound of her moans and whimpers. I was fucking aching for her. I gripped myself tighter and thrust harder. As I got closer, I braced myself against the white tile and twisted my grip around my sensitive head at the top of each stroke. I remembered the sound of Samantha groaning my name in pleasure, and that was all it took.

"Fuck. *Fuck!*"

My release erupted against the tiles in a torrent, faintly tinged with pink from the blood that invaded all my bodily fluids. I panted as I recovered from the intensity of the first orgasm I'd had in a very long time, then I cleaned myself and got out. A pair of gray boxers was all I bothered with before I climbed into bed.

I trained my attention on each movement I made and nothing else. Given the events of the previous minutes, it took a surprising amount of concentration to harness my brain that way. Which was the point.

Is this really happening? I groaned as my thoughts seeped through anyway. A million answers to that question paraded through my mind. Minutes passed, or hours. Finally, I sat upright in bed and combed my hands through my hair.

Yeah. It's happening. "It" being the fact I was in love. With a human. Who I had been planning to kill.

The shock of the admission drove me out of bed. I threw on clothes in a rush, ran down the stairs, flew out the door, and jumped into my car.

I drove the rest of the night.

On the highway, I blasted music on successive rock stations to drown out my thoughts. Four hundred miles and five hours later, I sped the Camaro up the gravel drive and parked, then got out and quietly shut the door.

Orchard Hill stood in front of me.

CHAPTER 8

Orchard Hill was a thousand-acre estate in North Ithaca, New York, my vampire family's home for the past 216 years.

The main house was white, a sprawling two-story with blue shutters and a red door. Newer wings flanked an older center block dating to the eighteenth century. Low limestone walls marked off paths and gardens, and a large pond sat behind the house. A gravel lane circled in front, surrounding an ancient cherry tree—one of many old trees embracing the house. I had always found the structure and the setting surprisingly charming.

Griffin was the first one out the door, surely alerted by the motion detectors at the beginning of the long drive. He was tall and lean and had close- cropped jet black hair. His deep-set silver eyes rested over defined cheekbones and under a pronounced brow and strong forehead. He was the oldest of our group and our leader, having changed everyone among us except me and William's wife, Anna. Griffin exuded power and authority, but could be extremely compassionate, which was what I saw in his eyes as I stood in the dark outside his house.

"Lucien? What's wrong?" He walked over to where I was leaning on the car.

I folded my arms and tilted my head back to look up at the predawn sky. It was going to be sunny. I shook my head once. It was enough for him.

The others assembled at the front door. Griffin raised his hand to them just as someone gathered a breath to shout a greeting. He had the strongest charming power any of us had ever seen—they all froze. It was a sure mark of Griffin's concern he was using his ability on them. Then he lowered his hand. They got the message and went back inside.

I couldn't bring myself to look at him, because if I did, I would have to say something. But I didn't know what to say. That was it. "Do you mind if, for right now, I don't say?"

"Come on." He placed a hand on my shoulder and pulled me along. "Everyone will be happy to see you."

I nodded and followed.

Rebecca was waiting in the foyer with a big grin. She was the youngest of the group, barely seventeen when she'd been changed. Her immaturity most expressed itself by actually voicing those things no one else would. She didn't seem to have an internal filter, but it wasn't a character flaw.

I melted under her gaze. Though I'd never shared this observation with any of them, her brown hair and pretty girlish features reminded me of Isabetta, or at least what I imagined she would've looked like if the events of that horrible May night had never happened.

"You came, Lucien!" She threw her arms around my neck.

Her delight invigorated me, and I laughed. "Yes, I did. Hello, Rebecca."

She released me, a huge smile still on her face. Her husband, Jedediah, stuck out his hand. Jed was average in height, with unkempt brown hair and gray eyes. He'd always been like a brother to me and never hesitated to set me straight when needed, which was often. "Did you come to see me, too?"

I took his hand and smirked. "Hell, no." He squeezed my hand hard. I shoved him away playfully, then looked around. "Where's everybody else?"

Griffin shut the door behind us. "Hen just went out back in her garden. William and Anna are at their cabin. And Catherine went out last night and hasn't yet returned."

Given my strange state of mind, I was happy William wasn't around. Our relationship had always been rocky and competitive. I wasn't up to his verbal sparring at that moment.

Rebecca threaded her arm through mine and walked me over to the sofa, then pulled me down next to her. She looked at me expectantly. "The last time we saw each other you promised to play for me. So...did you bring your violin?"

I laughed again and smiled sheepishly. "Sorry."

"Lucien! *Fine*." She flew out of the room and returned several minutes later with a wrapped package. "I was saving this for Christmas. But since some people are difficult..."

She set the package down on my lap and motioned for me to open it. Jed and Griffin settled themselves down in the surrounding chairs and smiled openly at Rebecca being Rebecca.

I tore the paper off the long rectangular box and lifted its lid. Inside was a pristine black violin case. My eyebrows shot up. "Rebecca."

She grabbed the case and shoved the box and paper to the floor next to me. Then she laid the case on my lap. "Open it!"

I undid the clasps and tilted the lid back. Inside was a shiny black violin, a sleek and darkly beautiful Luis and

Clark. I lifted it, sliding the case to the sofa next to me. It weighed less than my Ceruti.

Rebecca pulled a bow out from behind her back and handed it to me. "Try it out, Lucien. The sound is supposed to be particularly resonating."

I looked at her as I lifted the instrument to my shoulder. I launched into one of the Bach pieces I'd played the other night and was stunned by the sound. After a minute, I lowered the instrument to my lap. "It's incredible. Thank you. But, why—"

"It's made by hand of carbon fiber, which is supposed to be very durable. I, uh, peeked at your other violin while we were at your house last time." She was mildly embarrassed, but her feelings were more triumphant than anything. At nearly two hundred years old, the Ceruti showed its age. "I thought you might like a new one to play sometimes."

I loved that she knew nothing could ever actually replace the Ceruti. I set the Luis and Clark in its case. "Wow, Rebecca. Thank you so much." I hugged her into my chest.

She leaned back and stroked her fingers along my cheek bone. Her eyes were full of sisterly love for me. "If I had known this was all it would take to make you happy, Lucien, I would have gotten you a new violin years ago." She smiled. "Will you play us a concert later?"

"Sure."

"Okay, then. My work is done here. Come on, Jed." She flitted over to her mate's side and took his hand. He half smiled, half smirked at me and followed her upstairs.

I looked at Griffin. "I'd like to go say hello to Henrietta."

"Of course. She's going to be thrilled to see you."

I walked through the living room into the newer part of the house. Through the french glass doors at the back of the room, I spied Henrietta as she knelt in front of some rose bushes and clipped long stems for her basket. She had long black-brown hair and sparkling silver eyes. She and Griffin looked like the couple they were, matching in beauty, stature, and demeanor. I pushed through the door.

She glanced up and smiled. "Lucien." Even if I couldn't have felt it, she communicated so much love through just that one word.

"Hello, Henrietta." I threaded my way through the garden toward her. She stood and brushed her hands off on her jeans. The combination of her long dark hair and short-sleeved red shirt was striking. "Your garden looks wonderful. You really have the touch."

"Thank you," she said as she reached her arms out to give me a hug. "Oh, it's so good to see you again." Her healer's touch soothed me immediately, as it always did. It also made her able to sense my inner turmoil. "What's wrong?"

"Do you mind if I don't say just yet?"

"Okay, of course." She hugged me tighter and held on longer than normal for a regular hug. She knew I needed her touch. Even after she pulled back, she continued to hold my right hand casually. "What brings you to see us?" She added quickly, "Not that you need any special reason..."

I chuckled. "I just needed to get away for a few days. To think. You know."

She nodded, then looked up. "Hey. Do you want to take a quick run over to the cemetery before the sun rises? We could take some of these cuttings."

"That's a nice idea. Thanks." I knew some part of my trip here would entail a visit to the family cemetery. I needed to talk to Lena, although I didn't want company when I did it. Henrietta bent down and grabbed a thick bouquet of roses of all colors into her hands, and we took off.

Before long, we walked through the iron gate of the ceme-tery. Most of the remains dated to 1792, the year an Indian attack devastated this part of New York. Griffin saved a number of the victims by changing them and forming his—my—family. Though my human family had died far away in New York City, Catherine had tried to ease me by bringing their remains to rest with everyone else's families. That act was one of the many things that bound the two of us together so closely.

Unsurprisingly, bouquets of white roses already decorated each of the plots. I had arrived at Orchard Hill days after my change in 1895 and stayed for forty-three years before circumstances necessitated my departure. My last request to Rebecca had been to look after my family's graves.

Henrietta handed me the freshly cut stems. I selected a handful of roses for each of them, then knelt and leaned them against the headstones. I sat back on my heels. "I can't tell you how much it means to me that you and Rebecca have done this all these years."

She sat down in the grass next to me and crossed her legs in front of her. "You're welcome, Lucien. But you should know the others do it, too. It's not just me and Rebecca." My eyes widened in response. "We all miss you, Lucien. Bringing the flowers out to your family feels like a way of being closer to you. We all want that. So everyone has helped."

The warmth of her affection was obvious; she was not trying to make me feel guilty, but I still looked down at the ground. She took my hand again. The sense of peace was immediate. I smiled up at her.

"Hey, guess what I've been doing?" she prompted.

"What's that?" I shifted my position to face her, smiling at her excitement.

"I've been volunteering at the Ithaca Free Clinic. For about eight months now. I decided to finally put the medical degree to some use." She beamed. She'd finished her medical degree more than twenty years before but always feared the idea of practicing, feared that if she spent time in the presence of humans, someone might find her out.

"That's incredible, Henrietta. Congratulations."

"It's only two days a week, but it's been really great. And it's easier to pass than I thought."

I was so comfortable with her I almost blurted out she and Samantha would have a lot to talk about. The thought stuck in my throat like a swallowed canary. She noticed and smiled patiently. We talked for a few minutes more and then returned to the house before we pushed our luck with the sun. Minutes later, the five of us sprawled out on the couches and chairs in front of the flat screen in the great room.

"Let's watch a movie," Rebecca declared as she walked over to a built-in cabinet and popped open the door. "Thoughts?" She scanned the DVD cases. Everyone called out suggestions as the front door opened and closed.

We looked up to see Catherine standing at the top of the great-room steps. She was a beautiful creature, her long brown hair sleek and thick and her ice blue eyes a dazzling contrast. Her trim body and unusual height made her appear statuesque, as did her flawless porcelain skin. She was seductive in a pair of skinny jeans tucked into ankle boots and a mostly unbuttoned button-down blue blouse with short fluttery sleeves.

When she saw me, she paled and gaped. Her emotions were all over the place and washed through me: bewilderment, surprise, happiness, sadness, relief. The sensory overload threatened dizziness.

She felt what I was feeling. Of course she did.

She was an empath just as I was, only much stronger. Her power worked over greater distances, especially with those with whom she had had certain...connections.

"You're in l—" She registered my head shake and cut herself off.

The others looked back and forth between us. Our shared gift was part of what had drawn us so close together for so many years. It allowed us to carry out nearly wordless conversations.

I was torn. Part of me wanted to go off and talk to her privately and felt I owed it to her given our history, and part wanted to stay right where I was in the midst of the group so I didn't have to talk at all.

In the end, I just wasn't ready to have this conversation. With anybody.

She stared at me for a minute and registered my reluctance, then took a seat on the chair across from me. She kicked off her boots and wrapped her legs up next to her.

In the meantime, Rebecca and Jed decided on some stupid humor movie about actors who thought they were filming a war movie but didn't realize the director had been killed and they really were in hostile territory. It was over the top and hilarious. I laughed freely, which elicited several relieved and curious glances from around the room. My laughter wasn't a sound they heard often. Catherine didn't laugh once.

I kept my eyes on the television, but my brain was expansive enough to register she never stopped watching me. Her patience wavered.

When the movie ended, it finally ran out. "So, do you want to do this here in front of everyone or elsewhere with just me?"

Everyone gaped and their surprise tingled in the pit of my stomach.

"Come on, Lucien. You clearly came here to talk to us about this. You knew I would know." Catherine's voice sounded more calm and patient than her emotions felt.

I ran my fingers through my hair and rested my hands on top of my head. The room was silent. "Yes." I looked at

Catherine and knew she would know which of her questions I was answering. A long moment passed.

"Yes, *what?*" Rebecca, Catherine's sister in life and death, glanced back and forth between us, frustrated at our ability to communicate this way.

Henrietta gasped and threw her hands up in front of her mouth. Her eyes widened, but filled with love and happiness. She'd figured it out.

Rebecca looked at Henrietta. "Oh, for God's sake."

Taking a deep breath, I pictured Samantha and Ollie. "I...I have met someone."

"You're in love!" Rebecca bounced on her knees on the couch. Jed hugged her into him.

I nodded and failed to hold back a grin. The atmosphere vibrated with their excitement for me. Griffin smiled with satisfaction, while Henrietta and Rebecca radiated absolute delight. They knew I'd almost never allowed myself happiness before for fear it would represent a betrayal. My gaze drifted over to Catherine.

Her concern had been replaced almost entirely with her acceptance and happiness for me. Although she was still confused. "Why do you feel so tortured about this?"

Out of the corner of my eye, I caught Rebecca mouthing Lena's name to Catherine. I smirked. "Uh, no, Rebecca. Well, yes, but no."

Catherine's voice was nearly a whisper. "Oh, my God, Lucien. You are completely in love with this woman. Is she part of Laumet's coven?"

Suddenly, the sheer absurdity of my situation overwhelmed me. I laughed. Hard. I wrapped my arms around my waist and slumped over on the couch. Everyone looked at me like I was a complete lunatic, which of course I was, but I couldn't help myself.

I was having a hard time summoning the courage to

admit she was human, and I couldn't even begin to imagine a conversation wherein I admitted to her I was a vampire. Maybe this was one of those "if you can't talk about it, you shouldn't be doing it" things. That made me laugh harder. Altogether, I was nearly one hundred forty years old. Yet I felt like a teenager about to reveal to my parents I was dating someone from the wrong side of the tracks.

"Dude. You are fucked." Rebecca swatted Jed hard on the arm. "What? He is. Look at him. He finally went off the deep end. It's not like we weren't all wondering when it would happen."

"Jed!" Rebecca smacked him again.

I pushed myself up. I couldn't recall the last time I'd laughed that hard. It was physical proof of what I now knew I was feeling.

I took a deep breath and looked at Catherine. There was nothing but acceptance there. In that moment, I was so grateful for the reconciliation we had achieved twenty years before that enabled us to go from being exes to best friends once again.

Catherine smiled, then whispered, "Whoever she is, Lucien, I am so happy for you. I love her, because she has made you feel this way, because she has made you come alive after all these years."

I crossed the room to her, and she met me halfway. I embraced her and murmured low enough for her and her alone to hear, "Of all people, I so needed to hear that from you. Thank you, Catherine."

When we stepped apart, I led her back to the couch and pulled her down next to me. We continued to hold hands as I scanned the group.

"Sorry. I realize I'm a bit of a basket case—"

"A *bit*?"

I threw a pillow at Jed as I smiled. "Trust me, brother. I

am intimately familiar with my own insanity." I looked down at my hand intertwined with Catherine's. "Okay. Here goes. Please try to keep all editorial comments to yourselves until I get this out." I glanced at Rebecca who feigned offense.

"I am in love with a woman named Samantha Sutton. She is human. And she is the mother of a five-year-old girl named Olivia, although she prefers Ollie. And if that isn't awkward enough, I started out stalking this woman with the intent to kill her. I ran into her at the hospital where she works—she's a nurse." I looked at Henrietta and could imagine how they would get along. "Her feelings were so joyous and brought me such pleasure, euphoria even." I turned to Catherine then. "It was so intense."

Catherine nodded and squeezed my hand.

"I couldn't resist. I wanted her…that. I wanted more. I'm mortified to admit I planned to take her. But then I ran into her one day, and she talked to me. I told myself it was just another way to experience her as I planned her demise, but with each meeting, I got to know her. I convinced myself what I was feeling for her weren't my feelings at all, but was the strength of her emotions within me. And maybe that was true. I don't know. But then it hit me. I want her. But not in me. With me." I looked down. "For as long as she'll have me."

Feeling exposed, I clamped my mouth shut and waited for their reactions.

The room was tense and still, but then all hell broke loose. Everyone started talking at once.

Catherine's raised voice claimed the floor. "My original reaction stands. I am happy for you. I get it's complicated. But you deserve to be happy, Lucien. And if she is what makes you happy, then you should pursue her. Carefully."

Jed scoffed. "That's easy for you to say, Catherine. You

sleep with human men all the time. But having sex and having a relationship with them are two different things."

When Henrietta's quiet voice interrupted, everyone stilled. "Have you met the child?" Henrietta's young son died in the Indian attack, so I knew she would react to this part of the situation.

"Yes."

She let my answer hang there for a minute. "And?"

"I actually met her first. I didn't realize she was Samantha's daughter. I like her. And she really seems to like me. She *looks* at me, and meets my eyes. God, she *hugs* me. She held my hand the other day—"

Henrietta tried to suppress a gasp. "You love the child."

I had been so focused on Samantha, I hadn't thought as much about my feelings for Ollie.

Catherine put her arm around my shoulders. "It's okay to say yes, Lucien. It's not a betrayal."

She was right. That was my fear, the source of my hesitation. I wasn't convinced. I offered a small nod to Catherine, and then looked at Henrietta and did it again.

"Forgive me for asking. Please. But are you in control of yourself enough to know you pose no threat to the girl?" Her question was not out of line. While some consumed the blood of children because of its purity and raw power, it was a line most vampires didn't cross.

"Don't apologize, Henrietta. But she doesn't tempt my bloodlust. I've been around her, even alone, numerous times. I would never hurt her. I'm in control—"

"Lucien, how will you…what will you…ugh. Okay, they're going to notice you don't age or eat or anything." Rebecca's eyes were sympathetic.

"I know." I sighed as I tugged my hair out of my face. "I don't know." Thinking again of Henrietta's question, I met her eyes. "The way Ollie looks at me. She has completely accepted me. I can't begin to understand it. Samantha says she talks about me all the time—"

"You don't just love her...you feel fatherly toward her." Henrietta placed her hand over her mouth. "Oh, Lucien."

I swallowed thickly and looked down, realizing the truth in Henrietta's words.

"Uh, sorry," Jed interrupted, "I don't mean to be overly negative. But Lucien can't just start playing family with these people. They'll figure it out. Or something will happen." Jed looked at me. "Lucien, I get that the possibility of a family is appealing, but..." The rest of his words faded away.

The possibility of a family.

I had never thought of it like that. *The possibility of a family.* I let myself imagine having somewhere good to belong, having people who loved me. *The possibility of a family.* To have people who counted on me, people I could take care of. A sense of purpose.

The possibility of a family.

Then the ancient guilt hit.

"You have to stop that!" Catherine glanced around. "He's worrying he's betraying Lena and Isabetta."

I winced as she said their names.

"Lucien, you have punished yourself for more than a century. Enough is enough."

"Catherine's right." Henrietta squeezed my arm.

Jed huffed. "Okay. I agree on this point. You've definitely taken the self-hatred thing too far. It's time to let that go. And letting go doesn't mean you're forgetting or betraying them."

Just then, Griffin's quiet voice interrupted. He hadn't yet spoken a word. "Are you sure you can resist them?"

I sighed. "Yes." His face remained impassive. "I'm not saying the bloodlust isn't there. But I know now I could never kill Sam. *She* is what is making me feel good. Being *with* her. Would taking her blood feel good? Undoubtedly. But then she would be gone. So, yes. I'm sure."

He nodded. "But, if her emotions feel that good to you, how can you be sure you're in love with her and aren't just... sedated by her? Isn't it possible what you're feeling is the relief of being freed from your grief?"

"I know...I know because of how I feel *right now*. She's not here. But I feel good. She's not here. But I feel love. She's not here. And she's all I can think about." I looked at him. Hard. "Griffin, I feel *good*."

Griffin rubbed his hands against his dark jeans. "There are a lot of reasons not to do this."

My shoulders dropped at his words. Of course, he was right. He wasn't telling me anything I didn't already know.

"But you deserve some love and happiness. Plus, who knows what this could end up being? Maybe, just maybe it could be something. That makes it worth exploring. Slowly and cautiously."

I sat up a little straighter, hoping for his approval even though I didn't need it.

"But promise you will leave her if you cannot resist her blood. You don't want to lose her to that. And we don't want to lose you."

"Not necessary. But I promise nonetheless."

Griffin extended his hand and gripped mine, helping me to my feet. Then his face broke into a big grin. "I'm happy you're happy, Lucien. It's about time." He pulled me in to him, and we clapped one another on the back. Everyone else rose and started talking and laughing. The tension in the room melted away.

Catherine came up behind me and gripped both of my shoulders. "So...did you dress in the dark or is wearing your shirt inside out the new fashion?"

I met her laughing eyes and looked down. It was not only inside out, but backward.

I glared at everyone. "I sat in front of you for hours looking like this. Somebody couldn't have said something?"

I'm not sure they even heard me over their loud guffaws. I pulled the green tee off, flipped it around, and slipped it back over my head. They all laughed harder. Rebecca had thin pale red tears running down her face.

Dio, I was a mess, but I joined them. It felt too good not to.

My family celebrated the rest of the day. Jed and I obsessed over a guitar-playing video game I had never played before but turned out to be good at. Jed said my violin playing gave me an unfair advantage. But then Rebecca beat him too—he kept his mouth shut after that. Jed's mention of my playing reminded Rebecca of my earlier promise to break in my new violin, which I kept. It really was a striking instrument.

Later, Rebecca managed to convince everyone to sit down to a game of Trivial Pursuit, but we tied since we had all lived through the periods covered by the game's questions and had generally infallible memories.

As the night fell, the couples retired to their own activities. I sat on the couch and gazed into the dying fire. The elegant architecture Griffin had designed and built took on an ethereal quality as the light danced around the circular space of the great room.

"You wanna do something?" Catherine was the only one who remained with me.

"No. Not really."

"Are you going for a walk?"

"Yeah." I looked at her.

She gazed at me kindly. "Do you want company?"

"I don't think so."

She nodded, then leaned forward and kissed me on the cheek. "Night, Lucien." She pushed herself up and walked toward the hall steps.

"Good night, Catherine."

I gathered my shoes and stepped out the back door. The night air was cool, unusually so for July. I took a cleansing breath and walked off into the woods. I sat in the grass in front of Lena's grave all night, talking to her and Isabetta and telling them stories. I apologized for...everything and begged their forgiveness—and their permission.

When the first light filtered down through the trees, I knew someone would come check on me. But I was shocked by who it was.

"You mind?" William hovered over me. He was tall and well-muscled; his twenty-one-year-old face was boyish, but he had a man's demeanor and self-assurance. His dark blond hair hung behind his head in a ponytail.

"No." I looked forward again and my eyes traced the engraved letters on Lena's headstone.

CHERISHED WIFE, LOVING MOTHER

William didn't say anything as he sat. The palpable awkwardness came from decades of animosity, jealousy, and competition over my past relationship with Catherine, whom he had loved before his wife Anna came into his life. He studied the headstone of his human wife Maggie, who had died in the Indian attack.

Finally, he huffed out a breath. "We have a lot in common, Lucien." He turned back to me, his ice blue eyes piercing and, at that moment, full of wisdom.

I couldn't read him; he had perfected blocking Catherine and me after centuries of living with her. I pulled my knees up and rested my arms on top of them, then waited.

"I have been angry for most of the more than two hundred years I have been on this earth. When I was alive, I was angry my father didn't have enough land to provide for all his sons, angry I was forced out into this wilderness. When I held Maggie as she died, I begged her to stay with me, angry even as she took her last breaths. I felt relieved as my own injuries began to pull me under. When I regained consciousness after being changed, I was out of my mind that I had been denied my death and my reunion with Maggie. But then there was Catherine. She helped ease the pain. But she never loved me, not really. I know she cares about me. But when she couldn't return my love, when she sought out others, I was bitter. Then you came...Her feelings for you hurt so bad—"

He paused and his expression made me keep my mouth shut.

"My jealousy led me to one of the greatest mistakes of my life." Our gazes met. I remembered the despair in William's eyes the day we realized he'd created his own neophytes, of whom one died in transition and the other later became his wife. "But Lucien, sometimes horrible mistakes can lead you right where you needed to be, can bring a kind of clarity to your life. I was wrong to take Anna's humanity, and I try to make up for it every single day. Somehow, though, she has managed to not only forgive me, but to love me, despite the man I've been. She healed me."

He paused thoughtfully.

"Sometimes something good can come from something bad."

He pulled a leather-covered flask from his coat pocket and turned it around in his hands several times. His voice was low and soft. "We both lost our wives in horrific ways. We've both been miserable as a result. We've both been embraced by this family despite our issues and despite being royal pains in the ass. We have both loved Catherine." He looked

111

at me meaningfully. "And we have both been given second chances."

The others had filled him in.

"So"—he popped the funnel top off the flask and held it up—"let's drink to all we have lost." He tilted his head back as he drank, then passed the flask to me.

I hesitated and looked at him, then put the flask to my lips and took a swig. Deer blood. I handed it back to him.

"But let's also drink to all we could have." This time he took a longer draw from the flask before passing it to me.

I looked back to Lena's headstone.

"Would she want you to be happy?"

"Yes."

"Then be happy."

I tilted the flask to my lips and drained it, then handed it back to him. "You know, that might be the most you've said to me at one time in over a hundred years."

He smirked. "Shut up, smart-ass."

I laughed, releasing the tension I'd built up overnight as I sat and debated myself. I must have looked ridiculous, because he joined me.

"Come on. The women are all wringing their hands about what you're doing out here all this time." He stood up. "You know, because you're so *fragile*."

I sprang up next to him. "Yeah. And you're an angry fuck." He threw a punch, but I was too fast for him, as I had always been. I laughed at him from where I stood outside the limestone wall of the cemetery.

He smiled with resignation and walked over to me.

"Thank you, William. What you said means a lot. And it helped."

"Aw, man, we're not braiding each other's hair now. Come on."

After we returned to the house, I remembered Samantha

had days off on Monday and Tuesday. I decided to stay through the weekend and return to the city on Sunday night. It was nice being here with my family again.

But I worried Samantha might wonder what happened to me. I called a Detroit florist and ordered a big bouquet of flowers—sunflowers seemed most fitting—and dictated a note telling her I had to leave town unexpectedly to see my family but wanted to spend Monday with her if she was free.

Thunderstorms darkened the summer sky all Sunday afternoon. Griffin built another fire in the great room. I sprawled out on the rug in front of it, enjoying my family's company for a few last minutes before I had to leave. I gazed into the flickering flames and allowed myself to relax.

Griffin was right; it was too soon to pack too many expectations into this. Yet the possibilities now seemed endless, promising. The possibility of being loved. The possibility of giving love. Even if it was fleeting, it could be worth it.

William's words came back to me. Second chance.

My thinking suddenly crystalized. I loved Samantha and Olivia Sutton. I needed them in my life. I had to try to be good enough for them and make this work. For the first time in more than a century, I allowed myself to have someone to love, something to hope for. I could swear, in the hollow of my chest, my heart started beating again.

Lying there on the great-room floor at Orchard Hill, I came back to life.

CHAPTER 9

With a thrilling new resolve, I raced back to Detroit late Sunday night, eager to arrive with enough time to prepare for my day with Samantha. I had a surprise to plan and could barely contain myself until I could get in front of a computer to make the arrangements. Had the idea come to me before I left Orchard Hill, I could have taken care of it there. But it was only in the steady lull of driving my mind relaxed enough to generate the idea. By then I was too far from Ithaca to turn around.

I was so grateful to my family for their support. Even Jed had been willing to offer a "good luck" as we all said our good-byes.

This departure from Orchard Hill was different for me from every other. This time, I knew I would return again. At long last, I could let go of the belief that any happiness I experienced betrayed Lena's and Isabetta's lives and deaths. I knew I could, and would, allow myself the comfort of my family's company.

More importantly, this time I left in one piece, not as the shattered man I'd been so much of my existence. I'd let

Samantha and Ollie past my mind and into my heart, and they were already healing me.

I hadn't been to the Edmund Place house in a while. It felt still, empty. First thing, I parked myself in front of the computer and waited impatiently as it booted up. When the Internet was new, I found it a novelty and lost countless hours surfing it. Not that the time mattered to me. In truth, the Internet was a real boon—there was always something to read, watch, or listen to. And it had allowed me to expand my horizons in the world of music exponentially. I downloaded so much music, my album and CD collections hardly grew at all anymore.

Finally, my fingers moved over the keyboard. I found what I was looking for, made the arrangements, and pulled out the credit card of William Griffin to complete the transaction. Having just seen William and Griffin, a smile crossed my face. Multiple identities were necessary when you outlived the lifespan of a normal human.

Lucien Demarco officially existed, but as Lucien Demarco IV. My contacts in this city had long ago helped me create and paper an array of aliases. The multiple properties I owned provided residences for each of them.

Satisfied, I leaned back in the reclining desk chair and ran my hands through my hair, then rested them locked together on top of my head. All of a sudden, I sat forward and worked my fingers over the keyboard again. I typed Samantha's name into the search engine.

The hits were endless, and I realized I didn't know Samantha's middle name or initial to help winnow it down. I clicked on one promising link that led to a *Detroit News* story listing a Samantha Sutton as the contact for the annual Christmas toy drive at the Detroit Medical Center. *Thoughtful and generous too. I'm not surprised.*

Other links were less helpful. I clicked through several

pages and was almost ready to quit when another link caught my eye. This one also led to a newspaper website, this time to the *Ann Arbor News*. A kindly woman's face resembling Samantha's appeared in a photograph at the top of the page.

EVELYN MARIE SUTTON, Ann Arbor, MI

Died July 17, 2006, in Ann Arbor. She was born May 1, 1960, the daughter of James and Olivia Edwards. She was a lifelong resident of Ann Arbor and attended Ann Arbor Public Schools and University of Michigan, graduating in 1981. Evelyn was an avid Michigan football fan and rarely missed attending a home game. She was a social studies teacher in the Ann Arbor Public School System for twenty-one years. Evelyn was also an active member of the Junior League of Ann Arbor. Her parents and one sister predeceased her. She is survived by her daughter, Samantha J. Sutton, and her granddaughter, Olivia E. Sutton. Memorial services will be held...

I reclined in my chair. How hard it must have been to lose such an important relationship. I wanted to wrap my arms around Samantha, to shield her from the pain—pain I was relieved to remember she hadn't seemed to feel in the time since I'd known her. I was also surprised to see no mention of Joe and wondered if they'd been separated.

Reading the obituary made me realize just how little I knew about Samantha. I hoped she would give me the opportunity to correct that.

One final question had me at the keyboard again. A quick check on the weather reconfirmed the cloudy forecast. Full of anticipation, I closed out of the browser, shut down the computer, and went upstairs.

The hot water of the shower felt good against my cooling

skin. I was walking a fine line: I'd decided not to hunt in New York, because I didn't want my skin overheated from the fresh infusion of blood when I saw Samantha. But I also had to keep myself sated enough to ensure I had no difficulties holding the bloodlust at bay.

I made a cursory effort at towel drying, but was still wet enough when I pulled the gray Henley over my head that damp spots formed across my back and chest. I didn't care. I threw on a pair of khaki pants, shoved my feet in my leather boots, and pulled a comb through my hair. I grabbed a couple pieces of fresh clothing to take over to the Frederick house, then headed out to the car.

I took the Z, because Samantha liked it.

As I moved through the new house putting things away, it felt the most like a home of any place I had renovated over the years. I didn't have to think on that much to understand why.

By eight o'clock I was fidgety. It was too early to call on Samantha. But there was something I could do to pass the time. I pulled the phone book from a kitchen drawer and flipped open to the blue municipal government listings. A receptionist at the Department of Public Works answered, and I reported the busted street light Samantha had pointed out the previous week. Samantha was right, this section of the city was safer than some, but not so safe that dark streets were wise. I knew from personal experience just how unsafe the city was.

For forty years, I'd worked in Laumet's world and admittedly contributed to some of the danger in the city. And in the twenty years since I'd earned my freedom, circumstances reminded me Laumet continued to operate in much the same way he always had. While Laumet, true to his word, had left me to my own life, on two instances he felt compelled to interfere. Both were of my own making, as it turned out.

I should have put more thought into it, really. Laumet employed bad people to do bad things. And as a general rule, if I hunted humans, I hunted the bad ones usually while they planned or committed bad acts. I could perceive many things about my victims, but their relationships were not always among them.

Twice, just two years after I'd separated from Laumet and about seven years after that, I killed bad ones who turned out to be loyal, and important, to Laumet. He was less than pleased.

The first time wasn't as problematic. I'd killed and drained a man burglarizing a nearby house. I'd recognized his scent from a few other robberies, one of which included a murder, and was only too happy to be rid of him as his activities brought the attention of the police to my neighborhood. The vampire guard searched for the man when he didn't show up for work and found my scent at the scene. Laumet summoned me back to his old headquarters at Lee Plaza for a dressing down and easily justified my pardon given our history and the extracurricular nature of the man's activities.

The second time was more difficult for Laumet to tolerate and still save face. While scoping out possible historic houses to consider for my next project, a massive wave of fear, despair, rage, and lust slammed into me. I wrenched the car over in front of a dilapidated house in a bad block and tracked the emotions to the back yard. Three men pinned a young dark-skinned woman to a cushioned lounge chair on a covered patio. I snapped the neck of the rapist and savored the fear flooding from the other two who knew it was wrong but stood by. I incapacitated them in ways that wouldn't reveal anything unusual about who had participated in the attack.

I carefully charmed the distraught woman to calm her, then I replaced the story of my role with a fiction about a rival gang that showed up, interrupted the assault, and fought the perpetrators before fleeing. I found a towel and covered the woman's body, then dialed 911. Given the scenario, I couldn't feed on the men as I originally intended, so I fled as the sirens approached.

It turned out those three men were at the top of the organizational hierarchy of a gang closely allied with Laumet. Their deaths created a temporary power vacuum that disrupted business deals, resulted in further bloodshed, and required Laumet to renegotiate the terms of their business agreement, this time somewhat less advantageously.

As happened the first time, the vampire guard identified my scent at the scene, so Laumet summoned me back to Lee Plaza. Jacques was livid and wanted my head—literally. This particular set of business deals apparently fell under his purview. He was incensed at my interference in his affairs.

This one was trickier for Laumet to navigate. His solution was ultimately to offer a stern warning: If I interfered in his business again, I would pay for it with my freedom, life, or both.

He regretted the need for such a dire threat, but it enabled him to continue to protect me and save face. Reading his emotions, I knew his outburst was more for Jacques and his underlings than for me. I wasn't concerned.

Standing at my kitchen counter with the phone still in my hand, I nodded. I knew precisely how dangerous this city was. I would do anything to protect Samantha from all that, even if I had to climb that pole and change the damn bulb myself. I shoved the phone book back in the drawer and replaced the phone on its cradle.

A moldy smell caught my attention, and I frowned. I tracked the odor to my pantry and grimaced when I found a loaf of bread with significant green growth around the edges. *Huh.* That made me wonder about the food in the refrigerator and I opened the door and stared in, though I had no idea what I was looking for. *How long does human food stay good anyway?*

I pulled out the unopened carton of milk and turned it around. The date stamped into the top indicated it had three days left, so I put it back. I shrugged at the rest of it and chucked the spoiled bread into the trash. If I was going to continue to spend time with Samantha and Ollie, I'd have to figure this food thing out eventually.

Soon it was no longer too early to go visit Samantha. I smiled triumphantly at the overcast sky as I ran down my front steps. I tasted her sweetness as I turned the corner of my house into the grassy field that led to Samantha's townhouse. When I looked up, she was crossing the field toward me.

Samantha smiled when she saw me. The warmth of her affection lit me up inside. The sweet taste of her happiness wrapping around me, I picked up my pace, eager to have her in my arms again. When we met in the middle, I threw my arms around her and lifted her up.

She laughed and embraced my shoulders. "Hi."

"Oh, *dolcezza*." I reveled as always in her sweetness and continued to hold her tight against me, all the while pressing small kisses against the scar at her right temple.

She laughed. "Are you going to put me down?" She smiled against the side of my neck.

"I haven't decided yet." I enjoyed the feel of her feminine curves pressed against me for one more moment. "Do you have a preference?"

"Um, maybe put me down."

I loosened my hold and placed her back on her feet, although she kept her hands on my shoulders and her body close to mine. Her smile was so genuine and affectionate I didn't need to be an empath to read her feelings. "I couldn't do this when you were holding me so tight." She reached up on her tiptoes and brought her lips to mine. She cupped the side of my face as we kissed. I tightened my arms around her back and waist.

I kept my eyes open; I wanted to watch her give herself to me this way. Between soft kisses, I whispered, "Open your eyes, Samantha." Her desire smoldered. She moaned as our eyes met, and we continued to kiss. I caught her chin with my fingers and planted a last kiss on her lips. "I missed you," I murmured as I let my eyes roam over her. She looked lovely dressed simply in a teal blouse, khaki shorts, and flat sandals.

She smiled. "I missed you too."

"Shall we go get Ollie?"

"No need." She smiled mischievously. "Dad decided he wanted some quality time with her so they're going to the zoo today. They just left." She looked down again, then back up at me. "Thank you, though, for thinking of her, for wanting to include her."

I took her hand and raised it to my mouth, kissing the back of it gently. "How could I not? She is part of your life. I would always include her. Although I am, of course, thrilled to get to spend the day alone with you."

"Me, too." She bit her bottom lip. "Oh, and thank you, by the way, for the flowers."

"You're welcome. I just wanted you to know I was thinking about you." Her smile brightened further. "Is there anything in particular you would like to do today, Sam?" I tucked a strand of honey behind her ear.

"No, not really. I just hoped maybe we could just do something low-key, just to hang out, be together."

"My thoughts exactly." I squeezed her hand and led her in the direction of my car. "What would you say to being tourists in Detroit today?"

She laughed and nodded. "I'm game."

"Come on then. I have some ideas."

A short drive later, I pulled up next to the Detroit Institute of Arts. "There is a great show on right now," I explained. "Paintings of the modern masters. I thought you might enjoy it. We can walk around here before lunch." Art museums had long been a favorite pastime of mine. Catherine and I once spent years traveling and always made time to visit museums.

"You know, in two years of living here I've never been. It sounds great."

We entered the exhibit, which began with a section on landscape painting. Samantha studied each work. She seemed taken with the pieces by Monet and Van Gogh. As we moved through the sections featuring Picasso and the Cubists, she felt my eyes on her. The gallery was relatively empty, but she still whispered as she leaned over to me. "I think you're supposed to be looking at the paintings."

"I am. I'm just looking at them through your eyes."

She flushed brilliantly and rolled her eyes, though she smiled as she turned away to look at another painting. Of course, she couldn't know I could feel how she responded to the works of art on an emotional level. She stopped in front of Modigliani's *Portrait of a Woman*. Her emotions clouded.

"Tell me what you're thinking," I asked as I came up behind her.

"She looks so sad. Her eyes are striking."

I kissed her temple and after a few moments we continued along. She was remarkably intense in her study of the images, like she was soaking them in. I asked her to tell me what she thought of each painting that caught her attention, interested in any insight into how her mind worked. Finally, we came to the end of the exhibit.

"That was great. I haven't taken the time to just wander through an exhibit in so long. I used to do some painting in college, but I haven't in a long time. So, this was a nice idea." She looked up at me just as her stomach growled. She chuckled. "Sorry. I skipped breakfast this morning helping Dad get Ollie ready for the zoo."

"Well, then, let's head toward lunch." I took her hand and led her through the large lobby. "I'm glad you enjoyed the exhibit. And I would love to hear more about this painting you used to do."

"Okay." She smiled and nodded as we walked outside. "Where to next?"

"You'll see," I said as I helped her into the car. Within a few minutes, we pulled into a parking garage at the waterfront.

She looked at me curiously as we crossed the street to the sidewalk along the river. Then she glanced ahead of us and guessed our destination. "We're going on the riverboat?" She looked incredulous.

"Yes. Is that all right?"

"No." She snorted.

I stopped.

She took an additional step before she noticed. "Kidding! It's great! I've always wanted to do this, but my dad thinks it's too cheesy." She pulled my hand. I shook my head, smiling, and started walking again.

We had to wait briefly until the huge white boat boarded. Within a few minutes, we came aboard. Samantha headed right for the staircase. "Let's go up to the top so we can get a good view."

"You lead. I'll follow."

She climbed all the way to the top deck, delighted to find a large outdoor viewing area. She moved toward the stern of the ship where rows of benches filled the deck. She picked a seat nearest the railing, and I sat down beside her. "Too bad it's not a sunny day, although then it would probably be pretty hot." She turned in her bench, looking over every part of the ship we could see from our vantage point.

"It would be impossible to perfect this day," I said as I stroked her cheek and brushed a tendril of long hair behind her shoulder.

She placed her hand over mine and leaned her face into it. "I'm enjoying myself, Lucien. Thank you for spending the day with me."

"I'm the one who should be thanking you. The pleasure is mine, Sam."

"So, I suppose your work allows you a flexible schedule?"

"Yes. One of the benefits of self-employment."

"Oh. You own your own business?"

"I do."

"Wow. I mean, you just seem so young for that. It's really impressive."

I smiled. Young was not something I'd felt in a very long time. "I'm not so young."

"Twenty...?"

"Seven."

"And when do you turn twenty-eight?"

I smiled but was getting less comfortable with the topic. "November second."

"Ooh, a Scorpio."

I raised my eyebrows at her. She laughed.

"My mother liked astrology. She always read our horoscopes in the morning." A faint blush colored her skin. "She was a big fan of fortune cookies, too." I chuckled. She smacked my arm with the back of her hand. "Don't laugh. Your sign says a lot about you."

"Is that so?" My tone was all teasing, but I loved her a little bit more for helping distract me from the memory of the last time I'd celebrated my birthday as a human.

"Absolutely." She feigned a pout.

"And what does my sign reveal about me?"

"Hmm, let's see," she mused. "Scorpios are old souls, very sensitive, intense, and a little dramatic. They have difficulty finding happiness and are very loyal."

I stared and didn't know how to respond. So I turned it around on her. "And what does your sign say about you?"

She smiled. "Well, my birthday is April 14. That makes me an Aries. We are supposed to be outgoing and adventurous, but we're sometimes impulsive. We are also very trusting, resilient, and tend to believe the world's a magical place." She looked up at me as she bit down on her bottom lip. She was smiling, but her feelings revealed her uncertainty over how I would react to her interest in astrology.

"Well"—I picked up her hand and pulled it to my mouth to press a reassuring kiss to her knuckles— "with you the world is a magical place, Samantha, so I am now a believer."

She rolled her eyes and chuckled. "Shut up."

I laughed and, when she tucked her hair behind her ear, my eyes landed on the scar that ran from the edge of her eyelid, through her eyebrow, and into her temple. I wanted to know every last thing about her. "How did you get this?" I asked quietly as I traced the line of it with my finger.

"Oh." She reached her right hand up, and her fingers joined mine in touching it. She grinned sheepishly. "It's stupid, really. When I was eight, I tripped over some toys on the living room floor and fell headfirst into the corner of the coffee table. I don't think I've ever seen so much blood."

I winced—at the idea of her being hurt, at the thought of her blood. "Ouch."

"Yeah. And it left me with this lovely scar," she said as she fingered the leftover crease. Then she dropped her hands back in her lap.

I grabbed her chin lightly in my hand and tilted her head to look up to me. "I find absolutely everything about you to be lovely, Sam." The blush that blossomed over her cheeks mirrored the embarrassment and affection that washed over me. I leaned forward and pressed my lips first against the scar, and then her mouth. I sat back and rubbed my thumb over her cheek before dropping my hand. "So, how much more schooling do you have left?"

"I'll be done at the end of the fall semester. When I got pregnant with Ollie, I had four semesters left to complete. I'm so ready to finally get my degree and get a job. It feels like I've been in school forever."

I was curious about what I knew to be her relatively recent move to Detroit, but didn't want to reveal I'd found information about her online. "I imagine school and a child weren't an easy balance."

"No, it wasn't." Her hesitation prickled my gut, and then flared into a short but intense torrent of pain.

"Hey, are you all right?"

"Yes. Sorry. It's just...I don't usually talk about this stuff, but for some reason I always seem to spill everything to you." She smiled at me sideways, pulled her leg up on the bench as she faced me, and fingered the strap of her sandal. I didn't push. Finally, she took a deep breath. "It wasn't just that I had a child that made it hard. It's that...well, what really made it hard to get the motivation to go back to school was my mom died in the middle of it all."

I took her left hand in both of mine. "I'm sorry. Were you close?"

She smiled. "Yeah. My mom and I did everything together when I was growing up. We used to go to football games every weekend in the fall—I grew up in Ann Arbor, and my mom was a huge Michigan fan. She came to all of my high school events and meets. We got especially close after my dad left. Then it was just the two of us. When Ollie came, she was so excited to be a grandmother. She was so good with

127

Ollie. I don't know what I would have done if she hadn't been there to help me after Jensen left and Ollie was born. Ollie had just turned three not long before she died. Car accident."

An announcement by the captain over the loudspeaker interrupted our conversation. She met my eyes and forced a bright expression.

I squeezed her hand. "So then you moved here?"

She nodded. "After Ollie was born, my dad really started making an effort to get more involved in my life. He had tried when I was younger, but he was still working then—he was a professor at Wayne State. So he was busy, and I was busy, and after a while we were only seeing each other once every three or six months, despite the fact we lived relatively close. When Mom died, he asked me to come to Detroit with him. At first I didn't want to leave Ann Arbor, but I was all alone there. And I wanted Ollie to have what little family she had around her. So I moved here almost two years ago. But I couldn't go back to school that fall after everything that happened, so I took that semester off and then my dad encouraged me to start back the next spring."

The ship's engines came to life and the deck vibrated. Moments later the horn blasted and the ship got underway. The captain made another announcement.

"I'm sorry, Lucien. I don't mean to be so depressing. Let's talk about something else."

"Don't apologize. It's a part of you, and I'm interested in getting to know all of you, not just the happy parts." I was reassured by the sincerity of my words. It was no longer just her emotions attracting me. "But, by all means, what would you like to talk about?"

"How about your family?"

I choked out a laugh.

"What?"

"That story is just as depressing."

"Oh. You don't have to tell me."

I pulled her hand up to my mouth and kissed it. "I'll tell you anything you want to know."

She leaned into me involuntarily as my eyes held hers. A breeze picked up as the ship hit its stride. Samantha blinked and slipped her hand away to gather the hair blowing around her face. "Hold on a minute." She reached into her pocket and pulled out a bright pink band. Deftly, she worked her hands behind her head to create a thick braid of golden hair, then looped the band around the end to hold it in place. "Now I'm glad Ollie refused to let me do her hair this morning. Sorry." She turned her head so I could see the back. "Does this look okay?"

"More than okay. It looks very nice." Lena's practice of braiding her chestnut hair for bed flashed through my mind, although the memory didn't bring the crushing grief it once had. Just a pang that left me glad Samantha's hair was blonde.

"Thanks. And, yes, I would like to hear about your family."

"Okay." I hadn't told this story in decades. Forcing the words out of my mouth was difficult. But I wanted Samantha to know me. I wanted to share myself with her, however much I could. But now that I was in the moment, I found I wasn't sure how to begin.

Samantha took my left hand in both of hers, just as I'd done for her earlier.

I looked down at her small warm hands around my big hand, and then glanced up at her eyes, which were brimming with understanding and encouragement. "Okay, well...my...I..." I shook my head. She squeezed my hand and let me take my time. "Sam, I was married when I was very young, and we had a daughter."

A whirlwind of emotions erupted from her, although her expression remained unchanged, frozen by the revelation.

I took a deep breath and let it out with the painful words. "They were murdered."

"Oh God, Lucien. I'm so sorry." Her eyes immediately watered. I tasted the salt of her sympathy as a tear spilled down her cheek on one side. I reached up with my free hand and wiped it away. As I rubbed the moisture between my fingers, it occurred to me Samantha's was the first and only human tear ever shed for my family. I had cried—so many times—but I was incapable of such clean, pure tears. I closed my fist tightly around it.

"Thank you." There was simply no other way to communicate how much the grief she was feeling for them, for me, meant.

"Lucien, I'm sorry, you don't have to talk about this—"

"No, I want to tell you." I looked up at her. She nodded as she took a deep breath. "My wife's name was Lena. We were childhood sweethearts. We grew up on neighboring farms. I think our families always knew we would get married, so they weren't surprised when we did. Isabetta was born less than a year later. She was three when she died." As much as I appreciated Samantha's tears, they were hard to watch. "Please don't cry, *dolcezza*," I whispered. I leaned in and kissed her softly on the mouth.

She kissed me back and clutched at my face. The urgency of it communicated the sympathy and understanding I could feel within her. She pulled back and wiped her face with both hands. "Did they catch who did it?"

I checked myself before answering, making sure all hints of my rage on this point were well secured. "No." I shook my head. "Afterward, I moved from New York City where we had lived to Upstate New York, where my brothers live." After brainstorming with Griffin and Jed, this was the story we decided was best. "And then I moved here a while ago." I was trying to stay as close to the truth as possible. If she would allow it, I would keep specifics like dates vague.

"Well, that explains why you're so good with Ollie. It didn't occur to me you had a daughter. But seeing you with Ollie, it makes perfect sense."

I was stunned by the easiness of her compliment. I opened my mouth to respond, but wasn't sure what to say. Finally, I found my voice. "That's very kind of you to say, Sam. Thank you."

"No, I mean it. You're a complete natural with her. You know she couldn't adore you more. And what's so amazing is, after my mother died, Ollie kinda shut down for a while. I was really worried about her and even took her to see a child psychologist. Between her absent father and the loss of her grandmother, she had real abandonment issues. She's doing so much better now, but before we met you, I hadn't seen her so alive, so lively since my mom was with us. Just how she hugs you…she just doesn't *do* that with people."

Just then, the loudspeaker came to life again and announced lunch was about to be served in the dining room.

"Ah," I said, hoping to lighten the mood. "Now, back to taking care of that stomach."

She smiled as we stood. Then she threw her arms around my neck and squeezed. She planted a few soft kisses under my ear. I shivered as I pulled her tight against me, feeling the lushness of her feminine curves against my body.

"I'm sorry you've been hurt," she whispered, her voice a salve to my wounds.

I nodded my head against hers. "I'm sorry you've been hurt," I said softly with my lips against her ear. It was her turn to shiver.

She pulled her head back and found my mouth with hers. I moved my hand up her back and cupped it against her head, feeling the braid there. The words I couldn't say poured out through my lips and hands. I wanted her to feel my veneration.

After a while I realized we were the only ones still out on the deck. "Come on. Let's eat," I said, wanting to take care of her every need, even if it would cause me discomfort to dine with her. She nodded and, hand in hand, we crossed the deck in the direction of the dining room.

I was amazed at how right the whole day felt and how good it was to confide in her. And everything I perceived from Samantha told me she felt the same way.

CHAPTER 10

Samantha and I spent every free moment of the following month together, sometimes alone, often with Ollie. Few days were as jam-packed with activities as our date day had been. But the hours spent at the playground, watching movies, playing games with Ollie, taking walks, or just talking—the small moments that for most people made up the unnoticed fabric of life—meant so very much to me.

My love for Samantha deepened. We connected in ways I hadn't experienced in over a century. She let me comfort her on the second anniversary of her mother's death, and she climbed up on my lap and held me tight when I'd admitted I couldn't have any more children.

I just hadn't found a way to explain why that was. And this mother of all omissions was eating me alive from the inside.

Finally, the first weekend of August arrived and I could reveal the surprise—our first overnight trip—I'd planned that July morning when I'd returned from New York. I had made two special arrangements for the trip during the weeks beforehand. First, I surprised Samantha with an iPod and assigned her with loading it with enough music to last on a "very long" car trip. The only guidance I offered was I wanted the music to include her favorites and help reveal to me who she was. She balked at first at such an expensive present, but to her chagrin, I kissed her into accepting.

The second special arrangement I made was more of a long-delayed gift to myself: I bought a new car. The occasion of our trip justified the purchase as far as I was concerned. Samantha came along to help me pick it up. Since I'd known for years what I'd want if I allowed myself this indulgence, I'd already preordered the vehicle to my exact specifications. The black metallic Maserati GranTurismo S was a dream come true.

Samantha thought I was crazy, but since she got to ride in it, she decided it was a good kind of crazy.

By six in the morning on the day of the trip, I was already packed and ready to go, which was a problem since we weren't leaving until eight or nine. I tried but failed to be patient: I was too distracted to play and couldn't concentrate enough to read or watch TV. Finally I grabbed my phone and started typing: "Are you up?"

Several minutes passed without a response. Samantha was either still asleep or in the shower. I growled my impatience. My phone beeped.

Yes! What are you doing?

"Trying to restrain myself from coming over there and grabbing you so we can leave now."

Restraint is overrated.

Moments later, I stood outside her bedroom window with several small stones I'd found on the curb in front of my house. I tossed the first one up. It clicked against the glass. I tossed three more before Samantha's face appeared at the window.

She lifted the sash with a wide grin. "What are you doing?"

"I couldn't wait to see you."

Her wet hair clung to her face and shoulders. I swallowed hard at the picture of her glistening skin. Her scent was sweet and clean. Her love warmed me.

"Me either. But I want to have breakfast with Ollie, and she won't wake up for another half hour at least. So you have to be patient a little while longer."

"I thought restraint was overrated."

She smiled and bit her bottom lip. "It is. But, in this situation, it's necessary. Now, go away so I can finish getting ready so we can leave right after breakfast." She blew me a kiss and pushed the sash back down.

"Sam!" I said loud enough for her to hear but hopefully not loud enough to disturb her neighbors.

"What?" she whispered loudly as she pushed it back up a little.

"I love you."

"I love you, too. Now go home so I can get dressed!" She lowered the sash, then flattened her palm against the window in a gesture that bid me both good-bye and stay close.

I crossed the field with a stupid grin on my face.

I recalled the first time we'd exchanged those words. Maybe two weeks after our date day, Ollie fell asleep in the oversized chair in my living room while we all watched a movie together. Amazingly she stayed asleep when I lifted her into my arms, so I carried her back over to their house and put her in bed. Samantha stood in the doorway as I arranged the covers around Ollie, kissed her forehead, and offered my now regular words: "Dream sweet dreams, Ollie."

I stepped out of Ollie's room into the hallway as Samantha closed the door, then she took my hand and led me into her bedroom. She pulled us down to sit on her bed and looked serious. I smelled the scent of her anxiety.

"I just wanted to say something. I only say it now because I have Ollie to think about, too. And I know she feels the same. And I—"

I placed my fingers over her lips. "Whatever it is, it's okay."

She blushed as she looked up at me. "I...Lucien, I'm falling in love with you."

I groaned in delight and pulled her into me as I kissed her. "That's good," I murmured around her lips, "because I fell weeks ago."

Her breath caught in her throat, and she pulled back to look at me. "I love you, Lucien."

The warm satisfaction of her words filled me up. "I love you, Samantha." The freedom of giving voice to those feelings was like a weight off my shoulders.

"Will you stay? I'd just like to wake up with you by my side."

"I'd like nothing more."

So I'd stayed that night, and many after. But we'd agreed to take our physical relationship slow. Both of us had been seriously hurt by previous relationships, and Samantha had a child's welfare to think about, so slow seemed in everyone's best interest.

But there was no way I could keep my hands to myself entirely. *Dio*, I loved the feel of her. Her breasts were warm and heavy in my palms. She made the most seductive sounds in response to my caresses. And her taste—salty and sweet at the same time. I'd explored quite a few of her erogenous zones with my mouth—her neck, wrists, and the back of her knees were particularly sensitive. Being with her was a salve and a torment all at once.

By far, though, the most incredible thing was seeing her

come, and knowing I'd caused it. The first time it happened, she was actually asleep. She'd moaned and writhed, making it apparent she was having an erotic dream. She was fascinating and glorious in her arousal. I'd tried to wake her, but she was so deep into it. I'd kept my hands to myself but finally succumbed to the heat of her lust and whispered soft encouragements that soon coaxed her to orgasm. I was utterly captivated by the magnificence of her euphoria.

After that I needed more, needed to touch her in that most feminine place. I craved the feeling of her slick skin against my fingers, and finally I had the opportunity to discover the possessive satisfaction of using my hands to pleasure her. And, *Dio*, how I relished the scent of her arousal on me.

As good as these moments were, it was so fucking hard to be with her and restrain my vampiric instincts. My nature had caught me off guard the first time she'd brought us to orgasm together. She had straddled my clothed lap and ground herself against me. I hid my identity that time by clamping my lips shut when my fangs elongated and biting through the inside of my bottom lip. She gasped when she saw the blood, but it was easy to explain away, plus it healed quickly.

Worse, I didn't even need to climax to find myself struggling for control. The first time she took my shirt off, she saw the Blood Mark on my chest and gasped. Every vampire emerged from their change with a tattoo-like mark made of blood pooled under the skin on their left breast. Deep crimson in color, Blood Marks were unalterable designs that reflected a vampire's lineage. Mine was a pair of mirror image S-like symbols, the first facing forward and the second facing backward, centered over a truncated cross.

I didn't know who or what it represented, but I'd always interpreted the S's as representing myself before and after my transformation: the forward- facing S was my human self and faced the right way, while the backward S was my abnormal vampire self. I'd never seen another mark like mine, though I'd searched for it. It was one of the few clues I'd had in my failed search for my maker.

Samantha was captivated by the mark that first time she saw it and said she found tattoos sexy. I was so overcome with the immediate lust of her response I didn't realize what a perfect opportunity the moment might have represented to reveal myself to her until it was gone.

Because of the amount of blood pooled so close to the surface, the skin around the mark was extremely sensitive, and I sucked in a breath and flinched when she stroked her fingers over it. Then she ran kisses down my neck and over my collarbone and brushed it with her soft lips. The sensation of her tongue tracing my Blood Mark elicited a nearly primal reaction. She moaned and cried out as I flipped her over on the bed and channeled my blazing hunger into a series of orgasms for her. She was so far gone she hadn't seen me rip into my free wrist to avoid sinking my fangs into her.

So, our physical relationship progressed, but it progressed slowly, out of caution and necessity.

Of course, there was another argument for "slow" I hadn't shared with her: I wasn't sure I could make love to her without her being able to make a fully informed decision about me, which meant knowing who—what—I was.

So that night we first shared our words of love, I just spent the night. And I spent many nights thereafter, but we hadn't taken it much further than the use of our hands despite our bodies' aching readiness to do so.

The buzzing of my cell phone pulled me from my daydreams and reminded me of my impatience to get our trip underway.

Done packing.

I grumbled a sigh. Every few minutes, I'd get another one- or two-word text message from her.

Ollie up.

Fixing breakfast. Eating.

Then at 8:10 a.m.: *WAITING FOR YOU!*

I had the Maserati in front of her house in less than a minute. She emerged laughing. Ollie trailed behind, still in her pajamas.

"Good morning," Samantha said with a kiss as she handed me her overnight and garment bags. "How'd you make it over here so fast? Were you sitting in the car waiting?"

I laughed. "Something like that. And, yes, it is a very good morning." I walked back to the car and put the bags in the waiting trunk.

"Hi, Lucien!" Ollie stood on the curb and gingerly laid one finger on the car's pristine fender.

"Good morning, Ollie. How did you sleep?"

"Really good." She opened her arms to give me a hug as I walked around from the back of the car.

I knelt down and embraced her. "What did you dream about?"

"Santa."

I laughed and she joined me. "Well, that's good, I suppose. Be good for Joe, okay? We'll be back tomorrow." I kissed her on the forehead.

"Okay. Bye."

Samantha walked over to Ollie and picked her up. "Bye, big girl. I love you. I'll call you later, okay?"

"Okay, Mommy. Love you." Samantha put her back down.

I walked over to Joe who stood on the front porch. "Thanks again for this."

"You're welcome. Have fun now." Joe was a man of few words, and he still had reservations about me. But he loved

Samantha and Ollie and wanted them above all else to be happy, which was enough for me to respect him. Ollie asked Joe if they could play a game. "Duty calls," he said, as he turned to go back in the house with Ollie.

Within fifteen minutes, we were cruising west on Interstate 96. Samantha plugged in the iPod and adjusted the volume low so we could talk. She looked out the windows for a few minutes and hummed along with a ballad. Finally, she rolled her head against the seat back toward me. "So, do I get to know where we're going yet?"

"No."

"Oh, come on! I'm dying over here!"

I smiled at her outburst. "On the contrary, you look quite healthy to me, *dolcezza*."

She swatted my arm with the back of her hand but smiled at my now-common nickname for her. Sweetness. I grabbed her hand before she could pull it away and kissed her, then I rested our hands on the console between us and continued to hold onto her.

We alternated between long periods of comfortable silence and animated conversations about everything under the sun. She recounted stories from her childhood and funny things Ollie had said or done. She asked me to tell her more about Isabetta. I told her stories about my family in New York, and we talked about the possibility of going to visit them sometime.

Every once in a while she would pause the iPod and offer an explanatory introduction to a particular song. Some made her think of important times in her life, others made her think of me, and yet others made her think of us together. With each explanation, the space I had for her in my heart grew.

Occasionally, one of her song choices would so resonate with me it was overwhelming. When my favorite Beatles song filled the car, I surprised Samantha by getting off at a rest area on the side of the highway. I pulled abruptly into the first available parking space and released my seat belt.

Samantha looked alarmed. "Are you ok—"

My mouth cut her off as I landed a rough kiss on her lips. I pushed her back into the seat with the weight of my upper body and stroked her hair and face with my hand as I worked my lips over her mouth, jaw, and neck.

"Lucien?" Her heart hammered in her chest, and amusement and lust radiated off her in equal amounts.

"Hmm?" Her face drew into a smile, so I pulled back.

"Whatcha doin'?"

"Kissing you." I nuzzled my lips against her ear.

She smirked. "Yes, I got…that much. But was there something in particular that elicited such an urgent need to pull off the road and do that now?"

"Do I need a reason?" I licked the shell of her ear.

She shuddered. "No…but…"

"Besides, I always have an urgent need to kiss you." She laughed and I sat back, my heart full with the rewarding sense of how well she seemed to understand me. "'In My Life' is one of my all-time favorites." I shrugged. "I'm touched it made you think of me."

She beamed and leaned across the console to kiss me. "A lot of people have come before for both of us, but, for me, it finally feels okay. Because I do love you more."

With both hands buried in her hair, I pulled her lips to mine. "God, I love you," I murmured before the words were lost to the kiss.

Other songs elicited a more contemplative reaction, although I was a little surprised to hear "Somewhere to Belong" blare from her speakers. She leaned forward and turned the volume down.

"Linkin Park?"

She twisted her lips and shrugged as a mild wave of embarrassment washed through me. "You don't like them?"

"Actually, I really do." I had no problem identifying with the anger and angst and yearning in their songs, this one in particular.

"I might've listened to this song on replay quite a few times after I lost my mom."

"Yeah." I squeezed her hand where I was holding it between us and sighed. Samantha knew more about loss than I wished she did. "Sam," I said many miles and songs later, "no one has looked at me the way you do in so long. And you've helped me start to believe I deserve to be looked at that way again."

"Of course you do, Lucien. Why would you think you don't?"

"I...I just haven't always been as good as I am with you. I haven't always been the best...person. I've done things I'm not proud of, things I would give almost anything to take back." I'd expressed sentiments like this to her before.

"We all have, Lucien. We all have." She released her seat belt and reached her body over to press a kiss to my cheek as she spoke.

I didn't sense the least bit of suspicion within her at my words, which was remarkable. I could tell from her pulse and heart rate her body occasionally reacted instinctively to me, more like other humans. But more often than not she reacted to me as if I were a man, which is what she did at that moment.

And it meant everything.

~

Hours into our trip we were north of Chicago—which she thought for certain was our destination—and the expansiveness of Lake Michigan stretched out like a dark mirror on her side of the car. She'd shifted in her seat so her legs were partly underneath her, and she leaned toward me. As a sultry love song began, she brought my hand up to her mouth and kissed each finger individually.

My head felt like the world was spinning. "*Dolcezza*, if you don't stop doing that, we're not going to reach our destination."

"Is that a threat or a promise?" She slipped the tip of my middle finger into her mouth.

My chest rumbled softly.

"Did you just growl?"

When I trained my eyes on her, her heart rate picked up noticeably. I would've bet the hair on the back of her neck raised too. "If you don't stop, I won't be held responsible for my actions."

She shivered, then looked me square in the face and did it again. Purposely. And this time she leaned her head forward to take my whole finger into her mouth.

Madre de Dio. Heat roared through me as her lips wrapped around my knuckle. I closed my eyes at the sensation of it and concentrated hard on keeping my fangs retracted.

"Eyes on the road, Lucien," she whispered as she ran her tongue up the length of my finger.

Taking a deep breath that did little to calm me, I turned my head back to the road and shifted in my seat. She smiled triumphantly as she rested her face against my hand. She left me speechless and wondering what her expectations were for our weekend.

What I wanted and what I thought I deserved were two different things given my continued deception. While my mind shouted restraint, my body had been demanding more for weeks.

Finally, signs for Milwaukee appeared along the highway. "Okay," Samantha said with a pointed look, "so, unless we're going to Canada, which is pretty much the only thing north of here, I'm going to guess we're doing something in Milwaukee."

I smiled at her frustration, which was easy because her emotions were otherwise warmed with love for me. "Well, since you have done such a superb job of providing music for our trip, I guess I can finally reveal to you that, yes, Milwaukee is our destination." I exited the highway and followed surface streets to our hotel. The valet looked like he'd won the lottery when I reluctantly handed him the keys to the Maserati and a hundred dollar bill to ensure the car was cared for.

I then ushered Samantha into the warm, sophisticated lobby of the InterContinental Milwaukee. After checking in, we took the elevator to our fifth-floor suite. We stepped inside, and I pressed the five button as the doors closed behind me.

Samantha's slow seduction in the car still vibrating within me, I caught her off guard as I pinned her to the doors in a tight embrace. She laughed, then moaned when I ground myself against her.

"Sorry," I whispered fiercely. "But that was too long to go without holding you. I hope you don't mind."

She wound her arms around me and mumbled a response as she kissed me eagerly.

"Nothing in the world feels better than your body against mine," I murmured between kisses.

A soft ding encouraged me to release her so we didn't fall out the doors when they opened. Samantha stepped out first, then we walked down the hall hand in hand in search of our room.

I inserted the card key into the slot on the door and pushed it open for Samantha. Like the lobby, the room was well appointed, decorated with modern lines and warm earth tones.

Samantha set her purse on a table and pulled out her phone. "I'm just going to check in at home."

"Of course."

Minutes later, while Samantha was still talking to Ollie, a knock at the door signaled the bellhop's arrival with our bags. He placed them in the adjoining bedroom then departed. Samantha snapped her phone shut. "How are they doing?"

"Everything's good. Dad sounded tired. I think Ollie is wearing him out. But they both said they were having a good time." She pursed her lips.

"What is it?" I wrapped my arms around her waist and kissed her forehead.

She shrugged one shoulder. "Nothing, really, I've just never been away from Ollie overnight before." She smiled thoughtfully.

"Are you okay?"

"Yes. It's just weird."

"Hmm. It's okay for you to do things for yourself."

"I know. Thanks." She offered a quick kiss then pulled away. "Excuse me for a minute."

I let her go and watched her walk across the suite to the bathroom. I went into the bedroom, kicked off my shoes, and stretched out on the bed.

Samantha emerged from the bathroom and joined me. "Much better." She smiled as she crawled up into the crook of my arm and laid her head on my shoulder, just as I'd hoped she would. She stretched her arm across my stomach, and I wrapped my arm around her head and stroked at her hair. It was soft and fine. "So what is the plan?" she asked quietly.

"We're having dinner at six. Did you finally decide on a dress, by the way?" I'd told her only that she should bring a nice dress for an evening out on the town.

"No," she chuckled. "I still couldn't decide so I brought them both. You can help me decide."

"If you wish, I'd be happy to." She yawned and I kissed her forehead. "Would you like to rest for a while? It's only four now. You could sleep for an hour and have plenty of time to dress."

"I don't know why I'm so tired. You did all the driving... but, yeah, maybe I'll close my eyes for a few minutes, so I'll have plenty of energy for tonight." She tilted her face up and planted a moist kiss on my neck.

I hugged my arm around her shoulders and pressed her into me. With my other hand, I interlocked my fingers with the hand she'd draped across my chest. "Sleep, *dolcezza*."

Soon her respirations were slow and deep. Her heart thumped softly against me. It was an absolute miracle she was here, with me, like this.

I needed rest as well. I hadn't gotten as much lately, because I was with Samantha so frequently. I usually didn't permit myself to become entranced when I shared her bed, both because I enjoyed watching and feeling her while she slept and also because I feared what I looked like or did while I slept.

At that moment, however, with Samantha asleep on me, I couldn't relax because I was thinking. I was thinking relationships were built on trust. And I had yet to be completely truthful with Samantha. I had tried to bring up the Conversation several times. Mostly I couldn't force myself to say the words. Other times, Samantha would cut me off with reassurances.

I spent the hour Samantha slept internally debating the pros and cons of telling her during our trip. My hesitancy irritated me because it was evidence of cowardice. Surely Samantha deserved better than that.

Annoyed at myself, I slipped out from underneath her and went to shower. The hot water was particularly noticeable against my skin, which had cooled from a long stretch without feeding. I planned to feed as soon as we returned from the trip.

Thankfully, the bloodlust was no longer much of a problem, although I thirsted more when I let myself go for longer periods as I had been doing. But abstaining made me feel weaker and, for some reason, that didn't seem like such a good idea. I needed to be strong for my girls.

My girls.

I swallowed the guilt that came with that phrase, a phrase I had once used frequently. But Samantha and Ollie were not replacements; they were simply evidence that life goes on. And damn if it hadn't taken me too many lifetimes to figure that one out.

I stepped out of the shower and dried off, then flushed the toilet for the show of it. When soft knocks landed on the bathroom door, I secured the towel around my waist and opened it.

Samantha leaned on the jamb, her eyes widening as they locked on my bare torso. She reached up and caught a droplet of water running from my hair down my shoulder. Then she placed her hands on my chest, and the fingers on her right hand caught another stray droplet. When she brushed my Blood Mark, I sucked in a breath. Her lips fell open as she watched a third droplet slide around the base of my neck to my chest.

She leaned forward and kissed my skin over the stray droplet and let her tongue just meet my flesh as she drank the water into her mouth. I closed my eyes at the sensation. Her drinking off me was too fucking close to the fantasy of her drinking from me, and all at once the blood turned molten in my veins.

Oblivious to the seismic activity building under my skin, she continued to kiss across my chest. I wrapped an arm around her waist, the heat of her lust searing me. I burned from the inside and the out.

Ah, Cristo. I wanted her so damn bad.

Between kisses, she taunted, "So, I was just wondering if I could get you to growl again."

I gripped her more firmly against me, wanted her to feel exactly what she was doing to me. I ground the thick column between my legs into the soft flesh of her belly. She moaned appreciatively. Her heart thundered between our chests. And then she was successful in her quest.

She bit me.

She flicked her tongue out against my nipple and sucked it into her mouth. Then her teeth closed around the taut peak in a series of playful nips. And I growled.

She couldn't know the significance of her actions—for vampires, biting was very much a part of sex. And she also couldn't know how wild her bites made me feel.

Instinctively, I grabbed her roughly with both arms and spun her around so her back pressed against the wall next to the bathroom door. She gasped, but I distracted her with my mouth on her lips, jaw, ear, neck. I pinned her hands next to her on the wall. Her chest heaved against me. The scent of her arousal was thick and sweet in the air, making me want her worse than I already did.

She rubbed her thighs together as I ran wet open-mouthed kisses down into the V-neck of her shirt. I rolled my hips into her. She moaned. My teeth tingled, and I had just enough awareness to keep my fangs retracted. But I wanted to sink myself into her—my fangs and my sex—more than I'd wanted almost anything ever before.

"Lucien."

My name on her lips was an incredible invitation, so filled with need and longing. "God, I want to touch you."

"*Please.*"

I released her arms, and my hands flew to her body. She reached down and grabbed the hem of her shirt, then pulled it over her head and threw it to the floor. My hands met the swells of her breasts, and I groaned. I pushed a satiny cup out of the way, freeing a breast to my exploration. She arched into me. I caught her nipple between my thumb and forefinger. She whimpered as I teased her peaked flesh, then I replaced my fingers with my mouth, loving the way she tasted and freeing my hands to undo her shorts.

"Oh, please."

"Anything, Sam," I rasped as my hand slid under the silkiness of her panties. *Fucking hell.* She was hot and wet and slick and needful. I stroked my fingers against her sensitive flesh. She grasped my arms and sagged a little against the wall.

"Oh, my God. Please don't stop."

"Not until you're screaming my name, *dolcezza.*"

She moaned and rocked her hips harder and faster against my fingers, which alternated between long probing strokes through her wet folds and intense circular pressure against the nerves at the top of her sex. We settled into a rhythm and, though my erection was straining against the flimsy fabric of the towel, she so enthralled my senses I could almost ignore it.

When her breaths came in short gasps against my chest, I intensified my efforts. The nails on her right hand dug into my biceps, and I growled as the pain and her orgasm hit at the same time.

"God, Lucien!"

I kept my fingers moving until she was entirely played out and groaned as the heat and intensity of her ecstatic pleasure flooded my senses. Then I pulled my hand free and clutched her to me, relishing the feel of her against me and the sound of my name falling from her satisfied lips.

A moment later, I grunted as her hand found my erection and squeezed. I stilled her and she questioned me, but I cut her off, my voice low and rough. "Dinner is in"—I glanced over my shoulder to the bedside table—"forty-five minutes, my love. You need to get dressed." I stepped back from her and smiled as she held her position against the wall.

Her breathing was labored. Her face and neck were flushed, clothing disheveled. Her gaze dropped below my waist. "Dinner feels...optional right now, to me."

I had to avert my eyes. If she continued to look at me that way, we would indeed miss dinner. And tempting as that was, I didn't want her to miss what I had planned. I grabbed her shoulders and turned her body in the direction of the open bathroom door. "Get thee into the bathroom." I swatted her rear as she started moving.

"Hey! That doesn't help the situation here," she called over her shoulder as she grabbed her garment bag.

I shook my head in silent agreement and laughed as she closed the door, then sucked my wet fingers into my mouth with a satisfied groan as soon as it clicked shut. I closed my eyes at the exquisite flavor of her and exhaled a huge breath as I ran my hands through my hair.

Cazzo! Cazzo! Cazzo!

I palmed my erection and willed it to sleep, then with effort focused my mind on the task at hand: getting dressed. I towel dried my hair, then unzipped my garment bag. Within minutes, I was dressed in a beautifully tailored black suit over a white shirt and a silver tie.

After a while, the bathroom door cracked open. "Okay. Here's the first dress. Are you ready?"

I walked over to the bed and sat down on the edge. "Absolutely. Let's see it." My breath caught in my throat when she stepped out.

The teal dress was knee length with a flowing layered skirt and a tight V-neck bodice fitted over the waist and hips. Sparkling rhinestones adorned the neckline and wide straps. She'd styled her long hair in loose curls that hung down the middle of her back, which the low cut of the dress left bare.

I stood up. "I can't imagine how the other dress could begin to compete. You look exquisite." I kissed the back of her hand, then stepped back to admire her again, this time noticing how long and lean her legs looked in her silver heels.

"So you like it?"

"You look mouthwatering in that dress, Samantha." It was so true.

"You look pretty good yourself," she offered as she ran her hands across my shoulders and smoothed my tie.

"Shall we go?" I asked, trying to ignore my body's dire need of her.

She nodded and grabbed her purse, and I led her down through the hotel to the first surprise I'd planned for a woman in over a century.

Downstairs in the hotel's trendy four-star restaurant, the maître d' led us to a secluded table. I held Samantha's chair for her. She noticed the small blue box perched on the table at her place and looked up at me astonished. "Is this from you?" She picked the blue box up and turned it in her hands.

I shrugged innocently as I sat. "I don't know. I suppose you should open it."

She smirked at my words but pulled the ribbon off the Tiffany box and set it aside. She lifted the lid. "Oh, Lucien! It's gorgeous. This is too much." She delicately ran her fingers over the aquamarines and diamonds of the drop pendant necklace.

"Nothing is too much for you, *dolcezza*. May I put it on?"

"Please." She looked up at me. I was touched to see her eyes glassy with unshed tears.

I rose from my seat and came around behind her. She handed the necklace up to me. I secured the clasp behind her neck, then knelt down, admiring how it looked against her skin. "It's lovely."

I kissed her cheek and returned to my seat. "I've been looking for something resembling the brilliance and beauty of your eyes. I've just never seen anything quite like them. That necklace comes close, but your eyes remain the more remarkable by comparison."

"I don't know what to say." She fingered the stones against her chest. "It's so beautiful. This whole weekend. This is so magical being here, with you." She reached across the table and took my hand. "Lucien, I love you so much."

"That, my love, is the most magical thing of all."

The way she felt about me, the way she looked, was indeed wondrous. It made it easy to tolerate the hardships the weekend imposed on me, the biggest of which was how much human food I was going to have to ingest. But there was no way to avoid it and, at any rate, she was so happy there was no way I was going to behave in any manner that might diminish her enjoyment. So I ate.

After dinner, I led her out through the hotel lobby to the

street. "Wow, look at that building." Across the street sat, unbeknownst to her, our destination, the Marcus Center for the Performing Arts, which a changing light show illuminated at night. Currently the building glowed blue and purple.

I offered her my arm, and she hooked hers through it. We crossed the street and the plaza next to the Marcus Center. When we entered the lobby, a poster on the wall revealed what we were doing.

"Oh, my God!" She looked at me wide-eyed.

I grinned at her pleasure, at having pulled off the surprise. "You said it was your favorite."

"You brought me to see *Phantom?*"

"I did."

She threw her arms around my neck, oblivious to the stares of passersby. It was clear from the emotions of some of the passing men they were less interested in her public display of affection than in her body. I scowled in response and put my arm protectively around her waist, then led her to the large elegant hall where the musical would be performed. We found our seats toward the front of the orchestra section, just right of center. Samantha sat down and grabbed my hand, which she brought to her mouth and kissed repeatedly.

"I am so excited!" She pressed the back of my hand to her cheek. Her brow furrowed. "You're so cold, Lucien."

I gently pulled my hand away and handed her a program. "It's nothing. I've just been nervous about pulling all of this off without you finding out." We smiled, and she began paging through the program.

The result of having consumed multiple human meals had caught up to me. I probably appeared more pale than usual as well, although, if so, the dim lighting in the theater masked my pallor.

Moments later, the house lights dimmed. Samantha became engrossed in the show. Seeing it again in person, I sympathized with the Phantom's loneliness, understood the rash methods he used to woo Christine. Samantha focused so intently on the show, she didn't seem to feel my eyes on her. Her reactions and emotions were much more engaging than the show itself, which was among my favorites.

During several of the songs she especially loved, she moved her lips to the music and sang silently. Somehow, though she knew it would happen, she still startled when the chandelier fell. Her whole reaction to the musical was endearing. When the house lights came up after it was over, she wiped the tears from her eyes with both hands.

"Oh, that was wonderful. I love that musical so much."

"I'm glad you enjoyed it. I would do anything to make you as happy as you look right now." I kissed her on the cheek as we moved through the crowded theater. I concentrated hard on Samantha, my current state of undernourishment making it particularly difficult to rein in all of my instincts. I stopped breathing, which eased the situation until I locked eyes with a woman standing just ahead of me. Her heart rate spiked, and she blushed as her own instincts reacted. My hunger roared. I glanced away and forced myself to ignore the sound of her pulsing blood, then ushered Samantha through the straightest path I could discern to an exit. Once we were outside the theater, I sucked in a deep breath.

"Are you okay, Lucien? You look a little pale."

I blinked away the threatening rush of blood behind my eyes before I looked at her. "I'm much better than okay, *dolcezza*. I'm with you. I'm wonderful." She smiled. "Would you like to take a walk? There is supposed to be a path along the river over that way." The fresh air was helping.

"That sounds nice." She leaned into me and shivered a little.

I stepped away from her, needing the moment to collect myself, and then shrugged out of my suit coat. "Here." It was miles too big, but she made it look sexy nonetheless.

She pulled the fabric of the collar up to her nose and breathed deeply. The look on her face was complete satisfaction. I smiled to myself at such a small but meaningful gesture. Sometimes it was so hard to believe she loved me. But I knew she did.

I could see it. I could *feel* it. It was an inexorable truth. These thoughts alleviated the worst of the bloodlust.

We reached the river walk where a few other couples strolled as well. "So, tell me, what do you think of the Phantom?"

"Hmm. Well, I've always felt bad for him," she began. "He's clearly lonely. But he's also so desperate and angry he makes his situation worse."

"How so?"

"Well, despite the way he acts, Christine cares for him, at least on some level. Perhaps if he had been nicer and less manipulative, she could have both loved him and accepted him."

"Do you really think she could have found a way to love a monster?"

"He made himself into a monster. And he assumed she couldn't handle what he was, so he lied and hid himself. She might not have seen him as a monster if he'd been honest with her about his condition. I don't know. Maybe I'm being too idealistic." She smiled.

"What about you? If it turned out I was a monster, could you accept me?"

She stopped and looked up at me. "Hmm. What kind of a monster would you be?"

"Would it matter?" Something in my eyes must have

alerted something in her body, because her heart rate ticked up measurably and she shivered.

She tugged the lapels of my coat closed around her. "If you're a monster, Lucien, than so am I. In which case, we would still belong together."

"Samantha—"

Her phone buzzed in her purse. I bit back a curse in Italian at the interruption of the perfect segue into what I so very badly needed to tell her.

"That's odd. It's so late." She fished around in the small silver bag and pulled her phone out.

"Hello?"

The blood drained from her face.

"What happened? Okay…Okay…" A tear ran from her left eye as she listened. "I'll be home as soon as I can get there. Thanks."

My hearing had allowed me in on both sides of the conversation, but I still had to ask for appearance's sake. "What's wrong?"

"Dad…he collapsed. They don't know what happened yet. Ollie got up to go to the bathroom and found him on the hall floor. She ran next door to Mrs. Johnson, who called 911." Her face paled and her lower lip trembled. "I'm sorry…"

"I'm so sorry. Everything will be all right. Come on." I turned us back in the direction of the hotel, my arm around her shoulders. "We'll leave immediately. I'll get us back as quickly as humanly possible." If I could get her to fall asleep, it could be even faster.

Within thirty minutes we had returned, changed, packed, and were speeding out of Milwaukee.

CHAPTER 11

J oe never regained consciousness after the stroke.

He lived for seven days on life support. On the morning of the seventh day, Samantha requested the life support be removed. Joe had made it clear he didn't want to be kept alive by machines if something ever happened to him.

During his week in the hospital, I cared for Ollie so Samantha could concentrate on her father. Ollie was not doing well. Not only was she traumatized by finding Joe unconscious, but she was deathly afraid Samantha would leave her next. Every time Samantha left the house to go to the hospital, Ollie cried for her to stay. Samantha's heart broke over and over again as Ollie's old insecurities resurfaced.

The second day was so bad I resorted to charming her after Samantha left. I calmed her, and moments later she fell asleep in my arms from the stress. I held her on the couch like that for three hours before she woke up. When she did, she looked me square in the eyes and said, "At least I know you'll never leave me."

I had no idea what made her say that, but was desperate to reassure her. "I'll always be here for you, Ollie."

When I accompanied Samantha to the hospital on the third day, her neighbor, Mrs. Johnson, watched Ollie. Though she babysat for Samantha frequently, she was elderly and couldn't really manage a distraught child, so I had to use my power over Ollie then, as well. It was just hard for her to watch both of us depart at once, but her body was so worn out it was easy to will her to sleep.

I really needed to go to the hospital, though. Since we'd returned from Milwaukee, I hadn't had time to feed. It was critical I do so, given the heightened emotional states of my girls, not to mention, I was too pale, too cold, and too far out on the edge of my control.

When we arrived at the hospital, I offered to get Samantha some breakfast from the cafeteria. She went up to Joe's room while I met Langston at his office. I'd called him while Samantha slept on the drive home from Milwaukee so he could prepare for me to stop by sometime during the week; he had five pints waiting. I handed him an envelope as I entered his room. He stood watch outside the door while I drank. I disposed of everything in a bag he'd provided. "I'm done, Langston."

He easily heard my voice through the door and walked in and sat behind his desk. "You still look a little like hell, Lucien."

"Thanks. Appreciate that."

"What's the deal?"

As much time as I was spending at the hospital, he would figure it out soon enough, so I told him about Samantha. I could feel his surprise and even a little disapproval, but I respected him for simply saying, "Good for you, man." He had always been a good friend.

I left shortly after that and picked up a bagel and coffee from the cafeteria. Samantha was so absorbed with her father she barely registered when I returned. The only good thing about her distraction was she didn't register my temperature change. I kissed the top of her head.

She flicked her eyes to me and attempted a smile. Her emotions were a salty-sour mixture of sadness, guilt, despair, and hope. But she had too much medical knowledge to put much faith in the latter.

The next day Samantha asked me to stay with Ollie, who was still asleep when Samantha left. It felt odd being in their house without Samantha around. I wandered into her room where I had been "sleeping" lately, and lay down on her side of the bed. I buried my face in her pillow and breathed in her scent, then shifted and looked around the room, memorizing every detail of the place where Samantha was most herself.

Finally, my eyes settled on the slightly open drawer of the nightstand table next to me. Without thinking, I pulled the drawer open and saw Samantha's well-used journal inside. I swung my legs over the side of the bed and sat up.

Samantha had been so distant the last couple of days, which I completely understood, but I found myself longing for just a hint of her old happiness and suspected some might lie within those pages. I picked the book up and turned randomly to a page in the middle.

Samantha filled her journal with thoughts about raising a child as a single parent, her relationship with her father, and her achievements and friendships in her nursing program. I flipped forward several more pages and stopped when my name jumped off the page.

I met a guy at the hospital tonight named Lucien, I think. I say "I think" because when he shook my hand my brain seemed to stop working. I'm not sure if I heard him right. He was so gorgeous. I mean, just unreal. He was tall and had the best hair—brown and a little long and wavy. I felt like I could get lost in his eyes. They were the most interesting shade of gray. I made a complete idiot of myself in front of him, although he didn't seem to notice. I really hope I get the chance to run into him again.

A few pages later, my name appeared again.

How weird is this? That guy Lucien I met outside the hospital now rents a house right near mine. When I saw him I couldn't believe it. And then Ollie seemed to know him. Turns out she snuck out of the house last weekend and fell down. He helped her. AND she hugged him. I almost fell over when she did that. She looked so little in his arms, and he completely gave her what she needed. It was so sweet. I can't remember the last time Ollie reacted that way to someone. That must be a good sign about this guy. Ollie has always been a good judge of people.

I knew I shouldn't read her journal, but I was hooked. Just a few more pages, I told myself. Then I would never do this again.

Ollie and I went over to visit Lucien at his house this morning. Ollie insisted we make him an angel food cake of all things. I had to send Dad to the store for all the eggs. Lucien seemed surprised but pleased that we came. He gave us a tour of his house. I had always wondered what that old place looked like on the inside— he renovated it and it was beautiful. And he did all the work. He is obviously very talented. God, he is so handsome. He seems rugged and refined all at once. He's so tall and his hair looks so soft. I just want to run my hands through it and brush it behind his ears. And he has an incredible body. Can I just say? The width of his shoulders! Oh. My. God. But he's so gentle and kind too. I wonder what Mr. Cute-Sexy-and-Talented would think of being with a twenty-six-year-old mother of a five-year-old... Sigh. Just what every guy wants. Oh, and the weirdest thing happened, Ollie tripped down the steps and somehow he caught her. I swear it seems impossible that he did, but he did. Maybe he's like Clark Kent. That's too funny.

...Aaaahhh! I asked Lucien to kiss me tonight and he did and IT WAS INCREDIBLE! Okay, back up. He took me for an ice cream cone, and the next thing I know I put ice cream on his face. I have no idea what possessed me. But then he did it to me. For some strange reason he wouldn't eat the ice cream off his finger so I did it for him. I thought his eyes were going to bug out of his head. And I thought my heart was going to pound out of my chest. What a pair we would have been. But then I asked him to kiss me— and I swear it was the best first kiss ever in the history of the universe. And the way he wrapped himself around me! I made an excuse of wanting to say good night to Ollie so he would take me home, because I so would have ripped his clothes off right then and there. There's something quiet and brooding about him that is so sexy. Ugh!

...Today I told Lucien about Jensen and my decision to have Ollie. He didn't freak out! God, he seems to like Ollie as much as she likes him. She talks about Lucien all the time. It's very sweet, but it also makes me worry a little. She's getting all attached to *this man, and I have no idea what he even is to me yet, except he did say he likes me too! He took me on a date tonight to this great jazz place. An actual date! God, it felt so good. But before that he played his violin for me. I thought I would melt. It might have been the most beautiful, passionate thing I've ever heard. He was so sexy and intense when he was playing. He is really different from other men. I can't figure out what it is. The way he listens to me— he's always so attentive and intense. Whatever it is, I really like it. But I have to be careful. I think I could really fall for this guy if I let myself. God, I don't feel lonely for the first time in, well, five years. Lucien. When he looks at me he makes me feel like I'm the only person in the whole world.*

I closed the book.

I wanted to keep reading. Hearing her thoughts about me was just so damn gratifying, but it was also so wrong. The last thing Samantha needed to worry about was me invading her privacy while she was at the hospital with her dying father. Vowing I'd never open it again, I slid the journal back into the drawer and pushed it shut. *I'm sorry, Samantha.*

The next couple of days were sunny, so I stayed with Ollie during the day and visited Samantha at the hospital in the evenings to bring her home. She was grateful for my attention to Ollie, who was quiet most of the week and seemed to be watching me a lot.

By Saturday morning, Samantha had made her peace. She knew enough to know Joe wasn't waking up from what had happened. She requested they remove the life support and spent the day glued to his side, sure he would pass at any moment. He surprised everyone by hanging on.

Then, midmorning on Sunday, Joe Sutton took his last breath while Samantha sat by his side holding his hand. I was in the hospital cafeteria getting Samantha a coffee and a muffin. She had hardly eaten in the week since we'd returned from Milwaukee, and I was determined to help her keep up her strength. I knew the moment it happened, because a wave of pain so crushing swept through me I dropped the coffee on the floor where I waited to pay for it.

I fled out of the cafeteria and through the hospital, needing to get to Samantha as fast as I could. A nurse at the ICU desk gave me a look signaling what'd happened. I nodded, then pushed through the door to Joe's room.

Samantha sat next to his bed. Her face was stoic as she looked at her father and clutched his hand. I paused at the foot of his bed, not wanting to intrude on her moment with him. Slowly, she turned toward me. Her face crumpled in a wave of grief. I ran around to the side of the bed, knelt down next to her chair, and wrapped myself around her. She let go of Joe's hand and slumped into my arms.

I drew her weight down into my lap. She sobbed against my chest until she was hoarse and clenched her fist in my shirt. The intensity of her pain felt dangerously familiar; it mirrored the nearly paralyzing grief I'd felt at various times during my life. It was hard to take, but I had to. She deserved my support. I would be strong for her.

Some amount of time later, two nurses came in the room to disconnect the equipment. One peered around the end of the bed to where we sat on the floor.

I nodded to her as I lifted Samantha into my arms and walked us over to the armchair in the corner. I sat and settled Samantha on my lap, then brushed her hair back from her face. Between her tears and the sweat she'd worked up from how hard she'd cried, her face and hair were damp.

She looked at me and smiled weakly, communicating with one glance all the gratitude and love she felt but couldn't bring herself to voice in that moment. I kissed her forehead. She pulled the edge of her T-shirt up and wiped her face, then nodded to the nurse.

"Would you like to have a minute with him first?" the nurse asked.

Samantha pushed herself off my lap and approached Joe's bed. I stood up but stayed back. Samantha leaned over and kissed Joe's cheek. "I love you, Dad. Thank you for taking us in. I hope you know how much I always appreciated that and how much I love you. Say hi to Mom for me." After a long moment, she stepped back and nodded.

The nurses disengaged the brake on the bed and wheeled it from the room. When they were gone, Samantha gazed around the nearly empty space. Then she turned and looked at me. "It's just me now." Her voice broke. "I'm twenty-six years old, and I'm completely alone."

I flew to her, her sadness thick and salty in my mouth. "I know what that feels like, Sam. But I promise you two things. First, you are strong enough to bear this. I know it doesn't feel like it. But you are. And, second, you are not alone. I will be here for you as long as you'll let me."

She threw her arms around my neck and cried quietly, her breath catching every few moments as she tried to rein in her grief. She held on as if her life depended on it. And, to her, in that moment, it did. She sagged against me, drained from her outpourings of grief.

"Ssh, *dolcezza*. I've got you. It'll be all right." I folded my arms around her body and pulled her in, wanting her to feel me there, to have something solid, unmoving, unchanging, to hold onto. I knew what it felt like to lose your whole family at such a young age.

She released her grip and stepped back. "I have to tell Ollie. Will you come with me?"

"You don't even have to ask."

She nodded as equal measures of gratitude and worry rolled off her amidst the sadness. "Let's go home, then," she whispered as she took a deep breath and tried to put on a brave face.

On the drive home, Samantha's fear about the conversation with Ollie escalated. Sensing she needed a minute to collect herself when we parked, I offered, "Why don't you go in the house. I'll get Ollie from Mrs. Johnson's and bring her over."

"Okay. Thanks." Her voice was flat and a little hoarse. She grabbed my hand and squeezed it, then let go and walked toward her door.

I waited a few minutes to make sure Samantha had the time she needed, then knocked on Mrs. Johnson's door. Ollie came flying out. I thanked Mrs. Johnson as I picked up Ollie, who wrapped her legs around my waist and her arms around my neck.

"Hi, Lucien."

"Hi."

"What's up?" She studied me.

It wasn't my place to tell her anything, so I simply kissed her cheek as I walked her back to her house. Samantha was sitting on the couch and held her arms open to Ollie, who ran over and climbed on her lap. I sat next to them.

"Hi, Mommy."

"Hi, baby. How are you?"

"Okay. How is Grampa?" she asked quietly.

Samantha took a deep breath. "That's what I wanted to talk to you about, sweetie. Do you know how I said Grampa was really sick and might not wake up?" Ollie nodded and twisted a finger in her long hair. "Well, Grampa's not with us anymore now."

"Grampa died?" she whispered.

"Yes, Grampa died." Samantha was making a heroic effort to restrain her own grief.

"Did it hurt?"

"No, baby. It didn't hurt at all. Grampa didn't feel anything. I promise."

A tear stole out of the corner of Ollie's eye. "I miss him."

"I do, too, Ollie. Oh, baby," Samantha cooed as Ollie's face crumpled and her little shoulders shook. Samantha hugged her small frame in against her chest and stroked at her daughter's long hair. After a few minutes, Ollie quieted and Samantha alternated soothing words with soft kisses to her forehead. "It's okay to talk about missing him. Okay? You can talk to me about Grampa any time. Okay?"

Ollie nodded her head underneath Samantha's chin. When her breathing finally evened out, she slid across the couch onto my lap. "Can we live with Lucien now?"

I was amazed by both her actions and her words. That she'd think to be with me in this moment of need absolutely melted me.

Samantha managed, "No, Ollie. This is our house. We live here."

Ollie was about to protest when I had an idea. I reached into my pants pocket and pulled out my key chain, then worked a silver key off the ring. "How about this? I'm going to give you two a key to my house. And your mommy gave me a key to your house. So now we can come see each other at our houses any time we want. Okay?"

Ollie hugged the key against her chest. "Okay." Samantha looked at me and smiled weakly.

Waves of gratitude rolled off both of them and warmed me with a sense of belonging. It had been a long time since I'd felt as needed as I did in that moment.

Over the next several days, Samantha mostly operated on autopilot. I helped her make arrangements for Joe's funeral, which was on Wednesday. Joe hadn't belonged to a church, so Samantha chose a nearby funeral parlor. Dozens of her friends and colleagues showed up for the memorial service, along with a few of Joe's colleagues from his Wayne State days.

Samantha's eyes were unfocused throughout most of the service, Suddenly, she started writing on the back of the service program, then held it up for me: *I'm not sure I can make it through this without you. Will you please help me?*

I leaned my forehead against hers. Samantha had gotten me through my grief, there was no question I'd do the same for her. "Yes, Sam. Anything you need, I will be here for you."

She nodded, then rested her body against mine as she turned her attention back to the front. After the service, we followed the hearse to the cemetery, where there was another brief service. One of Samantha's nurse friends took Ollie back home, where she and some of the other nurses organized food for those who wanted to pay their respects. Within three hours, the house was quiet again. Just the three of us remained.

That night after Samantha put Ollie to sleep, she came in and sat on her bed with me. She looked drained. "I need your advice about something."

"What is it?" I grabbed her hand and brought it to my lips.

"School starts in a week…" Her eyes got glassy.

"You're wondering if you should return to school?" I rubbed soothing circles over her knuckles with my thumb.

She nodded. Her self-doubt and disappointment tasted bitter.

"I think you should." She looked up, ready to challenge, but I pressed on. "I think Joe would want you to. Remember how he encouraged you to go back after your mom died? He wouldn't want you to give this up, especially when you're so close to being done. And Ollie starts kindergarten in two weeks. If she sees you go back to school, I think it will make it easier for her to do it too. And maybe most important of all, you deserve to finish this. It might even help you to have something else to think about. With Ollie at school, you don't want to just sit around here all day thinking. Trust me. Idle time is not your friend in these situations."

How well I knew.

She took my advice and returned to complete her last semester of nursing school, and Ollie began kindergarten. They were putting on brave fronts, but their sadness and fear were palpable. Samantha's grief hardly abated as the summer turned into fall. For weeks, she fell asleep crying in my arms. I was desperate to help them, but wasn't sure what more I could do.

The interesting thing was I no longer craved Samantha's happiness for my own sake. I loved her so deeply, I cherished the experience of all of her emotions. I simply wanted to help her heal.

Halloween passed, then my birthday—which Samantha insisted on observing, and then Thanksgiving. We had small celebrations to try to keep things normal for Ollie, but Samantha's heart wasn't really into any of it. She needed a change. That's when it came to me. I called Griffin. After he checked with everyone, he enthusiastically agreed.

One early December night after Samantha put Ollie to bed, I suggested the idea: "How about for Christmas we go to New York to visit my family?"

Her eyes lit up in a way they hadn't for months. "Really? But I don't want to impose."

"Nonsense, Sam. I've already talked to them, and they'd be thrilled to have us. They'd really like to meet you."

She thought for a minute. "Okay. A change of scenery might do us good."

For the three weeks before Christmas, she and Ollie were both brimming with excitement about our trip to New York. I, on the other hand, was a nervous wreck. I didn't know how many phone calls and e-mails I exchanged with Griffin and the others. There were so many contingencies to anticipate and make plans for. I doubted whether an entire coven of vampires could fool a pair of humans in close quarters for five days. But they all scoffed at me. They reassured me they were up to the challenge.

The week before Christmas, Samantha and I sprawled on the couch together watching a movie after Ollie had gone to bed. Samantha had just finished all of her exams and was the most relaxed I'd seen her in weeks. "Sam?"

"Hmm?" She was absentmindedly combing her fingers through my hair as I leaned my back against her chest. I loved her hands in my hair. She seemed to love to play with it.

"I need to tell you something." *Well, two somethings, actually*.

"Okay."

"It's not a big deal, but I wanted you to know one of the people you'll meet in New York, my sister- in-law's sister, Catherine… well, I just wanted you to know I dated her for a while after Lena died." Again, the vague outline of the truth.

"Okay." She shifted so she could see my face more. "Is there a reason I need to know this?"

"No, not really. We're on friendly terms, and I know she's looking forward to meeting you. It's just…there are things about my past you still don't know that you should know." Of course, dating Catherine was not the most important thing about me she didn't know. I berated myself inside for that as we spoke.

She sighed. "Lucien, I'm about to meet your family. And we've just spent pretty much every day of the last six months together. You've seen me at my absolute worst and never wavered one instant in your love or commitment to me. Whatever I don't know about you at this point isn't that important." She reached her hand into a bowl of popcorn on the coffee table.

I sighed. I would need to talk to my family about this while we were there. *I have to tell her. Soon.* I could barely stand myself for not having done so already. I'd never been able to find the courage I'd nearly summoned that night in Milwaukee to attempt the Conversation. I couldn't imagine doing it in the midst of Samantha's grief. That had been a convenient excuse. And I knew it. I shifted so my ear was against Samantha's chest and concentrated on the rhythmic sound of her heart to distract me from my thoughts.

Soon, it was Christmas Eve. Samantha and Ollie were bubbling with excitement about our trip. We packed up the Silverado with luggage and presents and got underway. Samantha loaded more songs on the iPod, including a number of Christmas carols at Ollie's request.

It was the most alive I had seen and felt them in months.

Including a stop for lunch and several stops for the bathroom, we made it to Ithaca in about eight hours. I smiled to myself—it was the longest it'd ever taken me to make that trip.

If I'd had a heart that could beat, it would've been thundering as we pulled up the gravel drive to Orchard Hill. I smiled when Ollie gasped.

They'd gone all out. About a dozen trees in the front yard glittered with colored lights and every window in the front of the house had a white candle. A huge wreath with greenery, pine cones, berries, and a large red bow adorned the door. This was my family's first Christmas ever with a child in the house. They were thrilled.

I pulled the truck into the circular drive and parked

behind Jed's Infiniti Crossover—he'd loved when Nissan first introduced the Infiniti luxury line in 1989. He thought it appropriate for our kind and had owned some Infiniti vehicle ever since.

I looked at Samantha and then back at Ollie. "Well, girls, we're here. Welcome to Orchard Hill."

CHAPTER 12

All of a sudden Samantha got nervous. Her anxiety combined with mine was a bit overwhelming in the confined space of the truck cab. I hopped out and opened the door for Ollie, who promptly jumped down into the snow.

When the front door opened, I spoke so only the vampires could hear. "Do not overwhelm them." It was a fair reminder, for any one of us could do it individually, let alone a whole coven.

Griffin and Henrietta walked down the shoveled path toward us, while Ollie, Samantha, and I moved forward to meet them. I shook Griffin's hand and hugged Henrietta and made introductions. Ollie seemed puzzled as she studied them. She looked between them and me several times, but Henrietta distracted her and lured her inside with a dazzling description of their Christmas tree.

After stomping the snow off our shoes in the foyer and taking off our coats, we walked through the living room into the great room where everyone was gathered. In front of the windows on the far side stood a mammoth tree easily fourteen feet tall. There must've been a thousand ornaments and ten times as many lights. I was going to owe them big for this visit.

As we stepped down into the room, everyone rose from their seats. Ollie had already met them and was now walking around the tree with Henrietta, who delighted in pointing out different ornaments to her. Some of them were quite old and unusual. Ollie was absolutely enthralled.

With my hand on the small of her back, I made more introductions. "Sam, this is my brother Jed and his wife, Rebecca." Rebecca seemed unusually restrained; she felt nervous to meet Samantha. They all shook hands.

"And this is Rebecca's sister, Catherine."

Catherine kissed Samantha on the cheek and welcomed her with a warm smile. "It's so nice to meet you, Sam. We've heard so much about you."

"It's nice to meet you, too."

Samantha was doing so well, though her body was reacting to the presence of so many of our kind. Her heart rate was faster than normal and goose bumps sprang up on her arms when Catherine kissed her. She didn't seem aware of these instinctual reactions.

"And finally, this is my youngest brother, William, and his wife, Anna." Casting William as my brother was something of a stretch as we looked nothing alike. At least Jed, Griffin, and I had dark hair. But Samantha radiated nothing but acceptance as she shook their hands.

"This is a beautiful room," Samantha offered as she admired the central fireplace aglow with a crackling fire.

"Griffin designed and built it," I told her.

"Oh, Griffin, it's wonderful. So construction runs in the family, then?"

Griffin and I looked at each other and smiled. "Yes," he said.

"So, I know William is the youngest, but what's the order among you?"

"I'm the oldest," Griffin began as everyone found seats on the leather couches, "followed by Jed, Lucien, and William."

"Yes, but I'm the best looking," William countered. Samantha chuckled. William beamed at her reaction. It was stunning to me she accepted all of them so readily.

Henrietta's voice called from near the tree. "Samantha, Lucien, would you like something to drink?"

"No, thanks," I replied. Jed rolled his eyes. I glared at him in warning.

"A glass of water would be fine, please."

"Are you sure you wouldn't like something else, Sam? We have wine, juice, and soda."

"No, for now just water, please."

Henrietta nodded and led Ollie into the kitchen. "I'll be right back," I whispered to Samantha. I walked into the foyer where I found our stuff piled. Griffin must've brought it in earlier. I reached into my bag and pulled out the small flask I'd brought from home, then headed into the kitchen, which smelled of human food. The double ovens were both on and filled with pans and bowls.

Ollie knelt in front of the fridge and arranged letter magnets in rows. I raised my eyebrows at Henrietta who simply smiled. She'd thought of everything.

Henrietta set a cup of juice on the counter behind Ollie and filled a glass of water out of the refrigerator door for Samantha. I poured a few drops from the flask into Ollie's juice and again into Sam's water. Henrietta looked at me questioningly.

"Insurance."

She still looked confused. I hesitated for a moment and then splashed a droplet of the holy water on the back of my hand where it hissed. Henrietta's eyes widened as she understood. Her expression and emotions clouded with hurt.

I walked over and squeezed her hand. "Since day one, Hen, because I wasn't sure I could trust myself. Not just because we're here." She relaxed a little and nodded. I replaced the cap on the flask and stored it in the cabinet with the glasses.

Ollie looked up at me. "Can I stay here and play?"

"Sure. We'll be in here if you need us." I walked back to the great room and handed Samantha her water, then sat down beside her again.

Everyone had been asking Samantha questions about me, our relationship, and her school. They all offered a round of congratulations when she reported she'd successfully completed her degree and landed a job at the children's hospital that started in a month. Henrietta was particularly curious to learn about her education and work as a nurse. Griffin offered his seat to Henrietta, and the pair of them became quickly immersed in medical speak.

I joined the guys who moved near the tree and pretended to admire the ornaments so we could talk without Samantha hearing.

"She's wonderful, Lucien." Griffin smiled at me. "I can't believe she seems so comfortable among all of us."

Jed looked at Griffin. "Have you ever seen anything like that?"

"It happens, although it's not common."

William agreed. "The girl's the same way. Did you all notice how easily she meets your eyes?"

"Yes. I didn't even hear her heart rate accelerate when she came near us. Did any of you?" Griffin and William both shook their heads no at Jed's question.

Samantha came up behind me and wrapped her arms around my waist. "So, men don't typically stand around admiring Christmas trees. What are you boys plotting over here?"

I leaned my head back and kissed her forehead. Curiosity and astonishment radiated off the men. "No plots. We were just gossiping like old women."

"Oh. I want in." Her pout was beautiful. I smiled and turned in her arms to hug her back.

"Samantha, are you getting hungry? Everything's almost ready. I just have to get it all out of the oven," Henrietta said as she walked into the kitchen.

"Yes, but can I please help?" Samantha asked as she followed Henrietta.

Jed and William made faces at each other, and then Jed grabbed my shoulders from behind. "So, she really has you wrapped around her little finger there, huh, brother?"

I rolled my eyes. "No more than Rebecca has you whipped."

He gripped me harder. I shoved him away. They snickered and I smirked. Henrietta interrupted their teasing by calling us to eat.

The dining room table was already set. It looked like a spread right out of an interior design magazine. As Henrietta pulled the food out of the oven, Samantha moved it to the table. "Everything smells and looks wonderful," she told Henrietta, who smiled appreciatively.

As Henrietta, Samantha, and Rebecca made the final arrangements for dinner, the rest of us conspired in low voices in the living room. They teased me about what I'd owe them for all the human food they were going to ingest over the next several days. I felt their pain—there was simply no way for us to avoid at least one and probably two big Christmas meals with Samantha and Ollie here. I'd burned through more blood and thrown up more in the last six months than in the last six decades together.

They decided to make a bet of it. Jed came up with the terms. "Okay," he said, "whoever can go the whole holiday without throwing up, Lucien has to buy them the electronics of their choice." I rolled my eyes. "Lucien, of course, is not eligible to win."

"Aw, I so need a media room in my cabin, Lucien." William rubbed his hands together.

"So here are the rules," Jed continued. Everyone looked at him in anticipation. I was grateful for their willingness to make a game of this, even if it was going to cost me. "First, you have to eat normal portions, roughly equating whatever Samantha eats. Second, if Samantha offers you food at any point during her time here, you have to accept. Third, Samantha can never be allowed to eat by herself. And fourth, outside of our 'wine' at dinner, no hunting while she's here."

Everyone groaned at the last rule. I'd agreed we could try sneaking "red wine" at dinner, but if she seemed at all suspicious we wouldn't do it again.

We all took our seats in the dining room. Griffin and Henrietta sat at the heads of the table. Rebecca, William, Catherine, and Jed sat on one side and Samantha, Ollie, me, and Anna sat on the other.

"Samantha, it would be our great honor if you would be willing to say grace." Griffin looked at her warmly.

"Oh. Okay. Sure. Well, we had a tradition in my family when I was growing up. It went like this: 'God, we thank you for this food, for rest and home and all things good, for wind and rain and sun above, but most of all for those we love. And for those who are no longer near, please, oh God, do hear our prayer.' Then we would go around and say the names of people we loved who aren't with us anymore. I'll start. My mom and dad." Samantha looked at Ollie.

"Grampa." Ollie looked at Henrietta.

Anxiety bloomed throughout the room. Samantha could

not know it, of course, but she was asking them to delve into parts of their existence they mostly tried to avoid. Of course, her recent pain was as significant as our own. She didn't ask so much more of us than she'd done herself.

After a moment, Henrietta simply replied, "For Robert, Robby, and Lucretia."

"For Joseph and Thomas," Jed said quietly.

"For our parents and brother," Catherine said. Rebecca nodded.

"Maggie." William looked to Griffin.

"Charlotte and the children," he said.

"I would like to remember my parents," Anna said shyly.

It had come around to me. Samantha squeezed my hand under the table. Catherine braced for the onslaught. "For Lena, Isabetta, and Joe."

Two waves of surprise hit me. First, from Catherine, who was surprised because my saying their names hadn't been accompanied by the wave of pain she expected. Second, from Samantha, because I had included her father among my loved ones. A tear stole down her cheek closest to me. I wiped it away.

I picked up my wine glass, which Henrietta had already filled. "To our loved ones." Everyone raised and clinked glasses with those nearest them, repeating my toast in a chorus before bringing their glass to their lips.

"Please, everyone, dig in," Griffin said ceremoniously. A chuckle went around the table.

I handed the bowls to Samantha first, who fixed her and Ollie's plates. Ollie studied Henrietta with interest as she filled her plate with food. Henrietta looked at me. I shrugged.

Everyone kept an eye on what and how much Samantha was putting on her plate. Before long, the turkey, gravy, dressing, potatoes, green beans, cranberry sauce, and corn bread had circled the table.

This much food went back to the old days of our food dares. I knew the men were thinking of that as well.

The good news was Samantha was hungry. She seemed to have more of an appetite tonight than I'd seen in months. The bad news was Samantha was hungry. People kept making alternately funny, annoyed, and incredulous faces at me when Samantha wasn't looking.

The conversation was great. Samantha told animated stories about Ollie's antics, which Ollie added to by narrating her own versions of the stories. Ollie also entertained everyone by telling jokes. She was so earnest in her telling everyone laughed at them. Catherine regaled us with stories of her travels. Samantha mentioned our trip to see *Phantom of the Opera* and unintentionally set off a fifteen-minute debate about which was the best Broadway musical. Since they lived relatively close to New York City, they availed themselves of the theater frequently and all had strong opinions. Samantha laughed at how passionate they were in defending their choices.

As Samantha finished, Anna abruptly excused herself from the table. I didn't know exactly where she went, but it was close enough for the vampires to hear her lose her dinner. Everyone laughed. Samantha looked at me questioningly. I distracted her with a kiss.

As everyone rose from the table to help clean up, William went to check on Anna. No one was surprised she was the first one out. She was the youngest and therefore the least used to ingesting human food.

Once we'd cleared the table, several of us congregated in the kitchen to wash the dishes and put everything away. Ollie performed Christmas carols for the others in the great room and every so often we'd hear them clap or join in. She was the life of the party.

When we were done in the kitchen, Samantha pulled a

package out of the bags in the foyer and took it into the great room. "Would you like to open one present tonight, Ollie?"

"Yeah!" She grabbed the snowman-covered box and tore the paper off. She pulled the box apart and found a pair of Christmas princess pajamas. "Yay! Princesses! Thanks, Mommy." She tossed them aside. "Can I open another one? Please?"

"Nope. Santa will bring the rest late tonight...if you go to sleep in time. Come on."

"Lucien," Henrietta called, "put Ollie in your room. You and Sam can have the guest suite."

I nodded, then headed to the hallway to grab our bags and led Samantha and Ollie upstairs to my old room. A number of picture frames were gone from the dresser; they'd put away all of the photographs and other things throughout the house that would've been out of place chronologically for any of us.

Ollie jumped up on the mission-style queen bed and stretched out her arms and legs. "Wow! This is big!"

While Samantha got Ollie changed into her new pajamas, I walked our bags down to the guest suite. When I returned, we kissed Ollie good night and went back downstairs.

At the bottom of the steps, we retrieved three bags of packages and lugged them into the great room. Samantha knelt on the ground and spread the packages out under the tree. Most were for Ollie, but she also had presents for all of the rest of us there, too. I went out to the truck to grab my presents and added them to the piles she had started.

Everyone was gathered on the leather couches except..."Where are Rebecca and Jed?" I asked.

Catherine smirked. "They'll be right back. Rebecca wasn't feeling well and went...to take some medicine. Nothing serious." That made two.

Griffin and Henrietta walked out of the room and

returned several moments later with their own gifts. Samantha gasped when she saw the purple princess bike with training wheels and ribbons hanging from the handlebars. "Griffin, that's too much."

"Please, Samantha. It's not. She's the only child here for Christmas. Please let us splurge on her." I knew Griffin had to restrain Henrietta. If she'd had her way she would've bought the whole toy store for Ollie.

Samantha relented. She knew Ollie would absolutely love a bike. "Thank you, guys, so much. She's going to flip when she sees that." Before long, a literal mountain of wrapped packages appeared underneath the tree.

When Jed and Rebecca returned, she nonchalantly proposed watching *It's a Wonderful Life*. Everyone agreed and piled on the couches. Samantha cuddled into me. Griffin and Henrietta smiled.

I never imagined in a hundred years I could have all of this happiness at one time.

For the first time in an impossibly long time, I wasn't alone. I wasn't the odd man out. I was no longer a one. Instead, for the first time, I was one of two—one of three, actually. And I was finally free from the sense of guilt and betrayal that once plagued any effort I made for happiness.

In that moment, I belonged like never before. My family surrounded me, supported me, loved me. And Samantha and Ollie were fundamentally a part of that now.

I was home.

Everyone retired to their rooms around midnight. Samantha and I were sleeping in the guest suite, which was in the newer section of the house and featured a huge king-size poster bed and an adjoining bathroom with a Jacuzzi tub.

I threw my clothes over the back of a chair and walked into the bathroom in a pair of gray boxers and a white beater. I closed the door to give Samantha privacy to change and made a show of flushing the toilet. I returned to the bed and froze.

Samantha was sprawled across it wearing nothing but dark red lace lingerie that sat off her shoulders and closed with satin ribbons. Her golden hair cascaded around her neck and splayed out on the hunter green comforter around her. She looked exquisite. Pure and decadent at the same time.

She held one finger up and beckoned me to her. I crawled up her body and held myself above her. I had no idea how I was going to be able to resist her when she looked like this and looked at me like that. For months, the depth of her grief had put any progression of our physical relationship on hold. She'd never before tempted me like this.

"Merry Christmas, Lucien."

"It is, because of you. Merry Christmas."

She stroked her fingers from my cheeks, down my neck, and across my collar bones to my chest. Then she dropped her hands to her own chest and slowly untied the two satin ribbons that held the lace bodice together. The confidence she exuded was seductive, and the heat of her hunger coursed through my abdomen and groin.

I rested my forehead against hers and closed my eyes. *This is impossible.*

"Lucien?"

I opened my eyes and met hers. "If I look at you when you look this incredible, *dolcezza*, I won't be able to control myself."

"That's sorta the point. I don't want you to control yourself. We've been about as controlled as two adults should be.

I was aiming for a lack of control tonight." She pulled the lace completely off the sides of her chest just to make her point. "You're what I want for Christmas. Please? I want you so much."

The way she offered herself to me was so appealing. She looked beyond beautiful, flushed with her desire and literally glowing. And I loved her more than my life.

I lowered my weight onto her and found her mouth with mine, then ran my left hand down her arm, along the side of her breast to her hip, and back up. I stroked her tongue with mine and relished her taste. When I licked and nipped down her neck, I paused to suck gently over her carotid artery. *You're safe with me, Samantha.* And I knew it was true. Her existence was fundamental to my own. I could never do anything to harm her.

She rolled her hips up into mine, and we both groaned when she pressed herself against my erection. I slid down and kissed and licked between her breasts. She was so perfectly formed. I shifted to the side and licked over her nipple, then pulled it into my mouth with my lips. Her flesh pebbled harder as I sucked and tugged at her.

"Oh, God."

I caressed her other breast in my hand and rolled her nipple between my fingers. She moaned and arched herself up into my mouth. The smell of her arousal was intoxicating. I had to focus to keep my fangs retracted.

"*Dio*, you're beautiful. So beautiful."

I moved my mouth to her other breast. She wound her fingers into my hair. Then I ran open-mouthed kisses down her stomach as she gasped and squirmed. Her skin was savory and sweet, pure and clean. I stroked my tongue down her side to her hip bone, where the thin red strap of her lace panties sat. She moaned as I licked my way across the edge of her panties from one hip bone to the other.

"Off, please, Lucien." She raised her head and our eyes met.

I swallowed thickly as I hooked my fingers under the lacy material on each side of her hips and slowly slid them down and off her legs. She was completely naked before me, laid out like a sacred offering. I couldn't keep my eyes from admiring the glistening pink skin between her legs. "You're perfect," I praised.

Unclothed, her scent was much stronger and set my mouth to watering. I kissed up the inside of her right leg and paused to extend my tongue into the sensitive skin under her knee I knew pleased her. I nipped at the tender flesh along the inside of her thigh where her femoral artery pulsed under my mouth. A shiver passed through me, and I pressed my tongue hard against my canines to provide some of the counter-pressure they so badly wanted.

I pushed her thighs open wide, allowing space to situate my shoulders between them. She whimpered and let out a shuddering breath. "I want to taste you, Sam. I've wanted to for so long."

"Oh, yes." She used one arm to support her head as she looked down at me.

I licked my lips as I met her eyes, then pressed a firm kiss directly on her wetness.

She arched her back and sighed. "Oh, my God," she rasped as I explored her sensitive flesh.

"*Così dolce*," I murmured, tasting the exquisite sweetness I'd expected. Slowly at first, I laved her with my tongue. I was mesmerized by her smell and her responsiveness to me as I lapped at her slick folds.

"Please," she whimpered as her hands found my hair.

I groaned at her goodness as I stroked her with my tongue, alternating between hard and quick and deep and penetrating. Her taste was sweet and salty. I wanted to drink her down.

She moaned and writhed and attempted to thrust herself into my mouth. I placed my hands on her hip bones to hold her still. I had to control this for both our sakes.

"Oh. *More*, Lucien."

I sucked harder against her and slid a finger into her wet heat. I thrilled at being inside her as I always did. Samantha groaned. Her hands tightened in my hair as she tried to pull me closer. I added a second finger. She gasped and pushed harder. I worked my fingers in and out and curled them within her while I sucked at her tender flesh.

The sounds she was making—for me, because of me—were among the most beautiful and erotic I'd heard in my entire existence. I groaned in pleasure and need.

"Lucien. I'm… God…please…Unnhh…"

The breathy sound of my name out of her mouth was enthralling.

"You look so beautiful like this, Samantha. I want you to lose yourself. Lose yourself to me," I commanded as I continued to stroke her with my fingers, my thumb finding the center of her need.

"Mmm…oh God!" Her muscles constricted around me.

"That's right. Come on." I sucked her swollen flesh into my mouth once again and fought the stinging demands of my fangs.

She screamed and clenched around me, her body convulsing in pleasure, a pleasure that blazed through my entire being. I lapped at her offering and grunted in satisfaction as I swallowed greedily against her.

When she stilled, I pulled my fingers free and sat up between her legs. I held her gaze as I sucked my fingers clean of her sweet essence. *Cristo, she tastes phenomenal.* I was thrilled she allowed me the privilege of pleasing her this way and couldn't wait to do it again.

She licked her lips as she watched me through heavy-lidded eyes. Then she surprised me by wrapping her feet around my back and pulling me down on top of her. I allowed her to move me and groaned when she rocked her hips against my erection, still restrained by my boxers.

I took a deep breath, knowing I had things to tell her before we took this any further. I opened my mouth...

And she pressed three fingers against my lips. "I can feel you holding back. I know you think there are things about your past I need to know. But please believe me, there's nothing else about you I need to know before I make this decision. I know what I want. And I want you. Right now. Inside me. *Please.*"

I knew I should say something, but my voice failed as her unwavering honesty and guileless need shot through me. I kissed her fingers before she dropped them.

Determined, she tugged at my shirt. I helped her pull it over my head, still torn. She smoothed her hands over my chest, and I sucked in a breath through clenched teeth when she traced my Blood Mark. Then she hooked one of her toes into the waistband of my boxers and pushed it down.

I let her, giving in with each passing second. The desire and need radiating from her fueled my own, and I finally resolved to let her take the lead and have what she wanted. Hell, what I wanted too.

She managed to get my boxers down to my knees with her hands and feet, then I kicked them the rest of the way off. I had elevated myself above her in the process, enough for her to reach between us and grab my engorged length.

"Ah, *Dio.*"

She worked her warm hand up and down my heavy shaft. I was dying a slow, sweet death. She pushed at my chest and forced me upright, then wiggled her body between my legs so that— *Dio!*...when I realized what she was planning, I thought I would lose my mind—she could take me into her mouth as I straddled her. She licked up my length and moaned. Her satisfaction warmed me. A low growl rumbled in my chest. I was fascinated to smell how much my sounds heightened her arousal.

"God, you taste good, Lucien." She rested her head back against the bed and, with her hands on my rear, pulled me down to her waiting mouth.

I grunted. She gripped my hips harder. I closed my eyes as I let her guide me.

It had been years—decades—since someone had pleasured me this way, since someone had been so focused on taking care of me. I swallowed against the thickness that suddenly gripped my throat. Forcing myself to stop thinking, I opened my eyes to find Samantha looking up at me as she swallowed my rigid length.

I groaned at the visual. "Feels...so fucking good."

She moaned and the vibration stimulated me everywhere. The hot suction of Samantha's mouth around me was insanely good. When she dragged her teeth down my length, I growled louder, and she moaned and bucked underneath me, her nails digging into my clenching muscles.

The tingling around my canine teeth and the stinging in my eyes became painful. My instincts screamed for release. I could easily imagine the relief of my fangs stretching out and finding purchase against her skin. I clenched my eyes tight in concentration.

Samantha pushed at my hips, urging me off of her and onto my back. I whimpered at the loss of her talented mouth. She quirked a devious little smile at me as she crawled up and straddled me. Again and again, she slid her wetness against my achingly engorged length. I grabbed her hips and ground us together harder to heighten the friction.

She reached her arm across my face to the night stand. As

she did, I caught her breast in my mouth and suckled. She groaned and paused while I worked my mouth over her, taking in as much of her as I could and fantasizing about drinking from her there.

She pulled back and held up a square silver packet. "Do you mind? I mean, I know you can't...um...but I..." For the first time since I joined her in the bed, she blushed.

I reached up and cupped her face in my hand, grateful I wouldn't have to broach the issue. "Of course not, love." I would never deny her the ability to protect herself and, given the trace blood in my semen, she needed to.

She turned her face and pressed a kiss against my palm, then ripped open the silver wrapper and deftly rolled the condom down over me.

When she centered herself over my waiting body, one side of my brain screamed at me to stop her, while the other was so far gone I was hesitant to talk lest a feral growl erupt.

And then she lowered herself down fully and took me inside her. And it was over. At that point nothing mattered. Not the past, nor the future.

Only now. Right now. This second. This feeling.

I'm home.

I'd had other women. But everything I thought I remembered about being inside a woman was obliterated by the intense pleasure and sense of connection I felt with Samantha wrapped around me. Decades had passed since I'd felt the slick ecstasy of a man and woman joining together. More than a century had passed since I'd experienced how true love could make the act a spiritual experience full of bliss.

Samantha lifted her body up slowly, nearly to the top of me, before lowering herself down again. I watched myself disappear within her, a sight so full of belonging and eroticism, I simply surrendered to the perfection of the moment.

"Ah *Cristo*, I've wanted you."

"Me, too. So much," she moaned, her half-lidded eyes finding mine as we moved together.

She radiated above me, her skin flushed and moist, her golden hair tousled and soft as it dragged against my chest when she leaned forward. She held my gaze and never once shied away from letting me see and hear what she felt.

Her bliss flowed through me setting every nerve ending ablaze and fueling my own urgent hunger. I pulled her down and kissed her deeply, roughly. Her forward position allowed me to thrust up into her, but it wasn't enough. With my arms around her shoulders and waist, I flipped us over and pinned her to the mattress with my weight. My body covered her, encompassed her.

"Oh, Lucien. You feel so good." She grasped at my shoulders and brought her knees up against my ribs.

"So do you...oh *Dio*, so do you."

I moved in and out of her and concentrated on the way her slick walls clenched my hard length. I reminded myself not to be too rough, but found she responded eagerly when I moved harder rather than softer. I pumped into her relentlessly, giving in to the urge to lose myself inside her.

"Please," she whimpered.

"Please what, baby? Anything," I ground out, "anything for you."

She clawed at my shoulders and back, pulled my hair. "I just need you so...ungh...so bad. God."

"You have me, *dolcezza*. I'm here." Pressing a kiss against her forehead, I wrapped my hands under her shoulders and grabbed on as I thrust into her, rolling my pubic bone again and again into the nerves at the top of her sex.

She panted hard in my ear and nipped and kissed at my neck. Wrapping her arms around my shoulders, she leveraged herself and lifted her hips to meet mine with each stroke.

The added sensation fueled the burn in my eyes and gums. "I love you...unhh...so much."

"Me...too," she gasped. "Oh. More...*please*." Wanting to be the one who gave her everything she ever needed, I thrust faster and tilted my hips to work new places deep inside her. Supporting my weight with my left arm, I reached my right hand between us and stroked her. She screamed out. I thrust into her harder and rubbed my fingers in slick circles over her.

"Oh...I'm...again...gonna..." Her head wrenched back into the mattress, and her eyes rolled up. Her whole body flexed under me.

Her clenching ecstasy fueled my own. I ground my teeth together. Her fingernails dug into my lower back as I continued to slam into her while her body milked me hard. It was all too much.

With a grunt and a roar, I turned my head away from her neck as my instincts won out and my fangs protruded. The first wave of my release hit me in a series of delicious pulses. The convulsions of my body enflamed Samantha again and, as her body rocked through another orgasm, I sliced my fangs into my biceps to satisfy the fucking urgent need to bite.

We lay panting, our grip so tight we seemed melded together. Still looking away, I released my teeth and licked my wound shut, then retracted my fangs with a shudder. After a minute, I rolled off her and rested my head on her chest and listened as her heart rate slowed.

What have I done? I closed my eyes against the thought.

Then Samantha giggled and pulled me out of my head. I looked up at her and she kissed my forehead. "I have wanted that for so long. God, it was good."

I tasted her delight and satisfaction and the signature happiness that seemed such a part of her natural makeup. Her words were sincere.

How can I regret what caused her such obvious pleasure and happiness? Just let yourself be happy, for once. I took a deep breath and pressed a lingering kiss in between her breasts. "I feel exactly the same way, Samantha. I love you so much."

"I love you, too." She tilted my face up with her hands and kissed me, then pushed out from underneath of me. "I'll be right back." She walked naked over to the bathroom and closed the door.

I stared at the ceiling for a moment, then cleaned myself up and found my boxers. Partially dressed again, I pulled the covers down.

Samantha emerged from the bathroom and wrapped herself around my back. She kissed between my shoulder blades and squeezed. Then she leaned down to the floor and picked up my beater, which she threw over her head. My oversized shirt on her body was sexier than the lingerie had been by far. And that was saying something. She found her red panties on the other side of the bed and stepped into them before crawling under the covers.

I got in bed, and she settled herself into my side and used my shoulder as a pillow. She sighed, a sound full of contentment. I hadn't felt her this at ease in months.

Now that she had found her happiness again, I would protect it with my life.

Before long, she fell asleep. I turned on my side so I could watch her as she lay facing me.

Is it possible all those bad things happened to me so I could eventually find you?

I'd never been one to put much faith in fate, but how else could I explain how my painful journey had finally led to such bliss after so very long?

CHAPTER 13

Hours later, Ollie wandered the hallway. "Mommy? Lucien?"

The first light was just creeping into the sky. Samantha had warned me Ollie was likely to be up before the sun. I slipped out of bed, threw a clean T-shirt over my head, and opened the door to our suite. Ollie was tiptoeing as she looked for our room.

"Pssst."

She turned her head in the direction of the noise and smiled when she saw me. She bounded down the hall into my arms. "Lucien, it's Christmas morning!"

"I know." I wrapped my arms around her small form and picked her up.

"Do you think Santa came?"

"I do. You know why I think so?" She shook her head.

"Because you, Olivia, are a very, very good girl."

She beamed and threw her arms around my neck and squeezed. "I love you, Lucien."

The warmth and sweetness of her sentiment flowed through me. I staggered back against the wall. We expressed our affection for one another in countless ways, but it was the first time she'd said those words in exactly that way. *How am I lucky enough to have this much happiness?*

A door opened down the hall, but I didn't care. At that moment, my conversation with Ollie was the only thing worth knowing in the world. "That's so good to hear, because I love you, too." She squeezed her arms tighter.

Catherine stepped out into the hall a few doors down. There was no way she hadn't heard our conversation; I suspected the others probably had as well. I hoped they could approve, but I didn't truly care what they thought. I tilted my head against Ollie's shoulder, still holding her tight, and finally looked in Catherine's direction. When a tear worked its way free from my eye, I swatted it away.

For less than a moment, I tasted Catherine's sadness and jealousy, but they were quickly replaced with a warm wave of love. Catherine looked at me and smiled, then lowered her eyes and walked the other way down the hall.

I took a deep breath and placed Ollie on her feet, then peeked in the doorway behind me to ensure Samantha was still asleep. "How about we go downstairs and make some breakfast to bring up to your mom?"

"Yeah!" she whispered.

This was a small gift to my family, who wouldn't be forced to eat breakfast if Samantha ate in the privacy of our room. I led Ollie downstairs. We avoided the great room with its mountains of presents—Ollie was dying to look but agreed to wait until after we'd eaten.

Henrietta had apparently baked overnight, for a big basket of huge blueberry muffins sat out on the counter. A folded sheet of paper leaned against the basket. I flipped it open.

Enjoy all. We're out. —H&G

I chuckled and tucked the paper under the edge of the basket. I grabbed a plate and placed two muffins and two bananas on it, some for Ollie and some for Samantha, and filled two glasses with orange juice.

Ollie scrunched her eyebrows. "You're not gonna eat, Lucien?"

I shrugged. "Nah. I'm not much of a breakfast person."

We headed back upstairs and tiptoed across the guest suite. Ollie crawled up on the bed and sat cross-legged next to Samantha's knees. She placed her hands over her mouth to stifle her giggles. I set everything down. Samantha opened one eye at us and then closed it again.

Ollie couldn't hold back her laughter after that. Neither could Samantha, who finally rolled onto her back and opened her eyes. "Merry Christmas, baby." She reached for and squeezed Ollie's hand. Then she looked at me. "Merry Christmas, Lucien."

"Merry Christmas. We brought you breakfast."

"Mmm." She pushed herself into more of a sitting position and plumped the pillows up behind her for support.

Ollie handed her a napkin and spread one out for herself, then explained there was one muffin and one banana for each of them. Samantha picked up the muffin and laid it on the napkin in her lap. She pulled off a big piece of the muffin top and put it in her mouth.

"Mommy, why are you wearing Lucien's shirt?" Samantha coughed and looked at me.

"Oh. I lent it to your mom last night because she couldn't find her pajamas."

"Oh. Maybe Santa will bring you some new Christmas pajamas too, Mom. Mine have princesses. See?"

Samantha swallowed and motioned for her orange juice. I grabbed the glass and handed it to her. She drank and placed it on the nightstand next to her. "Yeah, baby, maybe he will." She made a face at me when Ollie was looking down. I stifled a laugh.

I left them to finish up and went in the bathroom to shower. In a rush to get back to my girls, I threw on a pair of worn jeans and a maroon button-down shirt and emerged from the bathroom to find Samantha selecting clothes from her bag while Ollie finished her banana.

Sam squeezed my arm and kissed me on the cheek, then closed the bathroom door behind her. Ollie was demonstrating her ability to do somersaults on the bedroom floor when Samantha finished up twenty minutes later. I looked up and smiled at her; she looked effortlessly beautiful in a pair of dark-wash jeans and a V-neck white sweater with a row of red snowflakes across the chest. She wore her still-damp hair clipped back on the sides with sparkly barrettes. Small pearl earrings her father had given her for a birthday adorned her ears.

I pushed myself up from the floor. "Who wants to see if Santa came last night?"

"Me!" Ollie yelled as she sprang up.

"Let's go then."

Ollie literally ran down the hall before Samantha and I made it out of the room. A chorus of "Merry Christmas!" sounded as we walked down the steps. The others were waiting for us. Ollie's surprised and excited response to the festive scene in the great room satisfied everyone's expectations.

A merrier Christmas had never been seen at Orchard Hill in its more than two hundred years.

Ollie tore through her packages like a tornado and demonstrated her riding prowess by making circles around the great room on her new bike. Griffin promised to shovel a clear path for her around the circular drive later in the day. The rest of my family demonstrated their affection for Samantha and Ollie by showering them with gifts. They were both thrilled, although Samantha was overwhelmed by their thoughtfulness. They had been drilling me for ideas for the girls for weeks.

Finally, Samantha couldn't hold back any longer and insisted I open my presents from her. Everyone else had been exchanging gifts with their spouses, but all the activity quieted as Samantha led me to a tall object hidden beneath a loose-fitting decorated bag with a big red bow.

"First, the little one." She handed me a red box with a white ribbon.

I looked up at her and smiled. Everyone watched me, and I think I would've blushed if I could've. Ollie danced around and tried to peer into the box when I lifted the lid.

It was an antiqued gold necklace with a tag- shaped charm. On its face were my initials: LAD. On the reverse was a hidden message:

the most magical
thing of all

I recalled those words vividly from our dinner in Milwaukee. I'd used them to describe her love for me. She was giving me her love to wear. I took a deep breath and nodded minutely in thanks when Catherine shot me a wave of reassurance and strength. I looked at Samantha and pulled her into my arms.

"I love it, Samantha. Thank you so much."

I stepped back and pulled it out of the box, then clasped the chain around my neck. It was long enough to lie underneath my shirt.

Her smile was huge. "Okay, now the big one," she said, pointing to the oblong bag behind me. The level of excitement in the room elevated.

"Can I help you, Lucien?" Ollie looked up expectantly.

"You take that side. I'll get this side. We'll lift it up slow, okay?"

She nodded and grabbed the edge of the bag. Samantha stood back and snapped a picture as Ollie and I pulled the wrapping over the top of the object. I dropped the plastic and looked at Samantha with an amazed expression. Standing before me was an antique mahogany two-sided music stand with elaborate carving. It was in excellent condition.

Samantha was so excited she could barely contain herself as she waited for my reaction. When I didn't say anything immediately, she explained, "One time you mentioned the name of your violin's maker, which I now know helps you date it. This stand is French but was made at roughly the same time as your violin—"

I took two long strides across the room and grabbed her face gently with my hands and pressed my lips against hers. "It's perfect." I kissed her again. "No two gifts in the world could have been more perfect—more thoughtful—than the ones you gave me."

She blushed. I wrapped my arms around her shoulders and rocked her gently back and forth. She smiled against my chest. Although I knew she had inherited money from her father, I was concerned about the expense of the gift. She was so proud of herself, though, I couldn't express any hesitation about it whatsoever.

"Open mine now, Lucien!" Ollie held out a small box she had clearly wrapped herself.

I ripped off the paper and found a key chain with a pocket-sized digital screen. Ollie turned it on and dozens of images played on a slideshow: pictures of the three of us together, of Ollie from all different periods of her life, and images of some of Ollie's angel drawings Samantha must've scanned.

"Ollie, this is the best present. Thank you so much." I

kissed the top of her head and handed the key chain to her when she stretched out her small hand. She sat with it next to Henrietta, who she'd taken to affectionately calling Henny —which Henrietta adored—and proceeded to describe the pictures to her as they changed.

I sat two presents from me on the couch next to Ollie. She eagerly ripped them open. The first was a collectible Golden Angel Barbie doll. She was beautiful with long golden hair, white wings with gold edges, and a flowing gown.

Ollie gasped and stroked at the plastic packaging over the doll. She set it aside but continued to look at it while her hands fumbled for the other package. Finally she pulled her attention away and ripped the paper until she could lift the lid. Inside sat a familiarly shaped black case.

"My own violin?" She gasped and flipped the clasps up on the lid to reveal a child's violin.

"You're always asking to play mine. I thought if you had your own, I could teach you, and we could play together."

"This is so good, Lucien! Thank you! Can we play now?" She ran her hand along the length of the instrument.

"How about after everyone is done opening presents?"

She nodded and picked up the angel doll box. She didn't seem to be able to decide to which to devote her attention. Henrietta laughed at her excited chatter.

I pulled Samantha down on the couch next to me. "Your turn." I handed her a familiar blue box. She looked ready to protest. I kissed her and tapped the box. "Open it."

She slid the ribbon aside and pulled the lid off, then opened the velvet box. Inside sat a solid circle of aqua-marines set in white gold.

"It's called an eternity ring, which is how long I plan to love you."

She blushed furiously, which everyone would've sensed even if they weren't looking at her. I slipped it from the velvet and placed it on her ring finger. To me, the gesture felt weighted with significance beyond the moment. She held out her left hand and admired it. "It's stunning, Lucien. I love it."

I brought her hand to my mouth and pressed my lips to the spot where the ring encircled her skin. "There's one other thing." I handed her a rectangular package.

She shook it. "It feels empty." She laughed as she tore off the paper.

She lifted the lid and set it aside, then pulled out a manila folder. She pursed her lips and looked at me curiously. I stopped breathing in anticipation of her reaction. She opened the folder and frowned. She flipped haltingly through several of the pages. Her breath caught and she brought her hand up to her mouth. Finally she looked up at me with glassy eyes and shook her head back and forth.

I slid down to my knees in front of her and took her hand in mine. "Please say something."

"I'm sorry. I'm dying here. What is it?" Rebecca's nervousness around Samantha appeared to be wearing off.

Without looking away from Samantha, I explained, "I made a donation to the children's hospital where Samantha works...Sam?"

She shook her head. "Lucien, 'a donation' is...fifty dollars, a hundred. This is...this is...I...How?"

"I sold a house."

"You sold a house?" She laughed. Then her face became serious. A single tear streamed down her face. "This is for real?"

I nodded.

"You sold a house and are making a contribution to the children's hospital in my parents' names?"

I nodded again and tried to interpret the multiple physical sensations her emotions caused.

"In the amount of"—she glanced at the papers again—"*a hundred thousand dollars?*"

"Yes."

To their credit, the others didn't audibly express the surprise they felt, but it tingled in the pit of my stomach.

She pulled a set of papers out. "I don't understand what this means."

"It means you get to decide how the money is used. I spoke with the hospital development officer about what a useful sum would be, but I wanted you to get to decide. You have a meeting scheduled for Monday with her, and she plans to make a presentation to you about the hospital's current needs. Then you'll get to choose how to allocate the use of the funds."

"I...I don't know what to say." Even her emotions seemed stunned.

"Say you'll take the meeting."

"Say I'll take the meeting? No, not about the meeting. About...about how much—"

I kissed her. "It's only money, Sam. I have a lot of it. You already know that. I don't need it. Having it has never made me happy. Having you makes me happy. Having you happy makes me happy. I just wanted you to know your parents were important to me, because they were important to you. And I just thought...if you saw their names there when you went to work every day, maybe you wouldn't feel like you were quite as alone as I know you sometimes feel."

She threw her arms around my neck. "I'm going to kill you for this!" she sobbed. Then: "Thank you."

"You're welcome, *dolcezza*." I kissed her hair and stroked her back. Samantha held on for a long time.

Jed nudged William. "It's a good thing Rebecca and Anna already opened their gifts. We would've looked like complete schmucks if we'd followed that." Rebecca thumped a pillow on his head. Everyone roared with laughter, breaking the tension that had built in the room.

Samantha laughed, too, and wiped her face with some tissues Henrietta passed her. "Oh, God. I need something to drink. And some chocolate."

"Hey, Jed? Pass around that bowl of candy over there." I smirked at him as he took a small chocolate and passed it around. Those who were already out of the bet passed.

Samantha took two, so I sent the bowl around again. Henrietta brought Sam and the others glasses of soda. Jed gagged a little on the fizzy liquid.

For the rest of the day, Samantha's emotions were a wild, curious mixture of happiness and sadness, elation and anger. She was also so aroused I thought I was burning from the inside out. At every available opportunity, we stole away for an intense moment of kissing or groping. She was more aggressive than I'd ever seen her. I was enthralled, but also concerned.

At bedtime, Samantha went upstairs before me. The bedroom door had barely clicked behind me when she grabbed and shoved me toward the bed. I fell backward, and she was on top of me, clawing at my clothes and ripping off her own. Whatever had been going on with her all day was now clearly finding a release.

"Sam?"

She kissed me roughly and shoved her tongue into my mouth. I groaned and pushed her back. Though we french kissed all the time, I generally kept her out of my mouth.

"Sam?"

Finally, she stilled. With her hands braced on my shoulders, her eyes burned down into mine. Her anger squeezed my chest. Her voice was strained. "Lucien, we'll talk later. I promise. But right now I want you, and I need you. And I need you to know it, feel it." Her words clarified little, but I nodded.

She unleashed herself on me, kissing and licking and roughly nipping at my upper body all while maintaining eye contact. I thrust my hips into her when she lingered over my Blood Mark. I finally had to grab her hair and tug her attention away from it. With a groan, she reached a hand down between her legs and worked herself as she devoured me. When I realized what she was doing, I moaned and gripped her shoulders and rolled on top of her.

I grabbed her hand and pulled it to my mouth, then noisily sucked on her wet fingers. I groaned at the sweet nectar of her arousal.

"You see what you do to me, Lucien? What only you do to me?" she rasped. "Take me, Lucien. I'm yours," she offered as she planted her feet flat on the mattress and pushed herself up forcefully against my erection.

Her aggression spurred mine, and I grunted. "You want me?" I asked as I ground myself against her wetness.

She ran a hand over the bedspread and found the packet she'd apparently laid out earlier. She slid herself against me as she opened it and then rolled on the condom. "God, yes," she whimpered.

I plunged forward and filled her in one hard stroke. She screamed and wrapped herself around me. Hard breaths and grunts and strained curses in two languages filled the room as we battled through Samantha's emotions with our bodies. She kissed me roughly and dug her nails into my flesh. The physical pain mingled with her radiating pleasure to coax what I was sure was going to be one of the most intense orgasms I'd ever experienced.

She came in a frenzy of screams and muscle contractions. And then bit against the taut skin at the base of my neck. Hard.

My fangs and release shot out at the same time. I growled and in a blur turned my head in search of my biceps. I missed the tender skin of her shoulder by a hair as the urge to bite down became irresistible.

Finally, I willed my fangs to retract and licked at the wound I'd made on my arm, then slid down a little and laid my head on her heaving breasts.

"I love you," I whispered breathlessly.

She hugged my shoulders and combed her fingers through my hair. "I love you, too." We lay together, panting, for a long time. "Lucien?" I lifted my head off her chest to look at her. "I'm ready to talk now."

"Okay."

She took a deep breath. "I will be thankful for your gift until the day I die. But I want to be clear. I don't want anymore grand gestures."

"Sam—"

"No. You have to hear me. I know you have some need to prove your worthiness to me, and in general. But I don't need you to jump in front of bullets. Or leap over tall buildings. Or lasso me the moon. I don't need grand gestures to know you are the love of my life."

The. Love. Of. Her. Life? I sputtered momentarily and then whispered, "I didn't mean it that way."

"I know you didn't, which is why I can accept it. I'm just saying."

"Okay." I grasped her hand and rubbed circles with my thumb.

"Deal?" She still looked stern. But her emotions were full of love and acceptance.

"Deal." I met her eyes. Her faith in me warmed and chilled me. I had yet to fully earn it.

∾

W e stayed at Orchard Hill through Sunday morning, when we departed to make the long journey back to Detroit. As we were leaving, Catherine and William both stepped forward to claim their prizes. Jed had been forced out when Samantha ate a couple handfuls of cashews on Saturday night; for some reason he just couldn't stomach nuts. William would get his media room after all; by comparison, Catherine's demand of a new camera with lenses seemed rather modest. I happily planned to pay up. I was so grateful for my family's support over the past five days.

By the end of the weekend, it seemed Samantha had known them forever. She and Ollie hugged them all freely before we left. Each member of my family had pulled me aside at some point during our stay to express their affection for Samantha and to say how good they thought we were together. And, of course, they were all head over heels in love with Ollie.

None of them, however, seemed to have any better ideas than I as to how to introduce Samantha to the elephant in the room.

As we drove home, I couldn't stanch the warmth the memory of the weekend caused in my chest. Though there was still an omission of fundamental importance I needed to rectify, I couldn't help but feel good about the developments in my relationships with Samantha and Ollie. I felt closer to them than I had to anyone in over a century.

Samantha was right. I did feel the need to prove my worthiness—my worthiness of their acceptance of me, which was a gift I so wanted to deserve.

As the miles ticked by, I found myself looking forward to the new year with the woman—the family—I so desperately loved.

CHAPTER 14

Three weeks after Christmas, the cold, snowy winter weather broke. For two days, temperatures hit the mid-forties. It was downright balmy.

After school on the first day, Ollie begged Samantha to let her ride her bike. Samantha finally relented, and Ollie rode the loop around the block, dodging still unthawed snow drifts while her mother and I walked behind her.

On the second day, Mrs. Johnson watched Ollie after school, because Samantha and I both had meetings. Samantha had a doctor's appointment in the afternoon. She'd been fatigued for weeks, which likely resulted from the stress of the last few months. Though she seemed to be regaining her appetite, she hadn't been eating well and had lost weight. The walk around the block on the first warm night convinced her to make an appointment, because it was clear the short walk had taken effort.

She hadn't even had the energy to offer her usual rant about the still-unfixed street light by the park. To the city's credit, they had come to replace the bulb only to find faulty wiring in the pole that required the replacement of the whole thing. God only knew when that would happen.

My meeting was with Langston at 5 p.m. at the hospital to pick up more blood. He'd become the sole source of my nourishment over the past months. I arrived promptly, eager to get home to hear what the doctor had to say to Samantha. Langston loaded the B-positive into my cooler, zipped it shut, and then sat down in the chair behind his desk.

"Lucien, you might have a problem." His expression was weary and serious. "And I might have caused it."

I sat forward in my chair. "What's going on?"

"It's Jacques."

"What about him?"

"It's probably nothing. But he overheard a conversation Antoine and I had about you. I'm sorry, but Magena saw my thoughts about your relationship with the woman. I ended up having to tell him."

I stood up in front of his desk. The scent of Langston's fear did little to suppress my panic. "And?"

"Antoine was fine, amused perhaps, but mostly he was just happy for you."

"Langston, get to the damn punch line. What's the problem? What did Jacques overhear?" As if their knowing about Samantha wasn't bad enough.

"It was something Antoine said. Again, it's probably nothing."

I growled.

"Okay, okay. Antoine said he was pleased his son had finally found some peace and happiness."

I winced, suspecting where this was heading.

"Then Jacques threw a chair through a wall, roared at Antoine he only had one son—him—and flew out."

I scrubbed my hands through my hair and locked them on top of my head.

"Antoine dismissed his outburst, but I just thought you should know. He sent some of the guard out to find him. Just watch your back, man, that's all I'm saying. You know Jacques."

I nodded once and ripped the cooler bag off his desk and fled. A clock in the hospital corridor read 5:28 p.m. Samantha should be home. I just wanted her and Ollie with me.

I wasn't sure what to think about Jacques. On the one hand, he was a hothead who hated me and felt I stole his father's affection. On the other hand, he was extremely loyal to his father, who had protected me on multiple occasions. I pondered whether the situation necessitated a meeting with Antoine as I left the hospital and regretted I'd walked. The warmer weather had brought people out of hibernation, and the darkening streets were full. I had to walk at a human pace, but calmed myself with the knowledge it would only take fifteen minutes to get home.

I was within a block of Samantha's when the chaotic sensations nearly leveled me—the stench and pain and rancid taste I registered as rage, jealousy, terror, and agony set me on full alert.

Witnesses be damned, I broke out into an unnatural sprint in search of the source of those feelings. I scanned Samantha's house as I approached it; no one seemed to be there. The feelings intensified as I raced across the grassy field. My house was dark; they weren't there either.

Then I hit the street.

I had found Jacques. He had found Samantha. He held her in a tight embrace and was clearly feeding from her.

I bolted across, vaulting over a parked car, and aimed for the dark spot shrouded by bushes and trees under the broken fucking street light. My only solace was he didn't seem to be reacting to the holy water in her blood yet, which I'd been giving both of my girls for months, so he'd just bitten her. I soared over Ollie's abandoned bike and slammed into them, trying like hell to avoid Samantha's body.

Jacques roared in outrage and dropped Samantha as he whirled on me. She slumped to the cold ground. I tore my now-inhuman eyes away from her to deal with him.

"You always did know how to ruin a good time," he spat.

The world went fucking red with my rage at the image of Samantha's blood dripping off his fangs. All I could see was my maker hunched in the darkness over Lena's body, his crimson eyes and gory fangs flashing to me when I'd interrupted. But Jacques was standing too close to Samantha's crumpled body to act rashly.

Then he coughed and sprayed a fine red mist into the air.

"How ya feeling there, Jacques?" I sneered through sharp fangs as I stalked closer.

A thin line of blood trickled down from one nostril. He fisted it away. "What the fuck?"

In the split second his eyes flashed down to evaluate the blood he'd wiped onto his knuckles, I launched myself at him.

We collided in a wall of muscle and will and hate.

Jacques stumbled back, propelled by my weight, and gripped my biceps to fling me off him. But my hold was tighter. He succeeded only in spinning us so that when we crashed to the ground, I was on top and pinned him.

Then he made the last in a long line of fatal errors: he turned his head to snap at my wrist where it held his down. In a blur, I leaned forward and sank my fangs deep into his exposed neck.

He roared in outraged surprise. I grunted in disgust as I wrenched my head to the side, tearing a gaping wound partway through his neck. Blood gurgled and splattered from the breach. His eyes were disbelieving as they angled up at me.

"You did this," I hissed as I released his arms and brought my hands to his jaw. I didn't pay attention to his newly freed hands until the cold steel pressed against my gut. He squeezed the trigger a split second before I ripped his head clean free of his body. Through a red haze, I watched as his head unevenly rolled under a bush. His body twitched then stilled.

Then the searing fire of the silver bullet registered.

I grunted and keened and clambered off Jacques's torso. I retched up the blood that had gotten into my mouth and throat. It tasted and stank of his evil and burned where Samantha's precious blood mixed in.

Samantha. I pushed through the paralyzing agony the silver caused and scrabbled over to her. "Oh, no. Oh, please."

She was unconscious. Blood poured from her nose, ear, and neck. The left side of her face was swollen and bruising. Her right arm sat at an unnatural angle. That was all I could see in that moment. It was enough.

I pushed myself up onto my knees and tore my shirt open to inspect the gunshot. The fist-sized wound was ragged and raw. My body was trying to heal, but the silver impeded my natural defenses. I reached into my boot and retrieved the titanium dagger I always kept there. With a grunt and a hiss, I plunged the blade into the wound and twisted it until I finally worked the poisonous slug out with the assistance of an old Italian prayer.

A tingling relief slowly—*too goddamned slowly*—replaced the burning pain, and a cursory glance down confirmed the now enlarged wound was starting to heal.

I sheathed the bloody knife and scooped Samantha's too-still form into my arms and didn't notice when her blood dripped onto my left hand.

Ollie. I staggered back to the sidewalk and forced my brain to calm and focus. With difficulty, I blinked and drained my eyes, then retracted my teeth. I scanned the street and sensed a rapid heartbeat from under a parked car twenty feet away.

Langston had told me others were looking for Jacques, so I moved quietly up the sidewalk and crouched down with Samantha. Peering under the car, I found Ollie's trembling form mostly balled up behind a tire. I shifted Samantha's weight and extended a hand under the car. Ollie screamed and retreated to the other side.

She couldn't see my face, so I laid Samantha gently on the sidewalk and crouched down. "Ollie, it's me, baby. You have to come out from there. Hurry. We have to go." I kept my voice low.

"Lucien?" It came out as a high-pitched whimper. Her terror sliced through me.

"Yes. Come on, Ollie."

"I can't." Her teeth chattered with the chill of her fear.

I didn't have time to coax her out. With regret, I placed my hand under the wheel well closest to her body and lifted the car enough to grab her with my free hand. She shrieked. I looked into her eyes, regretting the need to charm her.

Sleep.

It was amazing, but she fought it. Her eyes blinked open a half dozen times. "Mommy," she slurred before finally succumbing.

I scanned the length of the street. Empty. I raced Ollie down to my truck and laid her on the floor of the back seat. Then I returned for Samantha, who was bleeding enough the sidewalk was stained where I'd left her. I cradled her in my arms, then flew with her to my waiting truck, placing her limp body across the back seat.

Blood. *Cazzo! What happened to that damn cooler?* It seemed a minor point, but I might need that blood now more than ever. Not for me, for Samantha. I raced across the street and scanned the ground around Jacques's remains. It wasn't there. *I don't have time for this!*

In seconds, I retraced my steps and finally found the bag on the ground next to Samantha's house. I jumped in the truck and peeled out of Frederick Street, heading to a Victorian about five miles away I'd acquired during the fall and only recently finished remodeling and staging.

Passing the For Sale sign, the truck screeched to a hard stop in the driveway of the Victorian. I threw the strap of the cooler over my shoulder, then wrenched the rear door open and grabbed Ollie's sleeping body. I flew with her into the house and laid her on a bed in an upstairs room, where she grumbled and stirred in her sleep.

Then I raced back out for Samantha and moaned at how much blood coated the black leather of the seat. Her hair was thick with it on the left side. I kicked the truck door shut and ran inside. I secured the multiple locks on the front door and carried her up the stairs, then laid her gently on the bed in the master suite.

I paced and began to doubt my wisdom in bringing them to this house. The hospital would've been better equipped to care for her, but I feared we'd be hunted. And I had no idea how I'd explain the bite wound. But no one knew about this house. No one would know to look here.

I ripped the pocket of my jeans pulling my cell phone out, then pressed a button and counted the rings. My call waiting interrupted—Catherine.

"I need help," I answered in a hoarse voice.

"What happened?"

"Samantha was attacked. Put Griffin or Henrietta on the phone."

"Lucien, I'm not home. Hang up and—"

I redialed and called Griffin. He answered on the first ring. "Lucien, did you just ca—"

"Griffin. *Cristo*. I need your help. Samantha was attacked by Jacques Laumet." He sucked in a breath. "She's unconscious and bleeding profusely. I don't know what to do."

He put me on speaker phone so the others could hear. "All right, Lucien." Henrietta took over. "Describe her injuries to me."

"Oh, *mio Dio!* There's blood everywhe—"

"I know this is hard. But stay calm and start from her head and work down."

"Okay. Okay. Shit." I eased onto the mattress next to Samantha and winced as my weight shifted her body. "She's bleeding from the left side of her head, and there's blood coming out of her left ear. Her hair is so matted it's hard to see."

"That's fine. Keep going."

"There's blood coming out of her nose. Her left eye and cheekbone are bruised and scraped up like...like...ah, *Cristo*." The image of Jacques striking her boiled my blood with rage.

"What else, Lucien?" Henrietta's voice demanded I focus.

My eyes went red again as my sight settled on Samantha's neck. "Her neck is mangled, chewed, and still bleeding," I managed through clenched teeth. I forced a breath that failed to calm. "Her right arm is broken and probably a finger, too. Hold on..."

Silently apologizing, for the shirt and so much else, I grasped the top of her button-down and wrenched it open. "Oh, *Dio*. There's bruising all along her ribs. The bottom one looks obviously broken on her left side."

"How about her abdomen, Lucien? Is there any bruising or swelling in her abdomen?"

"Not that I can tell." My voice cracked.

"Okay, I've heard enough."

"She's not moving at all, Hen, and her breathing's so shallow..."

"Lucien, you're going to have to perform a Blood Healing. And soon. The head injury is the most worrisome and—"

"But I've...I've never—"

"I'll walk you through it, but you must. She cannot go without treatment for the four or five hours it'll take us to get there."

"*Cazzo!*" I roared as I tugged mercilessly at my hair.

It was far from an agreement, but Henrietta continued anyway. "You must open your wrist and get her to drink from you," Henrietta instructed as my mind whirled.

"Hen, I don't think I can do this—"

"You *are* vampire, Lucien. You are capable. And you must be willing. For Samantha."

"But I've never told her. I can't change her without having ever told her. I won't."

"Look, focus. You won't change her. The change can only take place if there's a full Blood Exchange, and you've injected her with the change enzyme from your fangs. Since you're not biting her, that won't happen."

"Okay. Jesus, okay."

"You'll be saving her, Lucien. Your blood will be curative. And her body's healing process will consume the vampire blood within her, leaving her human. Now, go. You can do this."

I dropped the phone from my ear and stepped to the edge of the bed. I was nearly frozen with fear and crippled with guilt. My heart lay broken and bleeding on the bed before me.

As I grieved Samantha's injuries, a footstep startled me from my thoughts, and I snapped around. Ollie stood in the doorway, her face white as a ghost.

I willed the blood out of my eyes and gaped at the child who by all rights should still be asleep. She had willed herself to consciousness despite the force of my charm. I of all people didn't need it, but here was further proof Olivia

215

Sutton was a special and powerful creature. She stepped forward and stood halfway behind an armchair near the door.

"Go back to your room." I trembled with the effort to keep my voice gentle as I spoke to her.

"I want to stay with Mommy." Her voice was shaky, but her resolve was strong.

"Ollie, I need to help her."

"Then do it."

"I can't. Do it. With you here."

"Yes, you can. I'm not leaving." Her eyes remained on Samantha's form lying on the bed.

"Ollie—"

"Do whatever it is you do." She looked me straight in the eye. "Just help her. *Please*, Lucien."

Whatever it is I do? Her words made my head spin. I walked over to her and gently pulled her body around to sit on the chair.

She placed her little hand on my cheek. "You can do it. I know you can. Angels have magic powers. Mommy read me books about that."

Angels? I knew Ollie was obsessed with angels—Samantha had ascribed it to having told her, "Gramma is with the angels now."

Samantha's heart stuttered. This conversation would have to wait. "You can only stay if you promise to close your eyes. Do you promise?" She nodded. "I mean it, do not open them for any reason until I tell you to. Do you understand?" She nodded more forcefully this time and squeezed her eyes closed.

I flew to Samantha's side and looked back over my shoulder to make sure Ollie was keeping her promise. I sunk my teeth into my wrist and tore my radial artery open, then I placed it over Samantha's mouth. I'd cut deep and the blood flowed freely. She gagged before swallowing once, twice, five times, more.

I glanced at Ollie, who sat stone still.

Samantha's heart thundered. Her face and chest broke out in a cold sweat as her body reacted to the presence of my blood. *Cazzo! How much do I give her?* I pulled my hand away when I estimated she'd received about two pints. Unthinkingly, I brought my wrist to my mouth and licked. The cut knitted itself together, though not as quickly as usual. My abdominal wound was still healing.

"Keep them closed, Ollie," I said gruffly as I walked out of the room. I flew down to the kitchen and grabbed some hand towels and a bowl of water. I returned and cleaned Samantha's body of the blood she'd shed.

"Can I open them yet?" Ollie whispered from across the room.

I pulled a blanket up over Samantha's shuddering body. "Yes. Stay where you are for a minute though, okay?"

She nodded and followed me with her eyes as I walked into the adjoining bathroom.

I dumped the bowl of bloody water into the tub, then set the bowl down so I could wash my hands, arms, and face. Between killing Jacques and carrying Samantha, I was nearly as befouled as Samantha had been. I'd need to find a change of clothes at some point, but not until I knew Samantha was stable.

When I came out of the bathroom, Ollie was standing by her mother's bedside. "Ollie—"

"Is she going to be okay?" She looked over her shoulder at me.

"I...I don't know. I've never...tried to save someone before." She searched my face and eyes before turning back to look at her mother. "Ollie, we need to talk."

"I won't tell anyone, I promise."

I frowned. "You won't tell anyone what?"

"About what you are." Her voice was matter of fact.

"What..." I gently pulled her arm so she was facing me and knelt down in front of her. Not sure I wanted to know the answer, I continued, "What do you think I am?"

She was full of worry for her mother and still badly shaken over the attack. But none of her fear was directed at me. "A guardian angel, of course," she said as she reached forward and brushed a strand of hair off my face.

A...*what?* "Ollie, I'm not an angel." My voice was almost a whisper.

"You have to say that. I know you're not supposed to tell. But I knew it the first time I saw you at the hospital."

Holding her little hands in mine, I asked, "What are you talking about? Why would you think that?"

The words spilled out as if she'd long thought about them but never before given them voice. "First of all, you're really pale, and your skin's all glowy, just like the pictures of angels in my books. And you don't eat. I didn't realize that right away, sorry about the cake, but angels don't need food and neither do you. Plus, you can do all kinds of superpowers. When you flew across the street that day with the truck, I knew for sure there was something wrong, er, uh, different about you, but I didn't know what it was until I saw a picture of an angel flying. Plus you flew down the stairs that day. Mommy was right. And you picked up that car."

Ollie was not quite six, but she spoke with the self-assurance of an adult.

I was stunned. My mouth moved but nothing came out.

I was equally dazed by the fact Ollie was perfectly calm—neither her emotions nor her heartbeat indicated any fear. I looked at Samantha, pale and still on the bed. Ollie followed my eyes. We stood motionless for some amount of time, keeping vigil.

"Ollie?" She looked back at me. "Angels are good, but I'm—"

"Not all angels are good. The one who hurt Mommy wasn't good. Was he an angel of death?"

I shook my head in defeat. *I don't know how to respond to this. Maybe it is better to let her believe I am an angel? God, I wish she was right.*

I pulled the armchair closer to the bed and lifted Ollie into it. I got her a glass of water. I could tell she was hungry, but I wasn't willing to leave them alone to get her something.

I paced. I stood. I knelt next to Ollie. Hours passed. *How long is this supposed to take?*

When a car pulled into the driveway, I flew down the stairs, fangs out and hackles raised. I peered out a front window and relief flooded through me when my family stepped out of their car. We exchanged solemn greetings.

Henrietta laid a hand on my arm and squeezed. My fangs retracted. The momentary infusion of peace and hope she gave me felt like water to a man lost in the desert.

Speaking low and fast so only we could hear, I recounted to them how I'd administered my blood to Samantha. It had been nearly five hours, but there hadn't been any perceptible change. Henrietta urged patience. The extent of Samantha's injuries meant the healing process would take time. Henrietta was about to head up the stairs to check on Samantha when I stopped her to explain one last thing: Ollie's theory. They were moved by Ollie's insightfulness and her obvious faith in goodness that led her to see light where others saw darkness.

As Henrietta and Rebecca went upstairs to check on Ollie and Samantha, Griffin asked me to tell the story of what happened from the beginning. I began with my conversation with Langston and ended with decapitating Jacques. The gravity of that action finally descended on me. I bent over and braced my hands on my knees with a groan.

Cazzo! I killed Jacques. I killed Antoine Laumet's only remaining son.

Thinking several steps ahead, Griffin dispatched Jed and William to retrieve and dispose of Jacques's body. "Lucien, I need you to stay focused. We're here now. We're going to help you sort this out." Griffin's voice was full of restrained anger and indignant protectiveness.

I nodded as he squeezed my shoulder.

Another car pulled up out front. Catherine's worry unsettled my gut. When I opened the door, she flew into my arms as her words rushed out. "I'm sorry it took me so long to get here. I was in Canada when I sensed something had happened. So, what did happen?"

Griffin recounted the story while I went upstairs to check on Samantha. I found Rebecca leaning against a wall and Henrietta sitting in the arm chair next to Samantha's bed with Ollie on her lap.

Henrietta met my eyes. "It's working, Lucien, although her internal injuries were extensive. I was able to…take care of her arm and ribs, but not…some of the rest of it. I might suggest another…dose."

Ollie looked up to Henrietta's face. Her voice was nearly a whisper. "Henny, you don't have to talk in code, you know. 'Cause I know." She held Henrietta's gaze for one minute more before returning her head to the crook of Henrietta's neck so she could keep an eye on her mom.

"Told you," I said as Henrietta gaped at me. I stepped to the edge of the bed. "Ollie, I need to help your mom again…" She closed her eyes before I even asked. "Er, okay."

I bit into my wrist and held it once again to Samantha's mouth. Griffin and Catherine walked into the room and hovered near the foot of the bed. Henrietta scooted Ollie off her lap so she could stand up and ensured as she placed her back on the chair her eyes were still shut. Then she placed one hand over Samantha's heart and one hand on her head, sensing the flow of my blood into her.

"I think that's enough, Lucien."

I pulled my wrist away and licked across the wound, binding it. It healed faster this time thanks to Henrietta's earlier touch.

"Now," she said, "we wait."

CHAPTER 15

The family sat and stood around the bed, seven of the world's most powerful creatures made weak and vulnerable by the worry and anxiety we all felt for Samantha.

"Lucien?" Catherine's concerned voice interrupted the tense silence after a while. "How much have you..."—she glanced at Ollie—"given?"

"About four, I think."

Griffin nodded at Catherine. "Lucien, why don't you go take a break with Catherine for a few minutes? We'll stay here with Samantha and Ollie."

I was about to argue, but Griffin's expression convinced me not to, so I decided on the route of least resistance. Catherine and I walked to a room down the hall. We stepped inside, and I pushed the door shut behind us.

"Sit, Lucien. You need to feed."

"Catherine—"

"No, Lucien. You don't look good. It's obvious you haven't fed recently, you were shot and poisoned with silver, and you've just given away more than a third of your volume.

You need to feed." She unbuttoned the sleeve of her blouse and rolled it up.

I remained standing. "I have a cooler full of blood around here somewhere."

"Good. You drink from me. I'll replenish with some of that. My blood is better for you anyway. You need to build your strength back up." She patted the bed beside her. "Sit."

When I finally sat next to her, she shifted so her body faced the side of mine. Then she held her arm up to me. Vampire blood was sweet and full of raw power. It heightened senses and intensified strength like nothing else. Usually only vampire mates exchanged blood, as Catherine and I had frequently done when we were together. So her offer was truly extraordinary and proved again what an invaluable friend she was.

I cradled her arm in my hands and laid a soft kiss on her forearm. She nodded when my eyes met hers. I sank my teeth in over her radial artery. She sucked in a breath but was calm. With her other hand, she rubbed my back in a gesture of comfort. It'd been seven decades since I'd last felt Catherine's blood within me. The strength of vampire blood immediately enlivened my senses and fortified my musculature.

"Okay." Catherine rubbed gently where my hair met my neck.

I immediately released her and ran my tongue across the wound. She pulled her wrist back and waited for the healing to complete before rolling her sleeve back down.

"Thank you, Catherine."

She smiled at me and nodded. "Hey, how's your stomach?"

I rose and tugged my hands through my hair. Her blood was at work on the wound. "Fine."

She reached for the hem of my ruined shirt.

I blocked her hands and pulled one to my mouth. I pressed a quick kiss to her knuckles. "I'm fine."

"Lucien—"

Jed and William's car pulled into the driveway. "Come on," I said as I turned away.

Catherine sighed and followed me out of the room and downstairs.

Jed and William came through the front door. Jed spoke first: "Somebody got to him before we did."

"The place reeked of vampire. Besides you and Laumet, I'd say there were three others there at some point," William said.

Cazzo! I nodded and ran my hands roughly through my hair.

"Oh, we grabbed Ollie's bike. It's in the trunk of Griffin's car," Jed added.

"Thanks. Listen, sorry to ask you to go back out. But they need food and clothes, and I could use a clean shirt."

Without hesitation, William handed me the button-down he had on over a T-shirt. I stripped off my bloodied thermal and ignored the collective groans and grimaces as the others reacted to the ragged hole in my gut. Tugging on the offered shirt with a nod to William, I rattled off a list of things I wanted for the girls and sent my brothers in the direction of a store not too far away.

Back upstairs, Ollie had fallen asleep on Henrietta's lap. I showed Henrietta to a room down the hall. She carried the child there to sleep. We rejoined the others in Samantha's room.

My phone startled us when it rang. I recognized the number. "Langston?"

"Lucien, are you all right?"

"Yes." I glanced at the others, knowing they could hear both sides of the conversation.

"Man, I thought you might be freaking out a little. The guard found Jacques's body."

I lowered my head. There was no way they wouldn't smell my scent on him.

"What the hell happened?"

I growled. "Jacques is what the hell happened. He fucking brutalized Samantha."

Langston hissed. "Shit, I'm sorry, Lucien. Hold on." Over a long minute, muffled exchanges sounded in the background on his end. "Antoine doesn't have time to talk right now, but he wants me to tell you he understands. He is furious at Jacques for going after the woman and creating this situation. We've all known Jacques's rashness was going to catch up with him sooner or later."

"Antoine's not calling for my head?" My gut tingled with everyone's surprise.

"Of course, he's upset about Jacques, but you know he always liked you better. He always considered you like a son. His first reaction was to inquire about your and the humans' fates. How are they, by the way?"

"I don't know yet. Samantha's critical."

"I'm really sorry, Lucien. Hey, tell me where you are. I can bring you some supplies."

I frowned. "Uh, I think I'm okay for now. I'll give you a call back if I think of anything."

"All right. Keep in touch. I'll check back in with you soon. Antoine will be in touch after all this blows over. He has to focus on damage control right now."

"Okay. Thanks for your call, Langston."

"No problem." The tension in the room ratcheted down at the news Samantha and I weren't being hunted. Now I could put my full concentration into getting her better and creating a cover story.

Jed and William returned a while later with bags of food,

drinks, and clothes. I thought about waking Ollie up to give her something to eat—she hadn't eaten since lunch time at school—but decided if her body was letting her sleep, then sleep was what she most needed.

We settled in the living room to talk and left Henrietta upstairs in the arm chair to keep watch over Samantha in case she regained consciousness.

"Okay," I began, "when Samantha wakes up…" Catherine looked at me and spoke gently.

"Maybe this is the time to tell her, Lucien."

Everyone remained quiet and watched as I sat thinking. "She's going to be too fragile. I can't ask her to deal with that on top of recovering from these injuries. She was already unwell before this." I didn't even know what'd happened at her doctor's appointment. "Plus, then I'd have to tell her about the Laumets and all the rest of it. It's too much at all once, even for someone as strong as Samantha."

Griffin sat forward and leaned his elbows on his knees, his measured tones full of the same thoughtfulness he always brought to his words. "Lucien, you have done an astounding job of walking in her world. But the reality is your world and her world exist together. They're the same world. Jacques demonstrated that forcefully last night. If you're going to be with her, she deserves to know the truth."

"What about Ollie?" Rebecca asked. "She knows about us."

"I don't know what to think about Ollie." I rubbed my eyes with my thumb and forefinger. "I charmed her before. She was almost able to resist it. And then she pulled herself out of it after we got here."

Henrietta appeared in the doorway to the living room. "She's a special little girl, Lucien."

"Yeah."

"I'll go up and sit with Samantha," Catherine said as she

rose from her chair. I tried to smile at her as she left the room.

Henrietta sat down on the arm of the couch next to Griffin. "I think I agree with Lucien. His blood will heal her injuries, but she's going to be weak for a while. I don't think it will help her recovery to have the added stress of knowing about him, us."

"Henrietta's opinion is enough for me." I rose and paced behind the couch.

Griffin disagreed, but nodded at the both of us. "You're going to have to charm her then, Lucien. You need to make sure she won't recall anything supernatural about last night's events." He paused. "Did Ollie see the attack?"

"I don't know what she saw. When I found her, she was hiding underneath a car farther up the street. There's a line of bushes that should've blocked her view of Jacques's biting Samantha and my...killing him." Those words were hard enough to think, let alone say. I hadn't been responsible for taking a sentient life in over a decade. "Oh." I swallowed. *They're not going to like this.* "Um, but she saw me pick up the car she was hiding under."

They gaped at me. "Lucien." Griffin's voice was full of disapproval.

"I know, Griffin, but she was too scared to crawl out, and I couldn't wait. I know."

"She chalked that up to your being an angel, too, though, right?" Henrietta looked thoughtful. "What's the harm in letting her continue to think that? She's clearly believed that about you for a while. It hasn't caused any problems."

I sighed. "For some reason, it feels worse to let her think I'm an angel than to think about telling her the truth."

Soft footsteps padded down the stairs. I walked out of the room into the foyer. Ollie was nearly at the bottom of the staircase. "Hey. What are you doing up?" I lifted her, and she wrapped her legs around my waist as I carried her into the living room.

"I don't know. I woke up. Then I heard voices."

I lowered us onto the couch and smoothed her hair back from her face. "Okay."

Everyone's anxiety tightened in my gut. What had she heard?

She lay quietly on my shoulder for a few minutes. The room relaxed. When she spoke, her voice was small but calm. "The truth about what?"

I froze. Everyone looked at me. In that moment, I made the decision. I pushed her body back gently, so I could see her face. "You're a smart kid, Ollie, do you know that?"

She nodded, but her face remained serious. "You know how you think I'm an angel?" She nodded again.

"Well, I'm not. I'm not an angel. But you are right, I am something different."

"What are you, then?" She met my eyes.

"I'm afraid I'll scare you if I tell you."

She fiddled with a loose thread on my shirt. "I can be brave." She took a deep breath.

I took her small hand in mine and squeezed. "I know that, Ollie. You are very brave." I thought for a minute while she searched my face. "Do you remember when you asked me if the man that...hurt your mom was an angel of death?"

"Yes."

"You said not all angels were good, there were good angels and bad angels, like him. Remember?"

"Yes."

I tasted the faintest hint of her anxiety, but overall she was remarkably calm. It felt so wrong to burden her with this information. She shouldn't have to know about things like this. I looked around. Griffin nodded at me.

Ollie watched me intently. "Lucien, you're good." She

surveyed the others and rested her eyes on Henrietta a beat longer than the rest. "And they're good, too." She looked back at me and whispered, "You don't want to tell me."

"I'm afraid to," I whispered back, meeting her eyes.

She cupped her little hand around my cheek. "Can't I just call you angels, even if you're something different?"

The love I felt for her in that moment—that came from myself and the others—was overwhelming. None of us had ever experienced that kind of unconditional acceptance in our long existences. I nodded and swallowed hard. "Yes, Ollie, you can. You are right about one part of it though. We are your guardians. Do you know that?"

She nodded.

"I'll always protect you. Do you believe me?"

"Yeah."

"Us, too," Griffin added softly.

She nodded. "Will you take me to see Mommy now, Lucien?"

"Yeah, baby, come on." I lifted her and carried her up the steps to Samantha's dim room. She'd shifted positions a little. That small evidence of movement gave me the hope I so desperately needed.

Catherine left as I sat with Ollie in the armchair. She lay her head down on my shoulder, but tilted it at an angle that allowed her to see her mother. Within fifteen minutes, she was sound asleep. I focused on the feeling of her heart beating against my chest and imagined for a moment it was big enough to beat for both of us.

I closed my eyes, not intending to rest. Before long, my ears tuned in to the conversation taking place in the living room. The consensus held I'd done the right thing by not telling Ollie the truth. It had felt right in that moment, but I remained unsure. There really was no right way to tell someone you're a monster. I shut the conversation back out.

Maybe that was the problem. They wouldn't have to know if I wasn't around them anymore. The weight crushing my chest nearly suffocated me.

The next instant, Catherine stood in front of me trying to understand the cause of the emotions she'd just sensed. Her flight from the living room had startled the others, who filed in behind her. Catherine knelt down in front of me and kept her voice low to avoid waking Ollie. "Lucien, I'm guessing by the sense of loss and grief you're feeling you're considering leaving them. Maybe that's the right thing, maybe it isn't. But I don't think it's your place to make that decision for Samantha without her having any input. Maybe one week into your relationship it would've been, or even one month. But you have been with her now for seven months. Their lives are entirely oriented around their relationship with you, am I right?"

I nodded.

"Samantha has no one else now, no family." She hesitated, then added, "And you're sleeping with her."

I winced. While I knew in a house full of creatures with heightened aural abilities our intimacy at Christmas wouldn't have gone unnoticed, I still didn't want it to be a topic of general conversation.

"My point is you've allowed the relationship to progress beyond where you can just make a unilateral decision without her."

"But—"

"No, listen to me. I know you're worried she'll be devastated by the truth and hate you for it, but I can guarantee you she'll be devastated and hate you if you just up and leave her or make up some hollow lie about not loving her anymore."

I heaved a breath and hung my head back against the chair.

"At some point, you're going to have to trust her with the

truth and let her make her own decision. You owe her that much."

"She's right, Lucien," Henrietta offered.

Griffin had said it best. Our worlds had collided. Samantha had been walking in my world all along, every bit as much as I'd been walking in hers. Only I knew it, and she didn't. My shoulders fell, and I sighed. Ollie stirred but settled back down.

"Okay, you're right," I murmured.

Catherine found my hand and squeezed some reassurance into me. I offered her a weak smile.

One by one the others left the room. Henrietta walked to the bed and placed her hands on Samantha.

"She's getting stronger, Lucien. It won't be too long now." She sat on the foot of the bed and leaned her back against the low footboard.

As I sat there with Ollie cradled in my lap, I could only hope and pray Henrietta was right.

Henrietta and I sat in silence for a long while. The morning had dawned just enough that the blackness at the windows turned dark blue. As the room continued to brighten, I realized the movement I was seeing through the curtains was snow falling. A storm front had passed through overnight. The normal cold of Detroit's winter had returned.

Ollie mumbled in her sleep. I pushed out of the chair, then carried her back down to the bed where she'd slept earlier. I was thankful she stayed asleep when I laid her down. Miraculously strong though she was, her little body needed whatever rest it could find after the events of the last fourteen hours.

I pulled the door shut and walked back down to Samantha's room. Henrietta inhaled to speak when Samantha's hand jerked. I flew to her side and grasped her hand in mine. Her eyelids fluttered, then fell closed again. Her cheek twitched.

"Samantha?"

A barely audible moan whispered from her chest. Her eyelids opened again, though her eyes remained unfocused, unseeing. Her mouth attempted to form a word, but it got caught in her throat. She turned her head to the side and with effort pushed her eyelids up again and struggled to make sense of what stood before her. She forced some air out of her mouth. "Thirsty."

Henrietta left the room and came back a moment later with a glass of water. The others gathered in the hallway, and I thanked them silently for giving her privacy. They always seemed to know the right thing to do.

I took the glass from Henrietta and, with my free hand, gently lifted Samantha's head. I tilted the glass against her lips and allowed a little of the cool water to pour in. She kept her eyes on me while she drank. Then she lay back down and shivered.

Too low for Samantha to hear, Henrietta quickly explained she would likely experience fever-like symptoms for the next six to eight hours as her body burned off the remainder of my blood. I pulled an extra blanket up over her body. She attempted a smile.

"Where am I?"

"At one of my houses. Don't try to talk, *dolcezza*. Just rest." I kissed her forehead.

She nodded and her eyes drifted shut, then flew open suddenly. "Ollie?"

"She's here. Sleeping. Don't worry, now, rest." Her head fell to the side as she lost consciousness again. *She's okay. Oh, thank God.* I closed my eyes as the realization swept over me.

The others quietly celebrated with me in the hallway. Henrietta smiled and nodded, then left the room.

I pulled the armchair close enough to the bed I could rest my weight in the chair but laid my head on the mattress near Samantha's hip. I gripped her hand in mine and closed my eyes. Four hours later, her respiration changed, quickened. I opened my eyes. Samantha was looking down at me.

"Hey," I said as I lifted my head.

"Hey," she managed with a hoarse voice.

I picked up the water glass and brought it to her lips again. She drank greedily, then pulled back. I returned the glass to the nightstand. She pushed herself up a little and grimaced.

"What happened?"

"What do you remember?"

She frowned. "I took Ollie for a bike ride. She was too impatient to wait for you to get home, so I agreed we could go early. It was so nice outside. I let her go over to the playground, but the equipment was still too wet, so we left. And then…" Her heart rate accelerated. "I don't know. I think I fell."

"You don't remember anything else? Why did you fall?" Was it really going to be this easy?

"I…I don't know. One minute I was talking to Ollie, and the next…I was…my head hit the ground." She worked her hand out from under the blankets and reached for her head.

"Does it hurt?"

"It feels numb and throbbing at the same time."

Ollie walked through the door. She looked at me, and I nodded. "Mommy!" She ran up to the bed and pushed her body tight against mine. "Are you feeling any better, Mommy?"

"Yeah, baby, I'm okay. Are you okay?"

"Yes. I was scared for you though."

I tensed.

"I'm sorry, Ollie. I'm sorry I scared you." Samantha looked between us. "What happened? I just can't seem to remember."

"We were going around the block and—"

"Ollie—"

"—you got wobbly and fell down. Your head hit the sidewalk hard."

"Shhh, it's okay, baby. I'm so sorry." Samantha worked her hand free of mine to stroke Ollie's cheek.

Ollie threaded one of her hands into mine and squeezed. If I lived a thousand years, I wouldn't be worthy of this child.

"Stupid," Samantha croaked. "My doctor's appointment... I'm anemic." She rolled her eyes. "I actually found out yesterday. There was a blood drive at the hospital. I got turned down because my iron was too low. The doctor confirmed it with some blood tests this afternoon, which made me feel a little woozy. I should've taken the time to eat something when I got home, but I figured I wouldn't be out that long with Ollie, and I wanted to go before it got much darker."

Her anger was a pang in my chest, a sensation made more uncomfortable by my guilt and betrayal at letting her blame herself.

She looked up at me. "You found me?"

"Yeah. You were just down the street across from my house."

She looked around, recognizing the house this time. "Why did you bring me here?"

Damn. She's sharp even when she's out of it. "Um, there was a snowstorm last night." *True.* "We lost power in our neighborhood." *Not so true.*

Her face relaxed, then she yawned. "You should rest some more."

"Yeah." She turned onto her side and brought her knees

up. "Just for a couple minutes," she said as she closed her eyes.

I looked at Ollie and led her into the hallway. At the top of the steps, I sat down and patted the step beside me. She sat too.

"Ollie, I want to thank you for what you did in there."

"I told you I wouldn't tell."

"I know you did. And I appreciate that. But I want you to make me a promise." She looked up at me. "I agree we needed to do what we just did in this one situation. But I want you to promise you won't lie to your mother about anything else. Do you agree?"

"Okay."

I needed to make that promise too, but couldn't. Not yet. "Let's shake on it." I held my hand out to her and she slid her hand around my thumb and laughed. "Come on. Are you hungry?"

She nodded, so we went downstairs. Everyone joined us in the kitchen as I rummaged through the bags Jed and William had brought from the store. I set three boxes of Pop Tarts on the counter and threw a look at Jed, who shrugged.

"Looks like it's Pop Tarts, Ollie. Is that okay?"

"Sure!" She grabbed the blueberry box, opened it, and lifted out a silver foil package. I handed her a napkin and a glass of water. I found a bunch of bananas in another bag and handed one of those to her as well.

"She didn't remember me being in the room before, did she?"

I looked at Henrietta. "No, it doesn't seem like it."

She looked at Ollie and hesitated. "Then maybe we should go before she knows we're here." I frowned.

"Henrietta's right, Lucien," Griffin added. "Our being here doesn't well fit with the story."

Ollie silently ate her Pop Tarts but paid close attention to the conversation.

"I know she would want to see you." The wisdom of their words was winning me over, though I really didn't want them to go.

"Why don't we just come back for a visit this weekend?" Rebecca offered. "That would make sense. We'd be coming to make sure she was doing okay and to help out around the house for the weekend while she was recuperating."

"I can't come this weekend," Henrietta replied. "I have to work. I can't cancel this late; they'll never find someone to replace me. I'm sorry, Lucien."

"What about next weekend, then?" Ollie hated to see them go as much as me. I smiled at her suggestion.

They looked at each other. "Next weekend should work. We'll come back," Henrietta said as she smiled at Ollie.

"Okay. It's a plan," I said. "Can you stay long enough to keep Ollie company while I help Samantha get a bath? I want to get her hair cleaned up before she..." *sees how much blood there is*.

They got the gist without me needing to spell it out in front of Ollie. "Of course. Go ahead." Griffin looked at me kindly.

As I walked out of the room, everyone settled down at the table around Ollie. I laughed out loud when she giggled and asked, "Anybody want some?"

They chuckled at her. Rebecca asked her to describe what a Pop Tart tasted like. Ollie's voice rambled as I walked into Samantha's room.

Balancing a glass of orange juice and a banana in one hand and a bag in the other, I shut the door behind me. I sat the food on the nightstand and sank into the arm chair. Samantha seemed to be sleeping peacefully. About thirty minutes later, a plow rumbled down the street in front of the house, waking her.

Her eyes settled on the orange juice. She reached out a hand for it. I helped her, and she drank half the glass. "Uh, that's good."

"How do you feel?"

"Better, I guess. Achy." She pushed herself up on an elbow.

"How about a warm bath? It might help."

"Um, yeah. Sounds good, actually."

"Here." I peeled the banana and handed it to her. "Try to eat a little something while I get the water going." She nodded and nibbled a tiny bite.

Within ten minutes, the bathtub was sufficiently filled. I pulled the shampoo and body wash out of the bag and sat them on the edge of the tub. I walked out to get Samantha and was relieved to see the empty banana peel laying on the nightstand.

She was in the process of pushing herself into a sitting position. I silently thanked the girls for coming in overnight and dressing her. It would've been hard to explain the torn and bloody clothes.

"Here. Let me help you." I scooped her up into my arms and carried her into the bathroom. I sat her on the toilet lid, knelt down in front of her, and grabbed the hem of her shirt. "Is this okay?"

She blushed a little—God it was wonderful to see that again—but nodded.

"I won't look. Promise."

She giggled weakly as I squeezed my eyes shut and lifted the shirt over her head. "Don't be a dork, Lucien. It's nothing you haven't seen before."

I opened my eyes and thrilled to see her smiling. "I've been called many things, Sam, but I don't think I've even heard the word 'dork' since the 1980s." She laughed. It was one of the most beautiful sounds in the world.

I grabbed the waistband of the sweatpants she wore. "Lift." She held her hips up, and I slid the fabric down. I met her eyes as I lifted her body and lowered her gently down into the warm water. "Is the temperature okay?"

She leaned her upper body against her legs and wrapped her arms around her knees. "Yeah. It feels good."

I grabbed a washcloth and dunked it in the water, then poured some of the soap into it. "Do you mind?"

"Not at all." She watched me as I ran the cloth up and down her arms. I washed her back for her. Then she took over.

"I missed you," I said. "I'm sorry I wasn't there."

"Lucien, you can't be there every moment of every day. And it wasn't your fault."

I ignored her last comment. "I always want to be there for you. If anything ever happened to you—"

"Shhh, baby. I'm okay." She reached out a wet hand and stroked my cheek. I leaned into her warm touch.

As she finished bathing, I walked out into the bedroom to retrieve the water glass from the nightstand. I knelt back down and dipped it into the water. She tilted her head back for me while I wet her hair. The water turned pink and she looked up at me.

"It's nothing. Don't worry. It just bled a lot."

Liar.

She nodded. She knew how much head lacerations bled, even when they weren't very serious.

I picked up the shampoo and filled my palm with it. I worked the creamy liquid into her hair, trying to be thorough but gentle with the injured side of her head. When I massaged my fingers against her scalp, she closed her eyes.

She loved when I ran my fingers through her hair. She said she found it relaxing.

I scrubbed the length of her hair between my hands, then retrieved the glass again. Within minutes, all the blood and soap had been rinsed out and she turned the drain lever with her toes. I turned and grabbed a thick decorative towel off a bar and unfolded it.

"Can you stand?"

She pushed herself up but grabbed onto my shoulders. I wrapped the towel around her body and lifted her feet over the tub's edge. She sat back down on the toilet lid, and I handed her another towel for her hair.

Someone moved out in the bedroom, then Ollie came through the bathroom door. I peeked out and Henrietta stood in the shadow of the hallway. She blew me a kiss and mouthed, "See you soon," then waved.

"Thank you," I mouthed in return. It wasn't sufficient, but they knew what their help meant to me. It didn't require words.

CHAPTER 16

We returned to Samantha's townhouse that evening. I had to smile at the kitchen appliance clocks blinking as if the power had gone out. My family was nothing if not thorough.

Samantha was weak and exhausted but didn't seem to be in any pain, for which I was eternally grateful. She made a concerted effort to eat since her anemia resulted at least in part from nutritional deficiencies, and she believed that was the cause of what had happened. My guilt at this train of thought grew since she was, of course, in no way responsible.

But day by day, she got stronger. And it was easier to let it all go.

Three days later, I finally gave in to her pleas to make love. It wasn't that I didn't want her. *Dio*, that was never the problem. I was just worried about harming her after what had happened. And I felt so damn guilty I didn't think I deserved to have her.

But Monday night, she was cuddled against me in bed trying, I thought, to fall asleep. Then the hand she had settled on my chest slowly slid down my abdomen and cupped me through my boxers.

Her rhythmic grip enticed my erection immediately. "Please," she whispered.

I couldn't stand her begging for what I was only too willing to give. I turned into her and gently took her face in my hand. I brushed my lips over her eyes and nose, and then leisurely nibbled at her lips and tongue until she was writhing against me.

Together we fumbled under the covers at removing our clothing. I grabbed some condoms and, when nothing stood between us, we settled back into the same side-facing position and softly kissed and lovingly stroked one another. I took my time before I reached for the heated cleft between her thighs.

"You're so wet for me." I groaned in pride and satisfaction as I dragged my fingers teasingly back and forth. The corners of her mouth quirked up around our kiss.

"That's because you drive me so insane." Her hands moved into my hair and tangled and fisted the way I liked. "I really need you."

I shifted my body lower and kissed my way down her neck until I was eye level with her collar bone, then I pressed a wet kiss over her pounding heart and hitched her thigh over my hip. I rolled on the condom and gripped my hard length and rubbed the swollen head against her drenched opening. She coated me with her arousal.

"Don't tease me." She pouted as she pressed kisses against my forehead.

I pushed into her. Slowly I filled her. When I was fully seated within her heat, I paused to suckle at her breasts. She moaned and pressed herself down and against me.

I threaded one arm under her body and gripped across her back; with my other hand, I grabbed hold of the curve of her hip. I rocked my hips against hers slowly and savored the sensations where we were joined. The sound of our love-making thrilled me as it always did—I relished the music of every shuddered sigh, wet kiss, pleasured moan, and shifting body.

Slow and sweet as it was, I was surprised by how much more intense it felt to be in her now that we had a Blood Connection. That my blood had run through her veins tied us together in primal ways that allowed me to sense and antici-pate her. The connection vibrated around us and pounded in my hard length. It made me need to be deeper.

Gently I rolled on top of her and grunted and swallowed as the new position enabled her body to take more of me in. I cradled one of her legs up over an arm and opened her to me further.

"Oh, fuck," I breathed, still trying to go slow, savor.

Samantha's hands sought purchase against my sides until she finally pulled me down to lie fully atop her. "I love…your weight on…me," she gasped around my thrusts.

The heat of her growing need enflamed my body and my mind. I grunted my agreement as a possessive, dominating urge ran down my spine. She buried her fingernails in the clenching muscles of my ass.

My restraint gave way. I gripped her shoulders and came at her with slow hard thrusts. Each time, I pulled myself almost all the way out of her before I hammered back in and rolled the base of my engorged sex against the center of her need.

Samantha groaned out her pleasure and lifted her hips to meet mine. "So good, Lucien, so good. Don't stop."

"Never."

We reached out with dry lips and wet tongues, but our labored breathing made lingering kisses difficult. So we panted and sighed and moaned into each other's mouths as our bodies met again and again. When her breaths started to come in gasps and her muscles started to tighten around me, I shortened the length of my strokes and thrust faster to concentrate all my efforts on stimulating her.

"That's it. Oh…God."

I didn't let up on her as she climaxed around me, on me. If anything, I moved harder, faster, dragging out her orgasm and chasing mine. When Samantha wrapped her arms and legs around me, the clenching in my groin told me to turn my head away from the sweating, pulsing life of her throat.

"Come in me, Lucien," she begged.

Her words sent me over the edge. "Fuck."

My release erupted, and my fangs tore into my biceps. The Blood Connection intensified my orgasm as well, and I ground my hips into her over and over as seconds turned into a minute. I wondered with amazement if I'd possibly had more than one.

I sucked my fangs and the blood on my arm back into my mouth and licked my wound shut as I panted on top of her. "Jesus Christ," I rasped with my head on her shoulder.

Knowing my weight must get uncomfortable on her, I pushed away with a kiss on her cheek. But she locked her ankles around my ass and held me in place.

"What was *that*?" she asked, her tone full of incredulity and appreciation. I opened my mouth, trying to figure out exactly what she meant, when she continued, "That was freaking incredible." Her smile was full and bright and coaxed one from me in return.

"Yes." I leaned down and kissed her. "It was." Minutes later, we were dressed and spooned in bed, though Samantha kicked some of the covers off with protests of being too hot. I chuckled as she shifted around and tried to get comfortable, and then stilled in surprise when the heat of her renewed lust snaked through my abdomen toward my groin.

Abruptly, she groaned and pressed her firm bottom back into my already-stiff erection. "Fuck, Lucien, I need you again."

"Your wish," I hissed as I sucked on her neck. She continued to grind her ass into me.

In one moment, I shoved her panties and my boxers down and sheathed myself in latex. Then I pushed her upper body slightly forward and found her wet entrance from behind.

The whole night went on like that.

We'd make love, and she'd sleep restlessly. Then she'd wake up, and one of us would need it again.

My blood in her veins was calling me home. And it was clear both of us heard it.

Samantha's new job was set to start on Wednesday. She was determined to go lest she end up having to work the weekend when my family planned to visit. Wednesday morning dawned, and she did in fact seem better, even excited. She demonstrated that first with her body before confirming it with her words.

"This is the first time I'll step foot in that hospital as a real nurse." She bounded out of bed and got in the shower. As she dressed in the bathroom, she called, "Don't take this the wrong way, but it'll be kinda good to get out of the house, too."

"Hey!" I pouted. But it was true. We hadn't left the house at all during the previous five days while she recovered. I knew she was getting cabin fever.

She emerged from the bathroom in scrubs—blue pants and a Snoopy shirt—with her damp hair in a ponytail. She leaned over the bed and kissed me. I restrained myself from pulling her back in with me. Barely.

"Don't work too hard today." I remained worried about her.

"I won't. Thanks again for today.'"

"No problem." Ollie had a bad cold and was staying home from school. I told Samantha I'd stay with her. "Your cab is going to be here in ten minutes. You should go grab some breakfast." I really wanted her to take a few extra days to recover. But when she insisted on going to work, I asked her to indulge me by getting a ride and not wasting her energy walking.

She finally agreed but wasn't happy about it. She rolled her eyes. "Lucien, I really can walk."

"I know. Humor me."

"Fine." She kissed me again and then ran downstairs. A few minutes later, a car horn blared and Samantha yelled, "Bye! Love you!" as she ran out the door.

It was a quiet day with Ollie, who really was sick and divided her time between sleeping in her bed and watching television. When Samantha got home at 3:30, Ollie was on the couch in the family room. Three hours later, we had her in bed for the night.

Assuming Ollie wasn't going to be well enough for school again the next day, Samantha asked Mrs. Johnson to watch her. I offered to do it, but she wanted me to get the Victorian cleaned back up and reopened to showings so it would be done before my family came. She was thrilled they were coming and didn't want anything to interfere with their visit.

I walked Ollie over to Mrs. Johnson's in the morning after Samantha went to the hospital. She seemed better but looked pale and acted tired. I left my cell phone number with Mrs. Johnson; if Ollie got worse, I wanted her to call me and not disturb Samantha at work. Ollie climbed on Mrs. Johnson's couch with a pink blanket and a thin brown bear she only seemed to want when she wasn't feeling good. I loved knowing that about her.

I kissed her on the forehead. "Bye, Ollie. I'll see you later."

"Bye." She laid her head down on the arm of the couch.

"Thanks again, Mrs. Johnson. Don't hesitate to call."

I jumped in my truck, still parked in front of Samantha's since we'd returned from the Victorian. As I pulled the door shut, the full power of Samantha's dried blood in the back seat hit me. I'd meant to clean it up but had completely forgotten. My fangs tingled. I powered all the windows down and pulled out of the lot.

I spent the day cleaning my truck and the spec house. I no longer renovated houses for Lena. I did it to provide for Samantha and Ollie's financial security. For the first time, I looked at the houses as investments in the future, not memorials of the past.

I'd just finished making up the master bed with the new comforter set I'd purchased when my cell phone rang. I fished it out of my pocket and placed it to my ear. "Hello?"

"Lucien, this is Betty Johnson."

"Is everything okay, Mrs. Johnson? How's Ollie?"

"Well, that's what I was calling about. Is Ollie with you?"

"What? No. Why would she be with me?"

"Well, she said she was going over to her house to get one of her movies about twenty minutes ago. She hasn't come back. I went over and checked, but she isn't there, so I thought maybe you or Sam had come home and got her." Her voice quivered with panic.

"No. Stay at your house, because she'll probably be right back. I'll be right there." I slammed the phone shut as I raced down the stairs. *Where could she be?* I jumped in my now-clean truck. Within fifteen minutes, I was parked in front of Samantha's.

The dark skin of her brow furrowed in worry, Mrs. Johnson met me at her door.

"Is she back?"

She shook her head. "No."

I turned abruptly and jogged over to Samantha's. I didn't hear any heartbeats inside, which didn't fully calm me. I ran through the house, but it was empty. I came back out to the front porch. *Where?* My eyes drifted down. Beginning at the edge of the sidewalk and continuing around the side of the house was a trail of small footsteps in the snow.

My house. I followed the trail across the snow- covered field and jogged up my front steps. The front door stood open.

There were no heartbeats in this house either. Ollie wasn't here. Her thin brown bear lay discarded on the floor. A small stack of DVD cases spilled off the coffee table. Her scent was strong in the air and—I seethed—tinged through with fear. She'd been here not long ago.

I froze as I stepped into the living room. Her scent wasn't the only one I smelled. Vampire. Someone, something, else had been here, too, had been here when Ollie came.

I went feral in that moment, my fangs punching out and my eyes flooding with blood. Giving over to my sense of smell, I stalked through the first floor. *It couldn't be.*

One of Ollie's angel drawings lay on the kitchen island picture-side down. *Please don't let it say what I think it's going to say.* I chanted a prayer as I picked it up.

Through a red haze, I read the curling script of Antoine Laumet's seventeenth-century hand.

I got tired of waiting for you. But this is so much better. A daughter for a son. Almost poetic, don't you think?

Unfortunately, she's just so little. She's really not a fair trade. So collect the girl's mother, and come to the Michigan Central Station at midnight.

Don't think of not bringing her. It will be so much worse if I have to track her down.

My eyes locked into a loop, reading and rereading the lines over again, willing them to shift the letters into different words.

My cell phone rang. Instinctively I knew who it would be. She couldn't help me now. No one could.

I thought back to Langston's phone call. I had been played. Betrayed.

The unsettling sensation of Samantha's worry broke me out of my reverie. The Blood Connection enabled me to sense her from even greater distances now. As she neared my house, she called my name. Her tone was filled with restrained panic.

I crumpled the paper and shoved it in my jeans pocket. I drained my eyes and retracted my fangs, then turned to face her as she ran up the steps and through the front door.

Her world was about to shatter in a million pieces. And I was going to be the one to wield the hammer.

CHAPTER 17

"Lucien, did you find Ollie?" She registered the look on my face. "Oh, God. What's happened?" She ran down the hall to the kitchen and stopped right in front of me.

"Samantha."

She grabbed my arms and shook me. "Lucien? You're scaring me."

"Sam, I need you to sit down."

"What? No. Tell me what's going on."

"Do you know how much I love you?"

"Of course I do." Tears filled her eyes. "What does that have to do—"

"I lied to you last week."

Her heart thundered in her chest. "What?"

Just rip it open, I thought. "You didn't fall. You were attacked. You were attacked by the son of a man I used to work for a long time ago."

She gaped and pushed back the wisps of hair that had fallen out of her ponytail.

"The son, his name was Jacques Laumet. He hated me from the day I met him. He attacked you to get at me."

The next sentence ranked as one of the three most impossibly hard things I was going to have to say to her today: "When I found you that day, he was killing you. Ollie was probably next. I killed him to stop him from doing it."

Her head shook back and forth involuntarily as she struggled to make sense of what she was hearing. Her fear and confusion roiled in the pit of my stomach.

"I'm so sorry I lied to you. I was trying to protect you. I thought we were clear of the danger."

"You killed someone?" She flung her arms down and paced between the counter and the island. "Defending me?"

I nodded when she finally looked at me. "Sam?" She continued pacing. "Sam!"

"*What?*"

"There's more. I need you to listen."

She braced her hands flat on the counter in front of her and leaned forward. Then she bolted upright. "What does this have to do with Ollie? Oh God, did she see what happened?"

"No, she doesn't seem to have seen most of what happened after he grabbed you. That's not the point. Listen to me." I paused. She focused. "The man I worked for, the father, his name is Antoine Laumet. He is a very powerful… man in this city. He runs a lot of the organized crime here."

The news devastated her—she paled and gaped. I'd just admitted to working for what she understood to be the mob. I steeled myself for the second of the impossible things I had to tell her: "He took her, Sam. He took Ollie to avenge Jacques."

She shook her head again. Then she came around the counter, walked straight up to me, and slapped me hard across the face.

I turned back to her and looked at her patiently. *That's the least of what I deserve.* She trembled and rubbed her hand. She raised her fists at me and slammed them into my chest. Finally, I caught them, though she twisted and struggled in my grip. "Sam...Sam, stop...*Samantha!*" But she continued to fight within my arms as tears streamed down her face.

"No. *No!*" she sobbed and futilely tried to pummel me. "She's all I have left!"

I hugged her tight. I needed her to work through these emotions, because the situation was far from over. My cell phone rang again in my pocket. I ignored it.

Finally, she pulled back and looked at me fiercely. "You're part of some criminal underworld, and you exposed Ollie to it?"

I blanched. "It is my fault, Samantha. But I'm not part of that world. I haven't worked for or with those people in a very long time."

She scoffed. "Lucien, you're twenty-eight. How *long* ago could it have been?"

"I'm older than I look, Sam."

She squinted and looked at me hard. "What the fuck is that supposed to mean?"

I walked right up to her. "You have every right to me furious with me. And you have every right to demand the truth—and I will give it to you, every last bit. But right now, that truth is not the most important thing. The most important thing is Ollie. I think we can get her back."

She sucked in a breath. I pulled the piece of paper out of my pocket and handed it to her. She uncrumpled and read it, a whimper escaping her throat as she did.

"Why the old train station?" She looked up at me.

"I don't know. The only thing I can figure is because I've never been there before. So he knows I'm not familiar with the building and its layout. Plus it's relatively isolated."

She looked at her watch. "We've got eight hours. We should call the police." She walked toward the phone on my counter. I grabbed her wrist.

"We can't, Sam." Her eyes and rage sliced into me. "If we do, he'll kill Ollie or take her away somewhere we'll never find. The police wouldn't be very effective against him anyway. Trust me."

Her voice came out as a high-pitched wail. "What are we supposed to do then?"

"We're going to do exactly what he says. I will gladly trade my life for hers. I need you to know that."

For an instant, her love and trust warmed me before being replaced by a noxious quagmire of hurt, betrayal, and fear.

I closed my eyes and breathed deeply. Then I walked to the kitchen cabinet over the sink. "Drink this." I pulled the flask down and held it out to her.

"*What?*"

"I know you don't trust me. But right now you're going to have to. You're going to have to dig deep down where some part of you knows I love you and find a way to trust me. Because Ollie's life depends on it. All of ours do."

Her blue-green eyes flashed with love and fear and malice. She grabbed the flask. "What is this?"

"It's just water. Drink it."

"Why—"

"*Please,* dolcezza, *just drink it.*"

I really hadn't meant to, but I charmed her a little. She lifted the flask to her lips and emptied it, then made a face. "Tastes weird." She shoved the flask back at me. "And don't call me *dolcezza.*"

I set the flask on the counter as her rage and terror wracked my body. Every bit of the pain I deserved. "Come on. You should change. Then there are some things we need to do."

She turned and stalked out of the house. She didn't wait for me as she crossed the field. And I stayed in her living room as she ran upstairs to change. Her distance was suffocating me, a tightness clenched my chest, but as it was entirely of my own making, I could hardly blame her for it. Finally, she came back down in dark jeans tucked into snow boots and a navy turtleneck sweater I'd given her.

It took everything I had not to pull her into my arms when she came downstairs. Instead, she shoved on her coat and walked alone out the door. I followed.

"Get in the truck, please. I'll tell Mrs. Johnson we're going to get Ollie, so she doesn't worry." Without responding, she got in the truck. I registered the door slamming as I knocked on Mrs. Johnson's door.

Several hours later, we returned. I'd made stops at four lawyers' offices and a bank. I also bought a prepaid cell phone just in case, a thick silver necklace I finally convinced Samantha to wear, and a silver-bladed dagger. I had weapons at Edmund Place I could've used instead, but I wasn't willing to leave Samantha alone, and taking her there seemed likely to raise more questions than she already had. I needed her as focused as humanly possible given what we were about to walk into.

She stomped up the sidewalk and into her house. I was about to follow when snow crunched behind me. I spun into a crouch, fangs bared. Catherine stood mostly hidden behind the corner of the next row of townhouses. I relaxed and flew over to her. We stared, silently conversing through our empathy.

"I've been calling...How bad is it?" She already knew from my emotions everything was coming apart.

"It couldn't be worse. Laumet took Ollie. Samantha and I have to meet him at midnight to try to get her back."

Catherine growled. "I'll come with you."

"No, you won't. He's going to have guards everywhere. He'll know you're coming before you're anywhere near him. I can't risk Ollie that way." She searched for alternatives, but there weren't any. "There is something you can do. Get the rest of the family here. If either of them makes it out of this alive, do everything you can to protect them. Take them out of the city if you have to. Give them access to any and all of my resources. I've made all of the arrangements, and Griffin knows who to contact. Just make sure they're taken care of."

"Why are you talking like you're not going to be here?"

I shrugged. "I'm not the most important thing."

"Don't you do that. Don't you fucking do that, Lucien. You come back from this. You hear me? Don't be reckless. They need you."

Kicking at the snow, I nodded, but refused to voice any promises I couldn't keep.

She grabbed my hands and squeezed. "We'll be here for all of you, Lucien."

I kissed her cheek. "I have to go."

"Wait." She ripped the clothing aside at her neck. "I don't know what you're walking into, but you need every possible advantage. Don't even think about resisting."

I met her eyes and sent her a rush of eternal gratitude. I embraced her and sliced my teeth into her neck. I drank and drank and was about to pull away when she gripped her hand at the back of my head and held me down. I could feel her concern for my safety, but I couldn't let her gravely weaken herself for me.

I pulled back more forcefully this time. She didn't fight.

I kissed her cheek again. A thin red tear stole from her eye as I ran back to Samantha's.

~

Soft snowflakes fell as I drove the truck up the long deserted approach road through Roosevelt Park to the ghostly grandeur of the Michigan Central Railroad Station. Built in the early twentieth century, the structure was imposing with its massive arched windows and neoclassical office building towering eighteen stories above. Its height was all the more pronounced due to the lack of any other noticeable building around it.

After refusing to talk to me all evening, Samantha's nerves had finally gotten the better of her. On the ride over she began tentatively talking and asking questions. Hearing her voice, even transformed as it was by fear and rage, was like a salve. All her words could be summed up by the ones she stated fiercely as we got closer to our destination: "No matter what, Lucien, we have to get her back. Promise me we can get her back."

I cupped my hand tenderly around her neck, groaning inwardly at the relief the physical contact provided. "I will gladly give my life to make that happen, Samantha."

She nodded and met my eyes momentarily, then glanced back down at her knotted hands.

I parked and scanned the area around us. I couldn't see or sense anyone, but surely they were there. As my eyes searched, I reiterated a list of rules to Samantha. "I need to say this one more time. You have to listen. You have to obey."

She met my gaze.

"First, I need you to avoid looking in Laumet's eyes. It would just be better in general to avoid meeting anyone's eyes." I could feel her wanting to question me again; we'd already had this argument. "Second, no matter what happens, you must remain at my side at all times so I can focus on how to regain physical possession of Ollie. Third, if I tell you to close your eyes, close them immediately and do not open them for any reason until I tell you to." I studied her to see if she was going to question me. "Finally—"

A shadow moved in front of the right side of the arched entryway.

I opened the truck door and stepped out, then motioned for Samantha to slide across the seat so she could get out on my side with me. As I shut the door, two more shadows—now taking shape as bodies—appeared. I grasped Samantha's hand tight in my own and walked around the front of the truck toward the building.

She tucked her body snug against my shoulder. I could smell her terror, but to her credit she was outwardly calm, steady, and focused.

I didn't recognize the vampires in the entryway. A tall black male radiating confidence opened the doors and indicated we should follow, while the other two males—one pale and bald and a muscular one with spiky blond hair—felt more curious and excited and followed behind to prevent our escape.

Samantha grasped me tighter as she lost her sight to the pitch black of the empty cavernous waiting room. My eyes scanned over the huge arched ceiling and the numerous classical columns, committing to memory as much of the physical layout of the building as I could. The space narrowed as they led us down a long arcade. Up ahead, I could just make out a hint of gray light. Samantha's heartbeat and the sound of our footsteps scattering unseen debris on the hard floor thundered in the stillness.

The walls around us opened up once more into another large hall—a row of abandoned ticket windows lined one side of the room. The light I perceived moments before came from ahead of us.

I pressed my lips against Samantha's ear. "Remember the rules and that I love you."

She nodded against my face and shivered like she was freezing.

As we stepped out into the massive rectangular concourse, I sensed and then saw a group congregated at one end of the long space. I surveyed the landscape: exit doors stood at each end, although Laumet's group blocked one set and the other appeared chained. A row of doors lined one wall, presumably the exits to the now defunct platforms. My shoulders fell as I calculated the odds. Including the three men escorting us in, seven of Laumet's inner circle and guard stood before us.

Samantha glanced up from underneath her eyelashes. She was looking for the same thing I was, but Ollie was not among them.

I locked eyes with Laumet from halfway across the hall. When we were within fifteen feet of him, I stopped abruptly. Samantha stumbled into me.

"Where is she?" My voice was coarse.

"Tsk. Tsk. All in good time." He glanced at Samantha. "I have not had the pleasure of your introduction."

Her eyes flickered up at him. Dressed impeccably in a dark gray suit, he moved toward us. At first her terror elevated. I took a step back, pushing her back with me. But then I was rocked with a wave of defiance and fury. I looked to Samantha, awed at her strength. She had stepped out from behind me and stood squared off, tall, erect. I wished I could read her mind, but I guessed by reading her body she'd decided she would not be cowed.

I raised my arm up in front of her. "That's close enough, Antoine."

He raised his hands in a gesture of assurance and stopped several feet in front of Samantha. He looked at me expectantly. Then he sighed and bowed slightly. "Madame, I am Antoine Laumet."

Samantha's eyes darted to my face before focusing forward again.

His smile was indulgent. "Is it not still customary to offer one's name in return upon an introduction?" A murmuring chuckle rumbled through the group.

"Saman—" Her voice cracked, and she cleared her throat. "Samantha Sutton."

He appraised her. His eyes made her uncomfortable. The confidence she'd demonstrated just a moment ago wavered under his intense gaze. The embarrassment his attention was causing her, however, stoked her fury.

"Where is my daughter? She has done nothing to you." Then, with some effort: "Please."

"Do not be concerned, Samantha. She will be down shortly."

"Antoine, let them go. They have nothing to do with this. I'm the one you want. Take me and let them go."

He walked right up in front of me. I instinctively pushed Samantha back with my arm. His emotions were all over the place and battered me: now pitying, then enraged; now bitter, then grieving; now regretful, then resentful.

I worked hard to block his and everyone's emotions. It was too distracting, and thereby made me too vulnerable. But months of keeping my power open to Samantha and Ollie had weakened the walls I used to throw up around my empathy.

"It has been a long road you and I have walked, Lucien. I took you in. I brought you close. I treated you as a son. I *cared* for you as a son. I gave you what you most wanted, your freedom." He shook his head. When his eyes met mine again, they glinted darkly. "*You* brought this on. I warned you not to interfere in my business. I warned you what would happen.

You have left me no choice. The gravity of your transgression against me demands redress. Jacques's death demands vengeance!" His voice bellowed and echoed through the hall by the end.

"So find your vengeance with me. Let the girls go. Olivia is but a child, for God's sake."

He spat his words at me. "You have been a miserable shell of a man the entire time I have known you. Killing a man who would like nothing more than to die is no vengeance at all. It's mercy. Jacques's memory and my empire demand vengeance. I need to make an example. They will help me make it."

My temper flared. *"How many times have I saved your life? You—"*

He flew at me, cutting me off with a blow across my face. I staggered back. Samantha choked on a scream.

"How dare you? I have repaid that debt several times over." He smoothed his suit. "And even if I had not, your destruction of my family has offended me so grievously as to render forgiveness or even leniency impossible."

Footsteps at the doorway through which we'd entered caught my attention. I whipped around. I could only focus on one of the four figures approaching our group: Ollie was slumped against Magena's chest, no doubt having been charmed into sleep. Perhaps that was a blessing.

Magena avoided my eyes. I couldn't get a good read on her. Walking behind her was a male vampire I didn't know and—my eyes narrowed— Langston, whose gaze flickered toward me before returning to the ground in front of him. I sneered at the false remorse flowing off him.

Samantha gasped and whimpered when her eyes could finally cut through the dimness enough to see her daughter. I had to restrain her from throwing herself at them. Her maternal instinct was strong and gave off a powerful energy.

They skirted around us and stood a little distance behind Laumet. Ollie was maybe twenty feet away—it felt like miles.

Tears spilled down Samantha's face. Her arms out, she took a halting step forward, which of course Laumet noticed. "Please...please, give me back my baby."

I could instantly tell when her eyes met Laumet's. She took another step forward, though this one was clumsier.

"Samantha!" The volume and urgency of my voice snapped her out of it as she whipped her head to me. Her eyes widened with some sort of realization. Laumet chuckled once at our exchange.

The sound pushed some button inside Samantha, who raised her head again and blurted out, "She's a child! An innocent child! We have nothing to do with this! *What kind of monster are you?*"

Laumet flew at her. I stepped between them in a defensive posture. My aggression caused several of the guard to move forward menacingly.

Laumet held up his hands. "Step back," he commanded them. "They are mine. I will brook no interference under any circumstances." He took the time to meet each of their eyes individually. They retreated. His direct order left them no other option.

He smiled broadly at Samantha over my shoulder. It struck even me as grotesque. He glanced back to me. "What kind of monster? *What kind of monster?*" He covered his laughing mouth with one hand as he crossed the other over his stomach. All of a sudden his face changed. He arched his eyebrows as he looked at me. "Oh, Lucien. It never occurred to me. You were always such a one for scruples."

I frowned, then blanched as I understood the meaning of his words.

He looked at Samantha with amusement as he spoke to me. "She doesn't know." He barked a single laugh as he paced back and forth before us. He finally walked over to Magena, drawing Samantha forward to stand next to me.

I growled fiercely when he brushed a wisp of blonde hair back from Ollie's face. Samantha stared at me in amazement. This wasn't the playful sound she elicited during our love-making. She'd never heard such a feral noise from me before.

Laumet turned on his heel to consider me in a sidelong manner. "You have been *passing*. Oh, that is too good, Lucien. Truly. You are a piece of work."

Samantha's confusion cut off abruptly as Laumet closed the distance between them at an inhuman speed and stood before her. A terrified curiosity washed off her. "What kind of monster, indeed, Samantha. Lucien, perhaps you—"

"Lucien?" The small voice came from behind Laumet, capturing everyone's attention. Ollie had regained conscious-ness and twisted in Magena's arms to try to see us. Magena held her firm, although she did let Ollie angle herself toward us. "Lucien? Mommy!" Tears streamed down her flushed cheeks. She was scared but remarkably composed.

"I'm here, baby. It's okay..." Samantha pressed her fist against her mouth.

"I knew you'd come, Lucien," she whispered. Her faith in me lifted me up and smashed me down. It felt miraculous, but was completely undeserved.

Ollie finally registered the others standing around her and surveyed the group. She cowered against Magena's body and flinched when she looked at Laumet. Then she pulled back to evaluate Magena, and her body relaxed. She ran her gaze over Magena's face and met the Native woman's eyes in the disconcertingly easy way she did with me and my family. Something tugged at the back of my mind.

Laumet grumbled and pulled everyone's attention back to him. "I am bored with this. It is time..."

"Antoine," I warned, "you should know if anything

happens to any of us, I've made arrangements to expose you. Several attorneys are waiting to hear from me. If they don't, they're prepared to distribute packets of information—"

"*You* think *you* can threaten *me?*" He belted out a strained maniacal laugh. "Lucien Demarco, you have violated my trust, tarnished my honor, challenged my authority, and murdered my son. This is my city. I make the rules. I mete out the punishment for the infraction of those rules. Your sins are too grievous for anything short of execution. I therefore sentence you and your humans to destruction." He looked at Langston and another vampire and barked, "Restrain them."

I hissed as Langston grasped Samantha's biceps. She shrieked in surprise. The bulky blond male from our escort grabbed me from behind. I seethed and bucked.

In a flash, Laumet flew to Magena and roughly pulled Ollie from her arms. Magena gasped and Ollie screamed, a sound Samantha immediately echoed. Something in Magena's face momentarily distracted me.

I scowled at Laumet and roared, "Antoine! *Don't!*"

CHAPTER 18

Antoine cradled Ollie in his arms. She struggled against him. He held her face still and looked into her eyes. A moment later her body went limp.

The next moments passed as if in slow motion. Laumet tilted Ollie's head back. Her long blonde hair cascaded over his arm toward the floor. Laumet's fangs protruded from his drawn lips. He lined his mouth up on Ollie's neck, sank his teeth into her, and swallowed once, twice, three times.

I slammed my elbows back into the blond male's gut, unsheathed the silver blade from my coat sleeve, and slashed his throat. Then I launched myself at Laumet. I silently thanked Catherine for her blood, which made possible these razor-sharp reflexes and my heightened speed and strength.

Samantha screamed Ollie's name over and over as Laumet continued to feed.

Then, he wrenched his head back in pained surprise. His eyes were bloodied, wide with shock and realization. His now-poisoned blood dripped from his nose. Just as I slammed into him, he coughed a stream of blood so forcefully it arced out over Ollie's body.

With one hand, I shoved him back hard. With the other, I flung Ollie's body to the side, flinching at the thud her head made as she hit the floor several feet away.

I was surprised to realize the others weren't attacking, and I concentrated just long enough to feel the frustration roiling off most of them. Antoine's order forced their inaction, which I prayed would keep Samantha safe for a few more moments.

I refocused on my target, who spewed more blood from his mouth and began bleeding from the ears.

Over Laumet's gagging and Samantha's shrieks, an authoritative voice commanded: "He told you not to interfere. As his second, *I* am telling you not to interfere."

Magena.

I finally realized what had been tugging at me earlier: *That must be a good sign about this guy. Ollie has always been a good judge of people.* Samantha's diary. Ollie had assessed Magena and relaxed. I hadn't connected it at the time, but Ollie had judged Magena to be good.

Magena is on our side. I tucked that away as I landed on top of Laumet. "Samantha, *eyes!*" I roared.

I couldn't delay to see if she obeyed. I needed to finish this before his body found a way to deal with and recuperate from the holy water now coursing through his bloodstream. If he got the command out of his mouth, the rest of them would be on me and this would be over.

I couldn't let that happen.

The blood pouring down Laumet's face burned his skin and, as I came into contact with him, it burned me as well. He struggled to control his body, but I knew from seeing him go through this once before—the day I twice saved his life two decades ago—his age slowed his healing abilities.

I had one option only and, as I sank my fangs into

Laumet's neck and ripped with all my might, I hoped my interpretation of Magena was correct. Because I killed her mate of nearly a quarter millennium. Laumet's head rolled to the side.

Just to be sure this was over, I slammed my fist holding the silver dagger into his chest and opened up a gaping hole that allowed blood to stream out in a gush. It set my hand on fire.

I jumped off him and landed several feet away, just far enough to escape his pooling blood. I wiped the bloody hand on my jeans as I crouched defensively and assessed the situation, looking for the next threat.

Remembering Samantha, I drained my eyes and retracted my teeth. Rage and confusion consumed me at the image of Langston's arm around her shoulders.

She pulled and twisted against Langston's hold and radiated a white-hot terror matched in intensity only by the murderous maternal instinct she felt for Ollie, who lay crumpled and bleeding a dozen feet away.

Laumet's broken body was in pieces at my feet. Where Ollie's blessed blood had spilled from him, his skin was blistered and raw. My hands, neck, and left cheek had similar marks on them, now in the process of healing. But none of that mattered.

I looked to Magena, who emitted an odd mixture of relief and anxiety. With Jacques and Laumet gone, she was the natural successor to the empire. She'd been Laumet's mate and was the next oldest vampire in his coven. She had to take decisive action to secure her ascendancy. She did.

"Do it," she growled at me.

In a flash, I was over Ollie.

Samantha screamed and fought until Langston finally released her. She sprinted toward us and fell to her knees just an arm's length away. I met her eyes and used my power on her in a forceful way for the first time. She stopped where she was.

"Sam, you have to listen to me. Ollie's life depends on it. Do you hear me? When I let you go, you may come over here, but you cannot interfere with what I am about to do."

I released her. She blinked lazily. When her eyes regained their focus, the look she trained on me was part incredulous and part livid.

"I know you have absolutely no reason to do so, but you *have* to trust me."

She made a choked noise filled with contempt. Wanting to spare her my fangs, I reached back and pulled the blade from my boot. Sensing Samantha's defensive instinct, I trained my eyes on her and held her in place to ensure she didn't attempt to stop me again.

"Here's what's about to happen. If you will please listen and stop trying to interfere, I will not do this to you again. We're running out of time, Sam; her head injury is stressing her system, and her heart is working too hard."

Her strength was simply amazing. Despite my hold on her she managed an obvious nod and a weak but clear, "Please."

I released her. "*Think* about it. I have saved your life once and her life twice. I would never— *never, do you hear me?*—do anything to harm you or her."

Her confusion flickered across her eyes, and a torrent of competing emotions coursed through her. Some deep part of my brain gasped in hope as the acrid betrayal and anger she felt toward me lost a little ground to the warmth of the love she had, or at least used to have, for me.

"She needs my blood. It's curative. It will heal her." I sliced the knife across my right wrist.

Samantha stifled a cry and glanced from my wrist to my eyes. "No, no, no, no."

"Sam, I'm her only chance."

"But you...you're a..." She looked at me wide-eyed.

"Yes, Samantha. I am a vampire." I met her eyes for one moment—which was all I could stand—and gulped down a massive knot of regret at this final impossible revelation.

"This will not change her. You've had my blood." She looked confused, then her eyes bulged. "It didn't change you."

She nodded almost imperceptibly. I'm not sure she even realized she did it.

I pulled Ollie's little body up against my leg so she was slightly elevated. I eased her jaw open and rested my bleeding wrist against her waiting mouth. The blood dropped in. After a moment she weakly swallowed, an involuntary reaction to the liquid pooling against her throat. I took the knife in my free hand and nicked the forefinger of the hand resting over Ollie's mouth, opening up a second small flow I wiped across the wound on her neck.

Within minutes, my blood started closing her throat wound. Samantha gasped. She sought my permission as she reached to take Ollie's extended hand.

"Yes, of course. It's okay." I looked up to Magena, who'd moved a little closer to observe my ministrations. "Magena, may we please have some water and cloths?"

She motioned to one of the others, who returned within minutes with a pitcher of water and several washcloths and towels. Magena looked to Langston and two other male vampires she'd made decades ago. These three men would form the beginnings of the inner circle of her guard.

Too low for Samantha to hear, she ordered everyone else out and commanded Langston and two others named Daniel and Michael to put the whole place on lockdown until she was done with this situation. Langston nodded, and the three flew out of the room. Only the four of us remained.

"Not too much, Lucien," Magena cautioned.

I nodded and pulled my arm away from Ollie's mouth, then lifted her body up slightly so I could rub my open wrist against the injury she'd received on the back of her head when I'd shoved her clear of Laumet's spilling blood. I cringed at the lump under her hair.

I'd caused that.

Magena stepped forward and placed her hand on my shoulder. So only I could hear, she offered, "You did right by her. She could have been changed otherwise."

I nodded and noticed Samantha's confusion at our seemingly silent exchange. "Magena, please speak loud enough for Sam to hear you."

"Oh. As you wish." She looked at Samantha. "Lucien feels guilty for Olivia's head injury, but I was assuring him if he hadn't knocked her free of Laumet's blood and it had gotten into the bite mark on her neck, it could have begun her change into one of us."

Samantha glanced back and forth between us and tried to keep up with the torrent of information coming at her from all sides. When I pulled my arm away from Ollie's head, I rested it in my lap. Samantha's breath caught and I looked up to see the cause of her alarm. Her eyes were wide and trained on my wrist. I glanced down to find my wound had healed.

"I heal," I murmured. "There isn't much that can permanently harm my kind. Those are the properties that will help make Ollie better."

She glanced at Ollie's face. "Now what do we do?" she whispered, still holding Ollie's hand.

"We wait for the blood to do its job."

I grabbed a washcloth and dipped it into the pitcher of water. I gently washed the blood off Ollie's face and neck. I threw the reddened cloth to the floor behind me. Her hair would have to wait until she could be bathed.

Magena picked up a cloth and dipped it, then handed it to

me. I frowned up at her in confusion. "For your face," she said. "You look as bad as she did." I roughly ran the clean cloth over my face and neck, and then cleaned my hands.

I looked up at Magena. "Why did you do this for us?"

"You know why, Lucien." I frowned. I really didn't. Her eyes darkened. "For more than two hundred years, I have hated what I am, what he made me into. I have hated the kind of person he was, the kind of world he doomed me to live in for all eternity. I have had to suffer hearing the thoughts of the very worst creatures. He did that to me. He subjected me to that." She paused and paced, glancing down at Laumet's gory remains.

"Then you came here. And you were different. You wanted to be different." She spun to look at me. "You *were* different, Lucien. I could see it. I could read it in you. You gave me hope. I was so happy for you when he let you go. And then when Langston told me you had found love, I was thrilled." She became lost in thought for a moment.

"When the guard brought the child in, I was so furious I had to hold back from striking at Laumet myself. Not only was she part of your happiness, but she was everything he was not: goodness, innocence, hopefulness, possibility. There was no way I was letting him take that away, from you or from her. I don't care what it costs me."

I gawked at her in admiration and gratitude. "Thank you" was all I could manage.

I was certainly aware of her resentment of Laumet and had been for a long time. And I knew she kept things from him. As I thought about it, she'd always seemed to have a special sense of protectiveness toward me. I never realized the significance of that feeling, however.

I looked from Magena to Samantha, whose eyes had been drawn away from Ollie by the forcefulness and passion of Magena's words. Samantha was fascinated despite herself.

"Magena, would you be willing to allow us the use of a room for a few hours until we can more safely remove Ollie from here?"

She looked between us. "Follow me."

I gently scooped Ollie into my arms, then extended the hand under Ollie's legs to Samantha to help her up. She hesitated but finally accepted it. I pulled her to her feet. She was more steady than I feared she might be, although I could smell the adrenaline in her blood and knew that was keeping her going.

Magena led us out of the concourse and down a corridor to a staircase. On the next level, we passed a few doors down a dark hallway when she stopped and pushed open a door to a large sitting room with couches.

The room stood out from everything else I'd seen here so far because it was clean, modern, lit, and well appointed. They'd clearly left the main level disintegrating to discourage intruders.

"I'll have some pillows and blankets brought in so you can make her comfortable."

"And some drinking water, please?"

"Of course." She returned with the items several minutes later.

I handed one of the bottled waters to Samantha who looked at me blankly. "Drink it, please, Samantha." She grabbed the bottle but didn't open it.

I arranged Ollie on one of the wide couches with a pillow beneath her head, then draped the thin blanket over her still form. *Come on, Ollie. Open your eyes, baby.*

I turned and found Samantha standing behind me. She stared at me intently, warily.

Not meeting her eyes, I whispered, "We have a while. Are there things you'd like to ask me?" Finally, I manned up and met her eyes. They were cold, flat, and filled with anger.

❧

"**W**as any...any of it...anything...true?" Silent tears spilled down Samantha's cheeks. Her body trembled as the shock set in.

"*All* of it was true."

"How could that be, Lucien? Huh? How?"

"If you'll allow me, I think I could prove to you— show you—the truth."

She looked between me and Magena and nodded, but took a step back. The shivering worsened.

"Please drink, Samantha. You're probably experiencing shock." This time she twisted off the cap and took a long pull from the water bottle. "Magena, would you be willing to help me?"

She nodded, knowing what I wanted. Her telepathic skill actually extended one step past where most people, including Laumet, knew. She could not only read minds, but she could project her readings into other people's minds. Her resentment of Laumet for changing her had over time led her to keep a number of things to herself, including the extent of her power.

"Please sit down, Sam," I urged as Magena and I approached her.

"I don't want to sit down."

"Please?"

"No."

"Okay. It's not necessary." I took a breath. "Magena is going to help me show you the truth. I realize this is going to sound crazy, but Magena is telepathic."

Samantha's eyes widened as she looked at Magena. "She can read minds?"

"Yes. If you'll let her take your hand, she can show you what she sees in my mind. Are you willing?"

"Do I have a choice?"

"Oh, God. You absolutely have a choice. I'm not going to force you to do anything. Sam, I'm not going to hurt you."

Her shivering returned. "What do I...?"

Magena extended her hand toward Samantha's. "May I?" Samantha nodded. Magena took her hand and mine at the same time.

A series of images ran through my head, beginning at the beginning. I pictured the night Lena and Isabetta died, what I recalled of how I was changed, my shock and horror at discovering what I was, and when I begged Griffin to kill me.

Samantha gasped.

Damn. Way to go, Lucien. I'd just outed my family as well. I shook my head and concentrated again. I showed her my despair when I left Orchard Hill and my intense relief when I left Laumet. I recalled my confession to my family of my feelings for Samantha and Ollie, and I pictured a million different moments the three of us had spent together over the last seven months which I hoped would show the depth and true nature of my love and devotion.

I looked at her and tried to communicate all of these things with my eyes as well.

Tears streaked down her face. She bit her lip, hard, to keep from crying out. All of a sudden, Samantha ripped her hand free from Magena, who made no effort to prevent her from doing so.

Magena stepped back to try to ensure Samantha didn't feel threatened. "Lucien, I need to put my house in order. I'll return in a while."

"Thank you. For everything." I worried for her. The challenges she'd face in making Detroit her own were going to be numerous.

She nodded, turned, and left.

Samantha and I stood and stared at each other for a long

time. Her emotions were so torn up I could barely make any sense out of them as they battered me. She was pale. Every once in a while, her body involuntarily shuddered.

But above all that was an extraordinarily strong woman. She'd held her head. She'd survived. I couldn't have loved or admired her more than I did in that moment.

"Sam?"

"Lucien." Her voice cracked.

I took a tentative step toward her. She eyed me warily but held her ground.

"Can I...?" I held my arms up to embrace her and slowly moved forward. Her face rippled with pain as she trembled. I took another step. *Please*. The next step put me within arm's reach of her. As I hesitated, she melted into me.

I wrapped my arms around her greedily and pulled her against my body, relishing a kind of touch from her I feared I'd never again experience.

Her voice was hoarse and strained. "You got her back for me..." All of the fear and stress and horror of the night began to pour out of her. She wailed and heaved against me for a long time. I whispered reassurances into her hair and told her I loved her, I was sorry, and I would do absolutely anything to try to make this right by her.

A rustle of fabric made us look at Ollie, who was moving in her sleep—a sign of progress. Samantha sobered up. We knelt at Ollie's side. Keeping her eyes on her daughter, she asked, "How does it work?" She nodded at Ollie.

"Um, I don't know the physiology of the mechanics. You were the first person I ever tried to save. Whatever it is that keeps us from aging helps cure injuries in the human body."

Her eyes snapped to mine. "You don't age?" She thought for a moment and frowned. "How old are you?" I looked down, hesitating. "You said you would tell me the truth, 'every bit of it'..."

I met her gaze. "And I will, without question. I was twenty-seven and a half when I was changed, Samantha."

"And when was that?"

"May 13, 1895. Almost one hundred twenty-five years ago."

Her heart rate spiked again. "You're...over a hundred and fifty years old?" I nodded. "And the others?"

"Which...?"

"Griffin..."

"They're much older. They found me after my family was murdered, after my maker changed and abandoned me. They were already old then. They took me in and taught me how to survive."

"How is this possible?"

The question was rhetorical, but I answered anyway. "I honestly don't know."

She glanced at me. Her sympathy tasted like tears. I was in awe of her capacity for such compassion, all things considered. "Lucien, I want you to tell me everything right now— don't leave anything out—you ever told me that wasn't true."

I wanted to answer truthfully and thoroughly. I took a deep breath and began. "Well, I already told you I lied about what happened to you. You were attacked." She nodded. "Um, I did fly down the steps the day Ollie fell." I glanced up at her, and she stared intently.

"And the day I met Ollie, she didn't fall down in the street. She ran in front of a truck. I grabbed her out of the way before it hit her. I didn't want you to worry. And, well, this isn't so much a lie as I didn't correct an assumption you made: I wasn't visiting a patient at the hospital, I was visiting a...friend who works there. Uh...I do own my own business, technically, but I really don't need to work in order to provide for myself. The length of my life has made it possible to accumulate money. I have more than I could need in many lifetimes. And I was born in Italy as a human, not New York, but I was changed there. Oh, and"—I rushed on now—"the mark on my chest isn't a tattoo. It's called a Blood Mark. It occurs when you're changed into...this...and is supposed to indicate your lineage."

Her eyes flashed down to my left pectoral despite the fact it was covered.

I thought again and sighed. "I would be remiss if I didn't admit my acquisition of the house on Frederick wasn't coincidental. I'd become intrigued by you and desired a way to be nearer to you."

"Intrigued?"

"Yes. The first time I saw you, Sam, I was so filled with grief. My whole life I've berated myself about my family's deaths. In my head, I know there was nothing I could've done. The attackers were so strong. But in my heart, I've punished myself every single day for not being able to protect them. The pain often felt crushing, suffocating."

I tasted the salt of her sympathy again.

"But then you walked by me at the hospital. And you felt so happy I—"

"Felt?"

"Oh." *How much more of this can she take?* "Uh, yes, felt. I'm empathic, which means I can sense people's emotions, how they're feeling." She frowned so I explained further. "I don't really know how it works. Henrietta thinks it has something to do with emotions being chemical reactions, and wonders if I'm sensing the energy that results from them. I don't know. But you felt so happy when I saw you that the relief was stunning. I wanted you, fantasized how to be around you all the time so I could feel that relief. It was challenging at first. I haven't allowed myself to become attached to humans in the past, because I didn't want to hurt anyone, but I found myself drawn to you, liking you, and then, well, loving you."

"Challenging? Does that mean…did you want…I mean…"

I sighed, expecting each confession to be the one that caused her to flee. "I struggled badly with my bloodlust for you, Samantha, at first. But it didn't take me long to realize harming you would only hurt myself."

Ollie jerked under Samantha's hand. We both looked at her, but she remained unconscious.

"Is there anything else?" she whispered.

I thought, hard. The problem was what and how much to tell her. In order to exist in this world undetected, much of my life was based on a lie. Lies of deception were a central tool of survival for my kind. I supposed that was something: "Um, oh, I don't eat human food."

She gawked at me.

"I mean, I can swallow it, but I can't digest it. While food gives you energy, it depletes mine."

"Mommy," Ollie's little voice croaked.

Samantha snapped her head back toward Ollie. "Hi, baby. Mommy's right here. Open your eyes." Samantha brushed soft kisses on Ollie's cheeks as she dragged her lids open.

Ollie finally forced her eyes to focus on her mother's, then she looked at me. "Hi, Lucien," she whispered hoarsely. I smiled at her, relief coursing through my body. "Thank you." She swallowed thickly. "For saving me. I wasn't too, too scared 'cause I knew you'd come."

Her faith in me was astounding.

"Was it like when you saved Mommy?"

"Yes, Ollie, and you're going to be okay." I squeezed her knee gently through the blanket.

"Did Mommy keep her eyes closed?"

Samantha looked at both of us questioningly. "I don't understand, Ollie."

"Save your strength. I'll tell her." She nodded. "When I was trying to save you, Ollie insisted on being in the room. I

278

finally agreed, but only if she promised to keep her eyes closed the entire time. I didn't want her to see what was happening. I didn't want her to be burdened with the knowledge of my kind."

Samantha's frowned and looked back and forth between us for a moment. "Wait, does Ollie already know about you?"

Ollie and I both spoke at the same time, then both apologized to each other at the same time. "Yes and no. Ollie is incredibly smart—somehow she deduced there was something different about me, which has never happened before. I owed her the respect to acknowledge she was right, but I didn't tell her what I was."

Samantha's mouth opened and closed but nothing came out.

"I thought he was an angel, but he told me he's not. But I think of him as my guardian angel. He looks out for us, Mommy."

Samantha's breath shuddered as she took in all we were saying. She squeezed Ollie's hand reassuringly.

Ollie groaned a little. "I don't feel so good." She weakly turned on her side and pulled her knees up into a fetal position.

Alarmed, Samantha looked at me then back at Ollie. "What feels bad, honey?"

"I feel like I might throw up. And my head hurts." She whimpered. "I feel dizzy."

Samantha brushed her hand across Ollie's forehead and feathered stray tendrils of gold back off her face. "She's hot. Lucien?"

"The fever symptoms are normal. Hold on." I fished my cell phone out. There were a half dozen missed calls—all from my family. My signal was weak, so I sprang to my feet and walked toward a window. As soon as I found a signal, I pushed a sequence of keys and waited.

"Oh, thank God. Lucien, are you all right? Are they all right?"

"Yes, yes, Henrietta. We're all right."

She reported the news to the others. I smiled to myself at their obvious relief and joy. "Where are you, Lucien? We'll come get you."

I debated. "I don't want all of you to come. The situation seems defused, but I don't want them to feel besieged by another coven of vampires showing up. You and Griffin come…" The others overheard me and protested. "I need your help, Henrietta."

She understood immediately. "What happened? Who's hurt?"

"Ollie. Laumet bit her."

Henrietta gasped and her voice was strained. "Were you…"

"It's okay, Henrietta. I was able to stop him. And I think I was able to address her injuries. But she's not feeling well now. I need you to look at her."

"Tell me where you are, and we're on our way."

I complied and snapped the phone shut, then returned to the couch where Samantha was softly singing to Ollie to distract her from her discomfort. The worry washed off her.

Footsteps echoed in the hallway and drove me back to the defensive. It was too quick to be my family. A vicious growled erupted from my throat as the knob to the hallway door started to turn. Samantha gasped as I leaped across the room to protect my girls from whatever new threat was about to walk through it.

CHAPTER 19

I wrenched the door open, surprising Langston as he was about to push into the room. Given his betrayal, I was immediately suspicious to find him trying to enter. I grabbed him by the throat and shoved him so hard against a wall the plaster caved in around his shoulders. I surprised even myself with my ferocity, but felt a primal urge to protect and defend my girls.

Samantha jumped up, her body positioned in front of Ollie.

"It's okay," I called out to her with a graveled voice. "Nothing to worry about." But she didn't relax her stance at all. I shifted my eyes back to Langston's shocked face. "What is the meaning of this?"

"Hey, man, it's okay. Listen, I don't blame you. Magena told me to stand guard. She didn't want anyone bothering you. I was just coming in to let you know."

I didn't sense deception, but I still didn't trust him. He'd been a part of this tonight. He'd called to tell me Laumet understood about Jacques. "You lied to me. You set me up," I

281

growled and flashed my fangs, leaning in menacingly toward his face.

He struggled, but my age and Catherine's blood were too much for him. "I know. I know. I didn't have a choice. When I hesitated, Laumet threatened to kill Magena if I didn't make that call. Man, I didn't want to do it. I'm sorry."

"Kill Magena?" This made me even more suspicious. "That doesn't make any fucking sense, Langston. She was his mate."

"You didn't see him, Lucien. Laumet snapped when they brought Jacques's body back. He killed the two members of the guard who brought him the news. He just lost it. Your scent was all over the body, confirming what the guard had already told him. He sent people out looking for you immediately. When no one could find you, he came up with the plan of trying to lure you out." He tried to restrain himself, then a wave of love and grief and embarrassment washed off him. "I love her, man."

"What? Who?"

He groaned. "Magena. You were gone by the time it started, but it's still been years. It's been unbearable."

"You're in love with Magena? *Did he know?*"

He appraised me for a moment. "He caught me looking at her a couple times. He must've suspected...I don't know. But that night, he grabbed Magena, he wrapped a long silver chain around her neck and declared I had to choose sides. If I chose his side, he would spare Magena. If I didn't do everything in my power to help bring you to him, he said Magena would die. The pain on her face...he took her completely off guard. He was so far gone. I'd never seen him treat her like that. Of course, he groveled apologies to her later, saying he was so overcome with grief..."

I released him and stood back.

He pulled himself out of the wall and brushed the small

crumbles of plaster from his shoulders. "I'm sorry, Lucien. I know it's not enough."

We faced one another for a long minute, both of us breathing hard from the confrontation. The pieces of a puzzle started falling together: Magena's sidelong glance at Langston that night at Belle Isle...her willingness to help us tonight...Ollie judging Magena to be good...Langston standing guard now...

"Does Magena know you—"

"Yeah." He folded his arms across his chest, a fierce protectiveness flashing out from him.

"And?"

"And what?"

"Does she love you?"

"Yes."

That was the missing piece. "Did you two...was tonight planned?"

"Not exactly. We didn't know how the whole thing would go down. But we hoped to get you and your humans out of this in one piece. And it was our chance."

"For?"

"Being together. And for Magena to finally be free of him."

"Shit."

"Yeah."

Until Samantha and Ollie were completely out of harm's way, I just couldn't find the full measure of forgiveness Langston probably deserved. But I could admit the situation was a lot different than I'd thought.

I ran a hand roughly through my hair. "Where is Magena now? I need to talk to her."

He seemed to appreciate the change in topic. "She, Michael, and Daniel are dealing with the others. Laumet's fall is going to have ripples. Magena has a following, though, because they know she's gonna be different. She's elevating all the guards who were here tonight, so garnering their loyalty should be doable. She said she'd be back."

"People are coming for me, to help..." I nodded toward the room. "I need you to let her know so they can get safe passage in here. It's a man and a woman—Griffin and Henrietta."

He nodded, then he looked over his shoulder into the room. "So how are they?"

"Okay. I don't know. I think okay." I watched Samantha for a moment. She sat on the edge of the couch rubbing Ollie's back.

"Good. Okay, so, I'll go tell her."

I walked back in the room, but left the door open to keep an eye on the hallway. "How is she?" I whispered to Samantha. Ollie's eyes had drifted shut again.

"Honestly, I don't know. She feels like she has a fever. If the rest of this night hadn't happened, I'd say she has a virus or something." She looked at me questioningly.

"I'm sorry, Sam." *For everything.* "Henrietta will be here in a few minutes and can better explain exactly what's going on with her. I suspect between my blood and Laumet's bite, her body is dealing with all the foreign matter."

"I thought you said it would cure her." Her voice was steady, but her emotions laced with panic.

I took her hand. "It is. It will. But—" *Cazzo!* Running footsteps pounded down the hall. I growled, wondering again about the near-insanity I felt to protect them. I shot out of the room.

Catherine slammed into me in a tight embrace. "I'm so glad you're okay." I hugged her back. Griffin and Henrietta walked up behind her, also clearly relieved. The looks on their faces told me there had been no keeping Catherine from coming.

284

I brushed a kiss against her hair. "Thank you. I owe you." I'd never been easy for her, but she'd been there for me so many times during my life. I appreciated her so much.

She stepped back. "How are Samantha and Ollie?"

"Come." I led them all into the room then hesitated, watching to see whether Samantha would be comfortable having so many of us near.

Momentary uncertainty pulsed from her before she spoke to Henrietta. "Can you please help her?" In a flash, Henrietta knelt next to the couch. Samantha described Ollie's symptoms while Henrietta nodded.

"Is it okay with you if I touch her, Sam?" Samantha tilted her head, and her eyes misted.

She and Henrietta had become close during our Christmas visit and had stayed in touch ever since. After a moment, Samantha nodded. "You don't have to ask."

Henrietta laid her hands on Ollie's head and then smoothed them over her little body, pushing the blanket down as she did so.

Ollie stirred and smiled up at Henrietta. "Henny," she said weakly.

"Hi, Ollie. How are you doing?"

"I don't feel so good." She glanced around Henrietta's side and noticed Griffin and Catherine standing there. "Hi," she whispered to them. They both smiled and returned her greeting.

"What doesn't feel good? Can you tell me?"

"My head and my tummy."

"Can you lie on your back for me?"

Ollie nodded and grimaced through a turn. Henrietta helped her.

"I'm just going to take a look at you, okay?" Henrietta embraced Ollie's face in her hands.

"Your hands feel good, Henny."

Henrietta smiled and turned Ollie's head a little to the side. She threaded one of her hands through Ollie's now tangled hair to cup the back of her head where she'd been injured. She held her hand there for a few moments and looked over her shoulder at me. I stepped closer.

"What is it?" Samantha glanced between us.

"Hold on," Henrietta whispered.

"Henny, that's feeling better. Keep doing that." Henrietta smiled down at her.

"What's going on? I don't understand." Samantha could tell Henrietta was trying to focus, so she directed the question at me.

I knelt down next to her. "Henrietta's a healer, Sam. Her power isn't absolute. She can't fix everything—"

"It's okay," Henrietta said reassuringly as she withdrew her hand from Ollie's hair. "Your blood healed the brain injury, but there was still a moderate subdural hematoma. It's gone." She looked at me. "Did she lose consciousness when she hit her head, Lucien?"

"I don't know. Laumet had charmed her before..."

Henrietta nodded and continued to work her hands down Ollie's body.

"Charmed her?"

I looked up at Samantha from where I knelt next to her and took one of her hands. She let me. "We have a number of heightened powers and special abilities, Sam. One of those is an ability to control other beings, like when Laumet made Ollie fall asleep before."

She glanced down for a moment and then looked back at me. "You charmed me."

"Yes, I'm sorry. I needed a way for you to let me help Ollie, and I could see you wouldn't let me near her otherwise. I'm sorry."

"Have you done it…before tonight?" Her eyes flickered to the others. I tasted her embarrassment.

"I've tried to avoid doing it to you. I didn't want to control you. I wanted you to act with free will." I sighed. "When I first met you at the hospital, I willed you to stay a moment longer when you were about to leave." I could feel the others' discomfort at being present for the execution of my confessions to Samantha, but I wasn't going to beg off her questions. I owed her that much.

"I felt dizzy when I stood up," she recalled. I nodded, ashamed. "Any other times?"

"When you drank the water at my house yesterday."

She nodded, thoughtful. "Is that why you told me not to meet anyone's eyes?'

Smart woman. "Yes. Our eyes are mesmeric, especially in combination with our voices."

"Laumet charmed me…"

"He tried to. You were able to break from it. Your will was more powerful than his."

"Hmm." Henrietta had her hands on Ollie's bare stomach.

"What is it?" Samantha couldn't hide her worry. The sharpness of Henrietta's rage sliced at me. I frowned at her. She shook her head and took a deep breath. "She will likely be nauseated and crampy for a few hours, maybe a day. From Laumet's bite."

That could only mean one thing: he didn't just bite her, he secreted his changing enzyme into her. That's what Ollie's body was struggling with. I shuddered in rage and disbelief, but also felt relief I'd shoved her clear of her blood. *God, if his blood had gotten into her wound…*

Henrietta was furious too and struggled to calm herself as she met Samantha's eyes. "But it will pass. She'll be okay."

Ollie pressed her little hands over Henrietta's on her stomach, holding them in place. "It helps," she whispered.

"Whatever you need, Olivia." Henrietta's love for her was complete.

Just then, Magena walked into the room. The others braced defensively before I quickly talked them down and made introductions, which were polite but stiff and formal.

"Are we free to go, Magena? I would like to get Ollie somewhere more comfortable."

"Yes, but there is one thing I need to do first, Lucien. Will you all follow me back downstairs?" Her words were cryptic, but her emotions didn't radiate anything that concerned me.

I nodded. Henrietta carried Ollie so her touch could continue to offer some comfort. I took Samantha's hand and led her and the others out of the room behind Magena and Langston.

My separation from Ollie, small though it was, rankled, and I realized in a moment of stunned clarity this protectiveness was the way the Blood Connection was manifesting between me and the child.

I tensed as we walked back into the concourse and saw other vampires gathered there. Magena led us over to the group. Catherine and Henrietta hung back with Ollie. I kept an eye on them as I assessed the others. "Magena?"

When she turned, the group stepped up around her. "Lucien, you are one of my favorite people in the world. But I am in a very difficult position right now, to a large extent because of things you have done. Don't get me wrong, I don't blame you. And I certainly feel no love for Laumet after everything...but there must be consequences. This city will devolve into wholesale vampire war if I don't decisively take charge."

"Okay, so, what—"

"You are hereby banished from this city. Leave and never return." I was stunned. "If you ever return, I will not protect you. There are too many forces, loyal though they may become to me, that will want to avenge the Laumets. I cannot have you be the source of further conflict or unrest." Regret and grief washed off her, even as she maintained her resolve and voiced her decision. "You can have a day to leave the city. You must be gone by dawn tomorrow."

I gaped and tried to process this turn of events.

"Do you understand me, Lucien?"

"Yes." I thought for a moment. "What about Samantha?" I squeezed her hand, which trembled within my grasp.

Magena looked at Samantha sympathetically. "She may remain. She has not wronged me. She will not be disturbed. Simply charm her to forget." Then Magena walked over and took both of my hands in hers. She kissed me on the cheek and whispered into my ear for only me to hear, "I'm sorry. There's no other way."

Given the enormity of the power politics I knew must be playing out, I actually did understand and said so.

"Take good care, Lucien." She stared at me. And just like that I was dismissed, from the room, from my whole life in Detroit. After a long moment, I nodded at Magena and turned away.

Her pronouncement was final. Nonnegotiable.

I shoved the shock of it away and concentrated on getting my girls to safe ground. Ignoring the confusion in Samantha's eyes, I whispered to her, "Will you allow me to carry you, Sam? I want to get us out of here as quickly as possible." She couldn't have agreed more, so I scooped her into my arms. "Close your eyes, please." She did, and turned her head into my chest.

Seconds later, we were all out in front of the station standing by our cars.

"Okay, *dolc*—uh, Sam," I said as I placed her on her feet.

She blinked incredulously at where we were and then

stared sadly up at me. A biting wind whipped at her hair as we stood in the circular drive of the train station.

Everyone hurried into the waiting vehicles. Henrietta rode with Ollie in her lap in the backseat of my truck while Samantha sat next to them. Griffin and Catherine followed us back to Samantha's house in their car.

As we parked in Samantha's lot, Rebecca, Jed, William, and Anna jumped out of a car parked outside of her house. Another round of relief-filled greetings ensued.

As we approached the door to her house, everyone stopped. Samantha looked at us, confused.

"You have to invite them in. We can't enter a dwelling inhabited by humans without an express invitation."

"Oh." She scanned the group, shivering. "Well, come in then."

Samantha and Henrietta entered and took Ollie upstairs. The others filed in and waited in the living room. I ran up to Ollie's room and found Samantha pulling the covers back so Henrietta could slip Ollie under. Henrietta's long dark hair spilled around her shoulders as she leaned down to kiss Ollie on the forehead. She smiled sadly at me, then turned to leave.

Shyly, Samantha caught her with a hand on her arm. "Thank you, Henrietta."

Henrietta patted Samantha's hand and squeezed. "Of course." Then she left us alone.

We watched Ollie sleeping peacefully as small children should. Safe in her bed. It was a miracle.

I watched Samantha. It seemed like she saw me looking at her, but she kept her eyes on Ollie. Several minutes passed that way. The room suddenly felt awkward, tense.

Finally, she looked at me. A tear spilled from one eye and streamed silently down her cheek. I took two long strides over to her and wrapped my arms around her. She leaned her head against my chest. Her pulsing warmth felt like life.

"You should get some sleep, my love."

She glanced at Ollie and pushed out of my embrace, then stepped out of the room and motioned for me to follow. I pulled the door closed behind me, and we stood out in the hallway.

She shifted on her feet and fumbled with her fingers. She heaved a great, shuddering breath that sounded of pure exhaustion. Then she met my eyes. "We need to talk."

CHAPTER 20

The hope I'd been feeling at Samantha's accepting behavior plummeted as those words left her mouth. But she was right, especially given Magena's pronouncement.

"We do need to talk," I agreed quietly, "but I think right now you should let your body shut down and recuperate from this day. Besides, you don't know how long Ollie will sleep. You should sleep now while she's out."

"Fine."

I followed her to her bedroom but stopped in the doorway and leaned against the jamb. Samantha moved aimlessly around her room. Finally, she pulled open a drawer and grabbed a set of pajamas. "What are you doing?" she asked as she noticed me.

"Standing here?"

She sighed and rolled her eyes. "Yes, but why are you standing there like that?"

"I...I just...didn't want to push you." I was screaming in my mind for her to please, please tell me I was being ridiculous, to just come in.

Instead, she thought for a moment, then nodded and walked into the bathroom. She clicked the door closed behind her. An eternity passed before the door opened again, and she stepped out.

"Will you be here when I wake up?" Her voice was flat. Her emotions an unreadable fog.

Is that numbness? I parsed her question in my mind trying to understand the meaning behind it. "If that's all right with you."

She climbed into bed and nodded once, then shut off the light. I stayed where I was for a moment, then reached in and grabbed the door knob.

"Can you please sit with me until I fall asleep?" A hesitant relief coursed through my body.

"I would love to, Sam." I longed to lie with her, to pull her in with my arm against my body, but I sat on the edge of the bed as she'd asked. The heat radiating off her abdomen warmed my hip and back. She watched me for a few moments before her eyelids drooped. I reached out a hand and stroked her hair back from her face. Within minutes, her decelerated heart rate confirmed she'd fallen asleep.

Even in the gray light of the dark morning, her beauty shone. I studied her—the splash of faint freckles, the fullness of her bottom lip, her thick eyelashes fanned out against her soft skin— committing every detail of her face to memory. *Just in case...*

Regretfully, I rose from the bed. Walking over to the dresser, I yanked my ruined shirt over my head with one arm. In one of the drawers she'd given me, I grabbed the first thing my hand touched—a long- sleeved black Henley—and pulled it on. Several minutes later, I rejoined my family downstairs and interrupted a low murmur of voices when I hit the bottom of the steps.

Everyone looked up at me expectantly. I glanced at the

wall clock in the kitchen, surprised to see it was 8:12 in the morning. It was still dark out, a result of the heavy cloud cover moving in to dump yet more snow on the world.

8:12 a.m. That left me twenty-three hours and forty-one minutes to forever leave the city of my residence for the past sixty years.

Catherine broke the silence. "Lucien, don't tell me you're thinking of trying to stay here."

I blinked at her. "No. Staying here is tantamount to suicide. I don't want to die, not when I have so much to live for." Catherine nodded. Everyone's relief warmed me.

"What can we do to help you then?" Answering Griffin's question necessitated I prioritize which aspects of my life here I was willing to abandon and for which I wanted to make arrangements before departing.

I formulated a plan, pulling out my cell phone and calling the attorneys I'd visited yesterday. I ordered two of the four to destroy the thick sealed packet of documents I'd dropped off in an attempt at blackmailing Laumet to release Ollie. The other two I instructed to courier the documents to safety deposit boxes at banks outside the city. One of these two lawyers was my long-time personal attorney James Bryant. I made an appointment with him for noon and gave him a series of tasks to complete in advance of the meeting.

I looked to Jed and William. "Would you go rent a moving truck and head over to Edmund Place? And get a trailer for the Camaro." They nodded and left, debating who would get to drive the truck as they walked down the front steps.

I tossed Griffin the keys to my truck. "Would you go get a couple dozen boxes and then come back here? Then some of us could get started here and some of us could get started at Edmund Place."

Griffin rose and headed to the door. "I'll come with you,

Griffin," Rebecca offered. She rattled off a list of other things we'd need.

"Lucien? *Lucien?*" Henrietta's voice finally caught my attention.

"Huh?"

Henrietta and Catherine exchanged a glance. I cocked my head to the side. "What?"

"They're leaving, too?"

I stared at Henrietta uncomprehending. Then I took two steps backward and sat down in a recliner.

"Lucien, did you and Samantha talk about what is happening when you leave?"

"No, Catherine, actually, we didn't. She wanted to talk, but I thought she should get some sleep. I told her we'd talk when she gets up."

"But, then"—she looked down into her lap—"can you be sure she's leaving with you?"

I put my head in my hands, then combed my fingers through my hair and locked them on top of my head. "I…I guess I don't know."

It was, of course, the obvious question. Only Samantha could make this decision. And after the revelations of the previous night, I had no basis for knowing what she might do.

Everything in me told me she still loved me. Even after she found out what I was, she'd talked to me and touched me and received my touch. I didn't perceive she was scared of me. Although given the way she'd felt in the bedroom, I had to admit I couldn't perceive much from her right now.

"We're sorry to even ask, Lucien. It's just—"

"No, Henrietta, don't apologize. Really. In fact, thank you for asking. You've reminded me to slow down where Samantha is concerned. I don't want her to feel pressured. It is her decision. But, still, we need to be prepared. Assuming she comes"—an assumption upon which it felt my future survival was now based—"we need to get to work on this place sooner rather than later. I don't want her to be in a position of having to leave anything behind."

Catherine sensed the turmoil beneath my words. She reached for my hand from her position on the couch.

I met her eyes and whispered, "She has to come."

"I know. She'll come. She loves you. They both do." Then she smiled. It didn't reach her eyes.

I pulled my hand away and stood up. "Would you two stay here? I want to run over to my house and grab some things." They agreed, so I ran to the kitchen and grabbed a black trash bag from under the sink. I left the house, and the cold air hit me like a brick wall.

Back at my house, evidence of Laumet's effort to destroy me remained, momentarily resurrecting the fear and loathing I'd felt when realization set in the last time I had stepped through this door. I picked up Ollie's brown bear from the living room floor and scooped up the scattered pile of DVD cases, then dumped everything in the trash bag.

I walked through the house collecting clothes, books, CDs, and framed photographs strewn throughout. I grabbed Ollie's pictures off the refrigerator and set them aside on the counter, then straightened some sheet music into a pile and laid it on top of her pictures. Finally, I secured Ollie's and my violin cases, still open on the kitchen table from a practice session we'd had the previous week.

I stood there for a moment. Having to abandon this of all my houses left an empty feeling in my gut. It had come to feel the most like a home of anywhere I'd lived. While in recent years that had become more true of Orchard Hill, during the time I lived there, my own emotional struggles and constant conflicts with William had kept that house from ever feeling like the sanctuary this one did.

I regretted having to leave. This was where I'd met them. This was where I'd fallen in love with them. This was where they'd loved me back.

I put the pile inside the bag and cinched it, then threw my violin case strap over my shoulder. I put Ollie's case under the arm holding the bag and with my other hand picked up the music stand Samantha had given me for Christmas. That was everything.

I locked the door on my way out and returned to Samantha's. Catherine held the door open for me. I thanked her as I set everything down on Samantha's living room floor.

"Griffin just called. They should be back in fifteen minutes."

"Thanks, Henrietta. Have you heard anything from upstairs?" She shook her head. That was good. They needed their rest.

When Griffin and Rebecca returned with the supplies, Catherine took the keys and code to Edmund Place. She and Rebecca went over to meet William and Jed with the truck to pack.

I glanced at the clock. 9:24 a.m. Twenty-two hours twenty-nine minutes. "Henrietta, will you please go up and check on Ollie? Just make sure she's still doing okay?"

Her face brightened. In a flash, she was upstairs.

I looked at Griffin's face, etched with concern, and blew out a breath. "I really made a mess of things, didn't I?"

He looked thoughtful for a moment, then jammed his hands into the pockets of his black jeans. "Yeah." My shoulders slumped. "But you know what, Lucien? Life is messy. I am a hundred times happier seeing you trying to live. It's so much better than how you used to be, just going through the motions, denying yourself any happiness. I mean this in the best possible way: you're more human right now than at any time since I've known you."

My eyes flashed to his and, as I struggled to find the words to respond, Henrietta returned. "She's still sleeping, Lucien, and her temperature has almost returned to normal. It's a good sign." She slid an arm around my waist and squeezed, then laid her head on my shoulder.

I slipped my arm around her in return, needing to indulge in her healing touch for just a moment. "Thanks, Henny." She smiled up at me.

"So, do you want us to start packing in here?" Griffin asked.

"Um, let's prepare to do it, anyway," I offered lamely. "Maybe start taping the boxes together—"

"Lucien?"

We all heard Samantha's whispered call. The agony in the tone of it nearly made me double over. I flew upstairs to Samantha's room, trying all the while to find the courage to face the conversation I knew we needed to have.

I took a deep breath and pushed gently through Samantha's bedroom door. She was still asleep, clearly dreaming. Her face was wet with tears.

I climbed into the bed and spooned myself against her, willing her to feel safe and secure. I draped my arm over her waist and tucked my fingers between her body and the mattress. Her shuddered breathing steadied after a few minutes, and she pushed her body back into mine. I sighed in relief.

She shifted onto her back, her face turned into my chest. I pressed a warm kiss of prayer against her forehead. *Please be okay with all this. I know it's impossible. But please.*

Over her head, the red light of her alarm clock spelled out the time: 10:01 a.m. Twenty-one hours fifty-two minutes.

Fifteen minutes later, her eyelashes brushed against my throat. She snuggled into my chest, warm with sleep. Then her emotions clouded.

I pulled back a little. "Are you all right?"

A long moment passed. She looked so vulnerable laying there curled on her side against me. "Yes. No. I don't know," she finally whispered. "I'll be right back."

She pushed out of bed and padded across the carpet to the bathroom. Several minutes later, she returned with a glass of water she placed on the nightstand, then she shivered, looked at me, made a decision, and crawled back into bed against me.

I closed my eyes in thanks. I'd been terrified she'd gone to the bathroom as a pretense. Her return nearly melted me. *Okay, I have to stop looking for meaning in every little thing she does.* But, honestly, right then, it was all I had to go on.

"Would you like to talk now?" I kissed her forehead as she nodded. "Do you want to start, or do you want me to?"

"Um, you?"

"Okay." I kissed her again, inhaling the smell of vanilla from her hair. I shifted down on the bed and lay on my stomach so I could see her face. I wanted her to be able to see me say what I had to say. "Sam, I love you. I love you so desperately it feels like my existence depends on yours. And I love Ollie. I love seeing the world through her eyes. Her goodness gives me hope. I love the three of us together. You, her, us—it all feels natural to me, like it was meant to be. You two feel like my destiny."

I reached for her hand and kissed it. "I should've told you earlier. I know it sounds pathetic, but I tried. I swear I did. But I didn't know how to force the words from my lips. Still, I know I should've told you. I know I deceived you. But, please, please believe I didn't mean or want to hurt you. Your pain is my pain, Samantha, literally. You must know that. So I'm sorry. So very sorry."

She heaved a deep breath and bit down on her lip.

"If the biggest contribution I ever make to this world is your happiness, Ollie's happiness, it will be enough, and so much more than I ever dared hope for. I promise I will never lie to you again, never keep anything from you again. If there is a way I can prove that to you, just name it. Anything. I will do anything to regain your trust."

Her emotions resurfaced, and the warmth of her love encompassed me. My heart swelled. I clasped both hands around the hand I'd been holding and laced my fingers through one another over her hand as if I was praying. I was.

"Please tell me we can be all right again, that you can accept me, that you'll let me make this up to you. I love you with my life, Samantha, please—"

She slipped her hand from mine and wrapped it around my neck. I moaned into her mouth when her lips found mine. Her heart thundered. I placed a hand on the side of her face and deepened the kiss, nearly euphoric in my relief. Too soon, she pulled away. She gasped.

She brushed her hand against my cheekbone and held it up to her face. Then she sat up and turned on the lamp on the nightstand.

Cazzo! I held my breath.

Finally she looked at me. "You cry blood?"

I ground the heel of my hand against my traitorous eye. "I'm sorry."

But she only felt sympathy for me. The thin bloody tear hadn't alarmed her, it seemed. In fact, she closed her fist around the remainder of the tear on her palm as if it was an object she was safekeeping. "Tell me about you. Please?"

"Anything, *dolcezza*." The nickname slipped out. I glanced up at her, expecting her reprimand.

"It's okay," she whispered, causing a dangerous current of hope to jolt through my heart.

"What do you want to know?"

"I want to know everything."

"Well, you already know my history. I only left the dates out before. I lived at Orchard Hill until 1938, then I traveled for a long time. I searched for the one who made me, who... killed my family, but I never found him. I came here in 1949 and have lived here ever since. Right after I arrived, Laumet's men found me and brought me to him. I was in a very bad place then. I felt like a total failure, like I didn't deserve anything better than the worst possible life. So I agreed to work for him. But you should know I tried to abstain from the worst parts of his business dealings. I feel things too acutely because of my empathy, and it was hard living in his world. I was losing myself. One time, I saved his life, so he let me leave. That was in 1990."

"Where?"

"Where what?"

"Where have you lived?"

"Oh. Well, you know I have a lot of houses. One has been my primary residence for most of my time here. It's not too far."

"I want to see it."

I thought about debating her, only because our time was so limited. But after everything, she had the right to ask for anything. "Okay. I'll take you this afternoon."

She nodded. "What else?"

"Last night you said you had special abilities. What are they?"

I met her eyes. "Besides being empathic and being able to charm, I also have heightened physical capabilities—strength, speed—"

"Like when you carried me outside last night."

"Yes. Um, also, our senses are heightened, so I can see, hear, and smell things you can't."

"Oh." After a moment, she felt embarrassed. "Whatever you're thinking about, you can ask it. You won't offend me."

"It's stupid." She pulled her knees up to her chest.

I pushed myself into a sitting position facing her. "I'm sure it's not. Just ask."

"Okay, well, um. Shit. I don't know how to say what I'm trying to ask. Okay, so I'll just say it: I'm thinking about movies, about what they show in the movies about…"

"About vampires?" She bit her lip and nodded. "Well, what exactly do you have in mind?"

"Um, wooden stakes, garlic, sunlight, coffins?" She traced a white flower on her comforter with one finger.

"Most of those things are fictions. Direct sunlight burns if we expose ourselves to it for any length of time, Griffin thinks because of the limited pigmentation in our skin. But otherwise all of those things are just legend. Would you like to know what can harm us, me?"

"Okay," she whispered.

"Can you guess any?"

"Um…you…his…" She stumbled, then made a cutting gesture across her neck with a grimace.

"Yes, that is the surest way to kill us."

She nodded and thought for a moment. "Why did he collapse after he bit Ollie?"

"One of the things that can harm my kind is blessed water or wine—holy water. I've been feeding you and Ollie holy water since I first got involved with you." She gasped so I rushed on. "Please try to understand, you were the first humans I'd allowed myself to get close to. I just wanted to protect you, to make sure I maintained my control around you. I've been putting it in your bottled water dispenser. It can't kill us, but it's like a poison, and it takes time to heal."

"That's why you made me drink that water yesterday? In case anyone bit me?"

"Yes. Having so much in your systems weakened Jacques and Antoine enough for me to save you both from them." She nodded. "Are you okay?"

She scoffed. "I have no idea. Go on."

"Um, silver. It also burns us and can be used to restrain us. Again, it wounds but doesn't kill—"

"Oh, God, Lucien. I'm sorry."

"Why?" I asked, surprised by her rapid actions.

Her hands flew to her throat. She fished under the collar of her T-shirt and grabbed the thick silver chain I'd asked her to wear. She wrenched it over her head and threw it on the floor. She looked at me horrified, her guilt lying sour in my mouth. "Why didn't you tell me?" she gasped. "I wouldn't have left it on."

At first I was mystified, but then I understood and hope seized me. I'd been working hard to give her space, but I threw myself around her. "Don't apologize," I rasped. "You didn't know. And even if you had, I would've understood if you wanted to keep it on."

"What? I don't want to hurt you!"

"I know, *dolcezza*. You can't know what your actions just now mean to me. You don't have to remove it, though, you know. I want you to feel safe. If it helps you feel safe, then—"

"Stop. Please." She heaved a breath. "Did you ask to become what you are?"

I sat back enough to see her but kept her in my arms. "Absolutely not."

"And can you change it?"

I looked at her for a long moment and shook my head.

"Lucien, I'm having a very hard time reconciling what you are with what I know of you. I mean, I never would've expected…this. But I can at least recognize what you are isn't your fault."

"Sam," I whispered, "is it too much to hope you can accept this?" I dropped my arms from around her but took her hand.

She let out a long breath. "I've just found out a world of myth and magic exists side by side with the real world. I don't know yet, okay?"

"Okay." *It wasn't a no. Right? At least it wasn't a no.*

"So"—she thought for a moment—"why do holy water and silver harm you?"

"I don't know the origins of my kind, but a lot of cultures ascribe religious significance and power to these items, so I can only assume their ability to harm us is evidence of our inherent sinfulness."

She played with her fingers. I feared the look on her face. "I don't know what to think of that, Lucien. You've always struck me as one of the most decent people I've ever known."

I looked up at her, in awe of the effort she was making.

Then her face clouded. "Do you sleep?"

"Not like you do. I don't fully lose consciousness, and I can go for some time without sleeping. I think of it as more of a trance."

She nodded and her anxiety spiked.

"What is the question you really wanted to ask me?"

She looked up at me surprised. "Are you reading my feelings?"

"Sorry. It's a little hard for me to avoid with you. But, since you know I am, you know I can tell you're feeling anxious about something. So, what is it?"

"I'm just wondering…about…what you…uh…" Her face flushed.

"Eat?"

"Yeah." Her blush deepened.

"Please don't feel embarrassed. You have the right to ask these questions." I ran my hand through my hair. "I assume you know the legends of what vampires eat?"

Her heart rate accelerated. "Yeah."

"That's true." The scents of adrenaline and fear struck me. "Don't be scared, Sam. I would never hurt you. Or Ollie. There are ways of getting blood that don't cause harm. I've been buying blood from a blood bank. I can also ingest animal blood."

She let out a shaky breath. Her fear diffused.

"But, in the spirit of complete honesty, I must tell you I have killed before. I know this doesn't make it any better, but because I can read emotions, I can sense evil. I rationalized that I was helping good people by removing the bad ones. I realize that's messianic…"

"Is…blood the only thing you can survive on?"

I sighed. "Yes."

"So, then, maybe…"

"What?" I concentrated on her hands in the comforter, twisting and gripping, twisting and gripping.

Her voice was low, quiet. "Maybe it isn't so much messianic as making the best of a situation."

I snapped my head up and knew my mouth was hanging open, but my gratitude to her was overwhelming.

She leaned away from the force of my stare. "What?"

"Just, thank you, is all." She nodded distractedly. I smelled her adrenaline again. Her eyes focused somewhere below my own. "What are you looking at?"

"Your…um"—a blush heated her face again— "mouth."

"Ah."

"So…how…"

"I just will it, and they change. Some situations cause it automatically."

She licked her lips and her eyes flitted between my eyes and my mouth. "Show me," she whispered.

"Sam—"

"Show me."

"Why?"

"Because I want to know you."

I glared at her and hated the idea she might define me by the vampiric nature I didn't choose or want. Her heart rate spiked. I cursed myself. I leaned my head into the cradle of my hands and tugged at my hair.

She stroked the back of my head. "Lucien, I didn't mean to—"

"I know what you meant—"

"No, obviously, you don't." Her tone surprised me. I dropped my hands and looked up. "I know...this isn't all you are. But it's part of you. I want to know it, too."

Good, Lucien. Keep being an asshole, why don't you?

"Please show me," she said softly as she fingered the side of my foot. Her small gesture of outreach melted my resolve.

Resigned, I glanced down into my lap. And punched out my fangs. I flinched when Samantha lifted my chin, but I didn't resist. Instead, I closed my eyes, not wanting to also see the fear I was about to feel. As if on cue, she gasped. But the scent of her fear never came.

"Please look at me." Her expression was filled with wonder and curiosity. "Eyes too?"

I frowned. "You didn't close your eyes at all, did you?" She shook her head. I rolled my eyes, blinked them closed, and then trained my crimson orbs on Samantha. Her heart worked harder in her chest but still the fear didn't come.

"Does it affect your eyesight?"

"Improves it," I replied in a low voice.

Out of nowhere, she reached a hand forward. "Can I touch—"

I flinched away. "No!"

"I'm sorry. I'm sorry," she cried.

"You can't...I can't..."

"Okay. Okay. It's okay. That was stupid of me."

"Sam—"

"What situations?" she deflected.

"What?" I panted.

"You said some situations make it happen?"

I groaned. "When I'm feeding, threatened, or, um"—I sighed—"aroused."

She gaped and licked her lips again. Finally she inhaled to speak.

I preempted her, not really wanting to hear her voice the question I just knew she'd ask. "Yes. And I hid it," I said as I looked away, drained my eyes and retracted my fangs, and got off the bed to pace.

A rustle of fabric told me Samantha climbed out of bed, too. Warm arms wrapped around my stomach. Samantha leaned her head against my back. "You're beautiful, Lucien, striking. I've always thought so. I still think so." I smelled the salt of her tears and turned in her arms.

We stood in silence for a moment. The alarm clock shone over her shoulder: 11:32 a.m. Twenty hours twenty-one minutes.

"Sam, I know there are probably more things you'd like to ask, and I promise you'll have the chance. But I need to leave in a few minutes to make some arrangements. There's something I need to ask you before I go."

"Okay." She dropped her arms and locked them behind her back.

"You heard what Magena said to me."

"You have to leave Detroit. Is that for real?"

"Yes. I have to be gone by dawn tomorrow. My question is —" *Please, God, please, God.* "—will you come with me? To

New York?" She sucked in a breath. "I realize a lot is happening all at once, and I'm so sorry. But this is for real. I have to go. My family is helping pack up my belongings right now. They're wondering if they should pack here, too. I'm wondering..."

She rubbed her forehead. "The room is spinning."

I gently led her to sit on the bed and grabbed the glass of water off the nightstand. "Here, drink this. It might help."

She grasped the glass and drank, squeezing her eyes shut. When she opened them, they overflowed tears. She brushed them away roughly. "I don't know what to say, Lucien. I don't know what to do. I can't think."

"Say you'll come with me, *dolcezza*. Say you'll be with me."

"I can't think." She stared at her lap.

"There's some time. I'm sorry, but I have to go for a while. I'll be back in a few hours. I can take you to see my house then, if you like." She nodded. "Oh, you should know Henrietta checked on Ollie earlier. She's doing better." Samantha's face lifted and brightened.

I leaned over and kissed her forehead. When I spoke, my lips brushed her skin. "I love you, Samantha. Nothing could change that. I'll be back soon. Griffin and Henrietta are downstairs if you need anything."

She nodded again.

Reluctantly, I left. The pull to stay with her was intense. But I had things I had to do in person. On my way out, I told Henrietta and Griffin they'd need to wait to begin packing. I didn't stop to hear their worried response.

CHAPTER 21

I returned to Samantha's house at 2:45 p.m. Seventeen hours eight minutes.

She'd showered and dressed in jeans and a green sweater and sat curled in the recliner with a cup of coffee in her hands. Her face brightened when I walked through the door. The wave of relief that hit told me some part of her was afraid I wasn't returning.

"Do you still want to see my other house?"

"Yes." She stood and sank her feet into her boots.

I held her coat for her and met eyes with Griffin and Henrietta as I did. Their expressions told me Samantha hadn't made a decision yet.

When we pulled up to the back of Edmund Place, she gasped. "I've been by this house before. I always thought it looked like a medieval castle or something."

I brushed her cheek with my hand and helped her down from the truck. We went in through the back door. "I've never renovated this place, Sam. It's not in the best condition, as you'll see."

Catherine and Rebecca were in the living room taping

boxes shut. A huge pile sat at the front of the room, full of my books, CDs, and albums, no doubt. William and Jed loaded the truck out front. "We're almost done," Catherine said. "This is the last of it."

"Thanks," I said as I watched Samantha survey the room out of the corner of my eye.

"Why have you never fixed this place up, Lucien? Like the others?"

"It just felt more right this way."

"You didn't think you deserved something nice, did you?"

My head snapped to her, and my dead heart expanded at her understanding and insight. "How did you know that?"

"Because this morning you said you were in a bad place when you came to Detroit and didn't think you deserved to be around people better than Laumet."

"Yes." I strode over to her and kissed her temple. "God, I love you."

I walked her through the house, which was relatively empty now save for the old furniture I was leaving behind. She remarked on the architecture but otherwise was quiet, observing.

When we came back downstairs, Catherine and Rebecca had joined the men in carrying boxes out to the truck. Catherine poked her head back in. "We're gonna head back over to Sam's."

"Okay. We'll be right behind you." She nodded and left. I locked up the doors and turned off the lights on the first floor, then set the alarm system as Samantha and I headed out the back. I peered through the glass of the now-empty garage. Then we were in the truck heading toward Sam's house.

"Sam, I don't mean to push, really. But have you given any thought to whether you'll come with me?"

"Yes. I...I just don't know what to do. I don't want you to

go. I don't want to be away from you. I'm so confused. And I'm scared."

I grasped her hand where it lay on the truck seat. "Of what?"

She stared out her window. "I can't get the images from last night out of my head. It just keeps playing over and over. And especially what happened to Ollie. I couldn't function if anything happened to her. I'm just still so scared for her."

"I understand, Sam. She's going to be okay. Nothing will happen to her now, I promise. Ollie is very important to me, too. You know that, right?"

She turned her head to me. "I do, Lucien."

It was 5:16 p.m. when we returned to her house. I had fourteen hours and thirty-seven minutes. We were all together again, including Ollie, who Samantha was overjoyed to find awake downstairs and eating a peanut butter and jelly sandwich. When Samantha leaned down to her where she sat on Henrietta's lap, Ollie threw her arms around her mother's neck. Samantha held her until Ollie protested for her breath. I reached down and pecked a kiss on Ollie's head. She smiled up at me.

We talked quietly for a while, just enjoying the good news of Ollie's improving condition. After a while, Ollie slipped down from Henrietta's lap and climbed into mine. Her words captured everyone's attention. "You're leaving, aren't you?"

"Uh…" I looked to Samantha for help. But she was clearly grappling with the whole issue of leaving and trying to find a way to a decision of her own. "Yes, Ollie. I have to leave."

"Can we come with you?" Her voice shook. It was clear it cost her to have to ask not to be left behind again.

"Sam?" I didn't want to contradict whatever decision Samantha was making.

"I don't know, Lucien." Her confusion and stress were apparent even to those of us who weren't empathic.

"Ollie, it's your mom's decision whether you come. And whatever she decides will be the right thing. But you are welcome to come. I hope you do." The thought of being separated from Ollie crushed my chest and made it difficult to breathe.

Ollie looked at me funny for a moment and then shifted around. "Mommy? Can we, please?"

Samantha sucked in a breath, then she glanced around at all of us. "Um, I don't mean to be...do you think Ollie and I can be alone for a while?"

"Oh. Of course," I said as I placed Ollie on her feet and rose to my own. Everyone followed my lead.

"I'm sorry."

"Don't apologize, *dolcezza*. Just give me a call," I said a little mechanically.

"I will," she whispered.

"William and Jed will be outside if you need anything. Just a precaution."

"Okay." Samantha offered strained words of thanks and farewell to my family as they filed out.

Then I grasped Samantha's face in my hands and pulled her into a kiss. She leaned into me as I poured my soul into her. I stroked her tongue with mine, needing to feel her, taste her. I approached everything as if it were the last time, because in my worst fear, it was. Finally, I pulled back, tried to smile, and left.

Each step away from them battered my body, like having bones broken one painful snap at a time.

William and Jed waved from their perch in my truck out front. I nodded, then the rest of us meandered across the darkening field to my house. It felt odd to return; I'd said my good-byes earlier in the day. But it made the most sense as a place to wait.

As time passed, everyone got edgy. "Lucien, we shouldn't

314

delay leaving until the very last minute," Griffin cautioned apologetically.

"I agree. I am acutely aware of the passage of time. But I can't push her into this decision. I don't want to push her into saying 'no.' "

He nodded.

We waited. The dread in the pit of my stomach grew with each passing hour. I couldn't imagine how Samantha would try to weigh this decision. *What must be going through her mind?* The suspense was killing me. I almost jumped when my cell phone beeped at me from my pocket. I pulled it out and flipped it open. She'd sent a text message at 9:06 p.m.

Can you come over?

A wave of nausea passed through me— everyone's anxiety, and my own.

"She wants me to come over," I said to them all. "Oh, *Dio.*" I slipped the phone back into my pocket and locked my hands in my hair on top of my head.

Catherine spoke for them all. "Go to her, Lucien. Make her listen. She loves you. You love her. So, fight for her."

I stared up at the ceiling for a moment, then nodded and left. The blackness of the snow-covered field closed around me. I prayed with everything I had I wouldn't get trapped by the darkness of loss again.

When I walked into Samantha's living room, she was huddled on the couch with a blue quilt around her. Her eyes were dry now, but her face was red and puffy from crying. I sat down next to her sideways so I could face her. She avoided my eyes.

I let myself do something I'd blocked when I came in—I reached out and searched for her emotions. They were a full-body experience for me: fear, grief, love, longing, sadness, pain. The constellation of emotions wasn't so different from what she'd been working through for the past day since we'd stood in my kitchen. But it filled me with foreboding nonetheless.

"I'm sorry, Sam. The suspense is unbearable. Please tell me you've decided to come with me." I stared at her still-diverted eyes. In a century, I'd never felt more powerless than I did at that moment.

Sensing she was wavering, I pushed on. "If you choose me, I promise I'll take care of you and Ollie. We'll make a normal life for her. I promise I'll love you forever, and I'll spend my days showing you how much over and over again."

I took her hand in mine. She let me. I shifted my body closer to her on the couch. When I kissed her forehead, she leaned into it just enough to offer me a spark of hope.

Eight minutes, thirty-six seconds—the amount of time that elapsed between the moment I walked in the door and when she finally spoke. I only heard it because of my heightened aural abilities.

"I can't." She finally met my eyes and bit down hard on her quivering lip.

I shuddered in panicked disbelief. "Sam, please. Let me make this right. I promise you this can work out. You said it yourself—you never would've known what I am. What I am doesn't have to change what we have."

She shook her head in a detached sort of way. Her torment constricted my chest and made it hard to breathe. I gasped as if I'd been punched in the gut.

"I'm sorry, Lucien, I can't." She fisted a stray tear away, adding to the redness of her face.

"Why?"

She heaved a deep breath. "I love you, I do. I love you so

much it hurts. Even with what I now know, as scary as that is to me, I…just…love you."

"Sam—"

"No. Please. Let me finish. This is so hard," she choked.

Please, Dio, no.

"I love you, but it's not enough. And it's not the most important thing. The most important thing is Ollie. That she's safe. That she's protected. That she gets to be a child, innocent of all that's complicated and dangerous and scary in the world. I have to be a mother first. I have to do what's in her best interest, which means I can't go with you."

"Sam, I would give my life to protect Ollie, to ensure her happiness—"

"I don't doubt that. But I don't want her to live in a world where someone might actually need to give their life for hers. One near-death experience with immortal beings is probably enough for one child's lifetime."

"Sam—"

"If I chose what I want over what I think she needs, I would not be able to live with myself. I would hate myself for that. And if anything ever happened to her, I wouldn't be able to forgive myself. I wouldn't be able to go on living."

"If you stay here, I won't ever be able to see you again."

"I know." Her sadness and suffering tasted like a bitter cocktail.

"Oh, *mio Dio*," I moaned as I got up and paced a circuit around the room.

"I can't do this halfway, Lucien," she rasped. "I couldn't take it. I'm already dying here a little tonight. There's no way I could see you now and again and not go crazy with wanting you. But more importantly, I can't do it to Ollie. She's crushed…" She took a deep breath. "I can't raise her hopes by letting her see you again. As it is, she may never speak to me after tonight…"

Think, Lucien! Cazzo! I swallowed down my frustration. At an impasse, I stared down at her while she pulled at a loose string on the quilt around her legs.

I involuntarily tranced out. But being inside my mind wasn't any better than being outside of it. The future I'd hoped for was gone, and the memories of another time I'd lost everything resurfaced and tormented me.

But this time, it was my fault. I didn't know how I'd ever be able to live with that.

"Oh, Lucien. Please don't cry," she said as she came to me. She reached up and grabbed my face into her smooth hands. I winced as her touch brought me back, but I let her wipe the thin red tears away. "I'm sorry."

"Please don't apologize. Just tell me there's something I can do to change your mind. I'll make any promise. I'll accept any condition."

A long time passed before she dropped her hands and her gaze. "I'm sorry. I can't."

I cut my eyes away and nodded. Struggling to keep my voice even, I asked, "May I say good-bye to Ollie before I leave?"

"She's sleeping…" She knotted her hands in front of her.

"I won't wake her, Sam, I promise. I can't bear the thought of not saying good-bye."

The internal debate played out on her face, then she turned and walked silently up the steps. I followed Samantha into Ollie's room, lit by a pink castle-shaped lamp that cast a low, warm tint. I knelt down on the floor next to her bed. Ollie was curled on her side and faced out into the room, toward me.

Il mio piccolo angelo. My little angel. She was the angel, not me.

Samantha was right. She deserved protecting no matter the costs. While I thought she'd be equally safe around me, I couldn't deny where Samantha's priorities were or that she thought she was doing the right thing. Even if her decision was tantamount to my destruction, my love for Ollie made me accept it.

I spoke quietly, keeping my promise to Samantha not to disturb her daughter. "I love you, precious Ollie. The way you accepted me, the way you looked at me—I'll never forget your kindness or your love. I hope you'll always be able to remember how much I loved and adored you. You listen to your mom. She loves you very much, and she only wants what's best for you. The two of you will have long wonderful lives together. And though we won't see each other again"—I paused, swallowing down the nauseating blend of Samantha's emotions and my own turmoil—"know I'll always be thinking about you, wondering what great things you're accomplishing." I took a deep breath, trying to steady my voice. "Dream sweet dreams, Ollie. Forever."

I leaned over and barely brushed a kiss on her hair. I inhaled deeply and tried to commit her innocent scent to memory. After a long moment, I stood up, and a tear-streaked Samantha and I walked out together. I pulled the door shut and rested my hand against it.

"Lucien? Is that you?"

Without thinking of Samantha, I pushed the door back open. Ollie flew off the end of the bed into my arms as the words spilled out of her.

"P-please don't leave me, Lucien. I love you. I'm s-sorry. I'll be better. I'm sorry I went t-to your house without asking. Mommy's always t-telling me. If I hadn't g-gone, I would've never run into him. *Please*," she wailed.

"Ollie, no, no." I sat down on the bed with her straddling my lap. "You can never think any of this is your fault. Do you hear me? You did absolutely nothing wrong." I hugged her into me and imprinted the feel of her in my arms into my brain. "I love you, Ollie. So much. I'm so proud of you. You have so many exciting things ahead of you in your life. Know I'll always love you and always be thinking of you."

"Lucien!" The tears streamed down her face now. Her arm muffled sobs as she used her pajama sleeve to wipe her face and nose.

The combination of their suffering was becoming incapacitating. My head and chest throbbed. "There, there, now. It's okay. Come, crawl back in bed. You're going to be fine. Just fine." My eyes burned from the tears threatening to flood into them.

She curled into her pillow. "Can you play for me, Lucien? I don't think I can go to sleep."

"I'm sorry, Ollie. I can't play right now, but I can sing to you." She nodded, her breath still coming in uneven heaves. My voice wavered through a lullaby I knew she liked.

"I love you, Lucien. You're still my angel," she whimpered as her eyelids drooped.

"Sleep now, baby. Dream good dreams."

When her eyelids fell for good, I flew out of the room. Samantha gasped. Her surprise tingled in my stomach as she followed downstairs, alarmed. I leaned against a wall bent over with my hands on my knees, trying to breathe through the chaos of emotions. I willed myself under control and rose to face her.

Her face was pale, drawn. An LED in the kitchen read 10:59 p.m. *Eight hours fifty-four minutes until my life is over.* An awkward moment passed.

Finally, I walked over to the trash bag of items I'd retrieved from my house earlier. My mind started to work in a more mechanical way. I knelt and pulled out Ollie's stack of DVDs and placed them on the coffee table. Then I found her brown bear. I held it up to my face, feeling its softness and inhaling its scent. Gritting my teeth, I set it on top of the pile of movies. Next, I pulled Ollie's violin case out from underneath the bag and slid it on the rug underneath the coffee table. I held my hand on the case a beat longer than necessary.

The rest of the bag was mine. I looked around. The others had already taken my music stand and violin with them earlier. I rose, emptiness a heavy weight within my very blood. Samantha approached me, slowly at first. Then she caught me off guard by throwing herself against me. We stumbled back into the front door as her lips found mine, pleading, urgent. I wrapped my arms around her and surrendered to the kiss. I tasted the salt from the tears she'd cried as I ran kisses across her cheeks and jaw to her ear and neck. We panted and moaned into one another.

It was pleasure and pain. Light and dark. Life and death.

"I love you, Lucien. I'm sorry. I love you." She looked up at me from underneath wet eyelashes.

"Never apologize. You gave me more than I could've ever hoped for. I love you, Samantha. I always will." I lingered a kiss against her forehead.

It's time. I looked into her eyes. She met mine, but the acrid smell of fear and panic flooded from her. She looked away gasping. "No!"

"Samantha—"

"I don't want to forget! Please don't make me!"

I scrubbed a rough palm over my face. Selfishly, I didn't want her to forget either. And charming them hadn't always worked anyway. I decided this was one infraction Magena could forgive. She knew charming wasn't fail-safe.

I nodded. "I told you I'd never force you to do anything." Then I reached down, picked up the black bag, and stepped out the door. I pulled it closed behind me and a thump and a brush told me Samantha had slid down against it.

My connection with both of them ached as I strained to break it. I swayed and gripped the railing.

When I regained my bearings, I looked up. "Meet on the street," I growled to William and Jed, still in the truck. Expressions filled with emotions I didn't want to analyze, they nodded.

I staggered around the side of the house and pounded a path back and forth while Samantha's hitching sobs echoed through the living room wall. The sound ate at me, and I threw the bag into the night with a grunt.

My knuckles grazed something. I reached out, needing to destroy. In a frenzy, I ripped out the row of boxwoods at the side of her house and hurled them.

It wasn't enough. I turned, almost behind her house now, and saw the large oak. A particular set of memories unhinged me: all those summer days I'd spent teaching Ollie to climb that tree.

I stalked up to the thick trunk and slammed my head into it. Blood trickled down my forehead as I reared back and with a roar planted my right fist into it over and over. The physical injuries didn't distract me from the emotional distress—mine or hers.

I had to get away. The others were all waiting on the street for me. The brine of their sympathy made it all worse.

"Let's go." I didn't wait for a response. I wrenched the door open and slammed my body into the Maserati and punched the accelerator. Tearing down the block and squealing around the corner, I careened in the direction of the interstate, the rear of the car fishtailing.

My body screamed against the separation, tearing me apart as surely as if I'd been drawn and quartered. I cranked the volume control up to its maximum setting. Some rock band screeched out unintelligible lyrics against a background of explosive percussion and screaming guitars. It suited me just fine.

My head was the last place I wanted to be.

In an effort to escape the agony, I succumbed to a light trance and allowed only enough mental capacity to remain in control of the vehicle. I forced everything else out.

There was just me. Alone. The road. The midnight sky.

～

Something nagged at me.

Despite my growing distance, torment and horror choked and suffocated me. The emotions' physical impact intensified and ripped me free of the trance.

That's when I understood it. Fear. Pain. Regret. Panic. Longing.

This was the cocktail of Samantha's and Ollie's emotions I'd felt earlier. My Blood Connections with them were stronger than my need for self-preservation.

The strangest thing was my family's feelings seemed to be reflected in what I was picking up. I looked in my rearview mirror. They weren't behind me. But then I'd torn out of Frederick Street with little expectation they'd be able to keep up.

A block before the on-ramp to the interstate, my cell phone rang. The noise enraged me. It took everything in my power not to crumble the phone into a pile of metallic dust. I rolled my eyes at Catherine's number on my caller ID.

"*What?*" I spat into the phone.

The voice that responded took me off guard. "Come back." Samantha. "We need you. P-please?"

I remained in a stupor of grief and rage and self-loathing. The only thing I could think to ask was why she was calling from Catherine's cell phone.

She ignored me. "Just come back, Lucien. Please."

I pulled a U-turn across four lanes of traffic, sending a beat-up sedan into a tailspin. In six minutes' time, I returned to Frederick Street, filled with equal parts dread and hope.

Unattended vehicles were parked haphazardly as if my family had returned unexpectedly. Everyone stood in the snowy field near Samantha's townhouse. I couldn't fathom the situation.

I raced across the field, but slowed as I approached them, still confused. In the center of the group, Samantha sat on the cold ground with Ollie on her lap. She rocked Ollie while whispering soft motherly reassurances in a panicked voice. Henrietta knelt next to them, delicately skimming her hands over Ollie's arm and shoulder.

"What—"

Samantha looked up, her face full of the same grief and despair I tasted. "She fell."

"*What?*"

Catherine placed her hand on my arm and pointed. My eyes followed her finger to the open window to Ollie's room where the pink light of the castle lamp still illuminated the inside.

"She fell...out of her window?" Samantha nodded, clutching Ollie to her harder and rocking her. "Hen?"

She evaluated Ollie's arm as she spoke. "Catherine felt her when it happened. She apparently landed on a surface tree root. She broke her arm and shoulder. It's taking me longer to heal her because her body is still weak from the earlier attack."

I knelt down, stunned. "Ollie?"

"I put her to sleep," Henrietta responded. "It was bad."

Samantha moaned at Henrietta's words. "I said I wouldn't go with you, to protect her," she gasped as she tried to hold back tears, "and then...I didn't."

"Sam, you can't blame yourself for this," I said, still dazed.

She shook her head. Her emotions were a gut- twisting frenzy of guilt and grief and sadness. "I'm making this huge sacrifice, on both our parts, but if I can't keep her safe, if she won't let me, then what's the point?"

"Sam—"

"Lucien, please, please, forgive me," she rasped, her voice a raw scrape as tears leaked from her swollen eyes.

Griffin stepped back so I could crawl in next to Samantha. I wrapped my arm around her shoulder, and she sank into me, Ollie's body falling slightly so she was between us, some of her weight on my thigh.

"There is nothing to forgive, *dolcezza*."

Samantha choked back a sob as she pressed her face into my neck. "Help me. Please?"

The taste and sound of her anguish pulled at the center of my chest. "With what, sweetheart?"

"With Ollie. Please? Help me keep her safe. I can't lose her. I can never lose her."

I didn't know how to respond to her. I couldn't stay. But I didn't dare hope she was asking to join me in leaving the city. "Sam—"

"Will you ask me again?" She pulled free of my arm so she could look up into my eyes.

"Ask you what?"

"Ask me. Please?"

Hope felt like the most dangerous emotion I'd ever known. But there was only one real question I'd put to her in recent hours. I swallowed thickly, then blew out a breath. "Will you come with me, Samantha?" My voice was a strained whisper. "Will you come with me to New York?"

She clenched her eyes shut and nodded against my shoulder. A wave of relief rolled through me so forcefully I sucked in a breath. "If you'll still have me, have us, then, yes," she whispered in a voice distorted by emotion.

I stopped breathing for a moment, half convinced I was still sitting in the Maserati on the way to New York and my grief had conjured up this hope-against-hope conversation.

"Lucien?" Henrietta interrupted. "We need to get Ollie someplace warm."

Samantha and I stared at one another for a beat longer, then we separated as Henrietta lifted an unconscious Ollie into her arms for the second time in twenty-four hours.

"Your face," Samantha said as she reached her hand toward my forehead.

I grabbed her hand before she could touch the blood crusted down the side of my face from my earlier encounter with the tree. Pressing a kiss against her knuckles, I murmured, "It's nothing."

She bit her lip as she continued to look up at my wound. When she finally looked away, down at the hand she was holding, she gasped at my healed but bloodied knuckles. A warm wave of compassion erupted from her. She tugged my hand to her mouth and kissed the back of it.

We returned to Samantha's house. I felt queasy passing through her living room, remembering the wrenching good-bye scene that had played out there less than an hour before and still echoed in the air.

We got Ollie settled in her bed, and Henrietta stayed with her, continuing to work her hands over Ollie's injuries. I walked to the window and pulled it down, but first noticed Ollie had pushed the screen out in her effort to flee the house. A wave of guilt swamped me for not registering her desperation sooner.

Griffin stood with Henrietta, a pointed look on his face. The clock read nearly 12:30, which only left us a little over seven hours until the sun rose. I guided Samantha into her bedroom and closed the door.

Tugging at my hair, I gazed at her, then walked up to her and grasped her hands. "Sam, you are welcome, of course. I want you. *God*, how I want you. But I don't want you to feel you have to be with me if that's not what you want. I can set you up somewhere safe, set you up with a whole new life. And we can watch over you, protect the both of you. But please, don't make the choice to come with me out of fear. If you come with me, I want you to be with me because you want to."

Samantha simply could not make her decision out of desperation. If she did, she would always regret it, always second-guess it, and I would feel every nuance of those emotions. I wouldn't be able to live with myself if Samantha felt cornered or pressured into this.

Samantha thought for a long while, staring down at her feet and shivering from the cold and her adrenaline. "Lucien, I love you. We love you. I won't deny I'm scared. And confused. And still overwhelmed by...everything." She heaved a breath. "But the main factor in my decision was Ollie's safety. I didn't want to risk it, to risk exposing her to unnecessary dangers. And then, not ten minutes after you left, she started screaming for you and then there was this thumping. I rushed upstairs and found her chair in front of her window and the broken screen. She was hanging from the tree limb whispering 'Don't leave' over and over, but she couldn't hold on. When she slipped, I thought I would pass out. Oh, God, the sound of..."

She choked on a sob and shook her head.

"She was crumpled on the ground, not moving. And I was so sure..."

I pulled her in for a hug, but she pushed back.

"No, no, please let me say this." She took a deep breath.

"I ran outside praying for her to be okay. My first thought after that was for you to be here, for your family to be here. And then I knew. I thought about the truck. And the stairs. And the fall from the window. And I realized there's danger everywhere. If you hadn't been here from the beginning, Ollie might very well have died when that truck hit her. I realized there are no guarantees—there's only living life today. But there are no guarantees."

We looked at each other for a long while. I finally managed, in a whisper, "Sam, please think this through carefully. I couldn't bear it if you changed your mind. It would break me completely."

"I won't. I promise. I'm only sorry I didn't come to these realizations sooner."

I froze and used every means at my disposal to evaluate her. She was sincere. But I was still concerned about her reasoning.

She cupped her hands around my face. Her fingers worried for a moment over the faint mark of the forehead wound. She searched my eyes for a long moment. Forever came and went while I waited for her to speak.

Finally, she smiled. A warmth so healing rushed through me I had to close my eyes at the goodness of it. "All that I am, Lucien, all that I have...it's yours. And it feels like it always has been."

My eyes flew open. I sucked in a breath. That was all I'd needed to hear. I pulled her into my arms and pressed kisses onto her hair and face, then leaned back so I could look into her eyes.

"Thank you, Sam, thank God. Your acceptance of me...it eases the burden I have carried for the sin of what I am. Your love has helped me forgive myself. And that is a gift, Samantha, a priceless gift, this feeling of absolution. I have been searching for it my whole life."

"Oh, Lucien," Samantha whispered against my lips.

Our mouths found one another, and we lost ourselves. The kiss was filled with love and acceptance and forgiveness and longing. It was glorious and life-giving. It might have gone on for minutes or hours.

A knock sounded against the door. We pulled back but remained embraced.

"Come in," I called, still staring in Samantha's now-bright eyes.

"I'm sorry to interrupt," Griffin began with a small smile, "but the time..."

"Oh." I broke my gaze at Samantha and looked at the clock on her nightstand and nodded. We had only six hours to do whatever needed to be done. "*Dolcezza*, time is short. May I ask my family to begin packing the house?"

She nodded and offered instructions about what could stay and what needed to go. Much of the furniture in the house was a mishmash of things her father had gathered in his bachelorhood. That fortunately left us with a smaller job than if she'd wanted to take everything. William pulled the moving truck around. Soon the house was a frenzy of activity.

Griffin came to me once work got underway. "Lucien, I think you should leave the city now. I don't want you here anywhere near the deadline. I don't want any of us here then. You should take Samantha and Ollie and leave now."

Samantha and I debated him for a bit but eventually agreed. Samantha packed overnight bags for herself and Ollie. After I cleaned myself up, I scooped Ollie out of her bed, hating to disturb her yet again from her slumber.

As I lifted her, I pressed a kiss to her forehead. "Thank you, Ollie," I whispered. "You saved my life tonight. But don't you *ever* do something like that again." I hugged her to me, so incredibly grateful to this child. She had seen me, accepted me, loved me, and saved me. Time and time again.

Ollie remained asleep, even as I lowered her into the back seat of the Silverado. The Maserati had little back seat to speak of, so William and Jed engaged in an almost immediate negotiation over who'd get to drive my sports car back to New York. Their good humor was welcomed.

Henrietta came with us in case Ollie needed her assistance in the night. Griffin kissed her good-bye and then shook my hand. "We'll be right behind you, old friend."

"Thank you, Griffin. There aren't words."

"You are family, Lucien. None are needed." Then he nodded, waved to Henrietta, and jogged back to Samantha's house.

Soon we were turning off Frederick Street. I was once again en route to the interstate. The similarities ended there.

Whereas before, I'd been filled with grief and despair and rage and self-hatred, now I was filled with hope and love and intense gratitude. Before, I'd been broken, and now I was whole. Before, the future appeared bleak and empty, but now the future seemed full of possibility and potential. Now there was a future worth living.

And the difference?

The difference was Samantha and Ollie, here with me.

The difference was love.

EPILOGUE

It was the first May 13th in one hundred twenty-five years I wasn't wracked with guilt and grief. I hadn't forgotten—I would never forget. But life moved on. And for the first time, I moved with it.

Samantha even helped me mark the anniversary. She'd shyly asked if she could go out to visit my family's graves. She took huge bouquets of flowers she cut with her own hands and then spent an hour on her knees talking to Lena.

At her request, I'd stayed far back, wanting to give her privacy for her conversation. But I was curious beyond belief. Whatever she'd said, the very fact of the conversation further cemented my love for Samantha and endeared her to me impossibly more.

After the morning trip to the cemetery, we drove out to our house. Or, what would be our house whenever we were done building it.

On the way to Milwaukee so many months before, we'd had a long discussion about what her ideal house would be. After a month of living in Orchard Hill's guest suite, I'd surprised Samantha with blueprints for a new house, designed entirely around the things she'd specified in that conversation. We adjusted the designs once she had a chance to consider them and broke ground in early April as the soil thawed.

Samantha was intent on helping with the build, wanting the house to be the result of both of our efforts. For that reason, she'd yet to return to work. She regretted leaving her job at the children's hospital in Detroit, but knew she could find work in Ithaca when she was ready.

The upside was how much time we had to spend together. We made good use of it and got to know one another in ways we couldn't as long as I'd hidden myself from her. The time off also allowed her to be available to help Ollie adjust to the move.

Although, of course, she adjusted better than we could've hoped. I didn't know why we were surprised.

And so, on that beautiful May morning, we stood at the edge of the construction site and stared longingly at the big hole in the ground, the one that would literally and figuratively become the foundation of our life and love.

The future lay bright and open in front of me, in front of us. But I'd become a big fan of focusing on the here and now. The past was gone. The future was only an idea. It was now that mattered.

And right now, I had Samantha, warm and soft, her back pressed against my chest as we tried to envision the way the yellow farmhouse with the wrap-around porch and green shutters would look nestled amongst the New York trees.

I spun her around to face me and captured her throaty laugh with my lips as I kissed her over and over and told her I would love her for all time.

She said it back.

And I was freed, finally, forever.

~

Thank you for reading! I hope you loved meeting Lucien, Samantha, and Ollie. If you want more vampires, you might like Kael and Shayla's story of fated mates and in IN THE SERVICE OF THE KING in the world of danger and desire that is the Vampire Warrior Kings!

And if you enjoyed FOREVER FREED, you'll love my Greek Gods in my Hearts of the Anemoi series, which is about a war between the ancient Greek Gods that control the wind, the weather, and the seasons. This series starts with NORTH OF NEED, a hot and heartfelt story of second chances between a Greek snow god and a grieving widow.

Reviews are so helpful to authors and other readers. Please leave reviews of this book on Goodreads and your preferred retailers' sites. Thank you!

ABOUT THE AUTHOR

Laura Kaye is the New York Times and USA Today bestselling author of over forty books in contemporary and erotic romance and romantic suspense. Laura grew up amidst family lore involving angels, ghosts, and evil-eye curses, cementing her life-long fascination with storytelling and the supernatural. Laura lives in Maryland with her husband and two daughters, and appreciates her view of the Chesapeake Bay every day.

Visit Laura Kaye at LauraKayeAuthor.com

Subscribe to Laura's Newsletter

facebook.com/laurakayewrites
twitter.com/laurakayeauthor
instagram.com/laurakayeauthor

ACKNOWLEDGMENTS

The story of my writing begins with Lucien, Sam, and Ollie in the summer of 2008. So much has happened since and there are so many people to thank. First, I must thank Eilidh Mackenzie, my editor at The Wild Rose Press, who saw something in an unusual male first person point of view story that made her willing to take the chance. Without Eilidh's belief in *Forever Freed*, it's hard to say what the trajectory of my career might've been.

Next, I have to thank my best friend and YA paranormal author Lea Nolan, who critiqued many early drafts of the book and helped me plot and brainstorm along the way. This journey wouldn't have been the same without her.

I must also thank my husband, Brian, and daughters, who supported me in my frenetic need to get this novel out of my system and down on paper when I had no guarantee of ever getting it published. That support is something I'll never forget.

Finally, I want to thank all the bloggers and readers who have read *Forever Freed*, loved Lucien, Sam, and Ollie, and let me know how much you want more. Lucien and Ollie remain very lively characters in my imagination, so I cannot rule out that one day I'll return to their story. It's on the list!

Thanks to each and every one of you for going on this incredible journey with me. It means the world. ~LK

MORE HOT ROMANCE BY LAURA KAYE

Vampire Warrior Kings Series
IN THE SERVICE OF THE KING
SEDUCED BY THE VAMPIRE KING
TAKEN BY THE VAMPIRE KING

Hard Ink Series
HARD AS IT GETS
HARD AS YOU CAN
HARD TO HOLD ON TO
HARD TO COME BY
HARD TO BE GOOD
HARD TO LET GO
HARD AS STEEL
HARD EVER AFTER
HARD TO SERVE

Warrior Fight Club Series
FIGHTING FOR EVERYTHING
FIGHTING FOR WHAT'S HIS
WORTH FIGHTING FOR

FIGHTING THE FIRE – COMING 2020

Blasphemy Series
HARD TO SERVE
BOUND TO SUBMIT
MASTERING HER SENSES
EYES ON YOU
THEIRS TO TAKE
ON HIS KNEES
SWITCHING FOR HER – COMING 2020

Raven Riders
RIDE HARD
RIDE ROUGH
RIDE WILD
RIDE DIRTY
RIDE DEEP – COMING 2020

Hearts in Darkness Duet
HEARTS IN DARKNESS
LOVE IN THE LIGHT

Heroes Series
HER FORBIDDEN HERO
ONE NIGHT WITH A HERO

Stand Alone Titles
DARE TO RESIST
JUST GOTTA SAY

Made in the USA
Las Vegas, NV
06 March 2023

68586165R00204